Now is the Time

Now is the Time

MELVYN BRAGG

SCEPTRE

First published in Great Britain in 2015 by Sceptre
An imprint of Hodder & Stoughton
An Hachette UK company

1

A CIP catalogue record for this title is
available from the British Library

Hardback ISBN 9781473614529
Trade paperback ISBN 9781473614536
Ebook ISBN 9781473614512

Typeset in Sabon MT by Palimpsest Book Production Limited,
Falkirk, Stirlingshire

Printed and bound by Clays Ltd, St Ives plc

Hodder & Stoughton policy is to use papers that are natural, renewable
and recyclable products and made from wood grown in sustainable forests.
The logging and manufacturing processes are expected to conform to the
environmental regulations of the country of origin.

Hodder & Stoughton Ltd
Carmelite House
50 Victoria Embankment
London EC4Y 0DZ

www.sceptrebooks.com

To S. R. 'Jimmie' James who taught history at the Wigton Nelson Thomlinson Grammar School from 1953 to 1983 (and continued to serve the school until 2010, principally as clerk to the governors), from one of his many former pupils who owes him a lifetime's gratitude.

The mixture of languages, the overlapping and intermingling of several impenetrable dialects, some impossible to write down with accuracy, probably two streams of French, some dog Latin, some Church Latin, and borrowings from every foreign crew that shipped in London, made the task of linguistic fidelity to late fourteenth-century England beyond this author.

I have occasionally quoted from documents and chronicles of the day. The rest is in the English that became our common tongue.

M.B.

There are three things of such a sort
That they produce merciless destruction
When they get the upper hand.
One is a flood of water,
Another is a raging fire,
And the third is the lesser people,
The common multitude:
For they will not be stopped
By either reason or discipline

John Gower
'The Mirror of Man', 1378

I

The Priest

It was the injustice of the intolerable taxes on the poorest and the anger against the tax-avoiding rich; it was the block on betterment and the loss of faith in authority; it was the erosion of morality and the fear that the world was about to end; it was an attempt to recover Eden, a leap for freedom, a cry from the depths of the souls of the people, the 'True Commons' of England.

＋—→＋

The accused priest stood before the court. He was dressed in the cheapest cloth. He might have been a beggar. From his scuffed and shabby habit, from his spare frame and plainness of manner in the ornately, hierarchically dressed company of the ecclesiastical court, he seemed to be just another casualty of the harsh laws of the Church. But there was about him a self-composure, which threw out the challenge of his independence too arrogantly for the taste of the court.

'This time, John Ball, you will be locked in prison until you are dead.' Archbishop Sudbury spoke evenly. Emotions were not to be wasted, he told himself, not on such a wretch, even though John Ball's popularly applauded sermons over the years had tested Sudbury's patience to distraction.

'By whose law?'

'By the law of the Church.'

'The law of God is the only law.'

'Who are you to know the law of God?' Sudbury, as

I

always, was inexplicably needled by this peasant priest's conviction. Once again he compelled himself to be patient.

'Because I am a man of God,' the priest responded. 'I am a man who speaks truth, the truth from the God you do not want to hear.'

Sudbury closed his fingers in a steeple and looked at them for a few moments.

'John Ball, you are of no consequence to anyone but yourself and the rabble. You are a man who has been excommunicated and put in prison three times since you came out of St Mary's in York many years ago. The last time it was on the authority of the King, of Edward III, and myself both. We have for too long been lenient and charitable to you. You have been a plague upon our Church ever since you became a priest.' Sudbury knew he need say no more but years of frustration would not be stoppered.

'You have been banned from preaching throughout Essex and Kent and in several other counties. Yet you have defied the ban, unsettled the people and prated in churchyards and fields, in hedgerows and in markets. You do not under-stand the traditions and authority of the Church! You have fouled the name of the great clergy and called on the people to dismiss them. You have tried to stir up riots against the aristocracy and become a petty hero, although you have achieved nothing! And you have attacked the King!'

'Not the King! God makes kings. I attack the wicked councillors who advise the King against the people of England. I will pull them down. And you with them, Archbishop Sudbury, who have persecuted me for many years. Your blood will flow. I see it. You sit here in judgment – but who are you to judge? "Judge not lest ye be judged." In your purple silk robes with a golden chain around your neck and a crucifix that would rescue hundreds of men and women from destitution—'

'Take this man away!' Any last sympathy with John Ball had been stamped out. Rule, order, obedience were fragile unless supported by law and authority. This man would tear down all authority.

'Your jewelled fingers steal the small means and lands of the poor and the unfree,' said Ball, as he was seized by the sergeants-at-arms. 'You cause fear and crush honesty, and this in the name of a God who does not know you and you do not know Him. You are not in His Book. He will be revenged.'

'Take him away!'

'And I will be His sword.'

'John Ball, you will live in solitude for the rest of your days. I will pray for your soul.'

The archbishop made the sign of the cross and kissed the jewelled crucifix as John Ball was taken from the ecclesiastical court into the dungeon.

2

The Princess of Wales

Joan, Princess of Wales and Aquitaine, popularly known as the Fair Maid or the Virgin of Kent, despite her seven children, was the widow of the Black Prince, whose victories against France had brought him glory from London to Venice. She was a friend of the pope and equally of John Wycliffe, the first translator of the Bible into English and the pope's enemy. The mother and mentor of King Richard II, in her sixth decade, still a beauty and a woman of fearsome influence in the kingdom, Princess Joan lay on her bed at Windsor Castle in the early daylight of a gentle May morning and played with her jewels.

She liked this dawn accounting of her treasure in luxurious solitude. She liked the clink of the stones one against another as she rolled and shuffled them. She liked the extreme wealth in her hands, the power at her fingertips, for this was a treasure that could be mortgaged for wars. And there was the unfailing romance of those prisons of rock in distant lands, so skilfully prised open to reveal lumps and slivers of rare material. Then they would be fashioned into the art of these dazzling, precious objects trickling through her strong fingers. That so much had been done to give her pleasure moved her deeply.

Joan had been picked out as a beauty from her childhood. It was a beauty so embedded in her character and so frequently polished by praise that its awareness never left her. Even as she aged, her manner and her history continued to expect unbroken tributes to be paid to it, and they were.

The jewels were proof. There they were on the velvet coverlet of her immense bed. Among them were four chaplets of gold enriched with gems. She slid these over her wrists, letting them dangle and brush softly, whispering against each other. She spent respectful time turning and turning again in the milky light a dearly bought brooch, with a large diamond, three balas rubies and three pearls weighing six ounces. Clink, clink, clink it sounded in the silence of the silk-clad room, as she pushed it gently through the scatter of sixteen smaller brooches, which were like its bridesmaids.

Many of the sapphires and rubies had been made up into rings or necklaces, small clusters of colour she liked to set against the large white diamond necklace. And there was a small golden sapphire and emerald jewelled hart. Her son's badge was a white hart (hers was a white hind) and she had four of these, waiting for the prime moment to give one to him as the perfect small reward. When he was a child, before he became king at the age of ten, she had presented him with twenty-two thousand pearls of different sizes among other gifts.

On it went, this carnival of artistry, her fabled riches, sensuously caressing her hands, objects brilliantly worked in jasper and ivory, in amber, jet and marble. And more, ceramics, ostrich eggs encrusted with rubies, clasps, belts, buttons, rosaries, mirrors . . .

Occasionally she would sigh, an exhalation of unfathomable contentment, and the sigh would drift around the room, a blessing given to herself. Her world was perfect.

When the time came to part with her harvest, she lay back on her bed and looked down, like a goddess, to savour, with a compound of happiness and ownership, that all that lay before her was hers.

The bed itself was her greatest pride. It was covered with red velvet embroidered with ostrich feathers of silver. At each corner a leopard's head of gold sprouted silver branches and leaves from its mouth. In her will, the bed was destined for her youngest son, the King.

She called for Jane, the favourite of her four young ladies-in-waiting. Joan would not have older women about her. Jane led in the two armed men with the caskets and iron-bound boxes that housed the jewels. With them was the steward of Joan's household carrying an inventory. Joan looked on intently as the jewels returned to darkness in the deep caskets. No one hurried. This was the morning of the jewels.

When they had been checked and sealed, the procession went from the Queen's Chamber, down the stone staircases, down, down into the treasure room, to which only the steward had the keys. He supervised the placement of every box among the plate, the gold and silver table vessels and the crowns. The crowns alone were worth a third of the annual taxes of the country. The guards left the room. And then the door was locked and one armed man stayed outside it. Great wealth, Joan knew, had to be closely guarded. Great wealth was power. And great wealth, such as Joan possessed, was, she thought, a divine gift to ensure her safety.

As her women dressed her, Joan rehearsed how she must deal with her son over the next few weeks. She had developed the unbreakable habit of learning by heart her responses to the possible course of any difficult encounter. Her fluency was famous and feared. She aimed to be the best-prepared negotiator at any meeting. She needed to steer her son more firmly, on his stammer, his affections and his exercise of royal authority.

This close contact with her son was an unexpected consequence of her sudden decision to leave her London palace and go to Windsor, with her bed, her jewels and her personal court. A rumour had come to her from Bristol that the

6

plague was back in England. It was said that half the population had already died of it. By God's grace she had evaded the Great Plague of 1348 and its virulent return five years later, then ten and again recently. But whatever God's grace might have in store this time, Joan took no chances.

She had thought of retreating to her Wickhambreaux estate in Kent, her home county, and the location of country palaces belonging to several of her rich allies about the court and the city. But Windsor was her safest haven. The cause of this apocalyptic disease, wave after wave for decades, had baffled all doctors save doctors of divinity. And the court was there in force at Windsor Castle.

Yet she had to get to Wickhambreaux before too long and from there to Canterbury to pray at the shrine of Thomas Becket. She had promised the Virgin Mary that she would do that and twice broken her vow. She dare not do so again. God's patience, like her own, was not infinite and Joan always kept her promises to Him, to His Son and His Son's Mother. It would have to be a fleeting visit, with two chosen maids in her new carriage, which required five horses to pull it. She would be guarded by knights. The shrine would have to be cleaned and cleared for her sole occupation. Prayers, she thought, were immeasurably more effective when you were not part of a crowd. How could God possibly distinguish individual voices in a crowd? For her son's sake, she needed the intercession of Thomas Becket.

3

The Mother

Windsor Castle was set apart, protected against all the world by its ancient walls, moated by water and further moated by reaches of open countryside. You could see the enemy coming from far off, and the plague too, spread like a deadly tide, destroying farms and villages; its rise could be noted from the height of the walls, its flood anticipated. She could feel both isolated and fortressed. Inside Windsor Castle there were smaller groups of buildings, each its own island and prepared as if for a long siege against the inevitable returns of the disease. The castle had its own well, its animals were set apart and penned in the garth, and the heavily thickened walls would hold off any who dared to try to board this Ark. If the plague could be avoided anywhere in England it was here in Windsor, Joan thought.

After the caskets had been taken away, Joan spent the next hour at her writing-table. She was compiling a chronicle of her life. The histories of kings were well known in her circle and relished with all the satisfactions of entitled tribal gossip. But few queens lit up the records. And although she was not a queen it was Fate, not character, that had denied her the crown. She felt like a queen. She acted like a queen. The people bowed to her as a queen, and for some years she had acted as a queen-regent would. She looked at her life with a deep and grand satisfaction, even above the pleasure she took in her jewels. They would be dispersed after her death. Her chronicle would remain for all time.

She had no doubt that her life was worth its own record. It had embraced amorous and marital boldness on a rare scale; it had known and created significance and intrigue, seen encounters with the finest men of her time, been on the side now of the highest authorities, now of philosophers in revolt at the society in which they found themselves. It had also, when she was a girl, known unjust, cruel treatment and bitter loneliness. During that youthful time, to sustain her spirits, she had made a cocoon inside her head, a secret self, and cast herself as an unacknowledged heroine, whom, one day, the world would have to recognise as . . .

Glorious!

The scribe who copied out her words was Burley, whom she had chosen to be her son's tutor. Confidentiality was essential. The tutor was sufficiently clever, a useful sounding board. His complete and perpetual silence on the project was guaranteed by his pride in holding such a comfortably remunerated post at court, and in the recurring clear memory of the flash of fear he had experienced when Joan had told him that if a word of it got out he would be executed. The memory of her sweet smile when she had said that could still make him panic.

Joan kept the pages in a casket that was always in her immediate vicinity. It was double-locked – she alone had the keys – and deliberately dull-looking. It declared itself in her ocean of splendours as an insignificant islet, worth no consideration.

Alone now in her room, silent but for the crackle of the fire, she sat at the writing-table, which looked out to the vast park and forests of Windsor, plumped for hunting. With a connoisseur's satisfaction she browsed through the history of herself.

Although everything that had formed her was, in her view, of unqualified importance, there were judgements to be made if the chronicle, as she intended, was to become her permanent memorial.

The first hurdle was on page one and concerned her father, the Earl of Kent. He had been half-brother to Edward II – which was good, she thought, and well worth including. But he had been executed for treason when she was two years old. That was bad. Would that help her or would it, from the outset, seed doubts? Treason was worse than murder. This was to be a chronicle, not a confession.

The sliver of redemption was that he had stood on the scaffold from one p.m. until five before an executioner could be found willing to make an end of him. This meant, surely, Joan reasoned, that he had been loved and admired, the father she had never known, whose ignominious death could still prick her eyes with tears.

Perhaps she would omit that and start on the next page. Queen Philippa of Hainault had taken pity on her and brought the child into her husband Edward III's Royal Household. She was the poor one, and she remembered the slights – but who would want to read about such trivial matters? What would interest them was that she was protected at court by a boy only a few years older than she was. He was the Prince of Wales, who would later be known as the Black Prince. She emphasised that. She had been grateful to him, and that childhood gratitude, she thought, had later led her to accept his offer of marriage, which gave her everything she could possibly want, save the love that she had, from the age of twelve until her death, for Thomas Holland. Now, how did she deal with him? How did you describe such passion? Passion in a woman was seen as weakness. How could that help her future status?

Just as she had paused over exceptional favourites among her jewels, so she paused, for much longer, when she came to Thomas Holland. Had there ever been another such dashing, handsome, fearless young man as that young knight of the Royal Household? He had declared his love for her when she was twelve and, without the consent of the Royal Household, had arranged their secret but lawful marriage just before her thirteenth birthday.

The Royal Household was not pleased. But how should she write about it? Had she got it right or did it need revision? Could she admit such love even now – with Holland long dead and herself unassailable? When her mother had taken advantage of Holland's posting with the army to Prussia and forced her daughter into what she saw as a much more suitable marriage, she had sworn that her daughter's first marriage was unlawful and had not been consummated.

Joan, as she roved over her chronicled past, remembered the anger of her mother when she had denied that. It had, the girl said, been wonderfully consummated and, looking back now, it was perhaps the triumphant way in which she had declared that which hardened her mother to a swift manoeuvre. It had led to the abrupt forced wedding of the declared maid Joan, already the Beauty, to William Montacute, second son of the 1st Earl of Salisbury. Until the day before the wedding, the girl protested that she was already a wife. Her mother's final means of persuasion was to tell her that, if she held to that in public, Thomas would be expelled from the army, tried for an illegal union, imprisoned, ruined and, if she could influence the matter, executed.

But she could not leave him out . . . Writing was like diplomacy, she thought. What mattered was the right words, seasoned with a little flexibility.

The seven-year marriage to Salisbury had been included, briefly. Her fury against him could not be let loose in her chronicle. 'Unhappy' was permissible, she thought, and 'ill-matched' – but little more than that. Apart from anything else, the current Earl of Salisbury, one of her son's closest advisers, was the son of her brother-in-law. An unthreatening but still sensitive connection. During her marriage she had never met the current earl. But if she painted her own Salisbury interlude as bleak as it had been, it might not be helpful to her son, the King.

So this part she had made a section of its own, easy to lift out if necessary when the manuscript was completed. But she hoped times might change in a way that would favour more openness. She wanted her chronicle to be vivid, to be singular – to be read! For the present she would put down the facts. Seven years, no children, pain.

She would not, in the currently authorised version, put down her loathing for that man, his sweating, groping paws, his foul breath, his attempts to assault her when she resisted his demands, her exile from the family, her life as an outcast imprisoned in the acred grandeur of aristocratic privilege. But one day, Joan thought, as she turned away from an episode that had tested her severely, it should be out . . . Every day on that barren estate she had prayed for Thomas to come back to her.

And then . . .

Thomas Holland did come back.

Back from Prussia, full of honours and booty, he had come straight to the Salisbury estate. Immediately this heroic knight, with nerve that had taken her breath away, had secured the well-paid post of steward of the Salisbury estate. For about a year Joan and Thomas lied and cheated their way into a ferment of happiness. But Thomas was not content. He lacked, he told her, a fortune to buy her back, but with Christ's help . . . He joined the Crusades, enhanced his reputation for gallantry, ingratiated himself with the papal party and came back a wealthy man.

Joan left out the lies but dwelt at length on his exploits in the Crusades. She was safe there. She glossed over their excitement on the estate together. The next stage, which was Holland's petition to the pope to restore his rightful wife to him, had to be delicately done. This could be found already in two existing accounts, but hers, she thought, would out-truth them both.

Holland had argued to the pope that she had been kidnapped by the Salisburys. Salisbury denied all knowledge of Joan's first marriage and set up delaying tactics that for a year looked as if they would prevail. After letters between Joan and the pope, Holland stepped up his campaign. He threatened to bring a charge of unlawful imprisonment against the son of the 1st Earl of Salisbury and, with more letters from Joan, plied the pope with evidence and arguments. He was listened to. The victorious English crusading knight was a valuable asset for the pope.

A papal bull declared Joan's marriage to Salisbury to be false. She and Holland remarried immediately and in quick order she had five children. The second-born was called Thomas, who became and for ever remained, her favourite.

How could she not include all this? Burley's advice was so trimmed to please that it was useless. At court the facts had been out for years. It would be foolish to attempt to ignore them now . . . Perhaps she would gain by admitting everything. Or the way to do it, she had thought, might be to dress it up as a Romance, the fashion of the time – innocent princess (she could elevate her status for the purposes of Romance) seized by brutal aristocrats, caged on a cruel estate, rescued by her lover back from the Crusades – stress the negotiations with the pope, play down the deceits practised by Tom and herself in the byways of the estate and the bedrooms of the great house. She still had not got it as she wanted it and she hated reworking her chronicle but this episode, with the love of her life, would surely bring a glow to her reputation and remind the world of his fame . . . Thomas had risen to become captain general of all English lands in France and Normandy until his early death.

The next episode, she thought, wrote itself. It was so much in the public domain. It was so much the history of England in France. She could still smile at the rapidity and unexpectedness of it all. Despite being her cousin (and therefore forbidden marriage in Church law) and despite being committed to a profitable dynastic marriage with Margaret of Flanders, Edward, Prince of Wales, already a national hero, insisted that the widow with five children, of no great fortune, marry him and soon, whatever laws were broken. In the presence of his father, Edward III, and the Archbishop of Canterbury, they defied Church law and were married at Windsor.

A few months later, as she recorded, they sailed to France, five children and all, for the new groom's idea of a honeymoon – further triumphs and conquests. From then until the coronation of her son Richard, fathered by the Black Prince, she had been treated as a Magnificence.

She had been very fond of her childhood protector. What had surprised her when she gathered together her memories of this period in her life was how spectacularly it had been lived. Edward, she wrote, or the Black Prince, as the world wanted to call him after his already mythical victories on the battlefield against the French, now went through France like a hero from legend. He rode, she wrote, from city to city and town to town, everywhere receiving homage, fealty and gifts.

It was here that Joan had developed her serious interest in wealth. In the chronicle she mentioned some of the jewels she had been given – she had let it be known to the French her particular affection for diamonds. In the chronicle she made a passing reference to her clothes – but only to score a point against the fashionable French ladies who said that her furred gowns, slit coats and rich materials were more the fashion of the mistress of mercenaries than a future Queen of England. They had no taste, those Frenchwomen!

But it was the public display she wanted to record. Four years into their residence in France, the Prince and Princess of Wales held the most costly and princely tournament in all Christendom to celebrate the christening of their eldest son. More gifts came in. But so did darkness.

The elder son died, leaving Richard the precariously sole heir. Then Edward contracted dysentery, which disbarred him from his obsession – war. Joan found it melancholy to track the irreversible enfeeblement of her friend and husband whom, she recorded, she nursed faithfully.

She wrote of their return to England but made little mention of her increase in power. As her husband's power declined, hers grew.

His relentlessly enfeebling illness had brought her closer to him than at any other time. To see such a warrior sink slowly into such infirmity. She feared for their son, who saw this great soldier as merely a dying man. In 1376 his father, too, the equally great warrior Edward III, was dying, losing his mind, kept out of sight of his subjects, often unable to speak, prostrate in a hooded royal barge as he came to say farewell to his dying son.

Joan could and did write at great length about the prince. Burley had copied out speeches made at the time. She selected from them. 'He never attacked a nation he did not defeat or besieged a city he did not take.' When the Black Prince died in May 1378, the chronicler Walsingham had written – and Joan copied into her own chronicle – 'on his death, the hopes of the English utterly perished'. His father died a year later and Joan did not spare the reader full and proud descriptions of the obsequies and burials.

From then on she saw the succession as her primary duty. She wrote carefully on how she had taken up the guardianship of the ten-year-old boy-king. She smothered with praise those who had been her rivals for power over him. John of Gaunt in particular, the brother of the Black Prince and well enough placed to claim the throne, was seduced by flattery, diplomacy and touching affectionate talk such as the rough, impetuous soldier had never known. Joan noted that it was she who had insisted – as if doing him a favour – that he be given his own army. But she did not record that the purpose was to get him out of London. He had been sent to the Scottish Marches or Borders for three years, to try to extend the peace treaty between the two countries and neutralise what she thought of as that perpetually tiresome and troublesome state, Scotland, which was France's best ally against the English.

In the chronicle she did not make mention of her own diplomatic corps; she included, however, a reference to the third of the revenue of Wales, which was assigned to her, and the twenty-six manors, her new barge, new carriage and London palace. She believed that a show of such great wealth commanded respect. Solomon was admired for his wisdom but his wealth – his glory – was the dazzling seal on his reputation, she thought.

Now to her son, the King: she must write about him, and it was this that gave her the greatest difficulty. People must know his strengths and his qualities. She still had so much to teach him – how to keep the city of London on his side for money for his wars and yet somehow persuade them to be pleased to present gifts as thanks for being permitted to contribute to the war chest. How could she help him rise above the cramping phalanx of old-style aristocrats on his council? How to find the new men of the age and make them his advisers?

She needed help. Her intelligence was that there were disturbing murmurs. In York some months before there had been unrest among the peasants. But that was the north, she thought, forever dissatisfied and forever doomed. Her ancestor, William of Normandy, had found what Joan believed to be the only effective solution to the north. He had laid waste to it.

And there were portents too. Just a few days ago, towards the end of May, there had been a storm of a ferocity never before experienced. Trees uprooted, rivers bursting their banks, the sea sweeping over the land, monstrous fish thrown on to the beaches, houses blown away, weird visions of spirits in the air, witches and goblins, the sky cracking open with lightning . . .

And unwritten in her chronicle – for how could she show such lack of faith? – the chief matter: what if it were true, as some of the prophets and the preachers said, what if it were true that the world was coming to an end?

She sent Jane ahead of her to the King's room. Jane was almost a beauty, puckish, bold, a girl for whom Joan had plans. She was to tell the King his mother was making her way to him. Princess Joan always walked slowly in what her courtiers and visitors noted and approved of as the appropriate dignity of such a magnificent Royal Person. She had a bad back and her corset was merciless. Her first five children had slid out effortlessly. The children of her marriage to her cousin Edward had arrived with strain, perhaps a little too late in her life, she now thought. Richard, her last child, had caused her to scream in a way she had never allowed herself to do before. It was to his birth that she traced the origins of the increasingly severe pain in her spine.

Doctors had been generous with remedies. Rare powders were mixed, heated and ostentatiously prepared before her.

17

Women and men had rubbed their muscular hands up, down and around her stubborn spine. Some of it helped. The most reliable relief she had found so far was ancient Egyptian massage. Mamoud was her man. She had brought him with her to Windsor.

She walked to the King's room along the chill stone corridors, as intent as a nun. She paused outside his room and looked out across the parkland. The dew had been replaced by a glistening of rain. She loved the sweet showers of the English spring.

4

The Dungeon

The dungeon was at the back of a palace built by Archbishop Ufford in 1348. It was just a few miles from his cathedral house in Canterbury but Ufford had relished the distance and the distinction it gave him. He lived like a lord. Those who led the Church came mostly from lordly families, overwhelmingly of French descent, who had owned the land and ruled it for more than three hundred years. The interests of Church and state were often identical.

The cell measured about twelve feet square. It was just above ground level facing the east. There was a barred window.

The gaoler, Will, a large and exceptionally strong man, was overawed by the fame of his sole prisoner. In the palace he was a drudge, confined to heavy, unacknowledged labour. He was often beaten and perpetually hungry. When the priest insisted they share his first meal, Will became his slave.

From early on John Ball had been encouraged by his father to watch the rising of the sun. The room in which the three of them – himself, his father and mother – lived in Colchester, between Estokwellestrat and Westokerillestrat, had a small window facing east. When the warmer weather came his father, a carpenter, would open it at dawn and, with his son, look out at the arrival of the light. It heralded the best story in the world, he said – the day. His father listened to the cocks crow, the birds call, the early creaking of carts, the slow clopping of horses, the festering and thickening of sounds in the town as the sun brought to life the living.

His father had come to Colchester with a new wife and the new-born boy, John, from the nearby hamlet of Peldon to look for work in what was then, in 1340, one of the larger, richer towns in England. More than five thousand people, two abbeys, a busy trade in wool, the wealthy spending and building, the artisans and yeomen proud of their traditions of liberty and independence, the women known in the town for the influence of their opinions. There was easy trade up to London. In his father's early years, Colchester was part of the great swelling of England to wealth and more than five million people.

As a child, John had woven himself into the town: its squeezed narrow alleyways, the small yards and half-concealed exits and entrances, the grand houses, the wild dogs, the ceaseless flow of people. The keen, quick boy was drunk with pride and excitement at the noise of it, and the variety of trades and people he saw as he flitted around the streets that became more his home than the tenement he lived in. He saw and came to know, by condition, by name, by trade, the blacksmiths, saddlers, skinners, masons, tilers, cordwainers, carters, butchers, fishmongers, bakers, brewers and, coming in from the country, the yeomen farmers, the shepherds and swineherds bringing their animals to market, the dairymaids with their milk and eggs, the scurrying servants of the powerful, the clusters of monks and the poor friars, farriers, bootmakers, bailiffs and the important, finely dressed men and women of the town. The eager boy spun between them and came to know the people and to love the crowd. He was oblivious of the stink and slime, leaping over the piles of garbage, playing the perpetual game of just being alive.

As he grew older he was drawn in, at times almost drugged, by the ringing of the bells, the processions of the clergy, the impenetrable holiness of the abbeys, the grave and beautiful chanting of the Latin words, the power of Mystery. And this bright spinning top of a boy, through the call of the bells, thought he heard the call from God to comfort the comfortless, help the poor and serve Him.

As a boy, he was of that tender character to be moved by the plight of the poor and the wretched: he saw them every day. He wanted to help them, as Jesus had done. He was seen to be a clever boy, picked out by the abbey and sent to St Mary's in York, as all the initiates from Colchester were. Some years later when he came bruised out of York he immediately headed back to Colchester where soon he became an outlaw every bit as hounded as those, often men who had fought for their country, who had taken to the forests of England and lived by robbery.

Now that he was a man, John Ball saw in the sunrise the perpetual promise of God and he, like his father, looked and listened. But he listened, too, for heavenly messages that whispered truth. He had learned how to pray through spiritual exercises in his priestly training in York. But also he had been granted visions. The rule of St Benedict was his guide. He had to gather all his forces to dissolve all thoughts so that his soul was open to receive, however faintly, the breath of the Lord. So now he stood alone in his cell, the light before him calling on a light to be lit within him. What did God want him to do? What could he do in such confinement? Here for life? He forced himself to bury deep that desolating certainty. For life?

The next morning, after meditation, John Ball went to the window and began to preach. He stood on the narrow cot provided for him and jutted the upper part of his long, lean body into view. There was a murmur of expectant gratitude when the people who had gathered outside saw through the bars the weather-chapped face, the strong prow of a nose, a stubble of beard, wide mouth and thin lips. Then they heard the voice. A singing voice, accustomed to the open air, using a chanted delivery, which carried his message much further than mere speech.

'Good people, I fear God will leave England,' he began, and paused, and in the moment of pause he saw the plague-blebbed face of his mother who had died a year ago. His prayers had not been able to calm her last hours. Since her death she had begun to break into his mind. What had she done so wrong that she should die like that?

'You all know of the Great Death, which first came here many years ago and took away so many of us.'

'We do,' they said. 'We remember.'

Once again he paused, and drew them in. 'And it came back again, and then again, and now yet again it is said to be among us. It scythes us down.'

'Yes,' they responded, and 'Amen' and 'God have mercy'.

'Why?' John cried out, and repeated, his tone full of sorrow, 'Why did He send down on us such a terrible punishment?'

'Save us, O Lord!'

'Is it because we denied Him? Is it?'

'Yes!' some said, and louder, 'Forgive us!'

'Why is He so merciless?'

He saw on his mother's body the black lumps of disease.

The growing crowd was caught up by the urgency of this priest.

'Is this the way the world will end?'

'No!' they cried. 'No!'

'But it will,' he said. 'Unless we listen to Him and follow His plan, we will *all* die of the plague. God is angry and His anger knows no limits.'

He felt the distress of the people seep into his soul. They were looking up to the barred window, waiting to be fed.

And he felt that he knew every one of them. Their familiar poverty and their longing for release – from God's plagues and the torments of men – stopped him in sorrow.

'Tell us what we must do!' some shouted. 'Tell us!' And the demand grew louder until it had the power of panic.

'Good people,' he said, his voice thickened with the desperation of it. He wanted to sway them, but he knew that all they could see was a face and hands behind bars. 'We can pray. But God is not listening.'

His voice rose, but he was imprisoned. He could not touch them.

'He wants us to have everything in common. Only then shall all be free as we were in the Garden of Eden . . . He made the Garden of Eden for us all – and LOOK AROUND YOU!' His voice soared to a fury. 'Look at what we have done with Eden! We have ruined it! Who can blame God? We deserve what punishment He has brought us! LOOK!'

'We do!' they cried. 'Good Lord, forgive us. We will repent.'

The crowd moved closer to the palace wall – those at the front were crushed against it. Perhaps even from this window he could touch their hearts.

The door of the cell opened. Two sergeants-at-arms rushed across to John Ball, hauled him back from the window and beat him. They boarded up the window and left him in darkness, huddled on the stone floor.

When he was sure the soldiers had gone up the stone steps and back to their quarters, Will came in. He had heard the beating of John Ball but been too afraid to intervene. He himself had been given too many beatings by those men.

He picked up the priest and carried him across to the narrow straw-bedded cot. The man shivered in his arms and

23

Will shook also at the sudden pressure of his precious burden.

Once he had laid him on the cot and covered him with the two blankets, he looked down on the fine face he had so swiftly come to revere. There was blood down one cheek. Will sought out a bowl of water. He offered it to the priest, who sipped painfully. Will saw that his lower lip was caked with blood.

When he had drunk enough, Will dabbed his index finger in the water and traced it across the wounds gently, rocking a little as he knelt beside the priest.

In the dungeon of Maidstone Palace, John Ball thought he would go blind. The sliver of light allowed him when, twice a day, Will brought in food and water, was too brief to be much more than a torment. Yet if God wanted him to be blind he would accept it. He would pray to find the blessing in it.

In York, where he had gone for his training and been proud for ever after to call himself 'a priest of St Mary's in York', he had taken, rather surprisingly, to solitude and meditation. This was in part because of the nervousness that had assailed him when he left the warm life of the streets of Colchester. In York he could best hide away by being alone in prayer. And in that solitude and intense contemplation he had found an ever-deepening vocation.

He was never at ease with his colleagues. They mocked and criticised his rough manners, his accent and his humility. Ball found the wealth of the Church disturbing. Such wealth was not in the Bible. And the discipline at St Mary's might once have been strict but now, he thought, it was slack, laughed at by most of the novices. Worst of all, his fellow novices were not serious about God. They talked of preferments, of the aristocratic connections of the abbots and envied how splendidly they lived. They rushed through prayers. They left care and preaching to the Black Friars.

Spiritual exercises were new to the young man and became his salvation. One elderly priest taught them to a restless, uninterested class. Ball sought him out and took counsel from him. Master and pupil cherished each other. The priest had a love for verse in Latin, which he translated into English. Ball memorised it. He emerged from York well educated, a believer in using English, and a priest with an ancient vocation.

Yet he knew his Latin and in the dark of his cell at Maidstone, he would chant parts of the liturgy. Will would lean outside against the door, entranced. His service to this priest now defined his character. And he saw signs of appreciation for him in John Ball that he had not seen in anyone before. The sound of the singing wreathed into Will's feelings and brought an experience of happiness. This is what Heaven will be like, Will thought. He did not understand the Latin but they were God's words, he knew, and he kept his head bowed as he stood outside the door, on guard, in thrall.

But at rare times Will understood the words. They were spoken in his own language, sentences and rhymes for sermons Ball would later write down in English uniquely among the priesthood of the day; now he polished them in the dark, speaking them aloud and memorising them.

Most of all John Ball tried to hear God. Silence and darkness helped. There was nothing of the world to distract him. His thoughts swam out across an ocean of unknowing. He held his fists as tightly as he could, then opened his hands and breathed deeply, more slowly so that the surge of colour and finally the white light began to stream into his mind.

He strained to find pictures, to hear words, to look for signs in the darkness. But his master in York had told him that he must not seek. He must let himself dissolve into nothing, go deep into the dark – and be found. Something would come from that nothing.

For hours, every day, he underwent his spiritual exercises. He had been taught to resist false images, hallucinations, easy resolutions . . . 'If nothing appears,' he had been told, 'then that is to test your patience. The patience of God Himself is infinite.'

Ball recalled the stone-still ecstasy of the female mystic Julian of Norwich, whom he had visited. He invoked her. He pictured the poorest beggar he had known in Colchester, a man who had survived the Great Plague but with disfigurements so monstrous that only the Poor Friars would go near to feed him. They had given John the courage to take him bread.

The image of the over-resplendent archbishop kept breaking into his meditations. Archbishop Sudbury was the devil, he concluded. His disguise was designed to deceive the people. Ball could not clear his mind of his hatred of the archbishop. He saw him holding open the gates of Hell in England.

He sat in meditation until his back ached and his limbs stiffened with cold and the rigour of it. For life?

It was matters outside himself, and outside the dungeon, that pressed hardest. Who would speak for them now? The unfree, the poorest, those who were chattels of the local lord and could be bought and sold. Who would speak for them? Those who could not quit a tenancy unless the lord permitted it, those who were not free to arrange the marriage of their children but had to submit to their local lord, pay him when a daughter married and give him the best beast in the household after the death of the father. Those who could not bring a civil action against their lord or even serve

26

as a witness, let alone a juror; those whom John Ball had seen eating the meat of diseased animals and trying to live on half the bread needed for life, let alone for heavy, constant farm work; those banned from fishing in the rich rivers, and hunting in the vast forests for the most common and numerous game. Who would speak for them?

From his earliest preaching days after leaving St Mary's, York, John Ball had seen no distinction between the salvation of souls and the liberation of bodies. When all were saved, all would be equal in all ways. He scorned the sins and, equally, the system that put the poorest into slavery. Death through hunger he had witnessed many times.

Who would speak for them now? The rich and the mighty took for granted that the poor and powerless were under their heel and, moreover, that this was God's order. The Church, Ball saw with despair, aped the rich. Even now, when because of the many deaths there were far fewer labourers and some were using this to their advantage to secure better wages, there were still the abandoned poor, bound by many laws.

John Ball saw them in the foreground of his mind. The poorest were his parish.

He, dungeoned in a world of lost souls and wasted lives, dumbed. Who would speak for them now?

5
The King

R ichard II was gazing at himself in a pearl-encircled hand mirror, one of the multitude of presents given him by his mother, this on his recent fourteenth birthday. Joan entered the room with some style, girdled by the quartet of girls of her household. She did not impose herself. She had taught him to make all others wait on the King and insisted that this included herself. She knew it gave him a needed feeling of authority.

She glanced briefly but comprehensively at his clothes because he would want her comments and, more importantly, her compliments. They would have to be as carefully embroidered as the jewels worked into the collar of his long velvet gown, another present. It was deep purple, recently arrived from Paris, and just as she had ordered it, trimmed with the ermine he loved, all the more because ermine was reserved for royalty alone. Beneath it he wore a shirt of fine linen from Rheims.

His shoes of Cordovan leather were pointed but not to excess like those of his friends, who had taken full notice of her presence, bowed, halted their game of dice and now stood attendant. His hair, merely down to his neck – not as long as the style of his father, which she regretted – had been brushed finely and slightly bunched below the ears. Like his father's it was parted in the middle and held in place by one of the lighter crowns. He had not yet chosen which rings to wear. He had waited to discuss the matter with his mother.

Meanwhile she took in the, at this hour, mostly young men around him. Thomas Holland was there but she had disciplined herself not to reveal how deeply she doted on him. He was in his twenties, partly idolised and partly envied by Richard. Thomas Holland, Earl of Kent, her second son, namesake of her great love and, disturbingly for Joan, the image of his father. Not only in looks and in his dashing, almost reckless character, but in certain gestures, which she could not explain to herself because he had known his father for such a short time. He stood before her, one leg elegantly, provokingly posed, and she saw a direct appeal to her young beauties, most likely, she guessed, to Jane. He was less richly but more daringly dressed than his half-brother, the King, which itself was a provocation, she thought.

Thomas wore the shortest doublet – bright green – he could risk. His tunic was shaped like an hourglass, a figure she herself could barely approach now even with the strenuous assistance of her well-designed and well-disguised corset. His hose were just as tight-fitting, his strong legs those of an athletic man, but she was glad they were not muscled to any disfiguring degree. The hose were scarlet, which, she thought, was a terrible mistake. She loved him for it. His shoes had longer points than those of any of the three younger men in the room. Joan liked these teasing new fashions, although Richard's taste was much less exaggerated, more elegantly royal, as it should be. Besides, his legs were scrawny and the less attention drawn to them the better.

There was a glow on the cheeks of all the young men, fresh from early-morning hunting in Windsor Forest. Richard had been well trained. He was a good horseman and, although he did not enjoy the sport as much as the others, Joan had been assured that he was unafraid even

in the roughest country. Indeed, they reported an un-
accountable carelessness about his own safety, which had
to be watched.

Joan had dressed conservatively. She wore a long purple
skirt (knowing that the matching of the colour would please
him), embroidered with heraldic symbols and trimmed with
gold. Her tunic in Lincoln green and gold, full on the full
bosom, hugged her figure, giving her a notable voluptuous-
ness. She had seen enough over-elaborate hair arrangements
at Philippa's court and again in France so her own finely
tinted hair hung long and loose in the traditional English
manner, lustred with small pearls. The only flesh to be seen
was that of her face and hands. The King bore some resemblance to her but it had to be searched for.

When, finally, he turned from studying his image to
acknowledge her, she made a small curtsy, he a shallow bow.

She went directly into the compliments on the clothes.
He could still be such a child. He returned in kind though
not in quantity. He praised her beauty most of all: he was
vain about his mother's looks. Then they chose the rings.
Jane was asked to come across and give her opinion, which
she did, sensibly, yet not without a little attempt at flirting.
Joan was pleased with her. She would not do for Richard's
queen – that place was already reserved for Anne of
Bohemia. One of Joan's agents had described Anne as a
'little doll dreaming'. Jane's role, as Joan saw it, was to
work up her son's lust. There was too much dreaming in
Richard, mostly about Richard himself. The men around
him, including her naughty Thomas, were easily able to
winkle out of him a passing affection that would speed their
advancement. She saw how easily his clever friends could
play on him and lure him on. She was determined that he
would develop enough masculinity for the breeding bed.
The Plantagenets needed an heir, the sooner the better.

30

The King sat down on the modest throne he kept in that informal receiving room. His nod gave others permission to follow. Joan's young women stood, their backs pressed against the wall nearest the throne, as she had instructed them, to show off their figures to full advantage. There was other game for them in this room besides the King, and already she saw at least one suitable alliance. Jane might be sacrificed but Joan would make sure she was well rewarded with an appropriate husband and an addition to her dowry. The pairing-off of the others was much more straightforward.

The King spoke to his mother: '*Je me demande si mon titre doit changer.* "My lord" – *c'est correcte, mais je préfère m-m-m-m* . . .' She held her breath, as did the young women; the men tried not to smile. His stammer entertained his friends and gave them, they thought, an advantage. Everyone had to be silent and to wait. His doctors had decreed that the King must not be helped.

'. . . m-m-m . . .' He struggled and blushed, his fair skin, already smacked pink by the hunt and the morning air, shot to crimson. He looked at no one. Carefully, he took a pebble from the purse that dangled from his wrist. He put it under his tongue and sucked it while they watched.

'"Majesty"!' he said.

Joan nodded. That silent applause was all that was permitted.

'My lord?' she said. 'I can't say "*my* majesty": I must say "*Your* Majesty". What of that?'

'*Alors?*' He sucked the pebble steadily still and the high colour drained slowly from his cheeks.

'English,' she said, switching for safety.

'*L'anglais? C'est seulement* spoken by *les paysans.*'

'That time is past,' she said firmly. And so, she left unsaid, is your attitude. Your grandfather Edward III embraced

31

English, even if only on the battlefield. As did your father. And all the intelligent people now take it into account. It is no longer the preserve of peasants, though we should be thankful, she thought, that they had preserved it despite French having been England's official language for more than three centuries. In conversation, French risked becoming the tongue of snobbery.

'English has it now,' she said briskly. 'And in poetry. That is the true sign. And I have brought you a scholar.'

At that signal, Jane took a servant to summon him.

'A Lollard?' Richard was not entranced by his mother's love of radical Lollard scholars.

'A Lollard,' she replied, and smiled. She knew that her smile made her look even more attractive and deployed it with skill.

'Shall we allow him in our presence? Will we not be testing the law? Are these Lollards inside our law?'

'Your uncle John of Gaunt and I both think we can learn much from these men.'

John of Gaunt, his father's brother, had been persuaded to protect the boy's succession to the throne. Richard admired him and was intrigued by his independent behaviour, which included offering protection – curious in such a loud-mouthed, bullocking, colonising warlord – to these quiet, subversive Oxford scholars.

Richard turned to his friends with the slightest of shrugs. She was his mother. What could he do? Their rather lingering complicit looks were too fond for Joan's comfort.

'My Archbishop Sudbury of Canterbury is an enemy to these Lollards,' he said, not going down without a fight. 'He says they must be r-routed.'

'I am a friend of John Wycliffe,' said Joan, unsubdued. 'He is our greatest philosopher. The Lollards take their inspiration from him but they are not him. He will bring the Bible to the people.'

32

'Why can you not be c-c-content with what we have? I was talking about this with Salisbury, Hales and others in London, and they said that what we have in our Church is the b-b-best possible arrangement. Why do these scholars want to change everything? Why must we have a Bible in English? Latin is a sacred language. We have had it since t-t-time began.'

'Our language must be like us,' she said. 'It is time to be English . . .'

The scholar was led in.

The young man, who was given no name but 'scholar', was dressed in his black Oxford gown, a crow among the peacocks. He bowed deeply to the King and to Princess Joan but she noticed, with approval, that there was no trace of fear or servility in that obeisance. He carried a slim sheaf of manuscripts.

'You are welcome,' she said. 'I would like you to talk to the King and his kin, his friends and his advisers.'

'Your letter dictated I talk about the English tongue and about this.' He held up the pages, manuscripts of the new translation. Joan nodded. She rather wished he had not sounded so northern. She saw a smirk flit around the room.

The young man looked about for a few moments and smiled. In that brief silence he assessed the languid, dutiful forbearance of the gathering. He had been in many households to bring the message of God through the first Bible in English. Had he been caught by the authorities he would have been imprisoned at the least, probably tortured and increasingly, as the fame of Wycliffe's English translation provoked implacable opposition to it, he and his kind would be executed. The Bible, the Church and the laws of state had to be in Latin. To put it into the vulgar tongue of England was a heresy punishable by death.

When challenged in the households that the young scholars of Oxford targeted across the length and breadth of England, they did as instructed and told the truth. English must be the language of God in England, they said. John Wycliffe, their leader, a philosopher and scholar renowned in universities from Paris to Padua, had ordered them to make this reply.

'There is no pure English in this country,' the young man began.

'No English?' said the King. 'So t-t-t-tell me what I sp-say.'

'You, the gentry, you speak an English that is riddled with French.'

'That is why I use the French. It saves time.' Richard looked around for, and received, assent from most of his friends. Tom Holland, he noted, was paying no attention, far too engaged in eye-mischief with one of the young women pressed against the wall.

'It is often the same word,' the scholar said easily. 'Your French *armée* is our army, your *garde* our guard, your *trône* our throne, your *cité* our city. And when I waited in the kitchen I had your *biscuit* which is our biscuit. And I see around us the French *lampe*, which is our lamp, French *boutons*, which are English buttons . . .' Once more he held up his sheaf. 'And so to hundreds of other words. Therefore by speaking our English language you also speak yours, but you would do us honour by speaking it in our way and also taking in our own ancient English words. A new language will be born. With your guidance we could preach the word of God in a common tongue understood by everyone and save the souls of many more in your kingdom.'

'Damn them, more likely. And who wants a c-common tongue?'

Joan sailed in with uncharacteristic docility: 'You did not think it common when the poet Chaucer came to

34

entertain us at Easter. You wept at his *Troilus and Criseyde*, my lord.'

'Poets are no counsellors.'

'Do you know it?' she asked the scholar.

'No.' The scholar paused. 'But I have heard *The Parliament of Foules.*'

'I see your course,' said Richard sharply.

'And there is Langland. His *Piers the Plowman*,' the Lollard said. 'It wrings both heart and spirit.'

'He is too sad for me,' said Joan, 'and he stirs up the people with his reports of misery. He is like those hedge-priests.'

The Lollard took this for the reprimand it was meant to be.

'We must strive for the use of our English – which Dr Wycliffe's Bible gives us – one English because among the English themselves there are so many different English languages. The south cannot understand the north, Kent cannot comprehend Northumbria, the west has its own tongues, as does the east. There is confusion between villages, while versions from the Dutch, Danish and German countries, let alone the Welsh, the Scots and the Cornish, obscure plain comprehension. And without that how can the word of God reach all the people save only in one common language, which I have here? Listen.' He looked at his manuscript, copied out in the subversive scriptoria of Oxford college libraries. '"Blessed be poor men in spirit, for the Kingdom of Heaven is theirs. Blessed be mild men for they shall rule the earth—"'

'No!' Richard was on his feet. 'Only kings shall rule the earth!'

Joan did not hesitate. Her son must have his way. 'Take him back to the kitchen,' she said. 'I will send for him later.'

The scholar was led away in silence. He had failed but his glance to Joan was one of thanks. It gave all the young university men strength that the Princess of Wales so unexpectedly and so staunchly should be their ally. She did not return his look.

A petulant gesture from the King cleared the room. Jane would have to wait another day. When the room was voided, save for mother and son, she bowed her head but spoke with great firmness: 'Your people want to be part of you,' she said. 'By speaking in their tongue you give what you can easily afford and what they would regard as beyond price.'

He nodded, then walked restlessly over to a window that looked across the meadows, softened by the warm light showers. His land, he thought, so effortlessly yielded up all the resources any kingdom could want.

'Archbishop Sudbury tells me that there are murmurings and unrest about the new taxes. I think he does not like being chancellor but I made him accept.' Richard smiled at the recollection of that exercise of his authority.

'You were right. The archbishop is exceptionally able. And these murmurings . . .' Joan was not entirely sure of her ground but she was sure of her role '. . . they will go away. You need the taxes for your wars in France and Spain. They must pay. We need the taxes and they must give them to us. We cannot let them believe that it is theirs to decide. It is you and your councillors who decide such matters.'

'We w-will not let them!' he said, and waited.

She walked towards him, took his face in her hands, and kissed him on the lips.

'My council will meet in the morning,' he said. 'I want you to appear to them before your journey.'

In the afternoon, Richard spent time with Burley. He was currently learning rhetoric.

When he saw his tutor, the King's thoughts flicked back to the day of his coronation when he was ten. At Westminster Burley had carried him on his shoulders through cheering, bowing crowds. The boy had felt most strange, most wonderful. Archbishop Sudbury had anointed him with holy oil and crowned him as king, as God's divine representative on earth. Then, as he was shouldered by Burley, his subjects had hailed him as their lord.

On that day London had been transformed into a heavenly city. Conduits in Cheapside ran with red and white wine; an eagle rose on a column in the King's palace and wine flowed from its beak. Bells pealed without pause. Children were dressed as virgins and angels. Music echoed from street to street. England had a new king! The Plantagenets were safe.

Burley had become his tutor and at first, Joan thought, he had been entirely suitable. But it was Burley who had foolishly allowed the boy to cultivate what was to become an obsession with alchemy, the black arts, and the occult. When she challenged the tutor on this, he claimed that the idea was the King's and he would not be dissuaded. Richard had embraced the influence of the Dominican friar Thomas Rushbrook, even though Burley had known the poet John Gower's description of him as 'a fawning confessor and professor of evil, a friar black within and without'. Richard would not be denied. He had been captivated by what Burley had originally permitted as an entertaining digression in his otherwise austere education. The boy loved the mysteries of alchemy.

Burley was now allowed to attend council and was flattered to be in such high company. Archbishop Sudbury was there with the treasurer, Hales, Thomas Holland, the earls of Arundel and Warwick, the Earl of Salisbury and the inner circle of constant courtiers, including Richard's cousin, Henry of Derby, and Robert de Vere, Earl of Oxford, his playmates, neither of them yet twenty.

'I have called you here,' said Richard, when he saw that they were in their proper order, 'on the advice of my lord Salisbury. But first we must bid farewell to the Princess Joan.' Richard never missed an opportunity to create a formal occasion. Joan could as easily have slipped quietly away at dawn but Richard enriched what he saw as the necessity of protocol whenever he could.

He bowed to her, she curtsied to him. She was vexed that she could not stay for the council but for too long she had not kept her promise to visit the shrine of Thomas Becket in Canterbury. Present portents – the storms, the rumours of misshapen animals, black demons and murmurings of uprisings – made it imperative. She would travel to her palace in London, the following day to her house in Kent and from there to Canterbury.

'My lord,' she began, aware of the slight frisson at her still not calling him 'Your Majesty', 'I come for your blessing on my journey. I will not be absent for many days. I wish you and your council God's help.'

Her son came towards her and drew her aside. 'Why are you taking such a small guard? They will think I do not love you.'

'You need to keep your men about you. I am known and loved in Kent. They will do me no harm.'

'You will take Jane with you?'

'I will, my lord.'

'Th-th-thank you. She is impure.'

His mother gave him the slightest possible stare. He smiled at her and held out his gift. It was a small brooch-sized hart, made of diamonds, suspended on a golden chain.

'This hart has secret powers to pr-protect you. I saw Rushbrook put them into its making. He has great art.'

She bowed her head. 'Then place it on me,' she said.

Pleased to bejewel his mother, he went behind her and locked the tiny clasp. The hart glittered against her black velvet gown. Jewels, she thought, seemed to make him happier than people.

'I must now go, my lord.' She turned to the assembly. 'Give your king good counsel, my lords.' She smiled. 'And use our English tongue.' Her smile was a discreet admonishment. Richard must be pulled back from the provocative exclusivity of the younger aristocrats who, she thought, traded on his weaknesses. And they were too much in love with their fluency in the excluding French language.

In the courtyard, her carriage stood in splendour. Five horses in a line would draw it. The eight knights were already in place. Mamoud gave her his hand to take the two shallow steps into the velvet- and silk-lined interior. Jane followed excitedly. The gates had been opened. Joan tapped on the ceiling and they were away.

'I understand, my lords, from the archbishop and my lord Salisbury, that Sir Robert Hales has disturbing news for all here. Step forward and speak freely, without fear. Be brief.'

'Thank you, Your Majesty.'

Robert Hales, the treasurer, was over-stout, but his height and fierce military bearing mitigated the effect. He had commanded high offices skilfully and bravely, but this disturbance over taxes called for a cunning he did not possess. He stepped forward into a space in which he was instantly uncomfortable. He felt marooned: any support he might once have had was already melting away. But he was no coward and he plunged in. 'The people are angry at the latest taxes, Your Majesty, and they are refusing to pay.'

'The people? *Les paysans!*'

There was the usual trickle of applause from his friends, as if the King had said something witty.

'Not just the peasants, Your Majesty, but also craftsmen, the merchants, the burgesses and bailiffs, some priests. They are calling themselves the "True Commons of England". They say the taxes are too heavy. They say they have been taxed enough over the last years for these wars . . . and that this new poll tax on every person above the age of fifteen is not just, Your Majesty. They say that it cannot be borne.' Hales kept the worst from the King. The number of tax evaders was growing out of control. Where could he find the money the King had demanded?

'They say that the Church and the aristocrats are not paying what they should . . .' he had not meant to say that but was now in deep '. . . and also that England is not protected as she should be. The French and the Castilian boats rule the Channel and there is a danger to England against which we should be defended before embarking on costly campaigns in France.'

This was almost a challenge.

Richard read the tension well. He did not like Hales. He did not like stout, sweaty, plain, blunt men. He did not like to be challenged. And he wanted his taxes collected without fuss.

'C-continue. *Même si ce n'est pas agréable.*'

'Reports are coming in of associations – that is what they call them – to resist the taxes. Many of your subjects refuse to pay. By lies and by flight they are evading the taxes in great numbers. We are not gathering what we need. In truth, Your Majesty, we are falling far short. We will not be able to pay your armies.'

'We have made a great demand on these Commons, my lord.' Salisbury spoke softly. He had found it an effective style with the King – like calming an excitable young horse.

'*Mais bien sûr! Parce que* we have great debts! What else are these people for?' said the King, and smiled at the applause his riposte drew.

'His Majesty is in fine form this morning,' they whispered, but loudly enough.

'I need more authority.' Hales could not disguise his desperation. 'I need to send in fully armed tax commissioners to interrogate those local men who are enjoined to bring in the taxes. We must make them co-operate fully and tell us why the tax roll has almost halved in some villages and boroughs. If not, they must be fined, imprisoned and forced to pay.'

'You are too hot, Sir Robert,' said the King. 'Bring our t-t-treasurer a little cordial.'

The court watched while the small drama took place. The pouring and bearing of the goblet of cordial had something of mockery in it. Richard enjoyed Hales's discomfort. The nervous sips. The return of the cordial. Silent as a mime.

'Thank you, Your Majesty.' Hales stood like one expecting a sentence of death and, for a moment, Richard flirted with the idea. What a memorable moment that would be! And in full council!

'These are dark times, Your Majesty.' Salisbury's words, though they expressed the general anxiety, had a soothing effect. Hales might well have dissolved into the air: he had been ostracised.

Abruptly Richard clapped. Hales started, alarmed. The King nodded towards the door. Hales bowed, then plodded, like a sleepwalker, towards a guard, who opened his way out.

'Now,' said the King, 'the council can begin.'

Princess Joan spoke little on the journey to Kent. Now and then she looked out on the rich pastureland of the Thames valley with the eye of a careful proprietor. She thought that the King was overcoming his stammer. Perhaps it was the influence of that dark friar. It would not have been Burley. He had turned out to be an unreliable tutor. But he was a useful spy.

6

The Soldier

He was a man you took care not to cross. Yet there was often laughter around him, and he had a cocky strut he would exaggerate for effect, a sense of play and strength. Walter Tyler was known to be his own man. Locally, he was revered.

The men he had assembled, stealthily, over the past few days, watched the outlaws' camp burn down. The smoke that swayed up from the middle of the woods was a signal of hope to the nearby tormented villages. The defeated men, disarmed and roped together, waited for their sentence. Tyler let them wait. They shivered in the cool of the morning.

Tyler had just beaten the dawn. Two of his men had worked in these woods for years. They knew the scarcely trodden paths. They were helped by a clear half-moon. Silence in their advance, Tyler had instructed them, was all that mattered. There would be time. The silence was blessed by his choice of Sunday.

It was a simple tactic but he had seen it work in France. The robbers, outlaws, about thirty, a number comparable to that of his own men, had thought themselves well dug in. The band who had built their quarters in the forest was one of many across the land, which had increased in size and number since the first Great Plague and following the fall-out of deserters and wounded from the wars.

Sometimes they were welcomed. Mostly they terrorised the neighbourhoods and did not hesitate to murder. When threatened with the drying up of supplies, they moved on, like scavengers. Mostly undisturbed by this, the local lords would only occasionally take action. The towns and villages made efforts with patchy success unless, as in this case, they could persuade a local man of Tyler's calibre and experience in war to do the job for them.

When he had given the signal, Tyler's men had rushed the sleeping outlaws. It was quickly done. The robbers were drowsy, many still drunk. Tyler had brought half a dozen bowmen; others had axes and vicious sickles. He led the assault with a short sword in his right hand and the precious dagger in his left. The encounter was fierce while it lasted but when the flames leaped up from the makeshift dens, and the outlaws sought escape only to run into a volley of arrows, they knew they were beaten.

Tyler bent down, turned over one of the dead bodies and looked closely at the man he had just killed. Eventually he said, 'I thought so.' He looked up, all ferocity drained from his expression. It seemed out of joint. 'We fought together in France,' he said quietly. 'He was a good man.' He glanced around, silent in his own thoughts, as if looking for explanation from the forest itself.

Walter Tyler was of medium height, still nimble, barrel-chested, his shoulders, his arms and his broad hands excessively developed through intensive action with the longbow since childhood. Most strikingly, his head had a distinctive cast, a Roman look, as if those early conquerors had left a living bust behind them as a reminder of their long occupation. The blue eyes, characteristic of the area, set off a skin permanently weathered. Like that of all bowmen, his grip was a stranglehold.

He had a horse, of which he was proud. Tyler had done well out of most of the campaigns in France and his work in England was not unprofitable. Besides, he was a man who attracted cases – such as this one – that satisfied his sense of duty and paid well. He had inherited his father's business and now had four men and two apprentices roofing and tiling for him. But his passion in life had been the wars in France.

A year after his marriage, at sixteen, he had gone south to the coast where he had been taken on by one of the King's ships hunting down pirates. That was his first commission in the company of men who were prepared to kill and aware that they could be killed. Tyler was excited and happy from the moment he boarded. And the sea itself, new to the young man, was another adventure. He was fortunate in that first year and went back to his new wife and their infant son in Colchester with coins and plunder enough to be considered a noteworthy man. He was a lucky one, they said, this man-boy Tyler. And he always looked after his money.

A few months after his return his father moved to Kent. An older brother, also a tiler, needed help with his business. He had no heirs. He had made an offer that could not be resisted. The family crossed the river to Dartford. Walter would miss Colchester.

Although he and John Ball had been near contemporaries in Colchester, with Tyler the older by a few years, they had grown up in different circumstances. Ball roved and revelled in the alleyways and side-streets. Tyler's father was a freeman of substance, who was proud of his status and of the high standing of Colchester, a town that had won itself a number of liberties from Anglo-Saxon times onwards. Tyler's father was determined that his son should be aware of the history of their town even though, early on, he feared that the boy would be off to the wars. Yet Walter was eager and attentive when his father told him about the privileges of being a freeman in Colchester. The town's liberties, he assured the boy, were equalled only by those afforded to freemen in London. He struck in his son a pride in place that would later bloom into a warring patriotism.

His father, a generally taciturn and irascible man, had a copy of the charter of 1189, which he had produced on several occasions to reel off the town's privileges. Walter would often coax him to talk of the town's fine qualities. At those times the older man's mood softened, his grimness dissolved. He knew the history by heart. He liked to recite to his son that, from 1189, the burgesses of Colchester chipped away at the Crown to gather liberties and privileges. And when the Crown chipped back, 'We stood our ground,' said his father. 'Colchester stood its ground. Just as it did when it was threatened by the Fitzwilliams, who besieged us for four months and tried to starve us out. And even when St John's Abbey threatened us. Colchester always stood its ground, Walter. Remember that.' The boy's heart swelled.

His father's glow convinced Walter that Colchester should be the model for all other towns and villages in England and that it was claiming freedoms which went back before the invasion of William of Normandy and his French army.

Throughout his life whenever he returned from the wars he would go across the river from Kent and walk through the streets of his old town, visit relatives and friends, note the variety of trades opening on to the streets, the craftsmen, the black flocks of friars, look with approval at the great Moot Hall, the centre of local administration, walk along the permitted stretch of the riverbank, and mourn the loss of friends to a plague more deadly than the causalities of war.

He was aware of the steady increase in the wealth of the townspeople after the mass deaths of the mid-century Great Plague. The survivors found more room in which to thrive. He noticed that the freemen now bought more expensive clothes for their wives, sometimes risking the wrath of the law, which laid down permitted attire rank by rank. There was talk among the richer merchants of holding a tournament, like those which distinguished the leisure of aristocrats. Tyler did not approve of that. Leave it, he thought, to those who had the means and the traditions to do it as it should be done. This was Colchester! It could stand its ground without borrowed show.

Tyler was widely reported to have done well in the wars. People praised him for it. His reputation went ahead of him. They wanted to shake his hand as he tracked through the streets, along the River Colne and across the fields on his youthful paths. When he was fifteen he had taken his sweetheart there and liked to visit the spot where he had settled the matter. It was a small clearing in a copse of oak trees, and whenever he looked at it, he smiled at the daring and forbidden love they had then.

Even a wife and then a child had not kept Walter at home as a young man. His father had seen that he must give his son his blessing to go to France for the wars or see him leave without it. Walter, wild and with the power of a young bull, had walked to Dover, this time to join the army of the Black Prince – 'to fight the French, as God wants all Englishmen to do', Ned, his closest friend, would say repeatedly.

Within six days of landing in Bordeaux, the contingent of which Tyler was part – the greater part of the force had sailed a month earlier – was bundled into battle. In the fighting and in the days of pursuit following, the young man was confronted by brutality – the axe wounds, the cascading

47

guts, the blinding and crippling, the mercilessness when the order came to take no prisoners, the howls, cries, pleas, prayers, promises, shrill as maddened beasts. Here, he thought, a man was seen as no more than a beast, often more bestial than the animals themselves. If this was war, he thought, so be it. He came through it. Friends fell. Ned was decapitated a few feet from Tyler and the blood from his neck streamed out full of life as the body died on the ground.

And yet. In the calm. When they found calm. In the reckoning. When they had time for it. There was the Black Prince. And there, with him, was the grace and glory of war. He was a prince indeed! The son of the great warrior king, Edward III, who had trounced the French. Those two the backbone of the Plantagenets. Young Prince Edward would be king himself one day. They all knew that. His glittering black armour. His uncontaminated courage. Tyler idolised him.

'They said that when he was sixteen at the Battle of Crécy leading his men in the thick of it, an earl who feared for the young man sent a message to his father, the King, asking for help. His father refused.' Tyler would never tire of telling this story. 'Refused,' he repeated, thrilled by the hardness of a father to his son. 'It was a day for the boy to win his spurs, the King said. The boy was sixteen! Later the prince told the earl that he was ashamed he had asked for help. When the battle grew hot as a furnace, he led his own guard right into the heart of it.' He imagined it, and every time he was proud to be an Englishman. 'My first battle under him came later,' he said.

Tyler was in the chief room of his father's home near Dartford. The fire lit the blackened beams and spilt over the stone surround to play along the surface of the rushes

48

that freshly covered the floor. There were three fat candles. His mother was in her place, his own wife and sons beside him. The dogs were laid out by the fire, one faintly snoring. The servant stood eavesdropping outside the circle of family. Tyler was back from his most glorious battle.

'It was near a place they call Poitiers.'

'I have heard tell of it,' said his father. 'Poitiers,' he repeated carefully. 'It is already famous.'

'And will be for all time!' said the young man, and his father smiled fondly. His son was lost to him now. But at least he was alive.

'Tell us, then.'

Tyler looked around and half closed his eyes, to see again the countryside of Bordeaux through which they had marched hard to keep in contact with the horsemen. Ahead of them, the supply force bought food. The prince would have everything paid for, he explained. This, he said, was his country and these people were his people. His army was not in France he said as 'thieves or robbers'.

'We got to what would be the battlefield just before night,' he said, 'and the prince sent a handful of his best knights to bring reports of the French. We were few and had been poorly fed for days. The French, they reported, were a big army, well provisioned, many times more numerous than we were. They – those who had spied out the land – said ten Frenchmen to every one of us. "Then the more glory for us," said the prince.'

The family's reaction around the fire gratified the young soldier. The story was true, but he could make it better in the way he told it, he thought. So now he paused, and they heard the hiss from the logs and watched the licking flames and nothing else stirred.

'Though it was nearly night he found a good place for us to pitch up. In front of us there were thick hedges, vines and bushes all entangled in a long, continuous line. He had us hack a gap in the dark, about four horsemen wide. Us bowmen were planted in the middle of the hedges. We were invisible!' He laughed aloud and repeated, 'Invisible!

'They said that the French king heard mass in his pavilion with his four sons. Our leader came into the field and we knelt with him to pray there on the field of battle. They had given me charge of men on the edges of the gap and it was there that he held mass. He was as near,' he leant out and touched his mother's sleeve, 'as you are.

'Then they were set to come at us. Remember, it is said that there were sixty thousand of them and seven or eight thousand of us. They had three divisions, the first led by the Duke of Orléans with thirty-six banners, the second by the Duke of Normandy and his two brothers, the third by the King himself. He sent men forward just to gauge our strength and positions.

'But nothing happened on the Sunday, because the Cardinal of Périgord went from camp to camp looking for peace.' He paused again. 'This is what they do in a very great battle.' His expression was set in solemnity. 'The cardinal tells them what God wants . . . But the King of France would not listen and neither would our prince. So the cardinal quit the field. And we tried to sleep, but . . .' he closed one eye '. . . we kept one eye open through the night.' His youngest son laughed and snuggled up to his knee.

'In the morning the trumpets sounded – oh! You should have heard them! I felt like leaving my spot and racing across to fight the French on my own. Such a sound you've never heard! So many trumpets! It shook me to the bones.' His voice rose and his excitement shivered through the room. To the bones!

'Old Sir John Chambers begged the prince to honour him

by placing him at the very front of our force so that he would be the first setter-on to challenge the charge of the French knights. He was granted that and he went out with his four squires and fought until the end of the battle. When the prince decided to move forward into the French storm his words to the good Sir John were "Let us go forth. You shall not see me this day turn back. Advance in the name of God and St George."'

Tyler paused, fingered the precious dagger in his belt, then decided against producing it. 'And I,' he said.

'Yes?' said his father. 'You, my son.'

'We bowmen rained arrows on them and on their horses so many and so fast they must have thought they were in a blizzard. And they fell, one falling over another, in their scores and then in their hundreds. We bowmen routed them!'

His boast rang around the room and he was emboldened by the impressive silence he had created.

'One thing more,' he said, 'for tonight. To leave more for other nights. Then I will tell how our noblemen were armoured and their fine horses and banners, and about the quarrels over who had captured the French king and how our prince took the defeated French king into his own tent after the battle and himself served him at the table and honoured his opponent as the bravest man on the field. But one thing more, just here, now.'

Again, for a final time, he paused and took a deep draught of beer. He looked around almost shyly. Then he began.

'My men were at the front of the bowmen, at the edges of the gap. When some of the French knights forced their way forward, the gap was all they had to make for. Four horses abreast was as much as it would take. Their swords slashed out at us and we had no shields, but we did have axes and we caused havoc on the legs of men and horses and soon the gap was blocked up. But still they came, the braver French knights, and had their horses leap or scramble across their own dead.

'Then a squire came up to me and said, "We have been watching you and your men. The prince commands that this place" – he meant the gap – "be cleared. He commands you to lay down your bows and clear a way." We did that. We hauled out the dead and dying knights, dragged away the crippled horses, killing them for mercy, and the gap was cleared. We had worked like slaves so I had not seen the prince approach, but when we had done and I had gathered my men together, there he was.' Tyler, moved by his memory, looked just beyond his father. 'Right before me.

'I knelt and I heard myself say, "My lord, I have seen the Frenchmen at work and they will be waiting for you. Let me and my few friends here, with our axes and daggers, go in front of you and your squires and keep the way clear. We shall be your dogs of war." I looked up and saw him full in the face. I will not forget that. And he said, "What is your name?" "Walter," I said. "Some call me the Tyler." "Do that," he said. And we took up the French shields and went ahead. Ten of us. Into the guts of the battle, into the sound and the great noise of it, and with our axes we cleared a way. Oh, Father, you should have been there! You will never see your son like that again.'

'You have brought it to me. You are a soldier now, Walter. But when that day is done, come back to us.'

'And . . .' Tyler produced the dagger that had been secured in his belt. It was plain, unworked, broad and of silver. '. . . there is this. The same squire came to me after France had yielded and he said it was a gift to me from the prince himself.'

The dagger was passed around the assembly, and when it came back to its owner, he unsheathed it and the blade seemed to leap with the flames. He tossed it from hand to broad, hardened hand and his smile was a smile of perfect contentment. The silence deepened into dreams of war.

A summons had come from Colchester. It was not un-expected. He had heard of the unrest and could guess that Colchester would be in at the start of it. Tyler lived near Dartford in the house of his father in which, long ago it now seemed, he had told his stories of Poitiers around the perpetual fire. He enjoyed his father's house. Since returning from his last campaign he had rebuilt some of it. It was made of oak on a stone foundation. Its three rooms added up to more than fifty feet in length: two of these rooms were interconnected for living and were where the servant slept; the third was a storeroom. A ladder went up to the family bedrooms. It was, for his station, well furnished, and embellished with quaint objects from his travels.

His father and mother were now dead. Three of his children – the boys – had been taken by the return of the plague in 1363 when he was once again in France. His wife and their youngest daughter had escaped death. He had insisted the name of his daughter should be Joan, in honour of the wife of the Black Prince.

Before he left he checked his forty acres. He grew veg-etables and some corn. There were pigs, ducks, chickens, three milk cows and a small pasture for his newest horse, on which he would ride to Colchester. He had taken care in his choice of a mount. He did not want a tall warhorse. That would not be fitting, and he would not be comfortable seeming to claim to be more than he was. On the other hand, ponies were too small. This young mare, bought at Dartford market, was perfect, he thought. A fine mount but not a showpiece. His daughter loved her.

He was now fifty-three, as strong as he had ever been, in command of his wits and his work, but content, he had convinced himself, to be in his village, his garden . . . Clearing out that outlaw band had drawn another line under his past. The shame and subsequent confusion at having killed an old brother in arms still clung to him. Better to stick to his business, he thought, than be the local mercenary.

But fresh news of the success of the French and Castilian pirates on the south coast had put the worm in that bud and he could not dig it out. His country, England, once the envy of the world, was now beggared and defenceless against the raiders who plundered her Channel ports at will. In France herself the English were defeated again and again. What make of country was she now? Where was her greatness? Although he kept these questions to himself, he was beginning to be ashamed of what England had become.

Tyler would not blame the new young King. No blame could go to the son of the Black Prince. But he knew that a fish rots from the head. It was the weak and wicked councillors who took shameful advantage of the boy, he thought. They were to blame. Their advice had brought England humiliation. The army no longer came back from France with victories to prove England's fame ran from Bordeaux to Constantinople. Tyler was an orthodox religious man. But his greater faith was his country. Now she was being driven to disgrace by men who could not lick the boots of the new King's father.

He let Joan ride the horse up the field and walked beside her until they came to the edge of their village, which stood a couple of miles from Dartford.

'Why can I never come with you?'

'Your mother needs you in the house.'

'You would take me if I was a boy. You wanted another boy, didn't you?'

'Until you came along. Not now. Off!'

She slung herself down from the horse. 'I am as strong as any boy.'

'You are more handsome than all the girls and that matters more.' It was Tyler who blushed at words he felt showed weakness but he could not repress them. She was his darling. 'Away you go now,' he told her.

But she waited, as he knew she would, until he came to a bend in the track, ready to respond. When he turned to give a final wave, she smiled widely and in return waved both arms. 'She'll eat your heart,' his wife had said, years before, watching him play with his child.

As he rode across the Kent countryside, he saw finely clothed dignitaries, who kept lavish houses yet did nothing to fight for the land they milked. As he took a ferry to cross the Thames he could imagine the French and Castilian ships daring even that mighty serpent of English water and sailing up to London. In Essex he went through a patchwork countryside similar to that of Kent; in some places greater prosperity of the labourers than ever before, in others half-empty villages, untilled strips of field, the pits of the plague-dead. Everywhere there was an unease, which he had tried to shut out in his retirement. Now it began to stir and could not be ignored.

He reached Colchester in the morning, and after he had eaten, he went to the river and let the horse graze for a while alongside it, then took her to be stabled.

7

At Northampton

In November 1380, six months before Tyler went to Colchester, it had been Northampton's turn to host the meeting of Parliament.

Simon Sudbury, Archbishop of Canterbury, who was also chancellor of the Exchequer of England, had had to take charge. Universally foul weather had discouraged several lords, and members of the House of Commons. Many of the great aristocrats were absent at war. The King and his court were marooned across swamplands in Moulton Manor.

Sudbury had been commanded to raise what he feared to be an outrageous, dangerous and certainly unprecedented amount of revenue. All the council were aware of the danger. The list rolled though the archbishop's mind, like a secular prayer. Armies in Normandy, Ireland and the north and the English garrisons abroad had not been paid for months. The uprising in Flanders had ruined the rich English wool trade. Aristocrats were accused of corruption and vanity campaigns; Plantagenet heirlooms and jewels had been pawned to city merchants. It was said that it was now the city, not the government, that controlled policy.

The archbishop had become the victim of his gifts. His wisdom at a time of brutish ignorance was rare; his integrity at a time of widespread corruption was a wonder; his dogmatic obstinacy about the traditions of the Catholic Church and the Catholic kingdom was seen as a rock.

But, he thought, as he wended his way through the mud and sludge of rain-blinded England, he should never have let himself be flattered into becoming chancellor. In his nightly prayers he asked forgiveness for his weakness. He knew now he had merely sought extra importance. This preoccupation with taxes was driving out God. He believed he could establish a country to save souls, if he bent his will to it, but to set up an equitable tax system was beyond him – and had nothing to do with the Church's teaching. Its sole purpose was to fill the King's coffers so that his favourites could indulge in impetuous foreign campaigns and hang the consequences.

But now, pinned into the cold, damp priory of St Andrew, Northampton, while the King played with his friends in the warmth of Moulton Manor a few miles away, while the city had emphatically proclaimed that there would be no more loans from them, while the House of Commons declared that they and their kind had been overtaxed on the last two occasions and the Church and the aristocracy shied away from appropriate contributions, as they always had done, Sudbury carried out his duty. He called Parliament together. Proceedings were opened with prayers and a complete reading of the Magna Carta.

There had been far too much change too quickly, the archbishop thought, as the many clauses of Magna Carta rolled out in medieval Latin to a restless Parliament. Change was not good unless it was slow and tested. Change was the enemy of stability; stability was the only guarantee of tradition; and without tradition all would be lost.

As the recitation of the Magna Carta droned on, so splendid a document, he thought, but so dreary in some of its detail, Sudbury reviewed his case. He had his history by heart. Until the death of the old King, Edward III, the Crown, since 1334, had relied on a subsidy that taxed a proportion of a household's movable property, usually a fifteenth. Land and capital were exempt from this but the clergy and the aristocracy were understood to contribute in other ways. It worked, despite the grumbles. But the death and destruction of the plagues had cut down the number of households, enfeebling the system beyond repair. The question was, what was to be done? The King's council, of which he was a member, had concluded that the only way to get the money was to increase the poll tax.

The poll tax dated back to 1377 when, for the first time in English history, Parliament had introduced a tax per head. Every male and female over the age of fifteen had had to pay fourpence – in contrast to the former tax, whereby a household could consist of half a dozen or more yet the tax stayed the same. Yet, with resentment, the new tax had been accepted and yielded £22,000 – squandered immediately, as all those at Northampton knew, on a pointless campaign in France. Once again, they murmured among themselves, as the King's favourites wasted the labour and the treasure of the tax.

Another poll tax in 1379 listed fifty separate categories, aiming to make it fairer – Sudbury had approved of this – but it had yielded only £18,600 and there were local accusations of corruption and bribery among administrators. Its inadequacy was highlighted by the £50,000 spent on John of Gaunt's failure to capture St Malo. The House of Commons, the mercantile classes and the lesser aristocracy felt themselves unduly picked on by this second tax and were in no mood to offer more for a good while.

The council had suggested that the common people should pay more. It was agreed that many of the survivors had benefited from the plague's dramatic cut in their numbers, which had increased their value and therefore their wages. But this new demand, Sudbury thought, would rightly be interpreted as most cruel on the poorest, the many who had not benefited and were still in servitude, often near starvation.

As he considered his limited options, the archbishop worried about the Plantagenet ancestral wealth, which rested largely in the extraordinary richness of the Crown's jewels. He had taken the precaution of speaking about this to Princess Joan at her palace in London before setting out for Northampton. Having first made clear that her own jewels and treasure were her private possessions and that the country had no claim on them, she had stoked his fears about the inevitable dishonour across Christendom if the King were to be deprived of his visible wealth. 'But,' she had added, 'the city will not fail to give the King money. They dare not. They will shout but in the end they will kneel. A few knighthoods will persuade them quickly enough.' That was what she wanted to believe, Sudbury thought, but what if the city stood firm? How could a king be a king without the outward show, the visible wealth, the precious stones that declared his grandeur? Who would follow a paupered monarch?

After completion of the reading of the sixty-three clauses of Magna Carta, Sudbury stood up and played his only card. The first poll tax had brought in £22,000, the second £18,600. Neither sum was adequate to meet the present danger of pirates in the Channel and the increasing number of failures on the battlefield. The chancellor-archbishop first made his case with pedantic precision, then boldly announced it was imperative that Parliament delivered £160,000! No less would be acceptable. The kingdom was in danger.

There was uproar.

Both the lords and the commons left the assembly. But Sudbury had made his case: pay or bring on the collapse of your country. He was implacable. In his archbishop's mind, this chancellor's request was severe but not fatal.

What would be fatal would be not to pay, to be invaded, and to do irreparable damage to this Christian country. He gave them no options.

Parliament buckled. Their consolation was that they voted to shift the burden onto the common people. Twelve pence would be levied on every man and woman over the age of fifteen. The House of Commons agreed to pay £100,000, a third of which would come from the Church. The poll-tax money would be collected immediately.

The local government's traditionally appointed collectors, with sub-collectors for each village and town, aided by local constables, mayors and bailiffs, had been effective for centuries. When told of this new levy, they knew they had an impossible task and said so, but they were not listened to. Sudbury feared it was a mistake, to challenge such bodies so savagely. He knew that the country needed its local government. It had given it ballast for centuries. But his directive from King and council was to get the tax through, and he had brought it into law. He had no power to prevent the consequences, however obvious and dangerous he thought they were. He had done his duty at the expense, he thought, of his conscience and the good sense of historic precedent, which he would summarise as 'Do not break the backs of the people with too much taxation.'

Even as Sudbury struggled through mired and swampy tracks back to London, he knew that England would need all the help God could give her.

But before he reached his palace in London, the flame lit in Northampton had set off what would become an inferno.

8

Colchester

A few minutes after his arrival in the Moot Hall, Tyler was introduced to a younger man, whose bounce and self-confidence made him smile.

'This is Jack Straw.'

'"Jack" will do. One name did for the Apostles. I've heard about you, Walter Tyler. They'll tell you about me. "Straw" came from a little lordling who thought he was a wit. Like muck, it stuck.'

Tyler shook hands with the spare, impish, gesticulating man. He felt that Straw's bones were fragile.

Tyler knew some of the burgesses of the town – Joseph Granger, Matthew Glasswright, Hubert Basse. 'Thank you for coming here, Walter,' said Basse, who spoke most carefully. 'We need advice from Jack Straw and yourself, and we need to talk openly among ourselves about the cloud that is pressing down on us – unfairly, we think. Something must be done, and here, by us.'

Tyler's spirits lifted. This was his true Colchester!

'I want us all to be sure of our ground,' said Basse. 'What we are faced with is perilous. I will stake out our position. We must all be of the same mind for what we may decide to do will not be easy.'

He took a sip of cordial from a small goblet. Tyler wished he had had a little more beer at breakfast.

'The Great Plague threatens to come back. Colchester has now lost rather more than a third of its people. Other towns and villages have fared worse. They say that London has lost half its people. Our world has been changed. I do not know why, but God has seen fit to let the change overcome us. We must change with it.' It was a pleasant voice, Tyler thought. He spoke as plumply as he looked. Despite what he was saying, Basse's tone made the world sound unthreatening.

'The villeins, the serfs – all the labouring men and women – will not any longer be bought and sold like cattle, or tied to a lord's land unable to leave him, and with no rights of their own. Nowadays when a man's labour is more valuable because there are fewer men, he has his chance. He can advance himself. So can we all. We must be free to do that. Yet we are still tied down in the old ways.'

For Tyler, the plague had destroyed his family but not his livelihood. The wars had taken him away when much of this unrest was growing. He listened closely. The bad news he was hearing about his country had to be borne.

'Now we have this poll tax,' said Basse, bringing out the heavy cannon. 'We have evasions all over our county. Thousands of our people cannot or will not pay. When the collectors come, wives disappear into the woods. Sons and daughters roam about the countryside where they can't be caught. People hide in abandoned buildings. They evade the tax in battalions. Many will not pay even if they could. We hear of riots and disturbances – and not only here in Essex. But even this is not the end of the matter.'

One final sip of cordial.

'Because these evasions are denying the Treasury its taxes, Archbishop Sudbury and the new treasurer, Sir Robert Hales, have been put in charge of the recovery of this money. They will push aside all the local men, like ourselves, who have collected the taxes of our own people since time immemorial. We are no longer to be trusted! Our liberties will be ignored!

'They are sending their own armed commissioners from London to interrogate us – us! – who have through the centuries until now raised good tax money for the King. They say that, by whatever means, they will force us to tell them where those who have evaded the tax are hidden. If we do not or cannot do as they say, we ourselves will be imprisoned. We, who have guarded and served our country well, are being treated as if we were traitors!'

'The rich are the traitors. They've never paid tax,' said Jack Straw. 'They should pay for these wars. They are the ones who benefit. Who else wants wars?'

'All of us must fight those wars,' said Tyler. 'We have always fought wars. Englishmen like to fight wars and, besides, France belongs to us.'

'But why should the people give their money to these aristocrats?' Straw was not so easily put down. 'Their own income and treasure could pay for all the wars without our taxes. And it is their war, not ours. It is the war of the French lords who have occupied our country against the French they left behind in their old country. Let them fight. But let them pay. They want the glory and the plunder but they pass on the cost to us. They are not really English,' said Straw, accusingly. 'They just suck us dry. And they make the King their mouthpiece. They trap him in their flattery.' Straw saw that he commanded the meeting and got to his feet. 'And there is more here than the evasion of taxes or the disgrace of those taxes. English people have been under the heel of these rulers for centuries. They took away our old English laws, tried to rip out our language and put many of us in bondage. They were the conquerors – and they still see most of us as slaves!'

There was unrest at the young man's vehemence but Tyler could see that he was respected. He could see also that this was a man who would not easily be silenced.

'Oh, yes! They have thrown us little privileges and duties from time to time – but what does that really amount to? We see now, as we have done before, in plain view, that when there is trouble, caused by them, we must pay, bow the knee and even be grateful that such long-titled, high-handed French-named de-this and de-that look after us! Well, the English can look after themselves now. We have our language back. We – you men – here in the Moot Hall and halls like it everywhere, can administer justice. We can raise our own taxes. We can see that our trade holds strong, that our churches are in good repair – despite the corruption of most of the French lackey clergy. We do not need them! And, above all, we do not need their wars! No wonder so many will not pay. We want no more of their rule over us. That is the deeper sound of England that I hear now.'

The young man's passion impressed Tyler. It was as if he himself had been shaken awake. He had been sleepwalking through his own country since he'd come back from the wars. Yes, the aristocrats had fought for their country in his day, defended it and brought it glory. But not now. Now they merely played at war and lost – they lost their honour too.

'But we must support the King,' Tyler said. 'He is just a boy and he is being badly advised. We cannot oppose him. We must rescue him from those who so badly advise him.'

There was general assent and a cracking laugh from Jack Straw.

'The reason we wanted to talk to you, Walter,' said Matthew Glasswright who, as a young man, had been a favourite of Walter's father for his steadiness, 'is that here and further afield we are forming associations of like-minded men who will be ready for any resistance that may be required.'

'They are in most of our villages in Essex already,' said Straw, 'and up country into Northamptonshire and Derbyshire, we're told, perhaps even further. It's time we were on the march.' His agitation suggested that he was ready to set off at that instant.

'On the march?' Tyler looked around the room. 'Where to?'

'Well said, Walter.' Glasswright quelled Straw's imminent continuation. 'We are not clear. But we know that we who are against this tax are determined men.'

'What arms do we have? What army? We are helpless,' said Tyler, and felt ashamed to say that word aloud. Helpless? How could they have let that happen? It stirred the first sensations of anger at what those false and corrupt councillors were doing to his country and countrymen.

'If there is to be a rebellion, it is we, people like us, who should lead it,' said Jack Straw. 'We are the ones who have held together this country through the plagues, starvations and those humiliating foreign defeats. And now it is *we* who are to be attacked by the King's tax collectors! Do you know what they're doing now? They lift up the skirts of our young girls with the points of their swords to see if they are still children or women! And there are even worse reports! These are bad men!' The gathering did not approve of Straw's graphic rage, but there was no denying it. 'Walter,' said Straw, earnestly, 'you know about battle.' The truth was made to seem flattery. 'We want you to go back to Kent and help us there, form associations and join up with us. Soon, Walter. Then we will sweep them all away. And we can begin again.'

Tyler went back across the river and rode into Kent.

By the time he reached home, a resolution had formed. What was needed now was for him to play his part. But to attack other Englishmen in England herself? And how would he proceed?

65

In Colchester he had bought yellow and red ribbons for Joan. She said they would be her colours, her pennant, and tied them to a stick. In Dartford at the market he had found an ancient brooch for Margaret, three intertwined circles, like a language locked into silence. Margaret would understand what it meant.

Both women knew him well and left him to himself.

From a distance, the next day, Joan watched him as he sat on the ground, his back against the wall of the house, in the spring sun, looking out as intently as if he were looking inwards.

Could he do it? That was the question. He had seen and heard enough to be sure there would be no turning back. The rebels were serious. The tax had broken their backs, their tolerance, their deference. Their anger was deep. He had heard that men were turning up ready to fight with pitchforks and scythes. This did not lessen his belief in the effectiveness of the rebels. A pitchfork in the hands of a strong man could take out a throat or rip open a belly. A scythe could lop off an arm or a leg. There were enough swords and daggers, and he knew where to find bowmen. But what part could he play? The Colchester men wanted him to stir up associations in Kent. And lead them? How could he be sure they would follow him? The people had to want him as their leader.

Tyler thought of the battlefields of France. He and his friends had talked tactics around the campfire night after night. Without realising it, he had accrued a detailed education in the arts and chances of warfare. He had become expert, experienced, hardened. But how could he apply this here in England now?

And there was the King. Tyler's fear was the ruin of England. The King had to be rescued from those who were leading him and the country into decline and defeat. Save the King and everything else would be saved. That was his belief.

At first wearily and then, as the hours passed, with increasing certainty, he knew that he would never be a man he could respect unless he took action to help put forward the grievances of the people and rescue the King from his advisers. He must be part of the battle for the country he had been born into.

The following morning, he told Margaret and Joan he would be gone for some days and rode away. He needed to test the strength of the support he could gather. The men of Kent were not in bondage as many were in Essex and other counties. Through prosperity and their closeness to the court, they had loosened the shackles of servitude generations ago. Yet they, too, as he gathered on his journey through the county, were outraged. But could that be steeled to action against those who ruled them? He needed to meet the Kent rebels.

9

The English Spring

On 30 May 1381, in the town of Brentwood in Essex, there was an unusually large crowd, many of whom had come in from surrounding villages, including the fishing village of Fobbing. Business was being transacted at the yearly spring peace sessions, bringing in the senior members of other towns and villages, men like those who had spoken to Walter Tyler in Colchester, men who believed the poll tax was unjust and that their long-worked-for liberties should not be overridden.

The festival of Whitsun in Brentwood was a mix of religion and hospitality. The finely dressed, the merchants, children, beggars and hawkers captured the streets. It seemed on that day, as it had always been, an interlude of leisure and a renewal of belief. But beneath that there was a darker strain. A good number of men had come armed.

The two commissioners – freshly briefed by Treasurer Hales – rode into the town on that day, high-horsed, escorted by sergeants-at-arms, bulked out with the weaponry of war. Neither Sir John de Gildesborough nor Sir John de Bampton was liked, trusted or respected by the elders of the towns and villages. They were not local men. Rumours of their corrupt appropriation of part of the new tax had already discredited them. They set up outside the Moot Hall and a crowd herded around them.

The commissioners summoned the leading men, calling them out by town and village. Their aim was to persuade or, if necessary, force them to bring in the poll tax from those who were evading or refusing to pay it. The leading man from

Fobbing was Thomas Baker who, in the previous four days, had taken courage and begun to rally around him some of the men of his village. They joined up with others, who in turn had contacted their friends and relations: Baker's message had passed speedily from village to village and area to area. They had become the new threat to order – an association.

Sir John de Bampton ordered Baker and his colleagues to make a diligent enquiry, give their reply and pay their money. Baker replied loudly that Fobbing would pay nothing: Sir John de Bampton had accepted a payment from them of the previous tax just a few months earlier.

Bampton immediately summoned two sergeants-at-arms, who drew out their long swords. They faced about sixty men, some of whom had been in wars and brought their bows for the day's sports, most of whom had been tipped off about Thomas Baker's intention. They shouted their support for what Baker had said. They would not pay the poll tax. They threatened the tax collectors and began to press in on their tormentors.

On orders from a rattled Sir John de Gildesborough, the sergeants-at-arms sheathed their swords. Bampton and Gildesborough scrambled onto their horses and, without dignity or order, hied off, empty-handed. They were sent on their way by a mocking flock of arrows, shot over their heads to spur them on.

It was a good day in Brentwood.

But at night Baker and his men camped in the woods for safety. They anticipated that retribution was sure to come. What they did not anticipate was that, within a few days, their action would have set off a rebellion of the people bigger, for the size of the population, than any ever seen in England before.

+— —+

Tyler had gathered around him most of the men who had cleared out the outlaw band. On the way to the next meeting place, they attracted almost as many others – about fifty in all, a compact, purposeful group.

He was still cautious. Despite the flattery and urging on of the men of Colchester and Essex, who were ahead of the men of Kent in the fermenting insurrection, he had quickly become aware that he must put aside any assumption that he would by right take over the Kentish chieftainship. He was about to meet with men – and some women – from villages and small towns well used to governing their own affairs and skilled at avoiding the imposition of over-weening external authorities. Tyler came to the gathering as a soldier offering what help he could give: he made no further demand.

The leaders of the villages were in council together in the grounds of the house of a corrupt tax collector, whose punishment had been the firing of his mansion and whose luck had been the opportunity to escape. The movement towards confident slaughter of known enemies of the people was beginning.

'Isaac Carter.' The speaker, a man even broader than Tyler, took the hand of the new recruit. 'This is Tyler,' he announced, unnecessary to many, but employed as affirm-ation of the growing strength of the movement rather than introduction.

More than a dozen villages were represented, each one settled in its separate space, most enjoying the fruits of the looted kitchen.

'Food like this!' said Carter. 'Most of these men have never seen the like of it before, let alone eaten it.'

'In that house,' said a man standing beside Carter, gesturing towards the burning mansion and eating furiously, 'the . . . what . . . the cloths . . . tables . . . candlesticks . . . what they have – and the *things*, all over the walls, the *things* they have – could keep us all here, all of us, for days, for weeks, for years! I can see why they never . . . didn't let us . . . get in . . . You should have seen the . . . all of it . . .'

'Was there an armoury?'

'There was,' said Carter. 'It is over there.' He nodded towards a heap of swords, bows, arrows, daggers, pikes and armour.

'Good,' said Tyler, and the weight he gave to that single word made Carter feel complimented. He warmed a little to the man he had feared would expect to take over.

'Is there anything we –' Tyler indicated his own force '– can do to help?'

'I am Simon Miller,' said another. 'I know about you, Tyler. What is it you want?'

'I would like to join you and help as best I can.'

More men had gathered around this caucus and sentences were thrown across at the three or four chief men.

'That's the right answer,' said Simon.

'Where should we head for now?'

Tyler held his peace and looked to Carter.

'Dartford was my plan,' he said – rather, he enquired of Tyler, who nodded. 'Dartford,' he continued, raising his voice, 'is where they are all gathering, and then—'

'Why don't we kill all the tax collectors?'

'What will we eat when this is done?'

'There's men and women here who have never known food like this.'

'We need to have a plan,' said Carter, again seeking Tyler's silent approval. 'If we just run amok they'll destroy us as soon as they get organised.'

'Isaac is right!' said Tyler, for the first time speaking loudly, but still deferentially. 'You, all of us – we are set on a path now. We can't turn back. They would just cut us down. But we have to go forward with a plan. Isaac, Simon and your other chieftains are right. I will follow them to Dartford where, from what we hear, we shall meet many, many men of our mind and we shall be a force. We shall be an army!'

The last word set off a cheer of relieved optimism. To be an army! To be an army was to be heard. To be an army was to be fit to face a king.

Tyler had sensed how to arouse those who had embarked on this rebellion. He saw excited men and boys, ill-prepared, ill-equipped, innocent of the ways of battle, though hardened to the injuries of life. These desperate people needed to be told how fine they were, how brave and bold, and how they would overcome whatever enemy stood in their way.

He took time to look around and pick out faces, and felt a sudden wave of sorrow. They deserved what they were demanding, and it was, he thought, little enough. But it was so believed in, this rebellion so swiftly become a crusade, a test long waited for of their dignity.

In his journey of reconnaissance, Tyler had seen the condition of his countrymen. It was pitiful for many. But their spirit was strong and becoming stronger by the day. As if a new faith had descended on them. Their optimism and blind courage ran parallel to his own conviction that England could be saved from herself by ripping out the weeds that choked the realm.

All they had, he had concluded, was numbers, the force of mass. And that rested on the strange alchemy of faith and boldness. What he could do to help, he knew now, was to praise and magnify their course and their courage.

While the men gathered themselves for the move on Dartford, Tyler did as he had done everywhere he had gone over the past three days. He walked around. He talked to anyone who seemed to want to talk. He sought out the men's mood and the strength of their determination.

'Do you think they'll listen to us?'

'Do you think it's right to execute the tax collectors and the lawyers?'

'How do we know they will keep their promises?'

And beyond these questions, he saw and felt sympathy with the poorest, often shy, desperate men who had everything to lose but were there because they had nothing left to give. Tyler had known men like them all his life. They were awkward with him. As if he were so above them that they could not approach him. Yet he approached them. These men, he thought, were at the heart of it. Out of their nothing must come something worth living for. He himself had had that all his life, but he had seen despair in the eyes of the bondsmen on the battlefield, lit up only by a great victory. The victory here had to be greater than one battle, he now thought. It had to be a victory for an England that did not lose her honour and entrap her king. The flags of St George were all about. The poorest he talked to blessed the King. Tyler felt among his own.

They set out, orderly, flags flying, for Dartford.

Tyler had missed this, the close-bodied smell, the comradely chaff, the jokes and the resolution, the talk of battle tactics for victory, the men. But unlike in France, there were some women too. They all felt inspired by the cause, their heads ringing with the righteousness of it, hearts bursting with pride to be part of it. They had been readier for action than he.

Some were beggarly dressed and carrying the rudest implements – but for them he felt an especial affection. They, like him, were out to rescue the King of England from corrupt advisers, and their bravery moved him. There were the village cohorts, many artisans like himself, small clusters led by local men whose life's experience had been in preserving the rights they had so obstinately clawed back through three centuries of occupation. Some of the local leaders were on horse, as were some of the merchants and even a few of the local gentry. As their numbers grew along the way, there were priests among them and lawyers.

Tyler had found fertile soil. He had also found some old comrades who formed the core of this as yet small army. He had been surprised to find his reputation so high and unaware that his modesty on that account was partly why people were turning to him. He was there, they said to each other, for their cause, not just for his. And he had fought on fearsome battlefields in France!

Now, just a few days after the clash at Brentwood, he was with a few thousand men making for Dartford. It was near his village and Margaret went to its market every week. Tyler rode into its high street, between the fine timber-framed shops, inns and houses, and made for that market where he was to meet Abel Ker, from Essex, another veteran of Poitiers. Like Tyler, he had stopped going to fight in France with the worthless new favourites and set himself up in the small Essex village of Erith. By now communications across the river were constant. The commerce of unrest was greater among the boats than the bustle of trade.

Tyler liked the confidence of Dartford. It was well placed for business and traffic from London to Canterbury and the Kent coast. It had a fine priory for Dominicans, built just a few decades before: Tyler liked to see the solid evidence of a greater past, and the monks about their daily work gave him a comfortable sense of the continuity of things in his country. Despite the plagues, the home-based woollen industry had kept Dartford rich. The town authorities were severe on all crimes, many of which were committed by strangers either begging for food and work or seeing the rich market town as plump with easy pickings on this popular route from London to Canterbury. Tyler approved of the town's policy of no quarter given to those who broke the law or disturbed the peace. Floggings and brandings were common, hangings not unusual.

Abel Ker and some of his men were to the east of the market as arranged. He and Tyler were not unlike in build and their aura of independence. That they had fought in the same battles gave them a powerful feeling of comradeship; time had grown their fame.

The men went into a small back room of the Dart and ordered food and beer.

'You have been busy,' said Tyler, at ease in the company of a man who had so precisely walked in the path of his own most vivid past in France.

'We started ahead of you, Walter – but you're catching up!'

'What sort of men have you?'

'Willing,' said Ker.

'Willing won't be enough,' said Tyler, 'but it's the best hope we have. So we have to gather more. The only way we can win is by convincing them that we are the whole of England.'

'Maybe you're right,' said Ker. 'But now I just want men who know how to use a bow or a sword, an axe or even a pitchfork. We're getting a few men like ourselves who fought across in France. When we used to win.'

'When we used to win.' Tyler laughed. 'Other times, Abel Ker, other days.'

'Some of mine are deserters,' said Ker, 'but they had no pay for months on end. Others were just sick of the – weaklings who led them to defeat. And then, when they came back to England, nobody wanted them. Some of them gang up and live in the woods.' He paused. 'But you know all about that, Walter.'

Tyler nodded and took a sharp breath. 'So where are you now?' he said. 'After Brentwood.'

'We'd been chipping away.' Ker had seen that Tyler did not flinch. What was done was done. There would be no gain in attempting to impose superiority over such a man by intimating that he had misunderstood the outlaws any more than that he was a latecomer. In fact, Ker sensed, it would not serve their cause at all to antagonise this man.

'The abbey of Cerne was our first conquest.' Ker smiled, and paused while the dish of steaming fish stew was put between them with the mild beer they drank – it was purer than water. 'The abbot used the abbey to add to his own treasure. Their rents to our people were too high, their church laws too drastic . . . And then this poll tax came along.'

'Everywhere they say the same,' said Tyler.

'Yes. Taking it was easy, and I had only about a hundred men then. But we made him swear an oath, the abbot. An oath that said he supported us and thought we were right to rebel and right to challenge the tax collectors.'

'That was good,' said Tyler. 'That was very good. An oath. And did you find any weapons?'

'I did. And I took every last one.'

'*Good*,' said Tyler. 'We are poorly armed.'

'But yesterday was even better.' Ker's tail was up.

'I have heard more and more about it all this morning, the nearer I came to Dartford.'

'It was a day!' Ker was up for a boast. 'We got Sir Robert Belknap and we pulled him down! Belknap himself!' Ker's eyes shone still from the outcome of a day on which he had feared that he and his men would be arrested. 'As soon as he came into Dartford – such a great man he thought himself that morning, a friend of the court and an ally of John of Gaunt—'

'That would stand against him around here. John of Gaunt!'

Ker nodded.

'Yes. But people still fear John of Gaunt. So Belknap swaggers with his armed men to make us pay the new taxes and find the evaders or we ourselves would be taken and then' – Ker spoke like one who had been afforded a miracle – 'the town rose up against him, Walter, the whole town it seemed. I had my plans and we were ready but, Walter, we were not needed! They rose against Belknap and told him he was a traitor to the King! And they made him swear – ON THE BIBLE – that he would never again hold such a session in Dartford or anywhere else and that he would never again act as a judge at such inquests as this! And *then* they – I was among them now – they chased him from the county, but not before they had forced out of him the names of those that told him who started the rising at Brentwood. We are tracking those men down, Walter,' said Ker, 'and when we find them – which we will – they will be executed, their heads put on poles and marched through as many other villages as we can reach to show the people what we can do.'

'We can't let it become a riot,' said Tyler.

Ker ignored the implied criticism. He was determined not to be forced into second place by Tyler. 'You've brought something of a small army with you,' he said, to be friendly.

'They're not mine, Abel. I am one of them, and they are no army.'

'Maybe not for now. But soon they'll experience war. You and me and a few others have done that.'

'I feel reluctant to make claims on them. They are voices. That's about the size of it. What can I give them but the sort of battle talk we used to get when we really were an army? And, Abel, we both know that is not the truth of it now.'

'It's not the words you say,' said Ker in admiration tinged with envy. 'It's just you, being with them. Among them. It always was. We will lead this together.'

When the men rejoined their forces, a small group of women barged to the front of the men crowding around them. One – lean, flaxen-haired, a face, Tyler thought, fit for a picture though by her dress she was of his own stock – spoke, or rather shouted at Ker, 'So what is your word?'

'I have not had time to think on it.'

'Well, think now, Abel Ker.' She stood, legs apart, arms crossed, making herself appear immovable. 'I won't leave this spot until till you tell me yes.'

'Who are you?' asked Tyler, trying not to smile. And, just in time, realising that a smile would not help.

'I am Johanna Ferrers,' she said. 'I know who you are. Everybody here knows Wat Tyler.'

'She wants to join us,' said Ker. 'She has, she says –'

'No "says", I *have*,' said Johanna.

'– more than fifty women already who will come with us and fight with us.'

'And more at hand, Ker! Many more at hand!'

Suddenly she smiled at Tyler and he felt it like a slap of fresh air. 'Tell him, Tyler. Tell him that women can fight. And tell him we're not coming along wherever you go for your enjoyment, as the women did in France – they'll turn up but they're not us. We've suffered just as much as you and we will come with you willy-nilly, Master Ker. It would be better for you if you held out your hand to us.' She held out her own to Ker.

'I think, Abel,' said Tyler, quietly, finding it difficult not to laugh, 'that if I were you I would surrender immediately.'

78

'I heard that, Tyler! You see,' she turned to the crowd, 'Tyler himself says we can march with you, wherever you go, and fight alongside you, and if we have to kill and burn we will kill and burn with you. Thank you, Tyler.' Once more she lassoed him with her smile.

She turned and, with her platoon of women about her, drove her way back through the crowd. 'Make way!' she shouted. 'Can't you see we want through, you oafs?'

'Who *is* she?'

'Johanna Ferrers.' Abel Ker sighed. She had not made his life easy. 'The family are vagabonds. Never on a grave charge but never far from it. But they are a clan to be reckoned with.'

'Would you trust her?'

'With my life,' said Ker, as they followed her through the crowd, 'but not with my purse.'

'Johanna Ferrers!'

She turned away from the group of women and looked Tyler full in the face, undisguisedly encouraging him. 'Have you come for some food?'

'I've eaten,' he said.

'I haven't eaten for many a long month.'

The women laughed.

Tyler felt embarrassed. 'Surely there's enough for you round here.' He glanced at the men crowding the meeting point.

'I like strong meat,' she said.

His intense determination lifted from Tyler, and for the next few minutes he spun in an old lightness of flirtation. 'Your husband can give you that.'

'My husband is dead, Tyler. I've been looking about since we buried him.'

'Any luck?'

'Not so far.'

Tyler remembered, almost as a scent, the feelings of those early days with Margaret, and the later unpursued affectionate exchanges that came and went, like promises made to be unkept, lives that could be only briefly imagined before they dissolved into the workaday regimen of the order of war. And then the roaring lust after weeks or months of battle. Times when this invisible tie would bind and control him as possessively as jealousy or a feeling of power. Even through so fragile, unexpected and light an encounter as this. It was as if there were out there a certain seed in the being of another that could not be disciplined but could come unexpectedly, be blown on the wind and find its true bed without apparent cause or preparation. 'Not so far,' he repeated to himself.

'I want you to help us,' he said, with a show of control that took in nobody.

'My pleasure,' said Johanna, dangling him at the end of her line.

'These men will need to be fed along the way.'

'So will we.'

'You could—'

'They can do what we do, Tyler. They can fend for themselves. We are not in our homes and hovels now.'

A cheerful assent came from Johanna's company.

'They want food,' he said, as forcefully as he could, but unconvincingly, he knew.

'We want axes and daggers, and if there's a sword going, I'll take it. We came here to get our liberties,' she said, flirtation abandoned, 'not to cook. I can do everything a man can do.'

Tyler knew he had to retreat. His request, pathetic as he now saw it, had been an excuse to see Johanna, to follow that strange scent – as if it was the time! As if he were someone else, in a previous time. She had seen through him. It had been a moment, a little pause of softness. It would go as it had come.

'I'll see you then, Tyler,' she said, as he turned and moved back among the men.

Tyler had not until now paid much attention to the law. He had led the happiest part of his life keeping to rules, following orders and, mostly, agreeing with them. His life at home had been grounded in work and a secure place in his society, which gave him the freedoms and opportunities of his peers and seemed to him to be enough. Now he was discovering that he was hobbled by this omnipresent might. Was what he was about to do within the law?

He had found a guide. Henry Long had been in the law in Canterbury until dismissed for poor discipline. The two men came across each other later that day in Dartford. It was no accident. Long had sought him out. His knowledge of the law was extensive, his dislike of its pervasive tentacles intense, and his desire obsessive to be revenged on what it had done to end his career.

Long had scared off many people in the two years since his fall from grace. His opinions were too sharp, his solutions too risky. To Tyler he was an education.

'You should see the scrolls, Walter.' His voice was low for secrecy in the fuggy dark room of the inn. 'You could pile up a fire of them that would burn all day. There are enough legal scrolls to wrap all Canterbury in burial clothes. And that is just there. Think of what there are in London – tombs of scrolls, and each one crammed with laws telling us what we must be paid, what labour we must do for our wage, how we must remain in bondage all our lives in the place where we were born, how we are to dress, where we can and cannot hunt, fish and even walk, how we must address each other . . .

'There is no life to be lived in this country on our own terms unless we are rich or titled or princes of the Church. The rest of us are ground down and we are told it is good for us. And it is enforced by the law. Are we such criminals and rogues that we need all of this?' Henry's pale, thin and faintly sweating face was tormented by what he was saying, as if the words themselves made him suffer. Tyler was impressed by the man's fierceness. Long had not finished. He drank a deep draught of his beer. Tyler's was untouched.

'Every path to greater freedom is shut down. The law is the King's secret army. You will see, Walter. Soon you and all the burgesses and commons will be trussed up, not by men you can single out and fight but by these scrolls of law.

'That is what they will invoke. The majesty of English law, they will say, sacred from the time of Magna Carta. But it is no more than a net thrown over all the commons and villeins, bondmen and serfs. And men like you, too, do not escape. It is a net that at first looks open to the sky and loose. But it is a net that is being tightened, Walter. We must burn these scrolls, Walter, and start fresh.'

'Magna Carta . . . isn't that where . . .' Tyler was too unsure of his ground to go further.

'What it says and what they do about it are two different matters.' Long saw in this man and the movement the chance to make good. He was dead meat for all but scavengers on the corpse of the law. With these new men he could exercise all his skills and show Them, show all of Them who had belittled, unsettled and finally thrown him out of the law and all its paths to wealth and power. The only way for him to take revenge and to get inside the pyramid of anciently layered and deliberately obfuscating privilege was to attack from the outside. And at last his day had come: this day.

'But you can't go against the Magna Carta, can you?'

'It is a charter for freedom, Walter.'

Tyler shook his head. 'You can't go against it,' he said. 'I know that much.'

'Are you frightened of the law, Walter?'

He did not like to be thought frightened of anything or anybody, and for a few ominously silent moments, he considered swiping away the pasty-faced lawyer and going along with everybody else. 'Won't we be as bad as them,' he said eventually, with all his concentration, 'if we break the law?'

'But that's where Magna Carta is on your side, Walter. They have complicated it with clauses that conceal its real truth.'

'What does that mean?'

'Magna Carta came about because the barons, earls and churchmen were determined to rein in the powers of the King. They led a rebellion against him, Walter. It came from the same grievances as yours – over unbearable taxes, unprofitable and humiliating foreign wars and, above all, injustices done by or in the name of the King. Men thrown into prison and worse on the whim of a king. The King's word said to be above the law.

'Nearly two hundred years ago they made the King bow to the law, Walter, and after a near-century of haggling they set it in stone. It is there for us all to use when we think we are in danger, as we are now.'

'We are,' said Tyler. 'We are in great danger. But . . . does it say we can rebel?'

'If the King breaks the law of Magna Carta, you can rebel.'

'What if his councillors persuade him to break the law?'

'You can still rebel,' said Long, his confidence growing by the minute, 'provided you condemn the councillors and not the King.'

'We do not condemn the King,' said Tyler. 'So we are—'

'You are acting with the law.' Long knew that he needed a clinching phrase. 'Magna Carta is the king of all our English laws.'

'And this is true?'

'This is true.'

'Let me think on it,' he said.

He walked to the riverbank and considered what Henry Long had said. Was he an honest man? Was the law with him?

At first Tyler could not decide whether this was poison or a policy being dripped into his ear. Yet in his heart he felt Long had spoken the truth. The king of all the English laws . . .

That evening, after more beer and a last meeting with Abel Ker, he let his horse graze its way through early summer lanes towards home, as the sounds in the air and the hedgerows became balm to his mind. He took in the inexplicable sight of the few drifting white clouds. The world before his eyes was a place of plenty and peaceful mystery.

Beer was good, he thought. It did as it was asked. In the morning its tang braced his body for the day, sluiced around it, cleaned it out. Before battle it gave him an extra pip of courage. It could make lovemaking more loving, friendship friendlier and even, sometimes, smooth the sharp edges of an argument. And it could, as now, take him into a space where no cares could reach him, insulated, as he was, by the God-sent drowse of ale.

He stopped, tethered the horse, found a good backrest on the bark of an ash tree and fell into slumber, shielded from the sun by the new young summer leaves, which were beginning to spruce up the twisting old branches. All was gathering in now, he thought, as he descended into sleep, all plans laid, and the enemy was in view. Fragments and images came up from the caves of his mind. He saw himself leading the men, commanding the field and, like his prince, never turning back.

It was near dusk on the first day of June and already Margaret felt as if it had always been summer. It was so easy, she thought, when you had survived, to shrug off the uncertainties of spring and the wear of winter when the first day of June promised such warmth and light. Walter was sitting on a bench beside the orchard.

Over the past days he had left the tiling to his men and the apprentices who were used to being without him and, also, to doing the job to the standards set by Walter's father. The business was sound and well managed, whether Walter himself was elsewhere in England, France or on the seas.

He had left orders that the house be prepared as if for a siege. Logs had been stacked high; his men had been over the roof to seek out and seal any holes. The walls had been scrutinised, the storage room freshly primed and supplemented, the small farm, which Margaret could manage with the help of an apprentice, had been checked for signs of affliction in the animals or prospective failings in the vegetables. It was in good order. The following morning he would go back to Dartford.

Margaret sat beside him. The sun still had enough heat to shine her skin and she turned her face towards it. Walter looked closely at her. There were still the lineaments of that born beauty, the slender, sensual face, despite the lines, the greying but still luxuriant hair. She picked up his attention and turned to him appraisingly. 'You're a fine man, Walter. And you were such a handsome lad!'

'And here's me thinking what a handsome woman you are.'

'Difference is, husband,' she smiled at him, 'I tell the truth.'

She looked across, as she always did, to mark the progress of the three oaks he had planted, one for each boy. She fingered the three-stranded brooch he had brought her.

'I'll never know why He took them,' she said. 'I prayed He'd take me instead. What had they done wrong?'

Walter, unlike Margaret, thought he could bury deep and leave behind a past that was too painful for the present. But at parting times like this . . . and those three young oaks.

'We have Joan,' he said.

Joan had been a late child, the more doted on for that.

'I couldn't live if she was taken,' said Margaret.

Walter shook his head and put his arm around her shoulders. 'You'll outlive us all, Margaret,' he said.

'Maybe. But only because He won't want me.'

She reached up and took the hand on her shoulder in her own and so they sat for a while, as the warm dusk gathered in the nesting evening. Eventually Margaret asked, as she always did, keeping her tone neutral, 'Will it be long this time?'

'There's no knowing.'

'Was there ever?'

'This one . . .'

'In our own country?'

'Is it our own country, Margaret?'

She shook her head. 'You've been saying things like that since you came back from Colchester, Walter, but I'll be blessed if I know what you mean half the time.'

'You understand it all,' he said, looking at her steadily. 'You always have done. Better than me most times. But you keep it to yourself.'

'Some matters are best not made known between us.' Her tone was forgiving.

'Here.' He passed her a carefully folded piece of paper. 'The instructions are there should you forget them.'

'I'll not forget them, Walter.' Her eyes glistened just a little. 'But I won't need them, will I? . . . Will I?'

He shook his head.

'You always come back,' she said.

Joan watched them from the cottage almost suffocating with frustration that she could not hear a word. They had told her to go to bed and there was no arguing.

They looked so gentle and kind and settled, she thought, even her father, as they sat side by side next to the orchard and murmured quietly to each other as the summer light reluctantly failed.

'You always wished I had been a boy,' said Joan. 'Confess it!'

'You always say that! You're trouble enough as you are.'

'So why can't I go with you?'

'You stay with your mother.'

'She has Anna, and the men will do all the lifting, if she asks them.'

'You will stay with your mother.'

She knew his final word when she heard it.

Walter noticed that she had begun to slow them down, to stretch out this dawn leave-taking. He had let her lead the horse, but he would want it back as the path swung sharp right.

Joan stopped, attempting to adopt a wistful posture. 'I can fight better than most of the boys around here,' she said.

'Walk on,' he said. He took the reins.

There was silence until the corner was reached. He looked at his daughter intently, embraced her strongly but briefly, and mounted the horse, which had the agility, he said, of a cat. 'Will you see me off with a scowl?'

His smile winked out a matching response. 'My blessing on you,' he said.

She watched him as he left the village and waved her ribbons and watched him until another corner took him out of her sight. He did not look back. Home was behind him now. What was ahead . . . It was hard to say, but as he rode to join the Kentish men, his spirits began to rise at the prospect of whatever struggle or battle there might be. It was a just cause.

It would be a fine summer's day, he thought. A man was lucky to be alive and fit for battle on a day like this.

10

Rochester Castle

'Am I not a murderer by law?' Tyler asked.

'It was the outlaws who broke the law,' said Henry Long, 'not you. And your raid is already a legend. Legends are outside the law.' He was pleased with that.

'It is no less a sin on me.' Tyler could not shake off the memory of his old friend. Why had he turned out like that? Someone who had been ready to die for his country.

Long was careful. He could not easily baffle and bluster Tyler with a few dog ends of Latin. Besides, he liked him and respected the way the uneducated warrior had picked up some rudimentary legal knowledge.

'God will understand.' Long was often uneasy about God. But He was still the only circumference of all understanding; His words and commandments were still the only available map of morality. Outside was anarchy and silence.

Tyler merely nodded. 'So in the law,' he said, 'I am not . . .?'

'An outlaw!' Tyler had been waiting for another meeting with Abel Ker when Long had seized his moment.

Suddenly Tyler clasped Long's hand and, as with many other men that day and others, the lawyer felt a visceral leap of loyalty to the man who could smile in that way, grip so strongly and play above the storm that was gathering around him. 'Well, Henry! I'll have plenty of work to keep you in beer, but not too much. If we're going to tear up the law and write it again we need to be sober. *You* need to be sober!

'I want us to have an oath,' continued Tyler. 'I want these men to know friend from foe. Something simple. Abel Ker thought this up but I added one word. "Who are you for?" our men should ask, when they see a stranger. If he replies "For the King and the *True* Commons of England," we let him through. Is that legal enough? "True" means that we are not the Commons in Parliament.'

'Yes,' said Long, with authority.

'Will it allow our men to kill those who don't give the right answer?'

'If it is a just war, then yes.' Long was on shaky ground.

Tyler saw this and let it pass. It would have to do.

'I want you to meet some of the leaders from the towns, especially Colchester and especially Jack Straw. He's a very clever man – more like you than I am. Colchester men know the law. But you worked in Canterbury. You will know what documents to destroy.'

Long swallowed the rest of his beer in one gulp. 'That will be the last beer until this is over.'

Tyler laughed. 'Let's see!'

'Why are you on oath for the King?'

'We must have the King.' Tyler was intransigent. 'Even if this one is just a boy. He is a Plantagenet. He will be like his father. And he is the *King*. It is his councillors we must destroy. We must rescue him from them. The King is sacred. Ask the men out there in Dartford. Have you seen how many more are joining us by the hour?'

'You sound like John Ball.'

'He comes from Colchester, like me,' said Tyler. 'I heard him preach once. Not long since I would have thought his sermons treason or lunacy. Now what I remember makes me want to hear him again.'

'That will be difficult. They've put him in the dungeon in Maidstone.'

'Excommunicated! Again!' Tyler shook his head in admiration.

'This time he's there for life.'

'We'll see about that. Here.' He passed Long a fat purse clinking with coins. 'They have trusted this to me. I want you to find men who know about the law so well that they can go anywhere, take out those bad scrolls and burn them.'

'It won't be easy for any lawyer to do that.'

'If you can do it, so can the others.'

The food was put in front of them.

Tyler stabbed his dagger into the thick cut of beef. 'We've talked enough,' he said. 'Now we must attack!'

He went out to talk to some of the assembled rebels. Tyler knew that such words were merely breath. Who was he to attack? He had talked this over with Ker and sent messages to Jack Straw.

Already in the villages and towns of Essex and Kent the uprising was well under way. The sergeants-at-arms, unleashed, had behaved like robbers. The commissioners had acted like tyrants, punishing and imprisoning at will. The people would stand it no longer. The rich locked themselves in their great houses. Rumour had begun to replace information. Those who had terrorised the people through the violent and corrupt execution of the law were now being sought out by the people and themselves punished with arbitrary violence. The tax commissioners and the sergeants-at-arms were being run out of towns and villages. The burning of the houses of those thought to be the enemy had begun. An audacious populace was gathering authority.

Tyler knew that this could gutter into anarchy. He wanted a battle. He had an army, a rough one but still, in mass, an army. The time was right for them to march. But where? Everywhere there was an urgency for battle. But where was the war? And how could he weld so many battle innocents into a force to take on the military armour of England? The stories that came from the villages of rampage and local revenge were of no comfort: mere riot in search of a cause. The excitement it generated was too like panic, and Tyler feared it might spend itself as swiftly as panic always did. The uprising needed a strategy.

It was with Abel Ker that the final decision was taken. Jack Straw wanted to make for London but Tyler thought that too ambitious at this stage. They were neither strong enough nor proven, not sufficiently credible.

And, with his new-found legal foothold, he thought he needed a proper reason to attack any prime object. Just to be on the rampage was not good enough. Abel Ker had told him about Belling, a labouring man illegally seized at Gravesend and taken to the dungeon of Rochester Castle. Ker saw it as an opportunity for action. The men of Gravesend felt themselves victims of an intolerable affront. Tyler saw a possibility. Surely to free Belling, unjustly imprisoned, would be on the side of the law. Henry Long reassured him that would be so: they would set free prisoners from injustice, as Magna Carta had said.

Tyler tried to think of what the prince would have done. He would, Tyler felt, have looked for a famous and surprising victory against the odds. He would have done what would never have been expected. He would have surprised the enemy and given the courage of triumph to his followers. Something astounding. He would have attacked Rochester Castle.

At dawn on 6 June, the rebels marched on Rochester. They carried the red cross flag of St George and the pennants from their villages.

Rochester Castle was one of the first fortresses built by the Norman colonisers. It was constructed to intimidate and subdue. It stood beside the Medway, commanding both that river and the London road. The keep had walls twelve feet thick and soared high above all that surrounded it. It had stood for the impregnability of the new French rulers and withstood all but one attempt to wound its authority, when it had been laid siege for months in the thirteenth century. It was a high, dark, cruel-looking thing. In that docile landscape, it seemed stronger than Nature herself. It was now a notorious prison. Over the past few days, such insurgents as could be captured had been incarcerated in what were England's foulest dungeons.

They would attack Rochester Castle and free the prisoners!

There was already some order in the rebel forces. Villages fought as units, with their own pennant, led by men used to command in their parishes. Tyler had brought together more than a hundred bowmen, who had joined the rebels along the way. They stood alongside Tyler at the front of what must have looked, Tyler hoped, from the ramparts of Rochester Castle, like a decently organised and indisputably vast army. Abel Ker had agreed reluctantly to take his force to the river entrance and block any flight or support from that direction. He was disappointed to be out of the most exposed location.

Tyler realised again, as he stood before the cliff fortress of Rochester, that his advantage was mass. So many he could not count them. They encircled the mountainous black prison. There were Ker's men and rebel boats on the Medway, the ever-increasing numbers of insurgents glutting the streets of the town and moving towards the dark object of hatred. Urgent prayers for the King were being said in the churches. Prayers were being said for the rebels, too, but in the streets and fields where the priests and friars who had joined the rebellion administered mass in the morning. Crucifixes, flags, pennants and staffs were held in the air, with the drilled copse of longbows, axes swirling in the bright, strong blue June morning, and before them the closed gates, the unbroken walls, the stone might of Norman rule.

From the scarce intelligence he had been able to gather, Tyler calculated there were at least fifty bowmen in the castle and as many soldiers. Sufficient, Tyler thought, to hold out for some time. The castle was under the command of Sir John Newton, who had brought his family there – a wife, two sons and an expensive household. Tyler had no information on the character of the man.

The True Commons of England were now in full spate. He stirred up the noise, called for shriller cries, ancient, chilling Celtic calls to do battle to the death. 'Tell the leaders,' he said to Henry Long, who had become an aide-de-camp, 'to watch me, and when I raise this flag to shout their loudest. To scream. And use these words – "SET THEM FREE! SET THEM FREE!"'

The sound, when it came, had the force of fear. The words, coming from the pit of men's stomachs and the strength of their hopes, hit the castle walls fit to bring them down like Jericho's. 'SET THEM FREE! SET THEM FREE!'

Walter Tyler felt the words penetrate his soul. This was all he had. This was the battle. 'SET THEM FREE!' he shouted in the rhythm, which had now become an unbearable drumming beat.

Tyler signalled to the core of bowmen close to him. He dismounted, and led them towards the castle gates. 'SET THEM FREE!' The words bore him up, like a gale from the heavens. He felt invincible.

They stood, Tyler at their head, all their might in voice and numbers only, sounds like giant waves crashing against the walls of black rock.

Then, like a miracle, the massive gates slowly opened and the prisoners, Belling among them, were freed.

Sir John Newton submitted to the rebels. On a Bible he swore an oath to support the True Commons of England.

Jubilation shook the earth.

Tyler's terms were harsh. Newton's men were to join the rebels. His own men were to man the castle. All prisoners would be pardoned. All weapons would be seized by the rebels. Sir John Newton would march alongside them as their prisoner and speak for their cause as a messenger should the time come.

His wife would be left behind, but his two sons would be taken with the rebels and killed if Newton did not obey them.

Tyler stood at the gate and looked over his army. He felt his body clench with the sinews of this first victory. He felt like a captain. He felt an almost physical transformation. He was walking in the footsteps of the Black Prince.

As they went towards Canterbury, Tyler wondered at how easy it had been. Why? With no siege weapons, no depth of arms, no mercenaries . . . why had Newton surrendered without a fight? Similar reports of inexplicable surrender were coming in from raids on the palaces of the lords and the houses of tax collectors, lawyers and landowners. Submission without a struggle. Flight the preferred response. Why? Was God on their side? Were the ever-growing numbers and the ever-growing rumours of more numbers spreading the fear? Tyler could not fathom it.

He had learned one thing. Those complex talks around the campfires in France, with reference to previous battles, ancient and recent, to the skills of knights and the strategies of leaders, the spot for battles so crucial, the timing, the testing, the absorbing art of war, which had fascinated them all, had no place.

All he had was mass. His present strategy, such as it was, must be to increase it as much and as fast as possible.

Canterbury

For God, Princess Joan wore her best jewels. She did not love Him. She considered that presumptuous. She feared Him and respected Him. She would dress accordingly.

Joan had stayed at her Wickhambreaux estate longer than she had anticipated. She had felt ill, been bled, felt worse, dismissed the doctors and taken to her bed for three days, with the warm wines of Burgundy and the plain fare of her Kentish cook. She had intelligence brought to her about the uprising. But she had concluded that it was largely under control. Crowds were milling around, she had been told, with no visible plan. More importantly, to Joan, the immediate neighbourhood, and Canterbury itself, five miles away, showed no signs of the rumoured new outbreak of the plague. That would have been a valid excuse to God. She pulled through her fever, and on the last day she wrote letters to the King and to his uncle John of Gaunt.

For a brief time John of Gaunt had moved to take power after the death of the Black Prince. He longed to tread in the warrior-monarch steps of his brother and his father, but as a soldier and commander he was impulsive, a bully, a blunderer and without strategy. Currently he dreamed of becoming King of Castile and took it for granted that England's treasure should be at his disposal to help him achieve it. Moreover, he saw himself as the real ruler of the city of London. He mocked its ancient liberties. He had barged into churches, defied the law of sanctuary and ignored sacred ground. He had insulted respected aldermen in public. Flaunting his looted wealth, he had built the most lavish, resplendent, costly palace in England, the Savoy, on the Thames, in full view of his enemies and the envious. He had fled from it more than once in a hurried escape boat, usually to be restored a few days later by the emollient intervention of the revered Princess Joan. Her most effective weapon was her ability to get him out of trouble. Through his faults she controlled him.

He had long been the most hated man in London but Joan liked him. This was mostly due to his unexpected loyalty to the distinguished theologian John Wycliffe. His tenacity to translate the Bible into English equalled her own. It was his fearless alliance with a new order and equally fearless contempt for the old that Joan found seductive. Wycliffe and his translation were anathema to the King and the court. But she was convinced that the Lollards would dominate the future. Joan wanted her son to benefit from them. Her unfashionable loyalty to Dr Wycliffe made her unpredictable at court – and dangerous. Joan regarded this as an advantage . . .

Her preparations were eventually completed and she went out to her carriage. The messenger had gone ahead. Her time in the cathedral would not be interrupted by others. A handful of ecclesiastical hierarchs would be her Praetorian guard, encircling her, but at a distance. Her holy vow was to be fulfilled alone. She took nosegays to fend off the stink of the open sewers, which she would have to endure on her passage through the city. By the time she reached Canterbury she felt herself to be in a state of grace. This was the most important pilgrimage she had undertaken since she had come here to pray for her dying husband.

Her carriage and escort waited at a safe distance from one of the gates to allow a party of pilgrims to ride past on their way, Joan presumed, back to London. There was no contact with them. The curtain was slightly drawn so that she could look out. It was sensible to travel in such a big group, she thought.

Princess Joan liked watching The People. Indeed, she liked The People, provided they gave her the respect she was owed. She was always assured of that here, in Kent. It was her home county, which she loved and in which she thought she was loved. Had she wanted to be recognised and fully drawn aside the heavy silk curtain, she would, she knew, have basked in their love, like a seal on a rock in the sun. She was still thought of as the most beautiful woman in the realm. She mocked that now (but only to herself), as she shifted in her corset and wondered if the oils and pastes applied to her face and neck were sufficient to last the day. Any one of her young ladies-in-waiting was far prettier now than she was. And yet . . . the prize would still go to her.

The carriage was ushered into the grounds. It was a place of ancient tranquillity – horses had to canter at the prescribed slow Canterbury pace. Joan had given the order that her horses would walk.

She felt the history and the spirit descend on her, like the Holy Ghost, as the two bishops offered their hands to escort her into the emptied cathedral. As she went inside she was bound more and more deeply into herself. She was beyond the noise of the city and strove to be outside her past. God needed her present presence.

She knew her history well: how Pope Gregory the Great had sent over Augustine to convert her ancestors, as she would always claim of the Anglo-Saxons, almost eight hundred years before; how through wars and invasions, through plagues, fires and storms, this cathedral had been steadfast, had grown and been beautified with stone from the quarries in Provence; how a glorious martyrdom had taken place when Archbishop Thomas Becket had been murdered at the high altar by four English knights, who claimed they were acting on the wishes of his former friend, Henry II. The assassination had made his shrine the holiest site for pilgrims in England.

Only the slippered sound of the bishops' feet interfered with the weight of stone silence. It was a hot midday but the walls kept out the heat. The illuminated windows let in only a little white light. Joan let her mind free itself from the world about her. As a child she had been trained in prayer, in absenting herself from the material world, and had found the discipline a consolation during her imprisoned years as the fraudulent wife of Salisbury.

The shrine was above Becket's original tomb in the crypt. There was a marble plinth, raised on columns, which supported what the chronicler Walter of Coventry described as 'a coffin wonderfully wrought of gold and silver, and marvellously adorned with precious gems'. Joan knelt on the stone floor. It hurt but she ignored it.

Here surely was God.

She waited for His word.

She wanted forgiveness.

She could not truly and convincingly love her son the King.

She wanted God to transform her affection, her loyalty and her pride in him into the love she bore so effortlessly for Thomas Holland. Love gave you power and the power could flow to the one who was loved. She needed all her loving powers to be devoted to Richard. She feared he knew that they were not.

She wore four of her finest diamond rings. One by one she took them off and placed them on the velvet cushion in front of her. She used it as an altar. First she kissed each of them, then held it for a moment's prayerful thought. The white brilliance glittered on the black velvet. She put all her hope in the saint, praying he would convert her to undisguised love for her son-king.

She had come to the cathedral, hoping her request to God would be granted so that she would be all she could ever be to her son, still a boy, so vulnerable.

'*In nomine Patris, Filii* . . .' she began, and later, those in attendance swore they saw an aura briefly encircle her, another small miracle on this long proven site of wonders.

12

The Meeting in Maidstone

John Ball set out to save Will's soul. He had a dependence
on the man, which was becoming increasingly affectionate as he perceived the goodness in him. There was an
innocence that, over the intense time they spent together,
Ball found he studied closely to marvel at. His life as a
hedge-priest had been one of constant movement, brief
lodgings with sympathisers and argument. Only now, for
the first time since his spells with his spiritual adviser years
before in York, had he been sufficiently settled to narrow
his concentration on one other human being.

How, he wondered, could Will retain such innocence?
Over the days, crumb by crumb, he had fed on Will's life,
and nothing in it had predicted this openness, sweetness
and, again the word that beguiled Ball, innocence.

His parents had sold him to a local abbey when he was
seven, already a strong and willing young body. He had
minded the pigs and eaten their slops. He had been whipped
for carrying too few logs, starved for minor lapses of duty
and incessantly mocked for his slowness of speech. His
size, instead of giving him protection, brought him more
pain as everyone learned he would never hit back. It looked
brave to punch Will. It was cowardly. He was the last to be
considered and the first to be blamed.

But his innocence, Ball saw daily, was intact. It had an
imperturbable quality. It realised itself in kindness and silence.
As the dungeoned days grew into one long twilight, the priest
felt Will as a blessed presence, unreal even, a visitant.

'We must teach you to pray,' he said.

The sun came through the chinks in the boarding that Will had made and could be used when they felt wholly safe. The light came in single streams, as if each one had a different message.

'Do you know how to pray?'

Will looked alarmed. He had only rarely been allowed in a church, and then at the back, cut off from the service by its language and its inaudibility. He had felt that he did not deserve to be there. And it was clear that he was not wanted there.

'God will listen if you pray to Him. You know that?'

Will's alarm grew. He shook his head and looked around the cell as if seeking to escape. God? Listen to him?

'He hears all of us. He answers our prayers. Sometimes He lets Himself be heard to us by sounds, like words, and in pictures.'

Will's discomfort intensified. He could not comprehend this.

'You begin "Our Father". Can you say that?'

His expression now was a plea. How could he talk to God? Why would God want to hear him? What did 'Our Father' mean?

'Say it. He is listening.'

Will moved his lips, as he had seen other people do when they were praying. But no sound came.

'We can say it together,' said John. 'Now, "Our Father" . . .'

With all his might he tried and a whisper resembling 'Our Father' crept into the dungeon. Ball reached forward, through a sliver of sunlight, and smiled as he took hold of Will's shoulder. 'Which art in Heaven . . .'

No, no, the eyes pleaded. Please, no.

'Hallowed be thy name,' said Ball, relentlessly. Here was a soul to be saved and prayer was essential to show God you were worthy.

But, no, the expression said, a face now in pain.

'Thy Kingdom come . . . Shall I just say it all myself, Will, so that you can listen and get used to it? We'll try at other times when you know it better.'

Will's face seemed to catch a shaft of sun and the smile of relief felt to Ball like a blessing. And so he continued, 'Thy will be done, in earth as it is in Heaven . . . Give us this day our daily bread . . .'

Will was now cradled in contentment, Ball saw as he spoke the words so familiar to him, so rubbed and smoothed by repetition. He thought more deeply on this imperturbable innocence.

He had a revelation. An innocent man was perhaps part of God's gift to the world. Will had been sent to show that in the middle of all the horrors and brutalities of life, there could be a living purity of soul. This was no visionary, no apostle, but a being whose existence alone taught us that goodness and innocence had been put on earth, often in strange places and circumstances, like secret and unacknowledged saints, just bringing to earth an essential part of goodness. It was too profound for any words.

So at last, Ball thought, I have met a holy man, ignored, despised, rejected, a true light of divine life.

'Amen,' he said.

Will smiled and nodded and mouthed, 'Amen.'

Then he heard his name called, loudly and angrily, and left the cell.

The day after the triumph at Rochester the rebels were in Maidstone. First, said Tyler, release John Ball. Then burn down the palace and take all the weapons.

As soon as he heard the shouts and noises of the rebels, Will went to the dungeon. John Ball understood disorder and began to pull down the planks barring out the light.

Will found relief in helping him, but when the rebels teemed into the small cell, he stood in front of the priest, like a shield.

'Where is John Ball?' said one.

Ball stood clear of his protector.

'You are a free man, John Ball, by the order of the True Commons of England. Come with us.'

Relief and hope cascaded through the priest and he went to them. At the door he turned and saw Will, rooted, helpless, as a man abandoned. The priest held out his hand. 'I cannot leave without you,' he said. Will's expression, suddenly radiant, warmed Ball's heart. Then he went about his mission.

Catapulted into urgent freedom, John Ball made for the nearest church to take mass. The clergy dared not resist him. Along the streets he had gathered his own congregation. When he came out of the west door of the church, there stood before him a crowd, some armed, who shouted his name in a rhythmic salute.

A man stepped forward and held out his hand. Immediately the fierce-eyed priest took it.

'John Ball, my name is Walter Tyler. They want you to preach to them.'

'I will.'

Beside the gate there was a stoop, which Will helped him to mount. It was as good a pulpit as he could have hoped for. He scanned the crowd, sharp-eyed at the bright morning, glittering weapons and helmets, the show of longbows, the red-cross flags, the pennants, the discernible formations within the mass. At peril to himself Will had prised away a plank of the blocked window some weeks before and at feeding times he had opened the gap to give the priest light. He would then station himself on guard outside. Ball did not exploit that window of light: to have preached from it would have led to Will's torture. The regular periods of light had strengthened his eyes, but even so, the glare of the June morning stung them to what might have seemed to be tears, which added to the passion of his delivery.

The priest spread his arms wide and the congregation calmed, the ripple of quiet almost visible as a wave that went from preacher to furthest listener.

So that his words carried on that calm summer morning he raised the volume and pitch of his voice, and used the reach afforded by chanting.

'John Ball, St Mary's priest, greets you,' he began.

The crowd returned, 'We greet you! We greet you!'

Will felt the longing in that response. He could scarcely contain his pride in being of help to such a man.

'All here come from one father and one mother, Adam and Eve.'

'*Yes!*' they cried. '*We do!*'

'Ah, good people, matters goeth not well to pass in England, nor shall they do till the lords be no greater masters than we be.'

Some of those present had heard that sermon before, over the years, but John Ball knew that what was familiar could be most powerful, and at a time such as this, comfort strengthened conviction. Sermons repeated, like the daily chant of prayers, knew the paths to hearts and to Heaven.

A few hundred yards away Maidstone Palace was burning, and the smoke drifted thickly into the placid sky. John Ball began to chant, letting each line stand alone, his hook secure in the hearts of the congregation:

'Falseness and guile have reigned too long . . .'

'Amen,' they cried.

'And truth has been set under a lock . . .'

'Amen.'

'And falseness reigns in every flock . . .'

'Amen.'

'Listen to the words in *Piers the Plowman*,' he said.

He dropped his voice. They were subdued. A few of them had heard of *Piers the Plowman*. But the poetry made it as sacred as a sermon. The priest spoke the words with a feeling that made them see their neighbours' and their own plight. They listened solemnly. He spoke in a calmer voice – a different truth was being brought forward:

'The needy are our neighbours, if we note rightly;
As prisoners in cells, or poor folk in hovels,
Charged with children and overcharged by landlords.
What they may spare in spinning, they spend on
    rental,
On milk or on meal to make porridge
To still the sobbing of the children at mealtime.'

He paused. Then, his voice dramatically raised, he called, 'Can we any longer let the children sob?'

'No!' they cried. 'No more. Amen to that.'

It was the anger and the passion in the delivery as much as the words themselves that moved Tyler so deeply. He was open to the full flood of change and rebellion. Rochester had sealed that – there was no going back – but at last he was inspired. The words and the truth-saying of the priest had turned his strategy into a crusade. Had John Ball called him to be baptised anew, this hard patriotic soldier would have stepped forward.

He experienced clarity and, at last, belief in his cause, their cause. John Ball was the soul he now knew he needed, and he watched with something of the same awe as he had looked up at his prince at Poitiers. The priest's words completed the new man in him. Tyler knew that in Maidstone he had been shown the vision.

Once more John Ball's arms were stretched out, and he waited until the crowd's excitement had subsided. He chanted again, with a rhythm that rocked them so that they became his drumbeat, and knew he was whipping their conviction ever higher. He closed his eyes, moved with the rhythm and so did the crowd. Back and forth went the words he had composed in the dungeon.

'Now reigns pride in every place . . .'

'*Yes*,' they called back. '*Amen.*'

'And greed not shy to show its face . . .'

'*Yes. Amen.*'

'And lechery with never shame . . .'

'*Yes. Amen.*'

'And gluttony with never blame . . .'

'*Yes. Amen.*'

'Envy reigns with treason . . .'

'*Yes. Amen.*'

'And sloth is now in season . . .'

'*Yes. Amen.*'

'God help us . . .'

'*God help us.*'

'For now is the time.'

'*God help us.*'

'Amen.'

And his 'Amen' was taken up many thousand-fold, turning it into cheers: '*Amen! God will help us! Amen! God is with us! Now is the time!*'

His voice and gestures embraced them. God could relent and forgive. They had to understand that. The world would not end if their faith was strong enough.

The sound of the crowd shook the air. The priest turned to Tyler and beckoned him forward. Will hoisted Tyler onto the stoop and the two men stood together, filled with the resolution of the thousands before them, authorised by acclaim to do all they could to uproot those who had crushed them, to build a new pasture, a new Eden in England.

'John,' said Tyler, brimming as if baptised anew, 'what now?'

'To save our souls, Walter,' he said. 'That is the law of the Lord. But first we must make this land fit for His mercy. And we can, Walter, we will . . .'

Jack Straw, on a requisitioned horse, with three of his Colchester men, arrived in Maidstone unannounced. This was unusual. There was a constant flurry of messages across the river, the county and, increasingly, to and from sympathisers in London.

'Too many are going to the wrong destination,' said Jack, as he slid gingerly from his unaccustomed mount. 'Salisbury has his spies everywhere. We two need to talk face to face and privately.'

He had come directly into the camp set up by Tyler and Ker. It was impressive. Tents had been found in Rochester Castle and at the Archbishop's Palace in Maidstone, as had heavy pots and pans, ladles, kitchen knives, all the furniture of mass feeding, as well as horses and ponies, and geese, ducks and hens penned in and available for later butchering.

Tyler, Ker and several other chieftains were eating their one meal of the day. Straw and his men fell to.

'Rochester,' Straw said, grabbing a heavy slice of lamb, 'was good for all of us.'

'I still can't fathom why he surrendered.' Ker looked across the grass towards Sir John Newton, who was with his two sons and a relaxed couple of guards. 'I don't think he can himself.'

'He did,' said Straw, firmly, reaching out for more food. 'And he did because he saw that we were stronger. That is why we will have our way.'

Tyler liked Jack Straw increasingly. He liked the bony energy, the absolute conviction, the speed.

'Now,' Straw said, after licking his fingers, 'we have to decide on our next move.'

'We were just discussing that,' said Ker, and the others nodded.

'I am here,' said Straw, with the clear implication that they were rather privileged to have him with them, 'to deal with two matters. The first is our joint strategy – because without working together we will be lost – and the second is to make sure that you have a leader or two leaders who are in agreement with that strategy, and have the confidence of the men who will follow them.'

'And what is our strategy?' Tyler asked, amused at the younger man's assumption of authority.

'To make for London and force a meeting with the King.'

Tyler sat back. The notion had been alluded to, debated, considered, but not as boldly as this. Especially when Straw added, 'And we must decide on that today. We are getting stronger as they fall apart. Their foolish wars have caught up with them – most of their soldiers are far from London, in Scotland and France, even in Ireland – and we have sympathisers in London. When can you be ready?'

Tyler looked to Ker, who nodded. 'We will leave here tomorrow morning, make for Canterbury and gather more people. We know many are on their way.'

'How many days do you need?'

'Two or three.'

'Why Canterbury?'

'They will welcome us,' said Ker. 'We know that. There we can pick up more recruits, many more, and arms, and treasure from the cathedral to pay our men.'

'And then we will be ready,' said Tyler.

'This is not good news. Essex is already on the march. But we need you to come in from the south.'

'We can make for London from Canterbury in four days,' said Tyler.

'I had hoped for better.'

'If we rush it, we will be weaker by far than we need to be.' Tyler looked directly at Straw. 'Our weapon is the people, Jack, these True Commons, mostly untrained, mostly poorly armed, mostly simple in their ideas of war or even of battle – but when they let loose their voices, and when the court and the councillors see the numbers, then we will have a chance. Our only chance. We need more men. We need to give people who are in with us the time to join us. We need the King's councillors to believe that all of England has risen up. When they look out from their castles and their palaces they must think that the woods and forests of England are moving against them.'

'We are better armed than you,' said Straw. 'But you are decided?'

'Yes.' Two or three joined Ker in the affirmation. Not everyone was convinced by the confidence of Jack Straw.

'Who is to lead you?' Straw looked around. He was an acute assessor of such matters – who would put himself forward, who was favoured, who could command the most substantial support. 'Or were you thinking of yourselves?' He looked to Ker and Tyler. Neither offered an answer. Straw kept his smile to himself. It was always like this. Comrades and equals till the final choice. He spoke now with a distinct change of tone. 'This must be settled,' he said. 'We need to know who to deal with. For Essex and all that Essex does, you deal with me and I will answer you immediately. I will not let you down. I need to know who is my man here.'

Still there was a shuffling of silent uncertainty.

'*And,*' said the Essex man, 'your leader must be chosen not from among you but by the people you have brought to Maidstone and who have found you there. That is how we must do things now. You must gather your men together – as we did – in their bands, villages and towns, and put it to them. They must be let judge and decide.'

Still they hesitated.

'This is not a royal army with its aristocrats and its command from the court, but men and women who at last see a chance to have their grievances heard and redressed.' He paused, then added, more emphatically than he had so far spoken, 'These people must believe that the rebellion belongs to them – the cause and the claims – and that the leader is their tongue. Do it now.'

Ker looked at Tyler. 'We must do this, Walter. It cannot work with the two of us. We both know that.'

It was said in sorrow based on unspoken truths. Ker resented Tyler's easy superiority in the ways of battle. Tyler was uneasily aware of Ker's advantages in local organisation. What had seemed a natural confluence did not work. The envy of the one and the impatience of the other barred it.

'Yes. That time is over. And we must do it now,' said Tyler. 'We will assemble them.'

'I will tell them why this is happening and what we want,' said Straw. 'Let it be done quickly.'

In the meadows beyond the smouldering castle the men and women assembled, many thinking they were about to set off for their next destination.

Straw had found a high wall, clambered to the top of it and commanded those before him. By now they were used to such occasions.

He told them who he was, and they cheered the Essex men. He told them that the victory at Rochester would be the first chronicled in the history of the new England, and they cheered themselves. Then he told them that their leaders – several of whom were grouped below him – had made a vow to have one leader overall and to leave the choice of that leader to those who stood before him now. They were five. He named them and after each name there was a response – already not difficult to judge. Ker and Tyler were clearly ahead of the field.

Straw leaned down and talked to the men. 'I judge this leaves Tyler and Ker to fight it out,' he said.

After some discussion, as much for show as for any other purpose, this was agreed.

'It is between Abel Ker,' Straw announced, 'and Walter Tyler. They will come up here beside me.'

The wall, the broad rump of a tower on the outlying wall of the castle, easily accommodated the three men.

'Would you like to speak?'

Abel Ker was first. 'You all know me,' he said. 'I have been with you since the start of this. We collected together when the King's men tried to force us to pay this unfair and cruel tax.' He was cheered. 'We stood up to them then and we kept on standing up to them until we all came together at Dartford, then Rochester – and see what we did there!' The cheers were even louder. 'I have worked with you and helped you here in Kent for many years and I will help you now. When we meet the King in his council, I will speak for you as before. Our grievances will be heard and we will be rid of the tax that crushes so many, beggars so many and . . . through and through is an attack on our liberties.' Ker raised his arms and took in the swell of applause.

Tyler waited until some thought he would not speak at all. 'Abel Ker,' he began, 'is as fine a man as you could find in Kent or in all England. I am proud to march with Abel Ker. We are blessed to have among us a man of such virtue and understanding. He is my friend. If you choose Abel Ker, I will be at his right hand.'

The crowd had not yet found a chance to cheer Tyler but there was a powerful sense of close attention, like a fishing line being slowly drawn in, needing strong hands because of the weight of its catch.

Tyler drew a deep breath, and then, unhesitating, said, 'But if you choose me I will promise you victory. I promise you that we shall summon the King to meet us and that he will come. I promise you that if they send their knights and men-at-arms against us we will find ways to defeat them in battle. I promise you,' his gaze scanned the mass before him, 'that I will bring back a better England, a safer land, a country that will no longer oppress the weak and feed the rich. We will rescue the King from the evil around him. We all, here today, want justice. We all, here today, want our ancient liberties brought back. We have left our homes and our families, our villages and our work to come together as never before. As never before have you, the True Commons of England, gathered to make your voice heard and obeyed. I promise you that, if you choose me, I will not fail you. And I will not let you fail.'

He folded his arms across his chest and bowed his head.

Ker and Straw looked at each other. Their glance said, 'The choice is made.' Cheers and shouts and shrill high bird calls rose, a sudden lift of sound, joyful, fearful, full of hope, like a horde of seagulls rising from the beach and crying out to sea.

Eventually he found a space and some time to be alone. So, he was to lead them. Surely he should mark the moment as princes did, as knights did, although he had no crown, no sword and no Bible. He stood alone, looking out onto the sweet Kentish countryside, bursting into summer, a rich earth ripe for all to live rich lives. He thought he should make a vow but that seemed above him. He was Walter, a Tyler, a man who had fought for his country alongside men like him, and worked for those he cared for when in England.

Perhaps 'England' was the word to be said. She could not go on as she was. He felt a tightening of anger and shame. His country must not be let fail, any more than these men of Kent should fail. The two were bound together, he thought. He could keep them together. Perhaps that was his vow.

As he walked back towards the tents, people left him alone, save one who came up to him as bold as could be.

'So you can't fail me, Tyler.'

'Johanna Ferrers.'

'You remember my name.'

'Begone with you,' he said, but the smile in his eyes gave the lie to his words as his spirits lightened and she stood implacably before him.

'Canterbury,' said Tyler, 'is our Holy City. We must have it on our side.'

'Canterbury is the centre of all the wickedness of our Church,' said John Ball. 'We must subdue it.'

They were two miles outside the city, seated on a hillock of warm grass. There were clearly apportioned feudal fields all about them, and around them the army of the True Commons of England, feeding on the last of their pickings from Maidstone, impatient for the hoped-for feasts in opulent Canterbury. But they remembered Tyler's orders after he had taken up the speech from John Ball: 'Remember, we come not as thieves and robbers. We come seeking justice.' It was remarkable how long the Kentish men had stuck to this order, which Tyler had heard from the Black Prince in France.

'They will welcome us in the cathedral,' said the priest, 'only because they fear us.'

'It is you they should be afraid of.' Tyler grinned at this unique, compelling man, who spoke truth. 'John Ball – I want to know – would you have us kill?' Tyler asked. 'Thou shalt not kill, said Moses.'

'God killed,' John Ball replied steadily. 'In Genesis, the first book of Moses. "And God saw that the wickedness of man was great in the earth and it repented the Lord that He had made man over earth, and the Lord said I will destroy man whom I have created from the face of the earth, both man and beast." As He is doing now,' the priest continued. 'The plague is back and we will all, man and beast, die unless we cut out the cause of our wickedness.'

'But that was God,' said Tyler. 'God can do anything.'

'He commanded Saul and the Israelites to destroy the Amalekites,' said the priest. 'When the Israelites came into Canaan He told them to "save alive nothing that breathed" but utterly to destroy the Hittites and the Amorites, the Canaanites and the Jebusites . . .'

'But,' Tyler countered, 'they were the Israelites. They were His chosen people.'

'We are His chosen people no less than they,' said John Ball, with such certainty that Tyler thought he could have been hearing the word of God Himself. 'The True Commons of England were visited by Joseph of Arimathea, and the spirit of the Son of God walked on this land. We, too, were chosen and He has looked over us no less than He looked over the Israelites. He killed them, too, by the plague, twenty-four thousand Israelites. It is written in the Book of Numbers. We are as they were. God is speaking to us.' As God had spoken to him in the dungeon and told him that twenty thousand men would come to release him. He had told no one of this. It did not do to boast of such help from the Lord God.

'And Canterbury?'

'Jericho was no less holy than Canterbury,' said the priest, 'and it pleased God to let Joshua destroy Jericho and "all that was in the city, both man and woman, young and old and ox and sheep and ass, with the edge of the sword. And they burned the city with fire".'

Tyler needed to take one final step. The priest saw that and helped him over the last hurdle. 'It is our only way now, Walter. It is too late to mend. We must begin anew and He has given us this chance. Have faith.'

On 10 June Canterbury welcomed them with ribbons, crosses and cheers, with food and companionship, and with promises to join this army of the True Commons, which was also for their king. The victory at Rochester four days previously had gone triumphantly before them.

Tyler, inspired by John Ball, used his anger carefully to direct his men to politic destruction. The Sheriff of Kent was captured and forced to open the archives of laws, which Henry Long and his men sifted then made the first of what would be many bonfires of such scrolls. As was now customary, the armoury was stripped and anything helpful to the rebels taken. Three Canterbury lawyers were accused of unlawful persecution and executed on the street. For some time there was a blood haze. The streets themselves were in a euphoria of legal riot. The carnivals that were imminent for Corpus Christi Day seemed to spirit their high humour forward in the calendar and imbue this occupation with the gaiety of a festival, despite the blood and fire, and the imminent terror.

John Ball was at the forefront of those who walked into the cathedral. Scarcely any of the men and women had ever been in there. The size of it, the historical weight of it, and the jewelled shrine of St Thomas Becket at first cowed and humbled but soon emboldened them even further. This was theirs now. The clergy scattered. The high ceilings bounced back their cries of thanksgiving. The rebels called for John Ball to be made archbishop. He refused, calmed them down, led them in prayer and eventually shepherded them out and back onto the streets.

'Yet,' he said, when he and Tyler met up at the end of that day, 'we must tame and diminish the over-mighty lords of the Church every bit as much as the lords of the state. They are even more wicked. I say again, where is it recorded in the Bible that there is to be a pope or an archbishop, or that the Church should gather great treasures, land and worldly possessions, like the aristocracy? I will say this until we grind it all to dust. Where does it say we need purple and golden cloaks and fine jewellery? They cannot be let off, Walter. They must be disbanded, all their lands given to the poor, and if it be the will of God, some must be sacrificed. We have to begin again. To remake Eden we have to destroy that which destroyed Eden itself.'

In the city, Tyler was always among his men. The crowd that formed around him were content with the food and drink that had come their way. Newton, the sovereign prisoner, was always nearby, under guard. Gifts to the rebels had depleted the shops, and bakers had worked harder than ever in living memory. More cheeses had been brought in and cellars opened when purses were produced. The order was to stock up with bread and cheese for a march the next morning. The village discipline was largely holding up.

'Now for London,' said Tyler. 'We will meet and rescue the King.'

'Will he even talk to us?' Long asked, a sceptic among the enthusiasts.

'We are too many for him to refuse,' said Tyler. 'But we have to go quickly. The only way to keep the men together is to move.'

Will had brought Ball a loaf of bread, which the priest broke, blessed and shared with the man who was already as close to him as anyone but his father. Ball was still puzzled by the depth of Will's devotion. To his surprise, he felt a reciprocal warmth.

'How are the people?' he added.

'Happy,' said Will, nodding emphatically. 'Happy.'

The women were outside the southern wall of the city. Three or four thousand, it was said, had joined the rebels on the same terms as the men. They, too, were emboldened. They, too, were armed, with whatever they had been able to gather up. Joan, Tyler's daughter, had brought as her weapon the hammer her father had used when he was tiling.

Princess Joan joined the main road from Canterbury to London a few miles outside the city. She had returned to Wickhambreaux after her visit to the cathedral. The pilgrimage might have increased her love for Richard but it had also brought on a return of her fever. She spent three days in her Kent manor. It proved too long. Her intelligence told her about the rising in Maidstone. Canterbury was of a different order. Archbishop Sudbury had fled just before the rebels had arrived. She, too, must leave. The fever would not abate. She thanked God there were no visible signs of the plague on her body. But, still, her illness seemed like a curse, a rejection by God of her plea to Him. She calculated that the rebels would spend some days in Canterbury. Her informants let her down. Tyler moved on after one night. Joan's entourage set off from Wickhambreaux on the same morning.

In what seemed no more than moments, her carriage was immersed in men as eager to be near her as bees around their queen. They rocked it. She ordered it to stop and, having drawn back the curtain, saw a swarm of heads. Her own men were all but paralysed by the surrounding numbers, who gave off what sounded, she thought, like a continuous animal shriek.

A few of the men asked her for a kiss. This did not frighten Joan. She had known their like as boys and, neither haughty nor stupid, she permitted a peck on the cheek and laughed with them while she calculated how to navigate her way through the dangerous mob.

The man who rode through it, a broad, cheerful, powerful man, brought her immediate hope. 'Make way! Stir yourself! Now then! I'll be through! Let me talk to her!' Willingly enough, though with no military snap of obedience, they let him pass. Those who had come with him formed a ragged circle of protection around him.

'You've come poorly escorted, m'lady,' said Tyler.

'I did not know I should meet the whole of Kent.' She smiled at him, knowing he was her saviour. 'And, besides, the people of Kent bear me no ill will. I am of them.'

Tyler composed himself and studied her closely. So this was the widow of the Black Prince. This was the Virgin of Kent, the beauty. This was the mother of their king.

He dismounted and stood – like a bumpkin, he thought later. But here he was, face to face with the woman who had been the wife of the hero of his old world. He wanted to say, 'I fought with your husband.' He wanted to say, 'I spoke to him.' He wanted to say . . .

'I will see that you get to London unharmed. Some of my men will go with you.'

She smiled. That was enough.

Tyler took a deep breath. 'Tell the King he will be safe with us. Tell him he will come to no harm from us.' He nodded. It might have been a failed bow. He organised her guard. He told her knights not to stop along the way.

The carriage, pulled by its five horses, carrying the Fair Maid of Kent, was cheered as it went on to London. Joan smiled and waved, deeply troubled.

So she is, truly, a beauty, Tyler thought. And a brave woman.

How would she describe this in her chronicle? The peasants had behaved chivalrously and sworn loyalty to the King. The local squires and nobles were pusillanimous. Lawyers and tax collectors were being disgraced and a few executed, usually, it seemed from her reports, because of corruption.

Sometimes, she concluded, it was more politic for a chronicler to write nothing.

13

In the Fields

E ngland was poised as never before: the rebellion of the
True Commons had begun as a series of local bonfires
and was transforming itself into a furnace. The alchemy of
circumstances, opportunity and the uniquely tuned temper
of the country had fused into rage. The state was crumbling
by the day. Two men had become the emblems of the insurgency: a common soldier and a common priest. One knew
how to make war; the other saw that as the final chance for
Eden to be restored in England.

Sir John Newton, the constable of Rochester Castle, knew
that he would never cast off the stain of his too easy, some
said cowardly, surrender of the great fortress. He had been
forced to join Tyler's rebels to save his sons. They were safe.
He was troubled by what he found among the self-styled
True Commons of England.

Over his short time in captivity, he had seen competence
and a clarity of purpose that, in his experience of courtly
diplomacy, had eluded their betters for some time. And these
people had not only survived the plagues but suffered the
worst of recent famines and threats of invasion from the
sea. They were subject to unjust and oppressive taxation,
humiliating labour laws and now violent enforcements.
Their voices had been denied for centuries.

Yet they held onto their unqualified devotion to their king.
He was of God. They believed that. He was to be preserved

but his traitorous advisers were to be destroyed. Newton agreed that some of them deserved it.

But most of all Sir John Newton thought that in the middle of this tumult, this excited new army of men and women on the road from Canterbury, there was honesty. It was like the cleansing fire that burned the weeds and choking scrub off the autumn hills. Newton admitted to himself some sympathy with their cause. He appreciated their high spirits and even – treacherously, now and then – found that he agreed with one or two of their demands.

Newton brooded over the defining attack on Rochester. In hindsight, he thought the débâcle had been due to the haughty, stupid and insupportable behaviour of that fool Burley. This man, now *Sir* Simon Burley, had been made a Knight of the Garter just a few weeks before in May. In Newton's view he was a pompous fraud who should not have been allowed near the young King, let alone as his tutor. And now a knight of the realm! For years he had been a ridiculous sycophant, a fawning fool, ceaselessly oiling his passage into favour, probably by trading in malicious gossip.

But his latest stupidity had been of a different order, he thought. Burley had pursued Robert Belling, whom he claimed as his serf and his property, and when Belling had fled to Gravesend, had sent two of his bullyboys to arrest him. The way in which he had organised this was a clear abuse of his royal connection. From the beginning Newton had seen that no good could come of it.

The bailiffs of Gravesend, who knew their authority and their laws, had refused to surrender Belling, but he had been arrested nonetheless and taken to Rochester Castle, where Newton had unwillingly imprisoned him. And that, for Newton, had set off the real beginning of this uprising.

Now Newton had seen for himself the military initiative of the man Tyler. But he wondered . . . no Belling, no Tyler? Such twists of thoughts tormented him.

Inside Rochester Castle, Newton had endured several hours of threats and murderous declarations. His men had been afraid. And then he had been faced with the nerve of Tyler – had he met a bolder man? – walking unarmed to the main gate. It had overwhelmed him. No one, he concluded, could hold out against such a power of numbers, without heavy slaughter. And of whom? Englishmen and, he saw, some Englishwomen. All for the sake of Belling? He had opened the gates. He would never lose the blame for that. But neither would he ever lose the memory of that man walking steadily towards the fortress cliff of Rochester, and the sound of the rebels, such a sound as he had never heard before in his life.

The rebels paused in fields outside Canterbury.

Tyler called together what was to become his council – Henry Long and the core leaders, chiefly aldermen from the major towns. He needed to make a reckoning. So much had happened at the edge of and beyond his vision. They sat in the shadow of elms, the sun blazing already at mid-morning. Below and around them was what Tyler had little hesitation now in calling an army. To others it might seem a mere mass but he could see the lines that, like ropes, held the men together in ordered units.

Groups of men were bringing in supplies from the farms. In the distance, he could see more men and women coming to join him. And each would be asked, 'Who are you for?' The oath had proved a useful glue.

He feared that hunger might set in. He feared there would be those who would tire or worry for their homes and turn back. He feared the enemy would have time to organise. Thanks to God, it was warm enough to sleep in the open. As his sense of wonder at what was happening melded into a sense of inevitability and rightness that it should happen, he forced himself to look back to his battles in France. Speed. Surprise. Those were the words on which he had to concentrate.

Messages flew across the counties, across the rivers and meadows, like swallows. He was in constant contact with Jack Straw and his men in Essex, who were heading for London from the north-east. Letters flew to and from St Albans and Northampton, and there was support from within London itself. Reports of more and more villagers swearing oaths 'to destroy divers lieges of the Lord King and to have no laws in England, except what they themselves made'.

Long and his new clerks drew up the lists of what had been done so far. The luxurious abbey of Lewes had been attacked and plundered, its abbot, a cruel lord, forced to take the oath of the True Commons.

The lists were fed fuller by the hour – local score-settling, the burning of lawyers' houses, the seizing of legal documents. One big prize was Cressing Temple, the estate of the order of the wealthy Hospitallers – crusaders, well connected, tax free and avaricious. Their enormous manor house was burned down, gold and silver destroyed, casks of wine drunk, food and weapons appropriated, but the cavernous barns, the greatest feature, were untouched. The rebels reported that they would be useful, later! In Chelmsford, royal records were publicly burned.

The executions in Canterbury had to be put into the records. Law of a kind was still recorded even as it was broken. Tyler and his men had taken Canterbury Castle and let loose the prisoners. He had seized the sheriff and, after making him swear the oath of allegiance, the man had been forced to watch Long gather together his legal records and royal writs and burn them all.

Some of the clerks disapproved of this wholesale attack on the law, the destruction of so many documents and the execution of so many lawyers. Long was not afraid to let them speak out and he reported this to Tyler, hoping for some discrimination.

'This is war,' said Tyler. 'And God killed his own people, the Israelites. John Ball says so. And we are His chosen people now.'

Tyler summoned Sir John Newton and told him to ride to London and tell the King that the True Commons of England wished to meet him on the following morning. He told Newton that if he himself did not return by sunset, he would not see his sons alive. Newton left immediately. To obey was the only course.

'This is war,' he repeated to Henry Long, who had demurred at the harshness of Tyler's threat to the children. 'And he will return. What will stop him? The King will want to see us. And we have numbers, Henry, and surprise. But not for long. We'll head for Blackheath. They will be gathering for the Corpus Christi Fair. We will find many recruits there.'

Some distance from Tyler's council, John Ball had set up a scriptorium. A number of priests, especially from the Poor Friars, had joined the rebellion and Ball made use of them. They wrote out scores of copies of lines from his sermons.

These short pamphlets were seized on by the literate – of whom there was a respectable number – and at points around the fields clusters of men were listening to messages as simple but as telling as John Ball could make them. They were written in English. This in itself was a challenge to the Church. He used language and images of their daily speech. They had a direct impact on men and women who had never before been included in such a way. They felt privileged to hear words written for them. They guarded the notes closely, and were increasingly united as much by Ball's evangelical conviction as by Tyler's success.

> 'John the miller hath ground small, small, small,
> The King's son of Heaven shall pay for all,
> Beware or be ye woe,
> Know your friend from your foe,
> Have enough and say "Ho,"
> And do well and better and flee sin
> And seek peace and hold you therein
> And so biddeth John Trewman and all his
> fellows . . .'

The sin they must flee was all around them, more now that they were off the leash of their enclosed local communities. John Ball's primary purpose was to save souls. The peace he preached was the peace of God, which meant complete obedience to God's demands. The warning to 'beware' and 'know your friend from your foe' was war-talk.

To make it inclusive of all trades, and to multiply and disguise himself, Ball often used false names: John Trewman was there and John the miller. These were characters who had often appeared in medieval folk tales. One message, especially cherished by the rebels, read: 'John Carter prays you all that you make a good end of what you have begun, and do well, and better, for in the evening a man reckons the day. For if the end be well, then all is well, and I will go with you and help as I can to prepare your meat and drink so that you lack not. See that Hob the robber be well punished for losing our grace, for you have great need to take God with you in all that you do. For now is the time to take care.'

The men would tussle with the meaning and find reassurance in uncovering a truth. They saw this priest, shadowed by Will, his mighty guardian angel, moving about the fields, administering mass, giving blessings, kneeling to pray beside those who wanted him to expel their sin. They cherished him. He gave them God and they saw him as their prophet.

And when he attacked their enemies, it was with the avenging sword they saw as clearing away all corruption, all injustice. Sometimes Tyler came and stood near to listen. John Ball was one of God's own. Tyler was mesmerised by him.

14

The Messenger

They arrived at Blackheath the next day, on 12 June. A deputation of London aldermen and the Bishop of Rochester was waiting for them with a message from the King, ordering them to go back to their towns and villages where their grievances would be assessed in full. Tyler would have none of this. His own plan was now set. Retreat was unthinkable. He would meet the King and he would meet him face to face.

As Sir John Newton was rowed up the Thames on the incoming tide that early afternoon, he felt as if he were going to the Tower for execution. Why should the King and his council let him keep his life after he had delivered this impertinent message? A command from a commoner, brought by a knight so lacking in his courtly vows that he had yielded a great castle and bowed to a peasant? They would see him as a man without honour in an age that made of it the inspiration for the noble life, an ideal as powerful as the love of Christ Himself.

He had lost Rochester Castle. There might be understanding of the odds against him. There might even be some comprehension of his reluctance to ignite a slaughterous encounter with an as yet largely unbloody rebellion. But, in their hearts, the King and his court would see him, he knew, as the knight who did not sacrifice himself when a local sacrifice might have saved the kingdom. What were sons compared to a kingdom?

As the eight watermen with their long oars rowed the boat easily on the calm summer surface of the warm Thames, Newton sat in the prow, for all the world like a proud captain. He tried to find consolation in the compelling demand of fatherhood. The words of the rebels at Rochester had been unanswerable: 'It behoves you to go with us, Sir John, and be our sovereign captain and do what we will have you. If you do not as we will have you, you are but dead.'

The same threat had been made to several other knights and gentlemen and all of them had sworn allegiance to the True Commons and the King.

Yet still Newton was tormented by the conviction that he should have given his life. He had been trained for that from birth, as had all of them in that comparatively small, closely related warrior family web. The reward of service was entitlement. The price of failure was death.

But there were the two boys. The boys had been in Rochester with their father for an induction into the life of arms and command to which they had been born. The boys, he had little doubt, would have been executed alongside him.

So he had surrendered the talismanic Norman fortress. He was conscience-blighted by what he had done. As a light spray from the river bathed his face, as the silent oarsmen drew nearer to the impregnable White Tower, he accused himself repeatedly: why had he not retreated to the keep in Rochester Castle? Tyler's men had not the resources for a siege. Why had he not held out?

It had been weakness. But there were the boys.

They were safe now. For a time. Guarded by men who had made them small bows. Who were, Newton observed, warmer and easier with them than he could be.

Sympathy, though, was a prologue to treachery. And as the boat drew up under the unassailable London fortress,

129

he tried to slough off the wounding memory, like the old skin of a snake. He stepped sure-footedly ashore and fell in behind the six waiting men-at-arms. The ravens cawed coarse menace as he was marched up from the Thames.

He went up steep flights of stone steps, out of the beaming June day into the intimidating gloom of the Tower.

They were waiting for him.

At the right-hand side of her son, and a pace behind him, stood the Princess Joan, head bent over an exquisite book of hours, dress plain black velvet, jewellery restricted to one ring, one brooch and the pearls in her hair. At Richard's other hand and, like Princess Joan, at a correctly respectful distance from the King, was the archbishop and chancellor, Sudbury. Like unfolded wings, those on either side of the King formed a ready guard and support.

There was Richard's half-brother, twice his age and his hero, Thomas Holland, the Earl of Kent, who stood close by their mother. Also in the semi-circle of reception were other members of the council and the court, the Earl of Salisbury, the Earl of Warwick, the Earl of Oxford, Sir Robert of Namur, the prior of St John's Hospital, the Lord of Vertaing, the Lord of Gommegnies and Sir Thierry de Senzeille. There was also a number from the city, led by William Walworth, the Lord Mayor of London, with several notable burgesses. But Newton's gaze fixed itself on the face of Sir Simon Burley, the King's tutor.

The King, who, on the advice of his mother, had chosen to dress plainly, beckoned Newton forward immediately. A large ruby ring caught a narrow shaft of sun that came through an arrow slit.

Newton felt that he was on trial. The gloating gaze of Burley was not encouraging. He sensed among these heavily dressed and richly protected men there was a fear of the rebels, which he was in no position to dispel. He had met most of the advisers during his time as one of the King's officers. He picked out little mercy in their collective gaze.

He knelt, and when Richard murmured, 'Speak', Newton began or, rather, it seemed that somewhere just ahead of him a voice like his own said, 'My right redoubted lord, let it not displease Your Grace the message that I must needs show you for, dear sir, it is by force and against my will.'

Richard had been rehearsed in this. 'Sir John,' he replied, 'say what you will. I hold you excused.'

The sincerity of the thin, boyish voice was of some comfort, and Newton found his own voice reconnected to his throat.

'Sir, the commons of your realm, who call themselves the True Commons, have sent me to you to desire you come and speak with them. They desire to have none but you. And, sir, you need have no doubt about your safety for I vow they will do you no hurt. They hold and will hold you for their king. But, sir, they wish to tell you of many things that they think it necessary you heed. I have no charge to tell you of these things and do not know them.

'Sir, I hope it may please you to give me an answer that may appease them so that they will know for truth that I have spoken with you.' He breathed in very deeply. 'For they have my children in hostage till I return again to them, which must be this day. If I do not, my children will be killed.'

'You shall have an answer shortly.' Richard indicated to Burley, who stepped forward and led Newton out into a side chamber where there was food, wine and beer.

Newton took the leg of a partridge.

Burley looked on with a carefully arranged mournful expression. 'We were dismayed about Rochester.'

Newton had his back to him and did not turn. He took some bread and cheese and drank a mouthful of the beer.

'We agreed not to mention it today,' Burley continued, with a forgiving sigh. 'Too painful.'

Newton swirled some beer in his mouth, then spat it against the wall.

Burley smiled at his little victory.

Sir John Newton prayed that he could save his sons.

And waited in silence.

'I will go to meet them,' said Richard, and glanced at his mother, who gave the merest nod, but that was all he needed.

'My lord,' said Salisbury, whose face was creased with doubt and burgundy, 'we should consider the dangers. My lord the archbishop has brought us alarming news of the riots of this mob in Canterbury.'

A troubled archbishop nodded, uncharacteristically lost for words. What words would serve? His life, secured by immeasurable wealth and land, had been robbed from him just two days before by the arrival of Kentish peasants. His informants had enabled him to leave before they engulfed the city – that sacred seat of God's ministry in England, that shrine of faith of which he was the keeper, that hallowed spot now brought low.

'My lord,' said Walworth, self-made, self-important and impatient with all prevarication, 'we must attack them before they attack us.'

'With what forces?' Joan spoke quietly. 'Gaunt is in Scotland with one army, Buckingham in Normandy with another, we have a fleet assembled at Plymouth and men in Ireland. With what forces, my Lord Mayor?'

'The city of London has men who can raise an army.'

'But of what size?' said Salisbury, slicing through to the heart of the matter. 'And of what mind? And who will lead them?'

'We are safe here,' said the archbishop. 'The mayor will not let them into the city.'

'Never!' said Walworth, seeing himself heroically cast.

'There are many of them,' said Joan. 'I have seen them. And they are for the King.'

'But the rest of us?' The archbishop smiled, rather weakly, and lifted his arms. 'Are they for us?'

'You will always be safe in the Tower,' said the King.

'And in the city,' Walworth added.

'What is to be gained by spurning this request?' Joan asked.

'Time,' said Salisbury. It was his favourite word in all diplomacy. Time was diplomacy itself.

'Time for what?' she asked.

'Thought,' he answered.

'On what?'

'Consequences.'

'Do we know what they will be?'

'Not yet,' said the earl. 'But they always show themselves.'

'The men I saw,' said Joan, 'who, to me directly, expressed loyalty to the King, seemed disinclined to wait. They are dangerous, my lords. They may at present be behaving like honourable men—'

'Honourable men! There is blood on their hands, my lady!' The archbishop uncharacteristically cut across her sentence. 'They have executed lawyers who were the friends of John of Gaunt. They have burned down fine houses and forced several of Your Majesty's loyal and distinguished subjects to swear an oath to their cause. In Maidstone they destroyed the palace.'

'And there will be much more and much worse,' said Joan, now fierce, 'unless we take action to prevent it. If we refuse to meet them and thwart them, who is to say what they will do?'

'I have been calculating,' said Walworth. 'In three, certainly four days' time the city could most likely give the King eight thousand fully armed men of experience in war.'

'The numbers we hear of,' said Salisbury, 'of these peasants as they truly are, seem to be in their tens of thousands and they increase in every town and village through which they pass. In London itself we hear already of many sympathisers . . .'

Each one then put forward an opinion but the decision was so firmly in the grasp of the King that the talk was little more than a formal exercise. Yet, thought Joan, at this crucial moment she could see in his eyes uncertainty and fear. He was so young.

'And you, my lord?' Richard turned to Thomas Holland. It was a curious but clever choice. Richard was painfully and often angrily jealous that his mother preferred Thomas to himself. All his life he himself had admired Tom's physical beauty, his elegance, his experience of life, his wit, boldness, even his temper. But he was still besotted by this older half-brother, this effortless hero.

'I think, my lord, that you should meet them,' said Thomas. 'They will praise your courage and be humbled by your courtesy.'

Richard looked at their mother. 'Was that not well said?' he asked her.

'Your own thoughts, my lord.'

'And yours?'

'Yes,' she said, as simply as she could. 'These are your people. Speak to them, my lord.'

'*Avec plaisir*,' he said, and smiled at Thomas.

15

Blackheath

Newton brought back the news to Blackheath. Tyler shook his hand and sat him down with the council for a while.

Newton slept between his sons. They breathed softly. Tyler would never let him go. He tried to count the stars, a childhood way to bring on sleep, but . . . There was singing from the women's camp; there was a murmurous tension in the thousand thousand exhalations of the men's sleeping breath. Not far away were the soft lapping sounds of the Thames, ever flowing, ever changing . . .

After Tyler and the men had gone to the Thames, John Ball stood on a mound sufficiently high above the crowd. Will was to one side. The priest's stillness brought a responding quiet among the massed congregation. The spot was some distance from the Corpus Christi Fair, which had begun in innocent gaiety as if nothing at all unusual was happening.

He began:

> 'When Adam delved and Eve span,
> Who was then the gentleman?'

His words sang across the heath, reaching many of the gathered multitude. It was a couplet he had used before, a simple couplet easily remembered. Inside its simplicity was the promise of a new life. In those few words his congregation were back with the firstborn of God, in the Garden of Eden, which He had told them about in Genesis, the first book He had dictated to Moses on Mount Sinai. In their rebel state of hope, apprehension, hunger, longing and frustration, they were ready to be captured by the spell of this man.

Then the words, repeated with all his strength, rang like the peals of a bell and they were taken up and chanted back to him by the eager thousands.

'When Adam delved and Eve span,
Who was then the gentleman?'

The question was returned, like a dread blood pulse. It was a full tide of crowd-sound accompanied by the waving of flags, pennants and weapons. Some saw the Garden itself. Others felt a cascade of faith in the certain prospect of Heaven on earth. Others saw bloody victory over lifelong enemies.

'Good people,' said Ball, when by gesture and his waiting presence he had poured oil on the excited waves before him. 'Good people.' They were embraced by these words: they were indeed the 'good people'. He paused and shifted the tone, just a little quieter, more coiled and concentrated as he leaned forward. 'We will not be saved until everything be common among us.' He rocked back and their assent swept over him.

'Everything must be in common. That is God's word! There are to be no unfree, no villeins, no gentlemen and lords, but that we may be all united together, and that the lords be no greater masters than we.'

'Amen! Amen to that!'

That was what they would have. John Ball heard the sound of God. It came, as it had done to Joseph, in his dreams. He turned these dreams into earthly words, but they did not lose their heavenly power.

Again the preacher paused, this time to signal by gesture and tone that he wished to be uninterrupted, even by acclaim. He closed his eyes, and they took this for a sign that God was in him.

'What have we deserved, or why should we thus be kept in servitude? We all come from one father and one mother, Adam and Eve. Whereby can they say or show that they be greater lords than we be, saving that they cause us to labour for what they spend?'

At that moment it was as if they saw and heard not John Ball, boy of Colchester, priest of York, but an apostle like those in the Bible, blessed and sent to them – and them alone – in England.

'*They* are clothed in velvet and camlet furred with grise, and *we* be vestured with poor cloth; *they* have their wines and spices and good bread, and *we* have the drawing out of the chaff and drink water; *they* dwell in fair houses, and *we* have the pain and travail, rain and wind in the fields; and by what comes from *our* labours, they keep and maintain their estates. We are called their bondsmen and unless we do them service, we are beaten.'

Then, with arms upraised and with all his force, he said, 'We will *all* go to face the King! He will listen to what we bring! We will demand the deaths of councillors. And he will say – *yes!* I, John Ball, have seen our God and these words to you are blessed by Him.' He made the sign of the cross.

John Ball was turning an untargeted feeling of riot into a common pulse of unity.

'Look at the sun!' Ball declared, and all of them looked up as the golden June sun crept towards its zenith. 'Who owns the sun? Now breathe the air. Who owns the air? God's work. Without the air and without the sun we are nothing. Now look at one another. Why should anyone own you?'

They were now ecstatic. They shuffled, they swung from side to side, they repeated the priest's words.

'This is the day of Corpus Christi. Did Christ have gold plate and silk robes?'

'*No!*'

'Did He own land? No! Did He force His countrymen to pay taxes and use speech that only a few could understand?'

'*No!*'

Ball's words bred a vast chorus of '*Mercy*' and '*Blessing*'.

'Now is the time, good people. This day is the day of Corpus Christi. This day we will be free.'

One last time he spread out his arms and became the Cross. They knew what he was calling for. He was the soul of the rebellion. They beat out the anthem sonorously and slowly and repetitively.

> 'When Adam delved and Eve span,
> Who was then the gentleman?'

Such a sound, Ball thought, was never heard before. Such longing, such hope and such a kingdom it could be with these good people.

Now the priest's eyes were closed and he clapped his hands, his face serene with the bliss of what he saw. His body urged on the congregation, the men, the army before him. 'Amen!' he would cry, and back '*Amen!*' would come.

'The Lord is our God!' he would cry, and that too would be returned. 'Save our souls!'

'*Save our souls!*' Men stamped on the ground in time to the beat of the exclamations of the mystic as he brought them messages from God Himself. Blackheath rose and fell with the voices and the ecstasy of prayer.

16

Greenwich

At dawn, Richard II had called all his lords to the chapel in the Tower of London. Archbishop Sudbury said mass in the Latin that he spoke so beautifully, his tongue tenderly caressing its sacred antiquity. Tall tallow candles were lit against the slow dissipation of the dark in this refuge, this place of peace in a habitation of war. Richard ate the bread and sipped the wine and knew that the Holy Spirit was in him. The subdued chanting was, he thought, the perfect balm for his soul. He was ready.

They let Tyler sleep as long as they could. He needed it. Men tiptoed around him. The orders were clear. About two thousand of them would go to the riverbank at Greenwich and it had already been decided who they would be. The others would wait on Blackheath and be there to greet their king when their leader brought him to them.

John Ball had told Tyler he would stay at Blackheath. One voice to the King was all that was needed, he said. But the men, too, needed a voice, to keep their faith in the rebellion. He would be their voice. They were in deep now. It was no time to lose heart.

Will came back with food and the two men ate together in silence, content in each other's company.

Princess Joan was there to see her son and his most select councillors step rather gingerly onto the royal barge. The tide was turning in their favour but a wind was getting up and the impatient slapping of the Thames against the small fleet of barges sounded, to her, like an omen. Yet there had been no celestial portents in recent days, no lightning or blazing stars, nothing but sun and calm. She watched them row downriver. The vessels glittered on the dull water and all other boats made way for them.

Tyler was unusually silent. More by example than by words, he shaped the men into a superficially disciplined army, then led them across the heath and down to the river. Henry Long was with him, Newton just behind, flanked by two guards. The war council accompanied him in formation on either side, taking care to keep up the steady pace. They would not be seen as a rabble. They would meet their king as his loyal and respectful subjects.

The Earl of Salisbury was not happy. He had always had a tendency to seasickness and even the light morning breeze on the waves set off queasiness. He sipped from his flask but the medicine had little effect. He doubted the value of this enterprise, which he considered over-dramatic and unnecessary. He could see the King, magnificently attired for the occasion, his golden collar and sleeves out-sunning the sun, relishing the adventure of the expedition. He had rarely seen this masked, elusive child so openly animated. But that was it, Salisbury thought, a boyish thing, the sort of theatrical gesture the lad liked too much. Little to do with the world as it was.

Princess Joan sat in her bedchamber, unable to concentrate on the letters that had come from Gaunt with detailed advice on how to deal with the uprising. Far too late, she thought, and, she smiled sadly, too brutal at this stage. It was better that she had not gone with the King, she assured herself. There were times when he had to be alone – and yet . . . She had an intimation of failure, a failure that her presence might have prevented.

The scribal priests of John Ball took his verses and sermons around the camps. In the women's camp one of the priests was told that the daughter of Walter Tyler was with them. On the other side of the heath, the music was beginning for the fair of Corpus Christi. Those who did not want to miss a minute of this holy day were already arriving, distinguished by their ribbons.

When Tyler and his men came to the riverbank they stood well assembled, an orderly wall. Tyler was proud of his army.

As they turned the final bend, Richard stood up to catch a first view. Tyler saw the boy and raised his arm in welcome. Behind him the men, seeing their king, shouted as loudly as their lungs would tolerate, a hail of greeting that whipped up the Thames and seemed to add to the agitation of the waves. Tyler nodded at how well it was all going. How could the King not warm to such a reception?

'Those men are mad,' said Salisbury. 'Listen to them. Those are the cries of wild beasts. We must take care.'

The King smiled. He was back at his coronation four years before, when the whole of London had cheered him, just like these men, wherever he turned, whatever small gesture he made. Once more they were here, the common people who loved him without reserve. His spirit, so secretly nurtured, so closely guarded, was let loose by the cries and he soared. He wished he had wings to fly from the boat to the land and be among them.

'They are not controlled,' agreed the archbishop. 'Their order is merely an appearance of order.'

Salisbury breathed deeply and held tightly to the side of the barge as it manoeuvred for space next to the shore and allowed the other barges to form alongside. There were several yards of water between boats and shoreline. The manoeuvres were accompanied by more cries, by whistling and the banging of one implement against another. Salisbury saw the longbows with apprehension. He also saw the pitchforks and sickles, which fed his need for contempt.

Tyler stepped forward, conspicuously, onto a small platform put up by his men. He commanded a lowering of the noise.

'My lord,' he said. 'We greet you as our king!'

Those simple words triggered another round, almost a spasm, of welcoming noise.

'Let us help you to land. It is only you we want to meet us, not the traitors with you.' Tyler spoke solemnly, fittingly, he thought. 'We have them named here.' He held up a fistful of papers. 'They must be executed.'

'Be ready to pull away,' Salisbury said urgently, quietly, to the boatmen. 'Master Tyler?' The earl paused and saw that the formal address had worked. 'Allow me first to have some words with His Majesty.'

Consulted as an equal, Tyler nodded, man to man. He noticed that the royal barge pulled away, but only by a couple of yards, an understandable trimming in the search for stability in the choppy shallows of the river.

Tyler knelt down, scooped cool water into his hand and splashed his face.

Salisbury cornered the King at the back of the barge, in the enclosed royal space. Man and boy stood apart from the others – one gesture from Salisbury achieved that.

He spoke rapidly: 'My lord, I beg you to let me speak freely,' he began.

The boy listened closely. He was fine-tuned to moods and Salisbury emanated danger.

'My lord, you have a kind heart for your subjects and that is good. But they want you to themselves alone, my lord. They will not have you take your councillors or your guards.' For which, given the cries for the heads of some of those councillors on the royal barge, Salisbury was grateful. 'You must know these peasants for what they are. Study them. My lord, as I speak to you, look over my shoulder at those who would have you surrender to them and be among them.' Richard did as he was bade.

'His grace the archbishop has told you what havoc these men made in Canterbury.' And here Salisbury spoke most forcefully. 'Those they robbed or executed included William Medmenham, Thomas Holte, from whom they took forty pounds, and Thomas Oferyngton, who was also assaulted. They broke open the castle and let the prisoners free. They burned the properties of Sir Richard de Hoo and Sir Thomas Foy, and stole goods to the value of a thousand pounds. John Tabbe was pulled off his horse and executed in the street. As were others. It was an inferno. My lord, look at these men carefully. Take off your gentleness. Do you want us to deliver you to them?'

He knew he had captured the King's sympathy. But it was an unprepared remark that clinched it.

'And think how they smell, my lord! How scabbed and ugly they are. More like animals than men. And look how they dress!'

Richard instinctively glanced at his own exquisite, fresh and unsoiled attire, and then at the splendour of the robes of Salisbury, the archbishop and the others. Finally he scanned the peasants. What common cheap smocks and pitiful cloaks, what filthy garments and faces. He shuddered, enough for Salisbury to pick it up.

'Who knows? They may carry the plague,' said Richard, adroitly giving himself an unimpeachable excuse.

'That also,' said Salisbury. 'I fear that most of all.'

He held the King's gaze, and the boy felt the power of the man's skill.

Salisbury turned, walked unsteadily but resolutely to the side of the barge, and to the barge commander, he murmured, 'As soon as I have spoken, move away and speedily.'

He called to Tyler and, over him, to the men: 'Sirs,' he said, 'you are not in such order or array that the King should speak with you. We will leave.' He turned to the oarsmen. 'Pull away.' The earl walked briskly to the north side of the barge, leaned over and vomited.

As the rebels saw the barge turn and point upriver, a cry came that tightened the stomachs of the King and his councillors. It was a cry from the depths.

Overwhelmed by disappointment, belittled, shamed before his men and distressed that the King had not trusted him, Tyler drew a deep breath and called, 'We will come to London.' He paused. 'And we will meet the King on his own ground.' He had not been angry until now.

The men parted as he walked up the rise, war drums beating in his head. First to Blackheath to collect their forces and then, this same morning, they would march on the capital.

Tyler forced himself to conceal what he saw as his scarcely believable public humiliation. In front of his men! He had promised that he would talk to their king. He had the names, including that of Sudbury, of those who would be executed for misleading the King and deceiving the kingdom. He had seen himself not as an equal to the King – no one was – but not as a mere petitioner to be dismissed, with the crushing excuse that he and his men were not finely enough dressed. Tyler's hatred of these councillors, his need for vengeance against them, fired him to a terrible shame and rage.

At midday, when the King and his party had settled back in the Tower, Joan asked to see Salisbury.

She made him go through the acts and words of the morning. She listened in a silence whose quality Salisbury immediately and accurately judged as antagonistic. Eventually he came to a halt and she let him wait. Then she said: 'What you have done, my lord, is to make the King act like a coward. To turn an angry rabble into a frenzied mob. And to give thousands of rebels cause to move on London. I trust your explanations are in good order.'

She turned to go, but Salisbury made a slight movement, which checked her. In the docility of his diplomacy it was too easily overlooked that Salisbury's courage on the battlefield had been the equal of anyone's.

'My lady,' he said, seeking her gaze, locking into it and never letting it waver. 'We all give the counsel we consider best for His Majesty. The leading rebels may be reliable. My people tell me that Tyler has done good service. But those he leads are an untutored mob, my lady, unaware of the danger of their own passions, of where they will lead, or how rapidly they will turn against what at one moment they embrace. They were not to be trusted with the King, your son and my lord.' The severity of his voice chastened her. He stepped aside and she left, thoughtful.

In her chronicle that day, she wrote of the King's courage in meeting the rebels face to face. She mentioned her own advice and found proud words to explain the King's refusal to meet the request for a conference. It was based on his loyalty: he would not abandon his council or his court. He would not deal with men who had sworn to murder his advisers. He had behaved as his father would have done.

Salisbury was not mentioned.

'I saw the King's face full on,' Tyler told John Ball. 'He wanted to talk to us, John. I could see that. I could see his father in him.' Tyler was passing his dagger from hand to hand.

'It was his councillors, Walter.' Ball saw the hurt in the man. 'Those men are the real traitors. They are the deceivers who have tangled the boy in a web. We must clear them away, Walter.'

'But no hurt to the King.'

'No,' said the priest, soothingly, 'not to the King.' He touched Tyler's arm, a very rare physical gesture, an affectionate one. 'And you are king of the True Commons, Walter.'

'Am I?' He grasped at that. 'Am I, John? Do they say that?'

The priest nodded.

'To London, then.' Tyler looked around the heath at the rebels assembling into an order of march, reluctantly preparing to leave the gaiety of the Corpus Christi Fair. 'And we will not look back.'

17

The Gathering

J ack Straw led the men from Essex to London. They had rallied most quickly to the cause, the first to rough up and drive off the royal tax collectors. Out they came to join the march, from Bocking, Coggeshall, Stisted, Braintree, Dunmore, Gestingthorpe, Ashen, Dedham, Chelmsford, Fobbing, Colchester . . . Like those in Kent who came from Erith, Dartford, Gravesend, Frindsbury, Chalk, Rochester, Dordra, Maidstone, Faversham and Canterbury. The dam gates had been breached, and they flooded through.

Other counties caught the fever. These assemblies were, in effect, England's great county regiments, built on reliable clusters of interrelated town and village friends, kith and kin, local references, local loyalties.

Again and again the ruling classes experienced amazement at the good order of the rebels, especially in the initial stages. They had thought of the peasants, if at all, as uncouth, undisciplined, illiterate. What they knew of England was London, the court and little replicas of the court across the shires. They had always ignored or been unaware of the careful layering and construction of an Anglo-Saxon-based town or village society. They were impressed that the rebels held on to Tyler's proud boast that 'We come not as thieves or robbers but as men seeking justice.'

This summer of rebellion released long-suppressed local tensions in a mixed manner across the country. In St Albans it gave opportune urgency to the long struggle between the abbey and those burgesses who had seen their rights brutally restricted, and their livelihood slighted, for more than a century and a half by the bishop and his clergy. By appropriating to itself the profitable grinding of corn and stripping the townspeople of their grindstones, the abbey had ruined the town's economy. Now St Albans men took up arms against the abbey and the monks fled.

The success of St Albans spread throughout Hertfordshire; in Derbyshire, the rebellion brought into the open a long dispute between the tenants of the powerful Stathams of Morley and those of John of Gaunt – the national enemy seen here, where he had substantial property, as a local oppressor.

Rebels were to seize Leicester, then sack and destroy another castle of John of Gaunt's. In Suffolk and Cambridgeshire, directly inspired by the Essex rebels, John Wrawe, a former priest, led some Essex men and attacked the manor owned by Sir Richard Lyons, a corrupt financier. Then they turned their attention to Bury St Edmunds, where they beheaded the prior of the abbey. They claimed, rightly, that he had unjustly persecuted the townspeople for many years. He had tried to escape on a ferry but Katherine Gamen, the lookout, had pushed his connecting boat out into the river to be swept downstream, out of his reach.

At Ipswich yet another priest led the insurgency alongside a tenant farmer. The house of the collector of the poll tax was looted, as was that of the archdeacon of Suffolk. In Cambridge, the forewarned wealthy took flight, save a miscalculating justice of the peace who was beheaded. The college of Corpus Christi was ransacked, because of its unchristian exploitation of the many properties it owned in the town.

Even in the Borders, where John of Gaunt was trying to fix a peace treaty with the Scots, the words of Ball and the deeds of Tyler flung out their challenge and Gaunt found himself critically disadvantaged in negotiations. The Percys of Northumberland refused him help, which set off another aristocratic feud. Sometimes a rebellion followed the same trajectory as that of Tyler; at others it used the local rupture to pursue private vendettas. It was a climate in which upheaval was tolerated. It was as if a string of beacons had been waiting, stacked, ready to be lit. The words of John Ball and the actions of Tyler were the model, and to and from Tyler there flowed messages and reports, spokes to the hub of this turning wheel of Fortune. In a few weeks it seemed that much of England was moving, like a slowly erupting earth, and being reconfigured, on the way to being occupied by the people, the True Commons of England, now aflame with a vision of their own promised land.

On their rapid march towards London, the Kentish rebels had paused nearby to gather intelligence and finalise their plans for the attack through Southwark, which lay directly ahead on the south bank of the Thames. The men were ready for action. The need for food and stores, the King's rejection and the prospect of arrival at their goal made them restless.

Tyler looked over to the city, smitten by its grandeur. It shimmered in the heat of the June day, he thought. It glowed, like, he imagined, the Holy City of Jerusalem. Such a Tower, so many steeples, such a number of boats on the snaking Thames, and the bridge across it crammed with workshops, merchants, taverns, butchers, bakeries . . . Walter Tyler had told the rebels, 'This will be ours.' And John Ball, unmoved by the romance of the place that had captivated Tyler, had said, 'There is the city of all wickedness, which must be brought down.'

Johanna Ferrers came to within a few feet of him, forcibly leading a young woman who was trying to hide behind her.

What a handsome woman she is, Tyler thought of Johanna. Young, long, fair hair, slim-faced, bold. He smiled at her and then more broadly as she returned his welcome, swayed just a little at the hips and thrust the reluctant girl towards him.

'She's yours, Tyler.' Johanna was used to seeing men attracted to her. But then Tyler . . . 'Look at her! The image of you. There'd be no argument about her father! Would there?'

The girl's head was bowed. He saw the ribbons in her hair.

'Look up at your father, girl!'

Joan's face was angry, as if unjustly accused, her hands clenched in preparation for defiance. She looked up at her father, and he saw himself.

'Where did you find her?'

'In Maidstone. I thought you should know that she's here. She wouldn't let us take her home. We're proud of her.'

'Your mother?'

'I sent word,' said Joan. Too late, he guessed, rightly, for Margaret to do anything.

'So you've joined these fighting women.' He smiled. 'I've found out more about you all,' he said to Johanna. 'They say some of you really can fight.'

'You're lucky to have us on your side.'

Her militant reaction immediately dispelled his fear that Joan might have fallen in with the women who always followed an army to fleece the men in exchange for favours. Johanna Ferrers?

'Ferrers! Didn't I see two men of that name in the stocks at Maidstone?'

'You did,' she said, not without pride. 'They were my brothers.'

'Are they with us?'

'All Kent is with you, Tyler. If not, we kill them.'

'*You* kill?'

'So do you.'

'God kills. John Ball says that.'

'John Ball is a prophet,' Johanna said. Her face was set in a cunning innocence. 'Isn't he? He can say whatever he has a mind to . . .'

He shook his head, taken with this bold young woman. Then he led Joan a few yards away to where the men parted and gave them a quiet space.

'Are you safe with them?'

'They are good women!' Joan had recovered herself. She could not let Johanna down. 'Most of them are married and they can't pay the tax. They hate the lawyers and the tax collectors. They do terrible things to girls who say they are too young to be taxed. They say they don't believe them and they . . . do terrible things.'

'So whatever I say, you will still stay with them?'

'I will. I am sorry, Father. Please don't send me home.' She looked directly at him. 'They say that you will make the King give us all that we want.'

He glanced towards Johanna, then back at Joan. 'You always said that you were better than any boy . . .' He held out his sheathed dagger. 'Take this,' he said. 'Use it when you have to. You thrust in and *upwards* under the chest. I will want it back when it's all over.'

She accepted it reverently.

Johanna had watched him, enviously, with his daughter. Most of all she had noted his gentleness. Yet all she had heard of Tyler were stories of his fierceness in battles in France and his violent efficiency at countering those outlaws who plagued the Kentish villages around his home.

Her brothers were strong and brutal, like their father.

Like him, they had treated her as their family bondwoman until her marriage to a man even stronger than they were. But he, in his turn, had shown little affection after the first months, and as time went on and she failed to conceive, he blamed her for it and beat her.

Johanna had been immeasurably relieved when he had been knifed in a brawl. She had found work in a tavern where the landlord had protected her and the customers made her something of a favourite. There, she had bloomed, listening to the talk of the more serious men, at last feeling free to join those women of strong opinion she had admired but from whom she had been barred by her brothers and her husband. A convert to liberty, she had become an immediate zealot in the rebellion.

But Tyler, as she watched him with his daughter . . . He had been known to her as a local hero. Even her truculent brothers would hear nothing but high praise of their man. And Johanna had imagined him as like them or, even worse, like her lout of a husband, but there he was . . . gentle but, as was said on all sides, not a man you would ever cross. She loved the frisson she felt when male strength was displayed before her. But its alliance – genuine, she could always nose out what was false – with gentleness moved her.

She had heard about love, the songs, the stories: she had seen women who had the difference in their expression and manner that she had put down to 'love'. One or two had even mentioned it, though tentatively and briefly, soon silenced by the raucous, bawdy men-baiting that was the currency of their conversation. Johanna had never anticipated that she would experience love.

But she felt, in those moments, brushed by this new sensation, somehow both fragile and compelling. Yet how could he have time for her? He was leading them to rescue the

King. He was deep in the lives and possible deaths of thousands. How could he have time for her? How could she claim time from him? Would he even remember her an hour from now?

These doubts were swiftly dispelled by the lust she felt. It gave her a sense of rightness. And she looked him straight in the face as he brought his daughter back towards her. Johanna knew men. She knew when men wanted her. She had become hardened in the skills of evasion.

But she did not want to evade Walter Tyler and he, too, she knew this as sure as she knew anything, had looked at her as she at him. Whatever might impede it, the exchange, a vow as unseen as the air, had been made . . .

'Stay as near us as you can,' he said, as he came up to her, and they tried to pretend nothing had happened.

'I will.' She forced herself to calm. 'I want to see you win.' She looked away: he was too close. 'We can't lose, Tyler.'

'We will not lose.'

He could hesitate no longer. It was time to move on. He looked across to London and saw the city of power. He had been there only once. He had experienced a world of intensity. Everything was bigger, richer, dirtier, more crowded, more dangerous, more magnificent, noisier, more various and exotic, poorer, more stinking than anywhere outside a battlefield he had been before or since. 'Capture London, capture all England.' He breathed it in. What glory that would be!

He glanced a last time at Johanna and then he turned to the men. 'With whom hold you?' he shouted, and the mighty return sent a shudder of joy through him.

'King Richard and the True Commons!'

'Harden your heart,' John Ball had told him. He felt for

153

the dagger that was no longer there. So be it. Unarmed he would take on London and the King. Now, on 13 June, from north, south, east and west, the rebels were marching on the city. On Corpus Christi Day. Surely, Tyler thought, that was a sign. On such a day they could change their world.

18

Richard's London

H is mother understood why he needed to be on his own, especially after such an encounter with the rebels. The Tower was occupied by numerous councillors, each with his entourage, and by a scurry of messengers, petitioners, London aldermen, knights-at-arms, and all the servants that attended to the comforts and maintained the magnificence of a king of England.

Solitude was a luxury but, to that lonely fourteen-year-old boy, increasingly a necessity. After the puzzling outcome at Greenwich, he wanted to think by himself. Richard had selected the turret at the north-west corner of the Tower and there he now stood in the late morning, looking with pride over London, the key to his kingdom. The sight calmed him.

The White Tower was its padlock. When he could not sleep Richard dreamed of the White Tower, beautiful, impregnable, the fortress of his sometimes fearful mind. It was in itself a kingdom, begun by William the Conqueror, fortified further by Richard the Lionheart and since then shaped into self-contained splendour and impregnability. At one stage nine new towers and a moat had been added at spectacular cost. Edward I had transformed it into England's largest and strongest concentric castle. It had been used as a prison from its first decades and its dungeons were still in service. It housed part of the Royal Mint. There was a Royal Menagerie, based on Richard's grandfather's collection of lions and leopards, a royal palace, with a great hall, a chapel, a library, private chambers, living quarters and kitchens fit for all the ceremonial feasts in the calendar. Richard, standing above the smells of the city and its sun-sparkling river, breathed in deeply and felt to his bones that he was loved by God and as safe as any man in Christendom. And beneath him, a city bedecked for the festival of Corpus Christi, the sounds and crowds filling the streets.

The ravens, which had cawed him to morning prayers, were now silent. He looked down onto the Thames where the immaculate swans glided commandingly among the infestation of boats and waste. The morning bells pealed eleven strokes.

This city was the real jewel in his crown. All the glittering treasure of his mother and himself were as nothing compared with the city, the most gigantic and invincible in all England. And it was his. The prayers that morning, led by the Archbishop of Canterbury, had been unusually urgent in their pleas to preserve both the King and the city. Surely the prayers of such a holy man would be answered. But were they necessary? he thought, as he surveyed the ocean of life swelling beneath him. Who could take this from him?

Richard counted his city as his mother counted her jewels.

He knew his London well. John of Gaunt had insisted he learn it. London, said his uncle, whose rascally reputation had filtered down to Richard in gobbets of anecdotal admiration, was the great book of his rule and he must learn it by rote.

He had begun by taking the child, aged ten, on a memorable procession around the city. At key points, scholars had been summoned and their words, read aloud but also written down, were gathered by one of the King's squires for future study. They had begun at the strongest part of London's wall. The wall was a marvel. It was eighteen feet high, and had seven gatehouses, Ludgate, Newgate, Aldersgate,

Cripplegate, Bishopsgate, Aldgate and Bridgegate. This last led to the nineteen arches spanning the Thames, London Bridge, congested with merchants' houses, craft works, St Thomas's Chapel, and at the city wall end, vast oak doors secured by heavy drawbars. At sunset, the whole of London was sealed up. If you were caught in the streets without permission, you were gaoled.

Richard looked across the bridge to Southwark, more crowded than usual because it was Corpus Christi day, but also, he knew, thanks to the rebels congregating there. They could not cross the bridge. They could not open the gates into the city. They could never force entrance into the White Tower. He stood above them, puzzled by the reports he had received of executions and destruction. Why were they not satisfied with their lot? Surely England was good to them.

A mile or so upriver was Westminster Palace, the place of government. John of Gaunt was not very respectful of it, but he said that the King had to know about such matters. Parliament met there; the Exchequer was housed there, as were the Royal Courts of Justice, the Royal Chapel and, most importantly for Gaunt, the King's Privy Palace.

Abutting this was Westminster Abbey. Even John of Gaunt took a step back in that crowning place of kings. There, Richard always found his greatest solace in the shrine of Edward the Confessor, plated with gold and covered with precious jewels. It was there, through the Confessor, in that treasured room, that all the young man's finest feelings and most material instincts came together. He wanted to be like Edward the Confessor.

From his towered height, Richard could pick out several private palaces – more, his uncle had told him, than any other four cities in Europe combined – although they were hidden from easy view, secreted in side-streets. Their entrances were modest, their neighbours often warehouses, but their interiors were princely – often large enough to house several hundred, including a private army.

Foreigners, Richard remembered proudly, wrote in awe of the fact that the leading men in the land kept houses and forces of such substance in the capital itself when they also had castles in the countryside. Richard picked them out like a bird spotter: there was Montfichet's Tower, and there the town residence of the earls of Derby, Gresham Court and Northumberland House . . . These loyal lords, knights and gentlemen, whose wealth originated from royal rewards since the Conqueror's era, the plunder from royal wars and the ceaseless revenue from local domestic taxes, would surely, he thought, be more than enough to ward off any rabble from the villages of Kent and Essex.

From that height, he could not distinguish the houses of the aldermen and the banking houses that gave the city its wealth, or the slaughterhouses, the tanneries, the bakeries, fishmongers, apothecaries and all the tumble trade and manufacture that steamed through the London streets in a fever of selling, making, buying, yelling, smelling and dying. Despite the plagues that, since 1348, had wiped out half of the population, traders, visitors, diplomats, thieves, adventurers and drifters were still drawn there in their thousands, tripling the city's population through the day, feeding on London and as unafraid of the black rats that infested the houses as they were of the pigs and dogs, which ran wild in the labyrinth of alleys.

Finally, in his consoling matutinal survey, there were the churches. He swore that he loved his churches better than his diamonds and sapphires. These, the boy thought, were his unique, most radiant and aesthetically perfect possessions.

There were more than a hundred parish churches in London, more than a dozen monastic churches, monuments to Roman Christianity such as the abbey and St Helen's, churches that marked Christian legends – St Bride's, St Paul's, St Magnus Martyr . . . It was called a town of steeples and bells. Richard thought they pealed for him.

He turned full circle, surveying his city, his people, his unconquerable bulwarks against all his enemies. His soul was settled.

His mind had been further assuaged by a visit to the study of Friar Thomas Rushbrook.

Rushbrook had realised early on that Richard, although intrigued by the alchemical disciplines and the quest to turn common materials into gold, was much more fascinated by how this transformation from an imperfect into a perfect state could be transferred to himself. How could alchemy make him more perfect? How could it give him everlasting life on earth? The apparent competition between his own everlasting mortal life and Heaven did not appear to Richard to be insoluble.

Richard loved the sound of the names brought to play in these lessons. Like the alchemist's room, dark, candle-perfumed, full of curious lamps and small pots, embroidered cushions, paintings of learned men with fine beards, at once a cave of elusive experiments and a taste of how alchemy might change Nature herself, its heavy books trapped the boy in their promise of scholastic truth. Like the curious zodiac-ornamented cloak the friar wore, Rushbrook's room thrilled him with its sense of mystery.

He was entranced by the names, the sonorous, scholarly names, the unlocking names. Gerard of Cremona, Adelard of Bath, both of them translators of Arabic alchemical texts. Aristotle and Avicenna, Hermes and Democritus, Abu Mūsā Jābir ibn Hayyān and Roger Bacon, Petrus Bonus and Geber. Richard could recite them like a prayer. The beautifully bound appearance of the books meant as much to him as their contents, which were summoned for him by the friar. Rushbrook displayed them artfully, even seductively, around his room, well aware that the combination of ancient learning and the aesthetic thrill of seeing such valuable and beautifully written manuscripts would reach deeply into the boy's sense of tradition and beauty.

Those names were uttered softly, with sly compliant glances at the young King, with smiles of enticement into this other world. The man knew how to charm the boy, and Richard felt dazed by what he promised to reveal of the dark arts.

As the names came on, like a lulling chant, through the mouth of the teacher, who swayed as he listed them, as if calling up spirits, Richard felt drawn further and further into this world of chemicals and transformations, copper into gold, men into beasts, men into gods, the four powers – fire, earth, water and air – all about them, able to change the world, whispered Rushbrook, change life. It could be captured, this spirit; a spirit such as the King's could divine it.

He ignored the attendant lords and other petitioners and sought out his mother, who had left her London palace and taken residence in the Tower. She was, deliberately by herself, waiting for him.

'I am safe,' he announced, striding across to her, face pink-flushed from the bright day, arms opened wide. A beautiful boy, she thought – too beautiful?

She submerged her fears and stood up to greet him with the smile that had deceived a thousand eyes. He held on to her like a drowning man.

'W-w-when this is over,' he said, as he reluctantly pulled himself away from her embracing reassurance, 'I shall r-r-rebuild London. I shall make it the fairest city on earth.'

'That is good, my lord. Many of your ancestors inspired great building.'

'Mine will outsoar them all.' She could see his spirits had risen since his safe landing back from Greenwich. And perhaps the alchemist was not as 'brimful of evil' as some said of him. But she must prepare him for the impending reality.

'And in times to come they will say "King Richard did that."'

'They will. But for now . . .' She waited to see how aware he was.

'London will withstand all assaults,' he said. 'London and w-w-we who live in it are safe. I shall not move to Windsor.'

'It is safer there, surely. The mob will not go to Windsor.'

'London is where the King of England must be when England is in peril.'

She smiled again, this time without guile. Now and then, like a flash from the polished blade of a sword, she heard in his tone and saw in his gesture his father. It was not courage the boy lacked.

'Are those t-t-traitors, my councillors, waiting on us?' He giggled.

She almost responded in kind. 'Most of them,' she said. 'Pity them, my lord. The rebels have already severed the heads of lesser lordlings. They are now set on grander ones.'

'They will be safe here. *On est hors de danger ici.*'

'But who will stop them, my lord?' she said, without emotion. 'If we are, all of us, in here.'

After the failed meeting, Tyler had sent to London the list of traitors he had held in his fist at Greenwich. It demanded that the King hand over those deceitful and disloyal councillors so that they could be executed. They included John of Gaunt, Archbishop Sudbury, Sir Robert

161

Hales, the prior of the Hospital of St John of Jerusalem, the Bishop of London, Bishop Fordham of Durham, who was clerk of the Privy Seal, Sir Robert Belknap, the chief justice, Sir Ralph Ferrers, a friend of John of Gaunt, Sir Robert Pressington, chief baron of the Exchequer, John Legge, the sergeant-at-arms most closely associated with the poll tax commissions, and John de Bampton, another poll tax collector. The Earl of Salisbury had escaped the listing.

'First I must see m-my archbishop. Stay as you are. I myself will summon him.'

He went to the door, charmed to be seen to be performing such a menial task, and called, 'The King will see his grace the Archbishop of Canterbury! These rebels are like a tide in a storm,' he said, as he came back to join her. 'They are swept up in its urgency, but that will soon be spent and the tide will ebb away.'

'They are bold men, my lord,' said his mother. 'I have seen them. And they are Englishmen who know how to fight.'

'I fear nothing.' His complacency was suddenly unbearable. But discipline kept her silent. 'We will t-teach them a lesson.'

Archbishop Sudbury entered the room, looking troubled. Charged by the energy he had drawn from his solitary survey on a peak of the Tower and the flattery of his alchemist, Richard emanated a playfulness at odds with the archbishop's unease. Joan stood aside.

'Shall I send for wine?' he asked.

'You are kind, my lord, but I fear it would do more harm than good in my present condition.'

'Which is?'

The archbishop had no time for niceties. 'Fear, my lord.' He paused. 'Which I share with many I have left in the chamber behind me. We are under threat of execution. Impending death has a powerful impact on the heart.'

'P-prayer can drive out fear.'

'Only if the prayer is answered.'

'Are not your prayers always answered?'

'No, my lord. That joy is for saints alone.'

'But surely an archbishop . . .'

'. . . Is full of sin, my lord.'

'I thought your prayers this morning would have moved all Heaven.'

'God is angry with us, my lord. He will not easily be won back.'

'I looked over the city this m-morning and I saw a place that would make God proud. Our churches glorify Him, you, your bishops and priests keep His sacred word. We show Him our d-devotion with treasures and prayers. We celebrate the festival of His Son.'

'Prayers, my lord, are answered only when God's ears are open. Now I fear they may be closed to us. And our treasure is seen as our sin by those who want to murder us.'

'Hedge-priests!'

'But the people love them, my lord. John Ball is no ordinary enemy. I know him. He claims he has the voice of God and the people believe him. He urges them to destroy our wealth and divide it among themselves. Why should they not agree? They do not understand that the Church on earth must be God's White Tower. You looked over the city this morning. I look over the Church every day and I see it in danger from the devil, from these wicked men and women, and from all the temptations we are heir to.'

The archbishop's urgency deflated the King's buoyancy.

'We need our churches, my lord.' Sudbury's tenacity would not be checked. 'We need to have places of prayer that the people will turn to. We need a house for their God.

We want to show in our treasures on earth something of His glory in Heaven. We want our psalms and chants to sing out our devotion to Him. Who will look after the needy if our abbeys, monasteries and nunneries are destroyed? Who will teach the children? Who will feed the poor? The Church in your country, my lord, is its chief pride. And now we quail as these men from Hell rise up to lay waste to centuries of our faith. It is they who must be laid waste, my lord, and it is you alone who can do this. For they do love you. And you alone.'

Richard felt a confused surge of vanity, pleasure and authority, a giddying sensation, as he absorbed with profound relish the words of the venerable cleric, whose passion was usually hidden under heavy vestments, complex rituals and ancient forms.

'What am I to do?'

Joan let the pause grow so that her intervention would not be seen as too eager a directive to her son. 'My lord,' she said eventually, 'your council is gathered together beyond that door.'

'All save John of Gaunt,' he said, suddenly petulant again. 'No one likes my uncle but I. If he were here he w-would act and not talk.'

'It is to you alone that this mob will look,' repeated the archbishop. 'Listen to your council but you alone, my lord, are the hope and only barrier against your country becoming a lawless realm.'

'I've heard that John Ball says we are at the end of the world,' said Richard, a little thrilled by the idea. 'What a fool he is!'

Joan and the archbishop exchanged the merest glances. It was the archbishop who spoke: 'If he were just a fool, my lord, we need have no fear. But the common people think he is God's messenger.'

164

'*Et vous? Qu'est-ce que vous p-pensez?*'

'I, my lord, am your archbishop and your chancellor. I will serve you as you bid me to.'

Richard looked for reassurance to his mother, but he could not read her expression. He turned his back on them and walked across to a window that looked up the river towards Westminster Abbey. Earlier he had felt that a cloak had been draped over him, which would protect him. And still he felt strong.

'There is a holy anchorite in the g-grounds of the abbey,' he said, 'I will visit him.'

He led the way to the council.

The council, so many of them, thought Joan, too many to move swiftly, bowed as a choir when the King entered the large chamber. They were like a flock of sheep, she decided, huddled in their rich, thick clothes on this sunny day, grazing the floor with averted eyes, none daring even to bleat, each waiting for another to make a move, to lead, so that they could shuffle close behind him.

It was her son Tom, the Earl of Kent, who stepped forward after the murmuring of formalities. Princess Joan avoided the gaze of the King, who, she knew, was testing her loyalty when he asked Tom to speak first.

'My lords,' said the young dandy, far and away, Joan still thought culpably, the most dashing man in any assembly and dressed for effect in crimson and blue, 'the cause we have is a just one. The King must have these taxes to fight his wars. Without them we could lose all that we have left in France and never regain what is rightfully England's. The Church has given its share.' He looked at the archbishop, who shifted rather uneasily, aware that the Church had much more that it could have given. 'The nobility, too, has rallied.' Now it was Salisbury's turn to shuffle: the nobility had been mean when it had not been evasive. 'And so it is the people, these "True Commons of England", who must pay now. We owe it to our king,' he inclined his head slightly, 'to beat them down. They have murdered our tax collectors and burned down their houses and palaces. They have looted, harassed, laid waste, and now they threaten London itself. We are here with one purpose, to help our king and to defend his city.'

His eloquence flushed him but he sensed that the response was warm.

He made to speak again. 'My lord,' he began.

'*Votre majesté*,' said Richard, suddenly, prickling with jealousy at this too-handsome sibling's easy command of the language.

Tom hesitated, then bowed. But he did not repeat the requested title.

'Earlier today I went to Southwark.'

Concentration in the room stiffened, as if a noose had been pulled tighter around their throats.

'It's been a busy place these past few days,' Tom said, knowing his news would command the room. 'The peasants have their spies in Southwark and already many of the rebels are there. And some are here, in London. My lords,' he swept his eyes around the now fully alerted flock, 'in Southwark there is anticipation. The light of Corpus Christi this morning was dimmed by the imminent lightning from Kent. Just as the men of Essex threaten their thunderbolts to the north, so these wicked men steal into the south and say they will take our city. They vow to kill every one of us who stands in their way and boast openly of themselves running all England. Save the King.' He bowed. 'They always add that. But it is we who must save the King, my lords, and he will save us. They must be barred from London. If they are let in, they will come down on us like wolves.

166

London is our only haven. The King is our only hope. And he alone can and will lead us to victory.'

The silence was unbroken until the King, his eyes threatening tears, walked across to Tom and embraced him. Joan's heart soared.

19

Southwark

Driven by hunger, impatience and boldness, sections of Tyler's army were making merry hell in Southwark. It lay at the southern end of London Bridge and looked as if it had been kicked out of the city in disgust. An exiled heap of outcasts – thieves, whores, jugglers, magicians, drunks, the diseased (there was a leper house) – and the notorious Marshalsea Prison were only partly redeemed by the ancient Cathedral of Southwark. It stood there in solitary sorrow, mopping up the sinks of London's underworld. To Tom and those like him who used the Southwark stews, the Flemish brothels, this outlaw suburb was forever tempting. There were eighteen brothels, incorporating varieties of bath-houses and lewdness forbidden in the city, save for trade in one sordid street, Cock Lane, which Tom and his kind avoided.

The sinless and profitable brothels – married men had no obligation in law to be faithful – were owned by the Bishop of Winchester and rented out by William Walworth, Lord Mayor of London. Tom knew both men, and when they spoke on high and solemn matters, his mind always slipped back to his latest pleasure in the stews. There was this black-eyed young filly from Bruges . . .

Tom Holland, Earl of Kent, could not wait to return to Southwark after the council meeting. He was more careful about his dress than he had been earlier in the day. The clothes of one of his stable-boys replaced his usual outfit. He had watched in exhilaration as the locusts, now in full strength, landed in the lanes of Southwark. What struck him forcefully was that the people of Southwark had been forewarned. They had been infiltrated and bent to the cause of the rebels, thrusting provisions on them. There were no confrontations between town and country. The afternoon sun and the continuing innocent high spirits of the Corpus Christi crowds intermingled amicably with the sudden influx of rebels. Many revellers instantly joined the rebels' cause.

A priest who was accompanied by a giant called on the rebels to march with him to Lambeth Palace. Another group was set on the destruction of the notorious Marshalsea Prison. Tom was torn between whom he should follow.

The prison's marshal, Richard Imworth, had got wind of the rebels' advance earlier in the day and bolted across the bridge into London. He had heard, as who had not, that these rebels released all prisoners. He had also heard that in Maidstone and Canterbury, the riots provoked by the arrival of the rebels were still raging. It was serious. He had no doubt that he would be a target. His viciousness and new methods of torture were infamous. His argument that letting out villains into such disruption was throwing oil on flames would be unheard. He was a lock on liberty, and thereby, to the rebels, an enemy.

There was much to wreck at the Marshalsea and after that there was the strenuous job of tearing apart Imworth's corruptly enriched house, removing everything in his bulging larder, taking his hens, chickens, ducks and geese, and comprehensively clearing his wine cellar. The harder element among the prisoners allied themselves to the rebels and swore lustily, many times over, by King Richard and the True Commons of England, promising on the sacred oath to help destroy all they were asked to destroy. They became fierce loyalists to the cause, and the drunker they got the more fiercely loyal they were. Tom spent some

169

time at the Marshalsea, then sped back to join the slowly assembled procession to Lambeth Palace.

The priest who led it, Tom knew, must be John Ball, the mystic. The march of rebels and newcomers that followed him was easy to join. They went alongside the Thames to the palace, the London residence of the Archbishop of Canterbury, though he had left it on the previous evening, the eve of Corpus Christi, when it became obvious to him that advance rebels were already in Southwark. By the time Tom reached the palace, he had become enmeshed in the crowd and felt safe.

The priest stood on a high wall outside the palace gates, the giant in front of him. The Thames was bobbing and twisting in the sun, clustered with many more than the usual number of boats. Some ferried rebels across the river to the city gates. Others ferried Londoners eager to join in the havoc. Tom was impressed at the silence the tall, thin preacher commanded. A man, Tom thought, sprung with wrath.

'Good people!' the priest called. 'Draw near,' and Tom, to whom this man was anathema, saw the rebels lean forward and felt himself do the same, drawn in by the cohesive intensity of the crowd and the lure of John Ball. 'It is in this palace that Archbishop Sudbury lives when he is in London. He has wealth that could clothe us all, food to feed us all, but he ignores us. *He must fall!*' Tom flinched at the sudden sound from the crowd, which burst open that hot silence, a growl from Hell, he thought, and for the first time he feared for his life. But he was penned in.

'This palace must be destroyed or all will be void!' The priest pointed to the gates. He led the people forward, as Tyler had done at Rochester. Again the guards surrendered and again the gates opened.

The archbishop's legal land-holding documents were found and they, with the lovingly and expensively embroidered vestments, were brought into the main courtyard, with books, furniture and tapestries. A bonfire was made, fed constantly by precious objects from the palace of the primate. The priest walked through to the next courtyard with his guard, indicating that his followers remain behind.

It was now, seeing so many fanatical faces mottled and distorted by triumph and drink, that Tom imagined he might be in an inferno. Those dirty, crude peasant faces, those gargoyles, were scarcely human, he thought. It was the opposite of the celebration of Christ: this, he thought, was a carnival of the devil.

After the burning had gone on for some time, the crowd quietened as their priest came forward, leading two cadaverous young men who walked shakily. A third was borne by the giant. John Ball noticed that he stumbled. His face was reamed in sweat as he carried the skeletal body, but that might have been the sun.

The priest spoke quietly now, but his voice carried even to the Thames, where boatmen had drawn up to be with the cut of events.

'These men,' he said, 'were in a prison. Yes, my friends. In the palace of the prime servant of God in England there is a prison. I have just been there. It is a place of shackles and chains. It is called Lollard's Tower, a dungeon in the sky. Three men were there. One is dead. The other two you see before you. And what was their crime?'

His voice deepened and strengthened. 'They preached the word of God in our own English tongue. This archbishop, who is the devil, will not let our language be the word of God!

'He hunts down young men like these and brings them here.

'They show no fear.

'He breaks their bones.

'His heart is stone. Is this a man of God? Good people, how can we let him live?'

Once again the cry of consent was so loud it made Tom tremble.

He slid away. He was now alert to his difference, as the deep-throated responses of the crowd became the sound of dogs about to attack. It had been a game to be part of a harmlessly rampaging mob: the darker mood had reminded him of which side he was on. He hailed a waterman.

The previous day the archbishop's barge had slipped across to the north bank from the same spot and taken Sudbury to Bridge Gate. From there he had gone to the White Tower and handed the chancellor's Great Seal to the King. Being devoted to God alone, not to God and the Exchequer, might just save him.

John Ball buried the young Lollard under an oak sapling in the garden at Lambeth Palace. The rebels knelt and he led them in prayer for his soul.

Corpus Christi Day in London always brought one of its most lavish celebrations. The festival marked the reality of Christ's body and blood in the Eucharist and affirmed belief in His presence at the altar. Over the years layers had been added, which included carnivals and clowning, the reversing of roles so that the rich could dress as the poor and the poor ape the rich and, above all, there were the marching pageants of the many guilds making a public competitive display of their wealth.

At the centre of these civic demonstrations was the ambitious Lord Mayor William Walworth, fishmonger, financier, proudly self-made, who, the previous day, had sent a delegation to Tyler at Blackheath ordering him not to enter the city. It had been led by one of his aldermen, John Horn, who was not unsympathetic to the rebels, which diluted the force with which he had been expected to deliver the message. Tyler had rejected it.

Walworth had been pleased to learn that the King's party at Greenwich had in turn rejected Tyler that morning. He had no fear they would dare march on the city. But by then Tyler's propaganda was working. The word from the rebels was that they came solely to rescue the King and abolish the poll tax. The people of London had had many reasons over the years to loathe and distrust the King's councillors. The rebels' call for wealth to be stripped from the rich and redistributed among the commons was attractive. And John Ball's reputation was high: extravagant claims for his powers of prophecy were the fat of rumour.

Lord Mayor Walworth was a man with no doubt of the strength of his judgement on all things. He would be reluctant on such a morning to absent himself from leading the grand processions of the guilds as they emerged from their churches. The city was safe: he had assured himself of that. No peasant rabble could force an entry! The guilds' members were preceded by luxuriously dressed clergy chanting prayers, dispelling incense, holding high statues of Christ Crucified. It was an important public event in which vanity could be excused and taken for authority.

Walworth knew he looked every bit the resplendent mayor as he peacocked in his robes, suppurating conceit at the thought that everyone who saw him knew him to be in command of the city of London; the body that was now so powerful, the indispensable banker to the King. So when at the height of the procession, outside St Paul's, he was warned of possible assault from the Essex rebels to the north, he replied that nothing need be done beyond closing Aldgate. To check the Kentishmen in the south he ordered that a chain be put across London Bridge and the drawbridge raised temporarily until, he predicted, the rebels lost heart. Meanwhile he would have his full glory of Corpus Christi Day.

The brothels had been burned and the whores – still in their distinctive yellow hoods – huddled in protective clusters against the walls of Southwark Cathedral, the traditional provider of sanctuary.

Johanna Ferrers was yelling above the rush of the leaping flames and the mixed exclamations of the onlookers. The object of her scorn was John Ball, standing nearby. 'How will these women live?' she shouted.

'They should not live like this.' His reply was sorrowful.

Johanna was not appeased. 'They do what they can.' Johanna pointed to them. 'What will they do now with no shelter and no protectors?'

'We should not let them live like this.'

'So what will they do now? Tell me that, John Ball.'

'In God's grace.'

'Will they be fed and watered by God's grace?'

'Take care. You blaspheme.'

'I can see what is in front of my eyes,' said Johanna. 'Women with nowhere to go, no money . . . They must join us. We must take them with us!'

There was only a lukewarm response. But Johanna went across to the Flemish whores. 'Some of them speak English!' she shouted, standing against the flames, waving her arms, something of the demon about her.

'These women belong to the Mayor of London and the Bishop of Winchester!' said Ball.

'Not now!' said Johanna. 'They belong to us. Lead on, John Ball.' To the women she said, 'You can take off those hoods.'

Newton went out of the sun into the gloom of the Tabard and looked across the tavern for Tyler. There he was, at the centre of eager followers, men forever claiming his attention, impatient to be heard by him, to hear him, to have a part of him. Men from St Albans and Norfolk, men from Gravesend and the Channel ports, so much better protected since Tyler had detailed the rebels there to ensure their security.

Newton noticed again the bowman's strength in the shoulders, the speed of decision, the quick grin that disarmed, the stare that silenced. In just a few days, Newton thought, since the taking of Rochester, this rough soldier had found in himself command of what could plausibly be called an army, and now he sat confident in his kingdom. Newton had come hotfoot from the city.

'It is as ready for taking as it will ever be,' Newton said. 'Walworth is bound up in his guilds' procession. The merchants and the nobles, whose armies are with them in London, are waiting to see what the King and his court will do. They, too, are against many of the councillors. And there is fear of you and this . . . mass, this army, which grows in rumour every hour. I think that many of the commoners in London are on your side.' He took a draught of the beer Tyler had passed to him. 'But Walworth has ordered the drawbridge pulled up. I was one of the last to cross it.'

'And Jack Straw?'

'He wants to come in now, through Aldgate,' he said. 'Their sympathisers have persuaded the gatekeepers to let them in. But Straw says that his men will only go in if you and the men of Kent also go in. They are moving in from Mile End. They found some provisions and more weapons in palaces, which they have burned . . . They are waiting for us.'

'Then we must go now,' said Tyler. 'John Ball can follow later.'

He had been in Southwark for less than an hour.

Among the decisions he had taken was to send orders that the men from the Channel ports must return there. He had implemented a policy of leaving a cordon of men across the coastal towns while he was at Maidstone. Rumour had it that the ships from Castile were now threatening to come upriver.

He looked up at the gate to the only bridge across the Thames and into the city of London. The walls could not be scaled. They had not the equipment for a siege. Tyler turned to his army and shouted, 'Tell them they must open the gates!' Turning back he felt the welt of sound from the thousands fronting the still embering brothels. 'OPEN THE GATES!' His words were repeated and chanted, but mostly it was a howl. The howl of a pack, voices hurled against stone. He hoped those charged with keeping the drawbridge up were feeling the first trickle of the panic that had gripped the soldiers in Rochester Castle. But would it work a second time?

Walworth was still enmeshed in the ceremonies of his Guilded day. The aldermen were not to be seen, save those few who said, 'We must open the gates or they will burn everything around the city.' Sympathetic Londoners were gathering at the northern end of the bridge, waiting to greet their new champions.

In the Tower, the King and his ministers came to the windows, stood out on the turrets, looked across at the drama. It was mid-afternoon. The meeting at Greenwich that morning seemed to Richard an age away.

Princess Joan joined her sons to witness this test of strength. The calculated screaming of the rebels made even her quake.

Tyler called up his bowmen and he himself took up his longbow. Since their raids on Rochester and other stores of weapons, they were much better armed.

'Fire over the gate,' he said. 'Two arrows each.'

There were now almost two hundred bowmen to hand.

The arrows went over in arcing flights of deadly beauty.

The royal party waited . . . They heard the conflicting orders, the loud commands, and then . . .

The drawbridge creaked, seemed to hesitate, paused, and then, like the slow apprehension of a miracle, it came down.

On Corpus Christi Day, thought Tyler, and on this morning, down that river, I met the King but I was not permitted to talk to him. So I have marched up to London and, by the grace of God, I will now see him face to face.

'We are invaded,' said Princess Joan.

Tyler smiled, in relief, in triumph, in joy, as he led the rebels into the city to save the King and to claim back their country. What a thing this was! Who had done such a thing ever before? What a force they were! And on one as yet unfinished day. At dawn to be spurned by the King's advisers, in the middle of the same day to force their way into their city. Who could stop them now?

20

The Savoy Palace

The rebels were greeted as liberators. The religious carnival of Corpus Christi spliced itself into what became the rebels' procession for justice. The figure of Christ Crucified bobbed above the crowds in the narrow streets, as did the flags of St George, the pennants and pitchforks, the bows and flags of the Kentish men from the south and the men of Essex from the north, making for the Temple to destroy all those laws that had for so long ruined their lives. Chants to God mingled with cries against the poll tax. The orchestra of bells competed with whoops from mouths too excited for words. As they surged across the bridge, such a tide, in their hearts they were already makers of a new England.

At the church of St Thomas, halfway across, John Ball, who had led the second wave an hour or so after Tyler, stood for a few moments and looked at the men who, so eagerly and so innocently, were on their way to ask their king to change their fate. He longed for it to be done. The priest had not been at rest since his release from the dungeon in Maidstone. This, he knew, was his last chance to bring God back to England. The cheerful surge of humanity in front of him gave him an unexpected feeling of hope. All would be well.

It was as if his soul went out to feed these people, many of whom had been so often hungry. They were desperate but determined men and women. They must not be denied. He thought he could feel every beat of their hearts just as, when in a trance, he could see the horizon's rim of the future and hear the voice that might be God's.

Yet he could have wept for them as he stood on the bridge and observed the tide grow and grow in its strength. So many souls given no time to build a life in God's image. So many lives knowing only the cruelties of man, not the goodness of God. Suffering faces flushed today with a rare radiance, pitifully grateful for the exceptional joy of hope. The meek shall this day inherit the earth, John Ball thought. Please, God, for this once in their lives, let them prevail. On this day of the Body and Blood of Christ, let them win back Your world.

He went in to the crowd, who chanted his name. Will had gone on ahead – as usual, Ball guessed, with a tender smile, to forage for bread. Like a biblical host, the True Commons of England went up to their capital to be saved.

London opened its shops, its kitchens and its cellars. London turned over the feast hoards for Corpus Christi to feed the rebels, whom they called brothers. Their loud, exhilarated parade passed by the traditional defenders of the city, who were hiding in their palaces. There were several thousand fully armed men in those mansions – all, it seemed, infected with the same epidemic of panic and paralysis that had gripped the guardians of Rochester and Southwark Bridge.

Johanna, who had tracked alongside him, thought that Tyler had never looked more the commander. His fine Roman head assumed an imperial character; his muscled body moved nimbly. He himself felt that physical fulfilment. He had never felt so stretched, so tested or more able to meet any test. There had been no opposition from a city of legendary defences! All the walls had fallen before them!

He pitched the tents in the open ground east of the White Tower. This would be his base. The enemy was all about him and facing him in the Tower. But it also held the King. First he must be prised away from his advisers and be assured of his safety.

Now he must seek out Jack Straw, whose men had begun their march towards the Temple. The Essex men, it had been agreed, would go to that hub of the law. The legalistic burgesses of Colchester, Tyler thought, would relish it.

Straw and himself had to co-ordinate their plans. They had two days to do it, Tyler reckoned. Two days before a drift of their forces would begin: those who had come merely for an adventure, those who feared for their families and their livings back in their villages, those who would surely return when they thought the goals had been achieved, and those who would just as surely go if they feared the goals would never be achieved.

Tyler had to persuade as many as possible to stay because he needed their mass when he unveiled his new demands, now enlarged by John Ball. And he would need the key men to stay on and make a government. He had to persuade Jack Straw to be less reckless. He had to secure the men from other towns whose reports and pledges of support could make such a difference. He had to keep the Londoners on his side. He had to curb the potential excesses of some of those released from prison. He had to keep his own men in order and have no robbing or thieving. He had to link up with the rest of the country. He had to find time to sleep. He had to talk to John Ball.

It was time he needed, and speed. God's speed.

Abel Ker and about a score of his men had camped nearby. As soon as Tyler saw them, he went across and sat with them.

'What do you reckon?'

'There's not much room to think, is there?' said Ker, smiling broadly. 'Who would have believed . . .'

'What do you reckon?' Tyler repeated, this time addressing Ker's men. 'Should we push on as hard as we can and force them to let us talk to the King?'

'Look what he did at Greenwich.' It was Isaac Carter.

Tyler nodded at him in recognition. 'That wasn't him, Isaac,' he said. 'That was not him. It's those around him. Once we get rid of them we'll get what we want.'

Greenwich burned still in Tyler's feelings so that he felt the heat of it flush onto his face. He needed only to think of that to feel not just certain but eager to get rid of those men who had poisoned the King. Their heads must be severed so that the head of England could see and act well for his country.

'They have armed men ready in those palaces over there,' said Ker.

'We must hope we can frighten them to stay inside, then.'

'So far,' said Ker, puzzled, 'no one has offered any resistance at all.'

'It is the will of God!' said Carter. 'John Ball says so.'

'To have got so far without a scratch.' Ker looked at Tyler with some admiration. 'I don't think I could have managed that, Walter.'

'We've all done it,' said Tyler, briskly. 'All of us – and you have been the real leader among the men here.' His eyes swept around the multitude. 'Look how they keep their order,' he said, 'even as they seem to be in nothing but confusion. They look up to you and your men, Abel. As I do.'

Ker took the compliment without flinching. Like Tyler himself, he was not comfortable with praise. But he knew that Tyler meant what he said and that his men had heard. The words would be passed on.

'In time to come, Abel,' said Tyler, as he stood up, 'we'll sit into the night, talk over these days and wonder how they happened.'

'Yes,' he said. 'We will wonder.'

Between the city, which created wealth, and the Palace of Westminster, where the business of Parliament and the affairs of court were pursued, between the intensity of commercial London and the amplitude of government lay the Strand. To the south of the Strand was the Thames, and between the Strand and the Thames, far enough away from the smells of the city of London, was the Savoy Palace. There were palaces inside the city, and palaces all over England, but none could begin to compare with the Savoy.

It ranged across a vast river frontage with access to the safest and fastest highway in London. It had been home to Prince Edmund, Duke of Lancaster. The present duke was John of Gaunt, he who, more than anyone else, was blamed for the ruinous taxes.

John of Gaunt, luckily for him, was on the Scottish Border. In his absence, his palace would have to stand in for him.

It had a great hall, stables, a chapel, cloisters, a river gate with a walkway and barges at the ready; there were gardens and fishponds, twin towers and many bedchambers. It had been crenellated and constantly extended. It turned its back on the Strand and faced the Thames. Poets and musicians had been welcomed and applauded there. It was at the apex of English culture.

The treasures it held were said to be bettered only by those of the monarch. The loot and purchases of decades had found their way there. The exceptionality of the Savoy Palace was sealed by its charter, which declared it to be a law unto itself. It had laws different from those in the rest of London. It enjoyed a special jurisdiction known as the Liberties of the Savoy.

Late on that hot June afternoon, on Corpus Christi Day, the Savoy Palace was to be erased.

Fire and the axe were the chief weapons. Some of the rebels, once over the bridge – fed and plied with unaccustomed wine – peeled off down Fleet Street. They broke open the Fleet Prison. By now some of the most vicious gangs in London, those who had just escaped hanging, were reassembling and they saw heaven in the anarchy on the streets. Many of the people of London who were on the side of the rebellion had scores to settle and now was the time. Moneylenders could be threatened, grievances redressed, bad neighbours attacked. Robbery could seem like sympathy with the rebellion. The law began to crumble.

But the discipline of the men of Kent held, especially at the Savoy. In those first hours in London, there was a consistent will among them to be regarded as seekers after justice, not as thieves. Though the Londoners saw the Savoy as an irresistible target for the most savage revenge possible, among the Kentish men Tyler's writ ran strong.

On their way to the palace, an obsessive object of desire, the rebels and their London sympathisers attacked any building that was owned by or connected to one who had been part of the making of the new tax laws. The master of the Hospital of St John, whose estate they had burned down on the way to Canterbury, owned many houses along the Strand. These were wrecked, as far as possible, and the armouries ransacked. Some buildings were pulled down and set alight. They sought out the house of the Bishop of Chester, near St Mary-le-Strand, where the bishop-elect of Durham, clerk to the Privy Seal, was staying. They raided his wine cellars, rolled out the barrels and drank deep.

But the Savoy was the prize: nowhere fatter, nowhere richer, nowhere more hated.

The gates were closed. Guards stood some distance away from them. Once again the cry, 'Open the gates!' Once again it grew into a wall of sound. Once again the guards, believing that surrender was the only path to survival, opened the gates. And so, unchallenged, the rebels surged into this palace, this fabled city in itself, which, they claimed, had sucked the blood out of them for decades.

The nature of the destruction was possibly unprecedented. All the dazzlingly jewelled clothes were torched. Headboards, some ancient and priceless, were burned, all. Rare jewels were hammered to dust. Silver was hacked with axes and hurled into the Thames. One man, a Londoner, who was seen stealing a silver goblet and hiding it under his smock, was thrown into a fire and let burn. Rare coats, half armour half splendour, were used for target practice by the bowmen, then flung into the flames. The great hall made a memorable bonfire, as did the chapel. Silver and gold coins, medals and vestments fed the flames, as did rare manuscripts, heraldic shields, tapestries, panels, lamps. All perished in the gorging flames, cheered on by the rebels.

They worked with an intensity that spoke more of a passionate crusade than a riot. They would destroy all evidence of the power of the man who, under the protection of inheritance, had so tormented them. Now it was his turn. His presence was this palace, and it would be no more. Gaunt was the enemy of God. His property was the infidel.

Some of the Londoners were less scrupulous.

Three barrels, thought to be full of precious ornaments,

were slung onto the fire in the great hall. They contained gunpowder, which instantly turned a fire into a furnace.

Below the great hall, in the fine wine cellars, about thirty Londoners, former prisoners, had set themselves to help in the task of destruction through drink. The explosion blocked them into the cellars. At first their cries and hammering could be heard, but as the blaze flared to the roof the beams collapsed, the cries grew fainter until they were heard no more . . .

But there was Joan. How could Johanna explain to her brothers that there was Joan? She tried. And she took them across the wreckage to point her out. What they saw was a strong young woman, not unlike a younger Johanna, immersed in the conscientious destruction of John of Gaunt's palace. They laughed at Johanna's fears so she, too, felt that Joan was fully capable of surviving without her for a few hours.

She went and explained to the girl that she needed to go downriver with her brothers but would be back on the next tide and would seek her out near the tents of her father. Joan was pleased to be granting a favour. She was pleased to be left independent. Of course she would be safe. Look at all the good people around her. She would stay with them. Johanna let herself be persuaded. She sneaked away her stolen goods – coins, jewellery, small precious ornaments easily concealed. All would be well.

Working stealthily and carefully on the waterfront, Johanna loaded her treasures into the small boat her brothers had brought upriver. With fine timing, they swung out into mid-Thames and took advantage of the strong outgoing tide to race downriver . . .

The palace would burn deep into the night and smoulder throughout the next day. The few dead included guards,

Londoners who had failed to give the correct response to the oath of the Kentish rebels and the thirty men trapped until their death, in the wine cellar . . .

'The jewels were ground to dust,' Tom reported.

'The jewels? All his jewels?' Joan could not immediately absorb such information.

'I saw them. So did he.'

He nodded at Edgar, her clerk and messenger, who had rushed to the Savoy with him.

'It was a marvel!' said the clerk. 'These brutes behaved as if they were on oath.'

'Brutes?' said Joan, who woke up from her daze. 'If they are only brutes, why are our knights hiding in their palaces?'

Salisbury murmured something noncommittal.

'Why did that fool Walworth let them in?'

Muttered equivocation, more mimed than spoken.

'My son the King is not rich in his advisers,' she said.

'They are moving all over the city,' said Holland.

'The King will be here soon,' she said. 'My lord Salisbury, call in the council.'

To her son Tom, Joan repeated, '*All* the jewels? Ground to *dust*?'

'Dust.'

'Dust?' she echoed. As we will become, she thought. 'We must act. The King must act.'

21

Lord Mayor Walworth

William Walworth, Lord Mayor of London, was the man accused of letting the gates to the city be opened to the rebels. Somebody had to be blamed. Walworth was finger-pointed by those who owned the city. Some said he was not only culpable, but traitorous. He knew he had a lot of ground to make up.

In that city of palaces and rooted aristocracy, in that land of ancient titles jealously guarded and a financial hierarchy tightly exclusive, Walworth was a newcomer, of no family, no shire acres, jumped up. He had overworked and taken questionable short-cuts, like many arrivistes before and after him; he had mixed duplicity with shrewdness and, like all *nouveaux riches*, taken the slaps and sneers of snobbery as part of the cost of ambition. He had on two occasions risked all his fortune for a greater fortune and won. To find himself now, when he had reached the pinnacle of status – Lord Mayor of London – the object of contempt and dismissive rumour was unbearable. As the rebels began burning the Temple and other law courts, and after the controlled savagery of the Savoy, he began his fight back.

To have the success that Walworth the fishmonger had had in that city of pyramidal privilege, you needed a brass neck. He ignored all criticism and would not answer it.

There were men of prodigal wealth in London and, over the years, Walworth had made it his business to know them all and entrap many of them into dependence on his loans. His access to capital was uniquely appreciated, even by grandees of city wealth, like Nicholas Brembre, and the richest merchant in London, John Phillpot. He had joined with them three years before to raise the private army that had swept away the Scottish pirate ships from the Thames. These men would be stunned at the fate of the Savoy Palace. They would now be planning how best to guarantee the survival of their own properties. That was his wedge back in.

It was to the palace of Sir Robert Knolles that Walworth went first. Knolles shared Walworth's background – and, for that matter, the background of Walter Tyler. Knolles could track back his ancestry one generation only, to yeomen. A uniquely successful fighting career of thirty-five years in the wars against France had brought him fame, wealth, a knighthood, property all over London and the means to support more than a hundred fully armed men in his London palace. The spread of his property brought him instant intelligence from outside the city – from St Pancras and Kentish Town to Barking and Cripplegate. His own well-trained men gave him the power to sustain it.

Walworth calculated that the support of Knolles was key. With him as an ally he could persuade the others.

The mayor took a decision to ride through the streets in style, but not in his usual pomp. He would not disguise his rank. He would have his guards about him. But they would be a mere half-dozen and he would school himself to good humour as his troop pressed through the roistering crowd, at this stage veering between religious ecstasy, rebellious success, carnival and drink. There was still, he reckoned, correctly, at this stage enough respect for the old ways to let him through. But as he gently pressed on, politely parting a path through the populace, he could sense that this might turn suddenly into unstoppable violence.

'That is why we must act tonight,' he said to Knolles, after he had described his ride through London.

They were in the knight's private chamber, decorated with some of the finest booty from Flanders and France, a room that the usually unsentimental Knolles loved to visit alone by candlelight and whisper to himself, 'Mine. All of it. All mine.' A chamber of trophies, burnished to impress.

'They are burning our manors, palaces and houses,' Walworth said. 'Cheapside is now a place of execution. It is already a bigger deathbed than Tyburn. The Essex rebels have burned down Highbury.'

The old warrior looked directly into Walworth's eyes. 'What do you suggest we do?'

'Attack them.' The mayor longed to redeem his humiliation.

'They are too many. London has embraced them. I hear that new men are heading here by the hour and in great numbers. If we attack,' said Knolles, 'we must win.' He hesitated; unlike him. 'And they are us,' he said, and his scarred, weathered, creased face lost its certainty. 'I went into the streets to look over them. I must have fought alongside some of those men.'

'They have been driven mad,' said Walworth, 'by wild priests and jealous rebels.'

'All of them? And all of them in London? And all those still making for London? All of them mad?'

'What are you saying?'

'I saw this in France. I saw the peasants in France rise up. And there are reports from Florence and from Germany but none, from what I hear, as big and strong as this. These men are almost like an army. Our army.' He took a draught of wine and encouraged Walworth to do the same. Outside the noise grew, penetrating the thick walls, a noise still more jubilant than inflamed.

The two men listened, as if they were at an oracle.

'If we had stayed in our fathers' lives, William, we would be out there with them!' said Knolles. 'We are not well ruled, are we? And for too long we have milked the poor to starvation. Yet still they fought for us, they fed us, they laboured for us . . . until now.'

Walworth let the silence build. Some of what the other had said found an echo in his past but he would not let it influence him.

'Who can blame them for wanting what we have?' added Knolles.

The old knight gazed beyond the mayor and his eyes settled on a shield given him by the Black Prince, now hanging splendid and solitary above the cave-mouthed fireplace.

'But they cannot have it,' said Walworth. 'We will not give it to them.'

'So we must win,' the older man said, rather sadly. 'Kill our countrymen to save our country.'

'Could you send out spies?' Walworth's abrupt change of tone and pace brought the knight back to the moment.

'I have done that.'

'How many men fully armed do you think you, Brembre, Phillpot, others and I could muster?'

'I've thought on that. About seven thousand. Some say there are seventy thousand rebels, maybe more. And they have London on their side.' He smiled. 'Even at Poitiers—'

'I'll go and talk to the others. There will be a council. We must all be there and of the same mind.'

Knolles beckoned Walworth and they went onto the roof. To the west, flames from the burning Savoy Palace licked into the drowsy summer sky. Crowds surged through the streets blindly, fiercely . . .

'They are so many,' repeated Knolles. 'And they are us.'

'And they are wicked men, all of them,' said Walworth, summoning up virtue to prove his courage. 'They will destroy our England unless we prevent them. They can no longer be called Englishmen, Sir Robert. They are traitors.'

The old knight could not take his gaze off the inflamed palace. 'I've fought with John of Gaunt,' he said. 'Now I watch while his wealth and reputation burn to the ground. I do not regret that. Gaunt attacked the city's wealth. He ignored sanctuary and trampled all over our city liberties. But . . . who will be next, my Lord Mayor?'

When the gunpowder had imploded in the Savoy, fright at the sound had driven many back into the Strand. It had seemed for a moment like the arrival of John Ball's Apocalypse. After Joan had been left by Johanna, she too made for London.

A crowd was pressing from the Savoy into the city and Joan was taken along by it. Once or twice she turned to look at the fires in the palaces and houses along the Strand but they disturbed her. She felt safer, being carried by the throng. The whole adventure was now in danger of becoming darker and her stomach tightened against what might happen. With her left hand she touched the dagger, well hidden but always ready.

Bad smells assailed her, the nearer they got to the city. Joan had been brought up in a village so small and wood-enclosed that such odours could be avoided by stepping into the land around them. A few yards – herding geese, fetching a cow, collecting fallen branches – would take her to places as sweet-smelling as the open midden in the village was foul.

But in London there was no escape. She saw the refuse of months clogging what should surely have been a stream. She saw and smelt as she came towards the city walls mounds of rotting food, slurries of excrement, black rats half as big as cats, wild pigs and stray dogs, half-naked children burrowing in the waste piles, and a pervasive dirt that made her nostrils recoil.

Inside the London wall, Joan felt almost lifted off her feet by the jammed crowd as she moved into the city. Such a size! So many spires, streets, shops, hawkers, so much bustle and noise! She was made dizzy by the variety, yet she felt alone in the middle of the whirl.

She heard languages other than English and even the English she heard she caught only fractionally as it sounded so far from her own district and dialect. And the clothes – fur-trimmed, silk-lined, gaudily coloured, all pegged by degrees. It seemed like a procession laid on for entertainment and show rather than people who lived their lives in this place, dressing and talking like that every day.

The big houses in the streets, the lanes walled in so tightly, armed men on horseback, rebels with axes and bows and pitchforks, priests with high-held statues of Jesus Christ – the Babel of voices became to Joan as just one sound, like the sough of wind sweeping through a wood, now blustering, now sighing, bursting, then dropping, but always there, testing the trees as these sounds tested the city streets.

And she heard her father's name! She glanced around but who out of such a crowd had uttered 'Tyler' or 'Wat Tyler'? It made her feel safe. So she let herself be carried in and out of the innumerable streets, part of one fluid body, which seemed to be looking for entrances and exits but was unsure where to find them and unsure which was which.

And then she heard the voice of John Ball. She put herself into the stream moving towards the steps of St Paul's. Joan could not credit that anything man-made could be as tall as that spire, which pointed at Heaven and threatened to reach it. She wriggled her way to the front, below the high step on which the priest stood. And the further she went, the quieter the crowd: here at last was the quiet heart of the city.

John Ball saw his task at that moment in the uprising to steady the mood. The first excitement was spent but successes along the way and the spectacular unopposed entry into London had fed an as-yet-unfathomed layer of possibility. Their will could be done. But now was the time to be steady. He could see what was to come: the blood tide that might be released.

There was no retreat now. If they turned back, they would be damned by God and slaughtered by the King's councillors. But if they could sweep away all corruptions in the body of England . . .

'I see the road before us,' he said, more quietly than was his usual style, his eyes almost closed – he swayed a little, moved by his vision, and some followed him, eyes half closed as his were, swaying as he swayed, 'your land, our land, a free land, a land of no hunger and no fear, a land that is full fed and light, where all who are born can live equally and have the life that God alone can give. I can see this, good people.

'John Ball prays you all that you make a good end of what you have begun.'

He made the sign of the cross and the people knelt before him. He incanted prayers, which they underlined, 'Amen, amen, amen,' and Joan felt a current of faith pass through her, as surely it passed through others, when the bells began to peal for vespers . . .

She followed John Ball. He went down towards the Thames and then east towards the Tower. He was followed by the crowds, which had scarcely left him all day. Beggars held out their hands to him – he was said to perform miracles by touch alone. He walked quietly, as if trying to shake off his followers. Will had still not returned and the priest's anxiety was driving out all other thoughts and feelings . . .

Joan fell away. And suddenly, quite abruptly, there was the White Tower and beyond it, massed across the land, the army that had followed her father. At first they seemed an endless solid block of men, scarcely moving, but the nearer they drew, the more she saw them, like bees about a hive. On the top of the mound were tents, one flying the pennant of Kent.

That, she knew, was where her father would be. She went there to wait for Johanna.

Outside the main tent there was a semi-circle of men around Tyler. A few yards away petitioners waited for their turn. The westering sun further bronzed the faces of the men. It was cooling a little now. From where he sat, Tyler had the Tower in full view. His men encircled it. Guards, usually women, patrolled the riverbank. It was a siege without siege weapons, save the mass of the rebels and the hourly increase in their numbers. Tyler could watch over the redoubt of his enemies and, he knew, his close presence was constantly observed by those within.

'They think they are trapped,' he had said to Henry Long, a few hours earlier when they had chosen this place as their encampment. 'They can't decide whether to meet us or fight us. They wait for us to move so that they can act. In the city, it's the same. The soldiers are armed and ready in those palaces but they won't come out. It seems that we have them.'

His council was in session for the second time that day, speeding through requests, punishments, news from up country, reports on current progress . . . Joan came quite near and, unobserved, watched him. She felt abashed. This man was far from the father who had asked her to help in the field and the garden, and let her ride his horse. He even looked different, she thought, his face more severe, his manner grander, and he was given such attention and respect. She was shy with pride.

John Ball went across to him, sat next to him and looked around for Will. He was not there. Tyler and Ball talked quietly to each other. Tyler glanced up and saw Joan, and she, understanding his look, knew she ought not to be there.

He went on talking with John Ball, then turned to the aldermen and burgesses, the village elders and Sir John Newton, to gather in their reports.

'Jack Straw and some of his men are on their way,' he said. 'We need to talk, all of us together. In the next hour.'

Then Tyler came across to his daughter. She lowered her head but he put his hand under her chin, lifted her face and smiled. The smile radiated through her. For a few seconds, daughter and father were back together.

'You must go,' he said quietly, only for her ears. 'What will happen soon will be dangerous. I do not want you hurt.' And, he did not need to add, I cannot spare a grain of time to keep a lookout for you. 'There are a few older men who are going back to Dartford in the morning. They will look after you along the way.' He pressed his hand on her shoulder. 'You will do as I say.'

Joan did not reply but nor did she indicate dissent. She could see as clear as the clear evening sky that her father was made now of one thing only: the will to have his way.

He held her shoulder firmly, but warmly, then went back to his men.

Joan slipped back into the crowd and quickly made off, aiming for the anonymity of the seething streets of London, guided by the spire of St Paul's.

22

The Council of the Rebels

J ack Straw arrived with a modest company of men but
with the flourish of a warlord. To command men who
had burned down such grand properties and overcome with
such ease all opposition as had been offered would have
made any man feel good about himself. Jack Straw, whose
rebel life had lain almost exclusively in the tactics of words,
felt himself transformed into a soldier. His Essex men had
scythed across the county, been patient in following the
strategies agreed with Tyler and, unloosed from their base
at Mile End, had targeted their enemies in the city with
good discipline.

He sat alongside Walter Tyler, Henry Long, several
leading elders from Kent and a similar number from his
own county. For the first few minutes, while small beer was
brought with meat, bread and cheese, Straw, like his men,
was mesmerised by the size and proximity of the White
Tower. What a fortress it was! Who could dream of taking
it? And yet here they were, with impunity, their men hurling
insults over its walls whenever the mood took them, and
Tyler confident that they would, and soon, possess it.

'We must first get the King out of the Tower,' Tyler said.
'When he is gone, we can take it.'

Jack Straw pulled his gaze reluctantly away from the
battlements. 'How?'

'God is on our side,' said John Ball. 'Why are those in
the Tower not shooting at us with arrows? Why are the
armed men shivering inside the palaces over there?' He

pointed to the city. 'Why did Rochester Castle open and why was the bridge at Southwark lowered? God's work is being done. We are God's army and He has struck down our enemies so that they dare not raise a sword.'

Tyler nodded. God, he thought, had been helped by many thousands of rebels but the greater cause of their so-far triumph he ascribed happily to John Ball and his God.

'We have scared them all,' said Straw, every inch the new warrior. 'They dare not show face. We went to the Temple as we agreed,' he nodded to Long, whose legal training had never been more useful than there, providing accurate lists of the documents relating to taxation and the terms of employment, which had been burned. 'And no one drew a sword against us. We took all the books and rolls. We pulled down the houses and destroyed the tiles so that what was left would be ruined by the weather. We were scarcely challenged,' said Straw, still groggy with the sleepless, boundless process of it all. 'Some of the apprentices in the Temple even helped us and showed us where to find the muniments and the more precious rolls in the Temple church. Those few who opposed us we killed.'

'The London apprentices are with us?' said Tyler.

'Oh, yes! Oh, yes!' said Straw, eating as if he had been starving. 'They helped us set fire to the Hospital of St John – it will burn for days! We looked for Robert Hales but he had fled.'

'He's in there.' Tyler pointed at the White Tower. 'With the others.'

'The prisoners from Fleet were like wild beasts when they came out,' Straw said. '"Kill!" they shouted. "Kill! Kill! Kill!"' Their malignity had excited him.

Tyler raised his hand. 'They must come in with us,' he said. 'They must not be left loose.'

'They have scores to settle.'

'Ours are heavier,' said Tyler. 'We must tell our men to check them.'

To find them, Straw thought, would be hard enough. Those men knew every rat-run in London and its suburbs and had been pitched in one move into toxic liberty.

'How do we go further?' Straw asked, impatient for more drama, more victories.

'We must take that Tower,' said Long, looking gravely at Tyler. 'We have come too far to retreat now. As long as they are in that Tower and we are outside it, they will have won.'

'But already we have won.'

'Not until we dislodge them from the White Tower.' Long was convincing.

'We have them penned in,' said Straw. 'Their friends in the city have deserted them. The armies are abroad. All we have to do is to wait. We can starve them out!'

Tyler shook his head. He was certain that this eruption could scatter into disorder and spend itself. Like fire, it needed to feed to live. The men who were ransacking the city, swilling free beer and wine and moving in a dream of conquest would soon want it to be over. They were far from the paid killers in the English army he had known in France. He had to build up a group from those around him now who would be ready and able to take up key posts in government the moment that victory was achieved.

'We have not time to starve them out. Go on,' he said to Long. Jack Straw was rebuffed.

'They,' Long indicated the Tower, 'the councillors, those who rule the King inside that Tower, know that you want them dead.'

'We do,' said John Ball.

'So they stay in the Tower. As long as they are in the Tower they are safe. As long as the Tower is safe, England is theirs. But capture it,' Long's usually even voice became intense, fully infected now with Tyler's ambition, 'and we will command the country.'

'I'll bring all my men here,' said Straw, 'and we will lay a siege.' The idea caught his unsoldiered imagination. But again he felt rebuffed when Tyler simply shook his head and did not offer the respect of a reply. 'Why not?' he demanded.

Tyler looked at the walls as if scrutinising each yard of them for a point of weakness. Once again he shook his head, but then he beckoned to Straw and the two men went apart from the others.

'We haven't the siege engines, Jack. And we haven't the time. We don't know how many men they have in there but it wouldn't take very many to hold out for some weeks. That's what they'll want. They'll want to wear us down and see us drift back to our counties and our homes. That's their best tactic.'

'Why don't we deal with all the others and leave them to rot?'

'Those we most want are in that Tower, Jack.' He took the younger man's arm. 'Once we have those who are in the Tower, all the others will know that none of them is safe and *then* we will have won!'

Tyler looked about him. A wash of noise came from the excited assembly, constantly swelling and dipping, an ocean of bodies. Surely, he thought, we are enough.

'So we have to get them out of there,' Straw said. 'Do you think if we sent the King our demands and asked him to talk to us, man to man this time?'

'They won't let him do that. Look at Greenwich this morning. Yet your way is the only way. But how, Jack?'

'Look what we have done in one day alone!' They gazed out over the burning city, smoking the summer evening air, cries filling it with either acclamation or anger. 'Who would have thought it?' Straw shook his head in awe and repeated, 'In one day.'

Tyler looked over Straw's demands as summarised by Henry Long.

1. Punishment and execution of councillors and traitors against the Crown.
2. Abolition of the poll tax and serfdom.
3. Mandatory rent at fourpence per acre of land.
4. Rights to hunt and fish and collect dead wood.

Only days ago these demands had seemed so bold. Now Tyler knew they would not satisfy either John Ball or himself. They would not cut out the gangrene . . .

Tyler felt the need to walk among the men, from one cluster to another, and he was greeted as both commoner and chief. It was hard to resist the pride this aroused in him, the spring of confidence those greetings and encouragement brought him. He loved to be so trusted. His resolution hardened as he saw mere pitchforks and staves, cadaverous faces and bare clothing, the poor of the earth who had followed him into one of the most fortified cities in the world. Not knowing whether they would be met by welcome or war, they had followed him. Just look at them! Thousand on thousand of them camped obediently outside the Tower wall. These were the people of England, he thought, whose time to speak had come.

He remembered John Ball's words when they had talked together on the march from Blackheath that morning. 'You must harden your heart, Walter,' he had said. 'It need not be as it is. Think of the wealth there is in the palace of the Savoy. All Kent, all Essex could have lived off it for years. Why should all that be the property of one man?

'Men like John of Gaunt could heal the England they say they love. But they do not love her. And they never will, as long as they can control and exploit her so easily. And that is the truth of it, Walter. If they are not rooted out now, they will grow again and again. England will be for ever a land lost to her people and we will be to blame. We have been given the chance. We have been chosen.'

With some difficulty Tyler pulled himself out of that recollection, which had been more vivid than the men in front of him. He knew what John Ball meant. He had to kill and kill again. The priest had understood that he had been flinching from this necessity.

He walked back to his own tent. Seeing and sensing his mood, the men did not trouble him. But he felt their plight and their hope in his bones.

When he came up to the men who were in his council, he looked to Jack Straw, nodded and said: 'You are right. We must get the King out of the Tower so that we can execute the traitors.' He shook off the tiredness that had threatened him as he walked among the rebels. 'We must tell the men to go to the castle walls and make a greater noise than they have ever made. Let us hurl threats. Let us call for the King, show him we mean a riot, say we will do *him* no harm but we *will* burn the Tower to the ground if he does not come and speak to us – and when he does, because he will, he is no coward, he is his father's son, we will demand that he meets us out of the Tower, and well outside the city walls, face to face, unarmed. And when the King is gone from here, we will take the Tower.'

23

The King's Council

P rincess Joan changed her clothes for the second time
that day. Her maids were hushed by her solemnity. She
summoned up the schooling in her Catholicism that turned
pain into strength. She was in serious physical pain, but the
harder the stab in her back the grimmer her resolution.
Princess Joan in the White Tower, candlelit as it might have
been for a romance, knew that it had to be war. The peasants had been in the city for less than twelve hours yet it
was already half destroyed and it was theirs. She wore only
one ring – the large ruby given to her by the Black Prince
on the birth of their first son. On her white hand, against
the dark burgundy of her gown, it looked like the seal on
a great charter.

A gesture dismissed her attendants. When they were gone
she walked over to a large deeply carved oak chair and
carefully lowered herself into it. There would be time enough
for standing when she went into the council meeting.
Meanwhile, silent to her ears through the thick stone walls,
she imagined the discussion under way. She bided her time.

She was aware of the stampede of policy, advice and news
rattling through the cool rooms of the Tower. She had seen
the King earlier, and she would see him again, but for a
while he must be let sink or swim alone in the twisting,
turning currents of opinion. Only she could tell him what
he most needed to hear, but she had to wait for the right
time. Her own people had brought further reports from
outside, which had pitched her into a sense of peril. She

had instructed Tom to bring her truthful news of the full danger.

Richard sat on his elevated chair-throne, wondering whom to trust. Although the room was murmuring with whispers and shaped by the movements of richly garbed men, he found it hard to peel his eyes from the pinched view of London outside the slit of window. He looked out on the least afflicted, less populous part of the city, but that made it all the more teasing. What was happening outside the restricted boundaries of his gaze? What would happen next? What should he do?

The advisers, in suffocating numbers, were, all of them, hovering to catch his ear. He had heard them all. Plans of action and inaction, soothing words, stirring sentences, promises, prayers, a confusion. He wanted to be alone. But he had not the authority in himself to command them to leave him. He had been coddled by continuous delegations of advisers since his coronation. Even his bedroom was guarded inside and out. The best he could do was to with-draw his mind from them.

He made it clear that he wanted no conversation with anyone.

Richard could read his own feelings. He was apprehensive but not fearful. He held the rebels in contempt, but he was impressed by their success. He could not resist fondling the oft-repeated password: 'We are for the King and the True Commons of England.' He repeated it to himself. For the King! But his city was being ruined. Places of magnificence and antiquity were being reduced to rubble. All over his realm the laws and commands of kings before him were being broken, like so many dry twigs. Then there was the confusion of his excitement. It was wrong, he knew, like sin, but he felt it thrill through him when at intervals a wild roar from the rebels would come in through his narrow view of the world and there would be wild cheering as another head was severed.

He was a young man already steeped in the appreciation of beauty. He found it in the woods and the fields while he was hunting, in the jewels he and his mother wore, in the music and poetry he heard; he found it in clothes and buildings, paintings and tapestries, in the sky, in the clouds and in the faces of those he favoured. And he was already a connoisseur of his unique position. As he sat, withdrawn, above the councillors, he was infused by an exquisite sense of his leading role in this play for his kingdom.

His advisers thought he was afraid. Each waited for the other to break through that wall of space set around their king. Richard wanted to secure and hold on to this moment, like the moment when the crown had been placed on his head, like the moment when he had been held up to be worshipped by the people . . . This it was to be a king.

'Thomas! What has happened to you?'

'My lady, I looked perfect!' The dusty, scruffy, exhilarated young priest, who had ripped into her room, strode across to his mother, gave a bow, which yet had a touch of mockery in it, as had his elaborate sign of the cross, and threw wide his arms. 'Out there,' he said, 'they are turning their world upside-down!'

'*Our* world,' said Joan, vexed but obliged to smile at this unpredictable rascal of a son.

'And what do we, here, do about it?' he exclaimed, still high on the disguise and the success of his raid behind the enemy's lines. 'Nothing,' he answered himself. 'Nothing but hide behind thick walls and hope it will all go away.'

'Will it?'

'No,' said Thomas, with rather too much relish, she thought. 'I know them now. I preached to them, men and women.'

'*You*? Preached?'

'I was listened to! I'm not like the man John Ball. But who is? I've heard him and, even standing far away, I felt the hairs on the back of my neck prickle. No one is like him. But I preached a sermon in Cheapside. You wouldn't have recognised me.'

'I hope not.'

'I laid into the rich – that story about it being easier for a rich man to go through the eye of a needle than to get into Heaven. They loved that. So I said it two or three times over in different ways.'

'Where did you get that appalling cassock?'

'Some poor priest I met in the street let me have it for fourpence. I gave him my rags. He was half drunk. Like so many of them. But not all of them. There are some proper men out there.'

'What do they want?'

'They want what we have!' Tom Holland was so cocky with his escapade that he was unguarded. 'Who can blame them?'

'I can! I do! They must be stopped.' Her sudden severity checked but did not stop him.

'We have no army near London,' he said, almost as if he were pleased, she thought. 'Our allies in the city are mice. They say that some of the guards here in the Tower are sympathetic to the rebels' cause.'

'Sit down. Tell me soberly and carefully what strength you think they have. What could halt them? What could defeat them? Tell me all that you know, and briefly.'

He sought out a chair not too near his mother, knowing the smell of him would irritate her. And, besides, it gave the potential exchange more formality and helped calm him.

The inadmissible truth was that he was in a whirl, his mood shot through with intoxication at such lavish destruction.

'They seem disorderly but most are not,' he began. And hesitated. 'And yet in some way they act as if they were drunk not only on beer and wine but on . . . the freedom they feel they now have and the greater freedom they will soon seize. The discipline that their leaders impose runs alongside mayhem. It may be that there are different parties. The parties of the counties, of Kent and Essex in particular, seem proud to be here to rescue and protect the King – that is the way they talk – and proud that they are not thieves but men of honour. But . . . in London – it is a mockery of our London. The heat, the crowds, with more sympathisers arriving by the hour, the streets full of men – and women too! – roving with intent for what? A spark would set them off. And rumour, rumour everywhere.

'They say that this man has used the rebellion to take revenge on his neighbour against whom he has had a grudge for years. That that family has taken possession of a house they claimed was stolen from them by deceitful lawyers. This man claims another's wife as his. A gang steals from every house in a street knowing they will not be apprehended. Lawyers are in hiding. Those foolishly released from all the prisons attack anyone they envy in the name of the Great Rebellion.

'They have set up an execution block in Cheapside. I saw two executions before my sermon – how the people cheered the severed heads! They say that on this day alone there had already been six. Everywhere there are people who fear for their lives . . . By mistake they threw a barrel of gunpowder into the fire in the great hall of the Savoy. They thought it was full of the duke's richest costumes. When it blew up it trapped dozens of men who were drinking in the cellars. They are still there and people say they will never get out!

They will die of drink!' He laughed. 'London feels to me as if a barrel of gunpowder has been thrown into the middle of it. Many people think they will never get out alive.'

'Rich people?'

'Yes.'

'It is all envy,' Joan said, fiercely. 'The rebels want to steal what they have not the wit to get by any other means. They are ignorant. They do not understand that a country needs leaders born and trained to rule. They do not respect the ordained and unchanging order. They must not only be defeated, they must be taught a lesson they will never forget.'

'May I speak freely?'

His mother's tone had risen from thoughtful to implacable, and he rarely dared challenge her in that mood. But the young man would not be silenced.

'I think they may already have won,' he said. 'They are strange men, the best of them. They killed their own kind who tried to steal from the Savoy. They destroyed that palace because of their convictions. A single jewel could have bettered their lives beyond their dreams. But I saw them and others did. And they love the King and will never see him come to harm. I say again. They think they have won.'

'We cannot let them win,' she said. And she very quietly repeated, 'We cannot, we will not, let them win. England will be drawn and quartered and all her noble heads severed. Our Heaven will be made Hell.'

'The rebels think it is Hell now.'

'It is no more than they deserve. They destroy the law – what then? We become like wild pigs. They destroy treasures and palaces. As the barbarians did in Rome. What then? Poverty! They sever the heads of all they claim oppose them – like barbarians. In their drunken stupidity they do not understand that the King and the Church and the law are there to guard a country that can stand like a rock against all the elements seeking to wreck it. We do not grind down our people. It is only because of us they are able to live at all! We are owed thanks.'

Thomas subsided.

'Go to your room and dress,' she said. 'Then come back and we will go into the council together.'

Unusually, there was no coquettish affection or teasing in her voice and her son left the room as if he had been whipped.

24

Resolution

'On the evening of this day of Corpus Christi, let us pray.'

Sudbury's words were welcomed. The council, from King to scribes, knelt on the stone floor and bowed their heads. The tall candles threw shadows on the walls and dimmed the high ceiling to a space of mystery.

Archbishop Sudbury, in the few hours since he had relinquished the titles and seals of chancellor, had gathered confidence. His intelligence was that the rebels considered him to be the arch-traitor, a man of God who betrayed God by wealth and corruption. He knew that if they caught him they would murder him. He would not welcome death but he thanked God that he would have time to prepare for it.

The Latin prayers were chanted unwaveringly and he led each amen with conviction.

He blessed the King, Princess Joan, those who were in the council, and he prayed for the safety of the kingdom and the Church. The pause for private reflection was unusually extended.

The men got to their feet with a greater feeling of responsibility. In their hands was the Keeping of the Kingdom.

The King resumed his throne. The council divided into two, each with their champion.

The Earl of Salisbury was on the King's right; his silken tongue was only one part of a character grounded in battle alongside Edward III and his son, and salted with looting and landgrabbing on an imperial scale. Flanking him were the Archbishop of Canterbury and Robert Hales, prior of the Hospital of England and royal treasurer. Behind them were John Legge and other favourites of John of Gaunt, who had come into the Tower after the burning of the Savoy. There was the Duchess of Brittany and her ladies, the boy Henry, Earl of Derby, others from the old aristocracy and a handful of knights from among the guards of the Tower.

Facing them were Walworth and the heavy wealth of the city, Nicholas Brembre, John Phillpot and, shoulder to shoulder with Walworth, Sir Robert Knolles.

The aim was to persuade the King to give his authority to one of what were radically opposed strategies.

Richard was thawing from that perfect dream world of his own unique significance. He saw, at the end of the channel between the two parties, which led like a carpet to the door, the entrance of his mother and his half-brother. She stood between two candles, which were as tall as guards. Her face was full lit, but its expression unreadable.

William Walworth, Lord Mayor of London, knew he had a lot to prove. The demon in his head was relentless. William Walworth had opened the gate! Or had he let the gate be opened? William Walworth had turned out, after much promise, to be foolish and a failure. Or, and this too had been whispered in rumour-fugged taverns, William Walworth was a secret sympathiser of Walter Tyler. William Walworth had a lot to prove.

At last, after what he thought of as the increasingly wasteful game of waiting on the King's attention, he was beckoned and could take the floor.

'Your Majesty,' Walworth began, in full, formal mode, 'with friends from the city I am here to offer you a plan that will rid it of these worse-than-rabid dogs. With these men, your loyal subjects,' he indicated the city magnates, 'who served your father in the field and have been proud to be of service to you in your wars, I wish to propose an action that will resolve this matter before dawn.'

Joan leaned her aching back against the comfort of the oak door. The man Walworth, she thought, was probably good of his kind. But she had no great regard for his kind. And why had he not guarded the gate?

'I have been through the streets,' he continued, 'and so have some of my most trusted servants. These peasants are many, but only, I would say, one in six or even one in ten is well armed or even armed with any real means of engaging in a battle. Many of them are drunk. Any order they might have had is breaking up. Their ranks are joined by London's scum. By midnight they will, most of them, be asleep.'

Joan glanced at Tom. His face was set. She knew that he wanted to leap in and refine this argument. She reached out, touched his shoulder and, when he turned to her, reluctantly because he knew what she wanted, she shook her head. It was an order.

You are a bully, Walworth, Joan thought, but you might, at this moment, serve.

Walworth looked around the council chamber, seeing it for what it was: a stage.

'We should kill them in their sleep,' he said.

Like the Massacre of the Innocents? Joan thought.

Walworth's arrow struck home.

'My friends here,' he turned to them and bowed them in, 'can put out more than eight thousand men in full harness by midnight. Properly armed for war. These are in our own palaces less than a mile away. There are the knights and bowmen you have here in the Tower and, surely, many others in the city who are already weary and angry at the ransack. When we begin, when we are seen to succeed, we will find allies, those who always fly to the side of the victor.'

'Will it be b-b-bestial?' asked the King. 'Will there be blood running through the streets of London?'

'That is what is happening now, Your Majesty,' said Walworth. 'And it will happen more and more as the days go on. This is only the first day and we have seen executions in Your Majesty's streets, assassinations in the law courts and in the properties of merchants. There will indeed be blood, theirs or ours.'

Joan felt a silent surge of consent fill her chest with satisfying aggression.

There was a quiet murmur. Much like 'Amen', Walworth thought.

The Earl of Salisbury stepped forward and, once again, Joan gave her dislike full play. Unforgivably, that very morning, he had made her son look a coward. Like Walworth, Salisbury, for Joan, had something to prove. He spoke softly. Slyly, Joan thought. Winding out his web to catch all the flies.

'We owe the city of London thanks that is hard to measure,' he began, bowing to the financial magnates, who were flattered. 'But my good Lord Mayor, though your loyalty and service to London cannot be doubted' – that hurt: Walworth felt the unspoken words 'The gate, the gate, why did he open the gate?' – 'I am not in favour of your bold plan. At least, not yet.

'We have not enough men, Your Majesty,' he said, addressing the King directly. 'We are scarcely ten thousand, they are in their tens of thousands. And you cannot kill in the narrow streets of London without cries and screams that would wake the dead, as well as the sleeping. And what would your men do, my Lord Mayor, even in full harness, against a biblical swarm of angry rebels, however partly armed, whose actions so far have been like a most mighty flood and swept all before them? Neither village, town nor,

Master Walworth, the once impregnable city of London has been able to stand against them.'

He paused to let this exert its full hurt.

'And what of your soldiers' formations and battlefield tactics in the alleys and yards, in those slit passages and crooked footpaths, where cunning can overcome discipline and especially at night? Will there be a moon, my Lord Mayor? If so, who will benefit? If they can see the enemy plain they can attack in mass. If not, the dark is the most loyal ally of the desperate.'

He saw that he had Walworth defeated. But he made sure.

'And what about London, my Lord Mayor, and the Londoners you know so well and control so tightly?'

Once again Walworth heard the cry, 'Why did he open the gate? Why did he let it be opened?'

'Our informants tell us that many of them have welcomed the rebels. And there are the prisoners foolishly released from the safety of so many of our gaols. They, we hear, are unmanageable.'

Initially Joan had resisted his argument but now found herself wavering. Salisbury's voice had risen. He spoke not unlike a prophet, she thought, warning his flock of wrath to come.

'We are not sure of our Londoners, Your Majesty. But we do know that they do not like being attacked. And after a day of carnival, of Corpus Christi, when the last is first and the greatest are lowest and all of us become our opposite for the day, they will be fuddled further by the liberty promised by the rebels.

'What if, Your Majesty, the Lord Mayor's well-intended midnight massacre does not succeed? Then all – all – will be lost to you, your heirs and successors, to us and those like us, to the entire realm of England for ever. And finally,

Your Majesty, do you want to acquire the reputation of the English king who killed sleeping Englishmen? Is that what any of us could live with? Would it not be the end of all honour?' Salisbury's voice rang out with a noble force. Walworth kept his eyes to the floor.

Joan could sense the words slapping into the mind of her proud Plantagenet son.

'Better by far tomorrow to promise the rebels whatever they ask,' said Salisbury. 'Give way on everything. Then we will survive for another day, and another, and they will soon enough grow tired and turn tail to their homes. After that, Your Majesty, we can take action. And may I suggest that, though they burn documents, we ourselves must offer them a document, sealed by you. They will honour and treasure it. I have a draft with me. And they can take your Great Seal home with them, the word of the King, the King they love – as we all do – and with that they will believe that they have gained a famous victory.'

A scribe produced the document. Salisbury took his time.

'"I, Richard, King of England and France,"' he read, '"give great thanks to his Commons for that they have so great a desire to see and maintain their king: and he grants them pardon for all manner of trespass and misprision and felonies done up to this hour, and wills and commands that everyone should now quietly return to his own home. He wills and commands that everyone should put his grievances in writing and have them sent to him; and he will provide, with the aid of his loyal lords and good council, such remedy as shall be profitable to him, to them and to the kingdom."'

Richard sought his mother's face.

'You would need to put your seal on the grievances only when they arrive. And do that in the presence of this council,' said Salisbury. 'I entreat you to send this out, now, to those rebels who crowd around the Tower, and especially to the

215

tent of their leader, the man Tyler, where it should be read out to him.'

'Who will take it?' the archbishop asked, in order that he himself would be excused the danger of doing it.

'I will, if there is none better.'

Thomas Holland walked into the space between Salisbury and Walworth. Richard gazed on him with, Joan thought, a touch of annoyance. Yet he signalled assent to Salisbury, who took the young man's hand.

'And I will read it out,' said Walworth.

Joan nodded to Richard.

'I c-command you both,' he said.

'Go unarmed,' said Salisbury. 'Neither sword nor dagger. You,' he addressed Thomas, 'must lead, carrying the King's ensign. When challenged, say that you are the son of Princess Joan, mother of the King. My Lord Mayor,' there was some admiration in Salisbury's voice, 'I beg you to be courteous to this man Tyler. They say he fought at Poitiers with the King's father. And already the people are calling him "king of the True Commons of England".'

Walworth bowed, then turned to the King. 'I thank Your Majesty for allowing me this honour. But may I speak once more, Your Majesty?' Unspurned, he went on, quietly this time. 'We in the city, too, were not happy to kill sleeping Englishmen. But, Your Majesty, it is their intention to kill us and those like us and they have begun. Their challenge is "Who are you for?" If you do not reply, "For the King and the True Commons of England," you are attacked. Many are killed. We pray that this declaration by yourself will heal many wounds. We trust it will. If it does not, those sleeping Englishmen, Your Majesty, will surely wake up to slaughter other Englishmen tomorrow.'

Salisbury was not pleased.

Joan, rather to her dismay, felt some regard for Walworth. As he and her son left the room, she allowed herself to look sympathetically at the mayor. Tom she did not face. Once again he was beyond praise.

Richard thanked the council and came towards her. 'We should see our city,' he said, 'and look over these rebels. There is a turret on the east side . . .' She followed him, summoning her courage for the stiff climb up the steep black steps.

Thomas rode into the middle of the vast crowd, whose faces seemed to fill his vision to the horizon. His horse was a neck ahead of Walworth's so that the King's flag could be seen to be in the lead. He looked neither to the left nor the right and kept moving. It was not a clear passage through the spilling cluster of people, hundreds of small campfires, animals, often belligerent rebels who had been by the Tower and now pulled back to follow the King's flag. It was the King's flag that proved to be the wand that opened the way, and eventually the two men came to the tent of Tyler.

Thomas immediately recognised John Ball. He did not pick out Tyler. It was Tyler who picked out Holland.

'You are?'

'From the King.'

'But who are you?'

'My mother is the Princess Joan.'

Tyler smiled. 'You've brought a speech?'

'I have.'

'Let us hear it.'

Walworth turned his horse to face the multitude.

'Dismount,' said Tyler. 'We'll not be spoken to from a horse, Walworth.'

Holland took the reins. A bench was brought.

'Stand on that.'

217

Walworth did so and was jeered, shouted at, mocked as he appeared on the small hummock, then the common bench.

Tyler held out his hands and quite soon a ripple of silence stilled the multitude.

'In the name of King Richard the Second,' Walworth announced. He unrolled the scroll and read, in a loud mayoral voice: 'I, Richard . . .'

Walworth had spoken to massed crowds many times. One sentence, then pause for it to be relayed, like a baton, to the back. Time it well and then the next sentence. And so it went on until '". . . such remedy as shall be profitable to him, to them and to the kingdom."'

They waited for the next sentence. Surely there had to be more. They had demanded charters to be given and under the King's seal, not merely the right to submit grievances. They wanted – now! – the ending of the poll tax, the abolition of villeinage, servitude and bondage so that they could move freely for work from place to place.

The angry sound of their disappointment buffeted Walworth and Holland. That unified sound of rejection was succeeded by angry cries on the issues unaddressed. Weapons were waved in the mild midsummer evening air. The ground shook as the mass shifted forward and stamped on the earth.

Tyler told Walworth to get onto his horse, then he himself stood on the bench. Eventually the noise abated.

'We do not accept these terms,' he said, and could get no further with the noise, which switched from jeers to cheers. When they were quieter he said, 'Tell the King he need have no fear of us.' Again, the sound of approval thunder-clapped around the city walls. 'But tell him we want to see him face to face and say plainly to him that he must let us deal with the traitors and we must make a new settlement here.

'Let these two men go through unharmed!' he said. 'Let them return to the King with our message.' He waited for a willing assent, which did not come. The mood was vengeful, especially against Walworth. 'We *will* let them go back unharmed,' he repeated emphatically. Tyler was not to be disobeyed. 'We will see they are safe back to the Tower. These men spoke to us for the King. Now they need speak to the King for us.' He came to Holland and said, 'Tell the King that there are men here who were with his father on the battlefield and would have died for him.'

Tyler cut through the mêlée. An encircling guard was recruited from the nearest armed men. Without consultation, John Ball took up one of the tall crucifixes that had come from the processions of Corpus Christi. He led the procession, chanting prayers. It became a vivid expression of the splicing of Christ Triumphant and the demands of the True Commons.

Richard looked down from one of the turrets in the Tower. Behind him his mother stood in the shadows. She knew what he was thinking.

She knew that he was jealous of the glory Tom was gaining in that simulacrum of a royal and sacred procession. She knew that he was entranced and captured by the unflawed respect of his councillors. And she knew that now they were alone he would turn to her and ask her what he should do, which he did.

'You must meet these "True Commons", as they call themselves,' she said. 'Face to face this time. And you must talk to them. They are your loyal subjects. And they are strong. Your father said that one of his Englishmen was worth seven men of any other country. They will listen to you. And only to you.' Joan knew that these simple words would soothe his jealousy and make him want to act. 'They will listen to you because of your great lineage, because of the victories of your father and his father, and because they know that you have been anointed by God.' In the vestibule of the small turret, her closeness surrounded him. He breathed in her perfume.

'We will now count Lord Mayor Walworth as a friend?' Joan nodded.

'And my b-brother Thomas?'

'He will be proud to have served you, my lord. He is your most devoted and loving subject.'

She knew that she had, in those few words, for a little while, dissolved the knot of jealousy. Her flattery rarely failed: it was an experienced weapon.

'I will reward him n-nonetheless. They will be approaching the council room. I will be there to greet them . . . And then?'

'Then, my lord, the plan is to command Lord Mayor Walworth to summon all able men, both rebels and Londoners, out of the city early tomorrow morning to where you and a few of your court will meet them, listen and grant all their requests. I will go with you.'

'Sudbury will write my sp-speech.'

'From your lips and not his.'

'From my lips?' He liked the unexpected word. 'Lips,' he repeated, and turned to face the city. His city. Burning wherever he looked. Burning churches, palaces, streets, and small fires by the thousand spread across the slowly darkening spaces. For the first time, he sensed anger. He could not let them win.

'We will go now,' he said to his mother, and he embraced her as he used to do when he was a child.

He was torn out of this healing embrace by a sound like rods of hail hitting stone, like . . . nothing he had heard before. He went back to the turret and looked down on such a great number that it seemed as if the earth itself had opened up and become a voice of the people. The King was stunned, drugged by the hail of sound hurled at the walls of the Tower. Then he let it stream into him. He bathed in it. He held his face open to it as if it were the morning sun.

He rejoined his mother and they came down the narrow stone steps from the turret, Richard leading, candle aloft, his mother stepping cautiously behind him. He stopped and turned to her, his exhilarated expression made lurid by the wavering candlelight.

'The sound!' he said. 'That sound! How can men make such a sound?' He was exalted by it.

Joan was glad to rest a while.

'When I went back to the turret I looked over the multitude of them – such a noise! Screeching, like a hundred thousand birds, like five, ten hundred thousand birds at dawn or in the evening when the sound is stronger. So shrill! But not screaming. Like sweet pain.'

Joan noticed that, in this curious extravagance of reaction, he had not stammered once.

'Why do you think they do it?' he asked her.

'They have no words to say what they want so they just open their throats,' said Joan, keeping to herself the absent stammer. 'Your father said that the cries of the Englishmen before a battle frightened him as much as they frightened the French!'

'Did he?' There was a warmth in her son's smile that she rarely saw. If only he could smile like that more often. Then she could love him. A smile like that could provoke passion. 'Did my father say that?'

'Yes,' she reassured him, as he craved. Sometimes she had to remember that the King was also a boy.

'I love the sound they are making,' he said. 'It is like a thousand lutes all playing the same note, their highest note, again and again and again. It is like a love-sound. It goes through my flesh like a blade of ice.'

Still he had not stammered. She wanted to congratulate him, to embrace him. But did she point this out and make him self-conscious or did she silently thank God that at last her prayer had been answered?

'The sound was so beautiful,' the boy said. 'It was better than music. It was better than a high wind in the trees at night.'

It was intended, Joan was certain but did not say, to terrify you. So: my son is not so easily frightened, Master Tyler.

At the foot of the steps they turned towards the council room, but before they reached it she touched his shoulder and he turned to her.

'I have a request,' she said, 'Your Majesty.'

He glowed, she thought, more brightly than the candle. Finally: she had said it. 'Your Majesty'. For those last two words he would concede anything.

'These are your people. You must tell them that you love them and not seem afraid. Say that you yourself will become their leader. Tell these commoners, as Salisbury said, that if they return to their homes you will grant everything they ask. These are promises you need not keep. God will forgive you. And, finally, I beg you at Mile End to speak to them in their own tongue. They are proud of their English. They want their king to share their pride in it.'

'Will you be there?'

'I will. I will be at your side, Your Majesty.'

25
Night

L ondon festered in the dark. Its gates stayed open, and throughout the night new recruits, torch led, came in through the open gate at Southwark to be at the feast of the rebellion. Its streets were glutted with sleeping bodies. The smells of burning mixed with the familiar city odours, made stronger by the defecation and debris that silted up the alleyways and gutters. Those with houses hid in them and fortified their doors with furniture, their spirits with prayer. Those in hovels anticipated the dawn with fearful hope, swinging sometimes to disbelief. Many of the city's aldermen slid away; a number had already decided that they would wake up for Tyler and these 'True Commons'. The city's rich, who had lain low, knew that their leaders aimed to command them to act: why should they, when massacre seemed the only outcome?

Men and women from the close counties sprawled asleep on the dampening turf. They had told each other that they could never outdo what they had done on that day. No dreams could match it. They had conquered London. Everywhere there were roving predatory bands, friends of the night. St Paul's, in the middle of it all, with its famous spire, stood miraculously unimpaired, reassurance of continuity. Bells from a hundred churches pealed out against the dark, and those who came from the country were disturbed even as they were inflamed. The bells urged them on, the bells spoke to them, the bells were at the heart of things, and so were the rebels. The city lay in wait for the morning and no one, despite the prayers, the confidence and the victories thus far, knew what would come of it. The Tower stood blank and unassailable. The rats, the fat black rats, were everywhere. They commanded the ground.

Tyler had drawn up his plans in the hour after midnight when the screaming cries of his men had been exhausted. His tent was overcrowded. The anxious allies from St Albans were asking him to send the twenty thousand men he had promised in the mid-morning; the news from Norwich was good from one messenger, dire from the next; Jack Straw was about to arrive, with his usual well-argued but lengthy Colchester suggestions. The morning's meeting with the King at Mile End would be outside the city walls, near where the bulk of Straw's men was camped. Tyler knew that the location would make Straw think of the occasion as his own. He thought that was as it should be: this would not be the only meeting. It was to show the King their strength, to extract some concessions and get the Royal Assent to the legal murder of traitors, but above all, to prise the King out of the White Tower, which he, Tyler, would then capture.

After that, Tyler calculated, the King would be badly weakened. Then he would once again summon the King and his remaining councillors to a final meeting at which the full radical picture of the New England, seen by John Ball and supported by Tyler, would be revealed for his consent.

His plan was laid. The cartloads meant for the White Tower would wait for the gates to be opened in the morning and would as usual be gathered together at dawn, ready to enter the Tower. Some of his own men would replace the King's in that food-train. They would retain its leader, who would give the password. Tyler himself would go to Mile

End with the majority of the rebels. The guard in the Tower would see them leave and relax. After the King had spoken, Tyler would return immediately and be let in by his own men, who had taken in the provisions.

Tyler had grounds to be confident. The knights and men-at-arms at the Tower had made no effort so far to show signs of defiance. The word was that some of them favoured the rebels, others feared them, few were prepared to risk life for the King and his council. And once inside the Tower . . .

But as Tyler left his tent and walked through the shadowy mass of somnolent bodies, reminding him in some ways of the defeated slain after a great battle, a treacherous thought ambushed him.

Were he and John Ball not asking too much – to push the whole world back into the Garden of Eden? Was this not bound to fail? Was he asking for too momentous a submission on the enemy's part when, at this stage, he could surely make a bloodless settlement?

He looked at the sleeping faces and saw not the gargoyles dismissed by Tom Holland in his adventure in Southwark but strong features, hard-lived but often fine, every bit as fine, he thought, as those they opposed. These were John Ball's 'good people'.

Was he right to ask them to follow him into what could be a furnace? For Tyler knew that this victory would be just the first battle. The armies would return from Scotland and France; the lords would surely fight back when finally they realised they were about to be stripped of their privileges. How prepared were his men for that? And where would he find councillors enough? Perhaps he should take the King around the country to show the people that the Crown of rule was still intact, though now in others' hands.

The load grew heavier. He was in deep now. He went back towards his tent, candlelit, like a beacon, on that small mound. The only way was forward. The only sure strategy was a quick victory. No turning back.

Neither could John Ball sleep. But he had been trained to use wakefulness. He had eaten little, and that, too, helped him. He had found a place a few score yards from Tyler and it was there that he meditated.

His body was soon racked with tiredness from kneeling. But that was good. Pain was crucial to revelation. He swayed in the balmy night, gently as the grass. But he could not concentrate on this call to God. Although it distressed him to acknowledge it, his thoughts centred on Will. He had not seen him since that morning in Southwark. He accepted that, in the hurry and confusion of the day, Will might have followed his own path for reasons that would become clear. But he could not expunge the picture of Will carrying the dead body of the young Lollard, the sweat running down his face, the uncharacteristic look of strain . . .

Joan Tyler was lost. She had found a group of women but then peeled off, attracted by the carnival remains of Corpus Christi and the exuberance of the crowds. So many, so full of happiness, it seemed to her, and her father's name uttered, always in admiration. She held onto her dagger more as a talisman than a weapon and, besides, there was nothing to fear.

She was hungry but a simple request secured bread. She was too tired to sleep. She thought she remembered where the women were camped but the seductive novelty and the labyrinth of London streets drew her in. She did not want to go to her father's tent yet. Out here was the new life! What a world it was! So much variety, so much energy, so many people, even now as the long mid-June day finally darkened. The streets were strewn with people, wild pigs, wild dogs, wild children. Men on high horses forced their way through those on foot; curses, songs, burning, burning. She was captured by it, and lost.

The street she ended up in was Cock Lane. It seemed just as friendly as many of the others she had passed through. But soon she noticed there were harsher men here, men boasting of how they had come out of the prisons, men shouting they held no allegiance to anyone, neither the King nor Tyler nor the priest John Ball. Men who pinned women against the walls and strode in packs into what, unknown to Joan, were brothels.

She looked for an ally who would take her back into the less threatening part of the city. Back to St Paul's. She ran into three men whose accents she thought she recognised. They were country men at any rate. And she walked towards them with relief. They were drunk and complaining about lack of money.

When they raped her she screamed so loudly she was sure someone would hear her, would come and save her. But her screams were just part of the night noises. She held on to the dagger but did not use it. It belonged to her father; she kept saying that to herself. One man after another. Then they were gone. And she lying bleeding, face welted, near out of her mind.

Finally she got up and walked. An old woman who was sifting through the remains of a chandler's destroyed shop pointed out the way to her father's tent.

She whimpered and cried, and made it worse by trying to silence herself. She had to be strong now. Her father would want her to be strong. But – what they had done . . . what they had done to her . . . Blinded by the dark and the violent shock of rape, she felt her way along the walls, by

227

touch, stumbling, lost, she thought, a lost soul, black in the Hell of the night city. Distant cries mocked her own cries. She shivered as uncontrollably as she sobbed. What could she do? What could she say?

The ribbons her father had given her had been torn out of her hair. A young scavenger picked them up the next morning.

26

Mile End

Tyler had slept well, but not for long enough, and woke lead-limbed, fug-headed, feeling more a carcass than a man. He ducked his head in a pail of cold water, rinsed his mouth, swilled it liberally and spat out the used water forcefully, as if ejecting a gobbet of plague. He called his council and they sat around the fire outside his tent.

All of them agreed that Mile End, near Straw's men, could not be thought of as a trap. They would willingly go there. All of them wanted their grievances settled soon. The rapidity of events on the previous day had given them a taste for immediate action.

In every direction the rebels were yawning awake, stretching into the new day. Embering fires were recharged. The weather was once more sunning them. Expeditions were sent out for food. Beer opened caked gullets.

'We will go,' Tyler said. He smiled. 'I suspect it's Walworth's plan. He wants to get us out of the city. He thinks that the King will then persuade us to go home. And after that? Will he close the gates? Yes. Will his friends with their armies come after us? Yes. He will get the King to make promises he will keep only as long as we stay here. But we'll outflank him. While he is at Mile End, some of us will come back to the Tower and take it.'

'But we must all meet him at Mile End?' Henry Long was anxious. This was too good an opportunity to miss. Promises could be turned into documents: documents could be validated with the Royal Seal. What they had set out to achieve – so few days ago! – would be done.

'So we will.' Tyler accepted the bread, broke off a piece and passed it on.

'Walter is right,' said John Ball. 'They will tell the King to swear to everything we ask. They will tell him these oaths mean nothing because we are only peasants and the King is in danger. They will make him lie on his oath. They will endanger his soul.'

'Harden your hearts,' Tyler murmured to himself, wondering again at the man's passionate certainty. So certain of everything that he made Tyler ashamed of his doubts. He must follow the priest.

The archbishop said mass in the chapel of the Tower and the King led the 'amens'. The bells had struck six. Lookouts had told him that the rebels were already moving north to Mile End. The chapel rustled with the sound of chainmail. Richard sought out the archbishop. 'I have commanded a barque to come alongside an hour after we leave the Tower. It will take you, Hales and others that the rebels wish to kill up to Richmond, where you will be safe.'

Sudbury bowed. 'Your Majesty. May God bless you.'

They followed the King out of the chapel. Tall new candles with a day to burn were unsullied by rivulets of wax. Princess Joan went out last of all, having stayed behind with the archbishop for a special blessing.

The retinue that assembled before the gate was impressive. Several knights had volunteered rather over-eagerly to leave the Tower. The night hail of sounds that had delighted their king had flayed their nerves. Reports came in of the growth in executions, murders, mutilations. Those in the Tower saw themselves as prime targets. They saw the rebels as a limitless body of avenging men whose stomach for assassination was strong. But it was said they would not harm the King: to be close to the King was to be closer to safety.

Some of those assembled to accompany the King were of the highest status. The key council members were with him. Tom Holland, Earl of Kent, the Earl of Salisbury, the Earl of Warwick, the Earl of Oxford, Sir Robert of Namur, the Lord of Vertaing, the Lord Gommegnies, Sir Thomas Percy and Sir Aubrey de Vere, who carried the Royal Sword. From the city, and waiting outside the gates, were William Walworth, Sir Robert Knolles, Sir Perducas d'Albert, Brembre, Phillpot, a dozen scribes and a proportionate modest number of men-at-arms from their households. The men were finely attired, though not in full battle dress. Their warhorses, too, were not in full armour. Princess Joan was in an open carriage, a whirligig, closely protected by ten knights from the Tower.

When the gates opened, and they went into what seemed a world wholly peopled by rebels, Joan noticed that the food-train, which had not been allowed to bring in the supplies on the previous day, was standing at the ready at its usual place of departure, a few hundred yards towards St Paul's. What should have reassured her perturbed her and she did not know why. As did the progress of the procession. From the outset the barely controlled rebels, who were moving in the same direction as the court, buffeted what had been designed to be a stately and impressive royal display. Hunger, hangovers and the dislocating speed of their triumphs had diminished respect. And while the counties largely held their formations, the pennants, the flags, the ordered disposition, newcomers from London streets and London prisons, and from villages around London who had teemed in, often looking for loot and trouble, were fast breeding the anarchy feared by Tyler. It was this mêlée of rebellion in which the grand royal party found itself to its impatient discomfort. Without respect, Joan thought, there could be no rule. Instilling fear, she believed, was the only alternative.

But the King did not pause and he was with men hardened in battle, used to high odds against them. The rebels were so many, Richard thought. At last, now, today, he understood their power. Pock-faced, some of them, pitchfork-armed, some of them, but axes flashed in the morning sun, some swords too, and the bowmen were there – the terrors of war, the English weapon of victory. Yet despite the push and pull of it the King did not halt.

When he came to the narrow streets there was an uproar. So many people wanted to touch him to be healed, to be blessed, and the royal party became like a ship in a strait channel of turbulent waters, constantly assailed by small pirate vessels nipping in and out, seeming to threaten, impeding their passage.

Some saw the King as providing them with a God-sent opportunity. The London captain, Thomas Farringdon, barged his way to the front of the royal entourage, slipped between the horses of the men-at-arms, grabbed the reins of the King's horse and demanded that the King order the execution of Treasurer Hales immediately because of an unjust seizure of his property. Such effrontery far exceeded the discourtesy that had so dismayed Salisbury at Greenwich. The earl rode forward, alongside the King, leaned from his horse and slammed Farringdon unconscious with the hilt of his long dagger.

A little further along, on that same street, Nicholas Brembre found himself threatened by a brewer for unpaid debts. A guard chased away the brewer – only for him to make for Brembre's palace and, with a gang of ex-prisoners, break in, pillage and extort money from Brembre's wife.

The rebellion was feeding and legitimising rivalries and grudges that the law had held in check. Unregulated was unconstrained. Thuggery thrived.

Richard called for Tom Holland. 'Take our mother back to the Tower,' he said. 'This is not for her.' Ahead, before Aldgate, the crowd was thick and threatening. The morning drunkenness was setting in. 'Then join us at Mile End.'

Tom turned his horse without comment. To take his mother through that! And then to make his way to Mile End! 'The King commands that I take you back to the Tower.'

'I will not go,' she said. Her legend and beauty had made her as big an object of curiosity as the King himself, but so far her reputation and sex had protected her.

'It is a command.'

'Tell the King I will not go.'

'It is his command, my lady. And mine.'

He took the reins of the lead horse and pulled the whirligig around in an arc, which cleared its own space and skittled some of the crowd. He ordered the guards of the princess to return with him. Then he led the small procession back to the Tower and, for a reason he could not fathom, the previously surly crowds cheered the Princess Joan all the way.

As the King went under the arch of Aldgate he looked up at the rooms above. His mother had once taken him there, to the lodgings of Geoffrey Chaucer, the diplomat and poet, some of whose lines Richard had by heart. Chaucer, he thought, was as clever a man as he had ever met and the most beautiful poet in the new language. He noticed that the lodgings were barred. He smiled to himself. Chaucer, he guessed, had made a fortress of this potentially dangerous location under which thousands of men of Essex had walked their warlike way into London.

And so to Mile End, already at that early hour resembling a ribald, rough-edged carnival. But when Richard arrived rather dishevelled and apprehensive, with his entourage, the rebels cheered him. Some knelt, even though he was at a distance, others waved their spears, bows, pitchforks and axes, some spiked with grimly reaped trophies. Waiting to negotiate with him was a cluster of men on foot, no more than two score, separate from the mass of the rebels, unmistakably their leaders.

Richard walked his horse steadily towards them. Salisbury and Walworth came up alongside as escorts; the rest of the entourage loosened their formation but copied the King and acted as diffidently as they could manage, unpolished though they were in understatement.

Jack Straw was at the front of the rebels. Tyler had insisted on this. 'I have brought some men here. But this is your ground, Jack,' he had said. 'Your men want to see you here. And you have Colchester men among you! I have other matters to settle at a later time. You speak for all of us.'

Tyler went back into the front line of the rebel army and let Jack Straw be seen as the leader the King must address.

The shrill sound was still there from the rebels. It was less threatening and in the background, but still clearly there – and Richard, unafraid, was curiously comforted by it. The sound was for him. God was smiling on him. It was a beautiful summer's morning. He was the safest man in England.

27

The King's Answer to the True Commons of England

Those nearest the King knelt. Those in the ranks behind bent the knee or bowed. Richard acknowledged their allegiance with a bow from the neck, and released them to be upstanding with a wave of his hand. All was well. He was through the bestial clamour of the city. He had made sure that his greatest ministers would escape these rebels. They would now be sailing up the Thames. His lines and arguments were well rehearsed, as his mother had insisted. In his conscience, deceit had alchemised into diplomacy.

'I am your king,' he began, looking down from his tall warhorse on Straw. 'What is it that you lack? What will you say?'

Straw took a step forward. Without ceremony, and without the expected respect of address, he said or, rather, shouted – he wanted to be heard by as many as possible of those behind, 'We want you to make us free. Ourselves, our heirs, our lands. And we want no more to be in bondage as serfs and not so reputed.' The words were passed along the lines.

'Sirs,' the King began, 'I am well agreed with you. Withdraw to your homes, your own houses and villages, but leave behind, here in London, three or four men from every village. I shall cause writings to be made and seal them with my seal, which I will give to them. Those writings will contain everything you demand.'

Jack Straw was nonplussed. It should not have been so easy.

Tyler – who could hear everything – did not believe a word of it. This was not the King talking. This was his corrupt and wicked council, who had poisoned him. He eyed the high-horsed councillors and saw beneath the attitude of compliance nothing but contempt. He fed on this. It strengthened his resolution.

Three Colchester burgesses, with scrolls, came up alongside Jack Straw and whispered to him. They wanted this assurance to be doubly sure.

'We wish to record aloud our demands,' said Straw. 'We wish our words to be copied by your scribes.'

The King waved them on. He enjoyed the formality. Their sense of occasion impressed him.

One of the burgesses stepped forward. Like a town crier, he unrolled the scroll and spoke loudly and clearly. After an opening paragraph, which identified the location, distinctions and loyalty to the King of these his faithful, devoted and True Commons, he repeated Jack Straw's demands, but with greater emphasis and at greater length. He paused constantly to look down at the scroll, as if to remind the King and his councillors that these were no peasants, these were men who could write out a charter for a treaty as well as any London lawyer ever could.

The principal demand was that they be made free for ever. The burgess turned to his right and then to his left as he said that; he repeated it twice to achieve his desired effect, which was to tell his own men that here in a written document, which they believed could never be denied, not only should they be freemen but so also their heirs and descendants. They wanted a rent limit of fourpence per acre, which would lead to a deep cull of what had become stultifying layers of regulation (listed in detail in the document) in which the landowners had given the lawyers permission to tie in knots and bondage for life those who worked the land.

The document asked that no man should be made to work unless it was guaranteed that his terms of employment were regularly reviewed. The King's officials, the lawyers and landowners, he said, were using the King's law against the True Commons and he asked the King to bring all this to an end.

Richard felt the relief of Walworth and Salisbury, who flanked him closely. No slaughter of the lawyers; no confiscation of the land of aristocrats; no attack on Church grandees or their wealth. This was a civil presentation of understandable grievances. These were still his loyal subjects!

Tyler noted their relief. Those behind the King were less sphinx-faced than Walworth and Salisbury and their relief was unguarded, sometimes expressed in intolerable smiles. And it brought from them a deepening contempt, Tyler thought. Was this the best that the rebels could come up with? Was this all they could do? The royal party shifted and sat more comfortably in their saddles than they had for days. But, Tyler thought, let these demands be sealed. Let those, especially the Essex men, who had taken the first steps in attacking the tax collectors have their day. They could force them into law later.

The King signalled to his scribes, who came forward and took the documents from the men of Colchester. Then he spoke again: 'To make you better assured, I shall cause my banners to be delivered to every bailiwick, shire and county.'

Straw turned to relay the news. It travelled swiftly up and down the lines and the young King swelled with happiness as the cheers enhanced even more his own exceptional status.

With his entourage in tight formation about him, he rode nearer the rebel lines and concluded, on the swell of that acclaim: 'Sirs, among you good men of Kent, you shall have one of my banners with you, and you of Essex another, and you of Sussex, of St Albans, of Cambridge, of Yarmouth, of Stafford and of Lynn, each of you one; and also I pardon anything that you have done hitherto, so that you follow my banners and return to your homes.' A few hesitations, no struggles. The stammer had been defeated!

He knew that Joan had noted it but said nothing. Presumably to give it time to prove itself. Well, now it had! He was free of that bondage of the tongue. Once again, as several times over the last twenty hours, he rubbed the rare stone given him by Thomas Rushbrook.

They would receive the King's banners, as if they were his real army in a great war! The King talking to them equally! The King's presence within spitting distance, and a more handsome, royally clad, gracious young king you could never meet. This would be the story of their lives. And these mighty earls and city financiers smiling down on them, surely smiles of thanks and understanding. What fine men! And how magnificent on those steeds of war!

Tyler went across to Straw. 'You must ask him one more question,' he said, as Straw waited for the King to return to his place. The King was confirming a promise – a promise he kept that morning – to employ more than thirty clerks that day to write out letters patent sealed with the King's seal before sunset.

As the King came towards them, Walworth said to Salisbury, 'Your plan is working, my lord.'

'The King has surprised us all,' replied Salisbury. Then he added, 'We must not show triumph.'

Richard ordered the rebels better to organise themselves and stand in line for no other reason than that he could make them do it. His rule was absolute not only on parchment but there, on the ground, at Mile End, over thousands of men who knelt to him, acclaimed him, obeyed him. His head was ringed with a sense of celestial invulnerability.

When he came back past Jack Straw he paused, seeing that there was another request.

'And the traitors?' Straw asked. 'What about the traitors?'

'Seize them!' the King said. 'Wherever they are in England. Seize them!' Tyler turned away and did not hear the King add, 'Bring them to me so that they may be tried by due process of law.'

'Seize them!' Tyler murmured to himself, as he called in his men and strode out for the Tower. 'Oh, yes. We will seize them!' John Ball had given him God's permission to kill. And the King had said enough to make it within the law. He had seen in the eyes of the King's advisers that they would certainly find the moment to take their revenge. He must immediately carry out the essential and now legally, royally, sanctioned executions of the traitors.

28

The Chapel

How had John Ball triumphed? Archbishop Sudbury could not get rid of that question. How had that destitute, excommunicated, ill-educated hedge-priest become poised to topple the head of the Holy Roman Catholic Church and all its powers and estates in England? And he would succeed. The archbishop now had no doubt. The base common man's imminent victory stabbed him, like a needle stuck under his foot, piercing more deeply with every step he took.

The royally planned escape by boat had been foiled. Tyler had put women on the lookout. As soon as they saw the archbishop and his party come out of the Tower, their calls had summoned the waiting forces Tyler had also left in place. The archbishop and his friends had retreated back into the Tower. The rebels had bayed mockingly at them. That screaming, that unceasing screaming, must be the sound of Purgatory, thought Sudbury. It sounded like souls in torment yet it was on earth here, the voices of men like John Ball. Why had he not had him executed years ago? There had been cause enough. Forgiveness had failed.

Up the stone steps they went, a forlorn, thwarted, glitteringly robed procession. They said little. Their chance had gone. The archbishop led the procession but could find no words to ease their state. Their time was run. But how – he could not wrench it from his mind – how could this have come about through the words of such an undistinguished peasant priest as John Ball? The man had made no mark in the Church! He had risen not an inch above the ground. He had turned his illegal congregations against all that the True Church represented, and all that he, an archbishop in direct line from St Augustine sent by Pope Gregory eight centuries ago, had continued and maintained. It had been no simple task! And now to be threatened and, he feared, cast down by this petty demon, this spawn of the devil, this . . .

Sudbury arrived in the council room and saw that no one would look him in the face. The Princess Joan had been brought back and gone immediately to her quarters. Her news provided the chief subject for such conversation as there was. She had reported violent crowds around the Tower. The plan to pipe all the rebels out of the city of London had worked as badly as the plan to send the 'traitors' to Richmond.

The archbishop went to the chapel.

He had to rid his soul of this poison. John Ball might be the ruin of his life in this world, but he must not be allowed to prevent his entry to the next.

The others who had accompanied him joined him in the chapel. After some minutes of silence, the archbishop turned to the subdued congregation and asked them to pray for the soul of John Ball. And, like the voice from the dawn of his faith, came the whispered question, might there be something in what that humble excommunicated man preached? Might there not be in him, said this unsummoned whisper, some of the divine revelations first heard on the shores of Galilee by humble men just such as he? Sudbury forced himself to admit that.

By this act of prayer, he believed he would be shriven of anger. He prayed silently that, having commended the soul of John Ball to God, he himself would be free of him, the incubus would leave him, the curse of hatred on him would be lifted.

He began to say mass, pausing only to ask, 'When will they arrive? Good God, when will they arrive? For already the time has come, if it pleases God they should come.'

But the rebels had not yet come, and the chants and prayers of Sudbury, Hales and their co-councillors filled the tranquil thick-walled chapel with hollow comfort. Was it too late for God to intervene on the side of Right?

Tyler had put his best men in charge of the caravan of royal supplies making for the Tower. These were the men with whom he had cleared out the terrorising gang around Dartford. They had stayed close to him throughout the campaign.

This, Tyler calculated, was the crucial strategic move. Once in the Tower, little could stop them, save their own blunders. And, of equal value, it was there that the first arrests of councillor-traitors would take place. This, Tyler thought, would give the rebels authority. The Tower was the traditional tomb of distinguished traitors.

The caravan of men had been about to go forward when they saw the small entourage of Princess Joan as she returned. She was cheered through a clear passage to the drawbridge. Perhaps some of the rebels were applauding their own victory in forcing the princess to retreat. But she was popular. The growing antagonism to her son's advisers had not led to a finger being laid on the Fair Maid of Kent. Sentimentality smothered radicalism.

But the moment the drawbridge had gone up, Tyler's Trojan horse moved forward. The password was shouted to the battlements and, once again, the slowly creaking platform into the fortress bowed down.

The men walked in at a steady pace. Observant eyes saw that there were substantially more in the party than usual. Observant minds worked out what was happening. No one acted.

Why did the men who guarded the Tower not fight? Like their fellows in Rochester, they did nothing. It was as if the topsy-turvy carnival of Corpus Christi, where the poor were allowed to play at being the powerful, had burst into reality. The rebellion froze its enemies. Perhaps it was a contagious panic. Perhaps, in some profound way, many people thought that the rebels, and especially John Ball, were right.

The supply caravan trundled in without challenge. Once inside, it revealed its purpose, with swords, axes, spears, bows, pitchforks and chains, and the guardians of the King's last redoubt stood aside and let them pass.

The only action took place when Thomas Holland, having settled his mother in her quarters, saw the drawbridge down, and charged his horse towards it, only to be torn out of the saddle by the rebels. His agility and quick wits wrenched and dodged him away from them. He raced into the heart of the Tower in which he quickly lost his pursuers.

They advanced through the fortress with great care. These men from Kent were unable to believe what was not happening. Surely this was an ambush. Who could explain it otherwise? Certainly the fear of the rebels had gone straight into the bloodstream of most of those whose duty and training it was to resist invasion. Perhaps, like Tom Holland in his report to his mother, they thought that the rebels had already won and the only course now was to negotiate for survival. Submission was the traditional first move in that direction.

Very soon Tyler's men had taken the inner sanctuary of the fortress. The men of Kent, a few of London, but mostly those who had been on the march from Kent, were exhilarated. They were also filthy from sleeping out, discombobulated by feast and famine, bewildered by their undreamed-of victories.

They stamped into room after room and still true to their leader's pledge, they destroyed but they did not steal. They jostled the soldiers, took their weapons in a friendly way and urged them to abandon their lords and join the men of Kent. They teased the knights and stroked their beards, marvelling at their handsome chainmail. The stroking of beards for a few minutes became all the rage as these countrymen romped in the novelty of liberty, luxury and being in the treasury of power.

Finally they went into the chamber of Princess Joan. What splendour! What beauty! Some sat on the edges of the bed and one or two, dared by others, asked for a kiss. They liked Princess Joan. Was she not the most beautiful and the richest woman in all England? And here they were, bouncing up and down on her bed, tickling the beards of her guards, tearing down luxuriant tapestries, asking for a kiss.

Joan saw no one in command, save herself. Her knights might have been cut from stone. Her son, the court and the council were outside the city. The peasants were getting bolder. She was not afraid of their robust familiarity and could even smile at their unbuckled delight at being in her chamber. But action was essential. She acted.

She gasped a little, put her hand to her throat, stared around imploringly, attempted but failed to say something, saw her tormentors fall back in alarm and then, most convincingly, Princess Joan swooned.

Joan saw her father go into the Tower, but he did not see her. She was glad of it. She wanted to be invisible. How good her father looked! How strongly he strode. And the men about him, she could see, were so proud to be with him. Those he passed raised their weapons in the air in salute as if he were a king. She, too, was proud of him. But she wept for shame. She had let him down. She had shamed

244

both herself and him. How could she even speak to him again? A solitary young woman, shivering under the morning sun, withdrawn in a closed circle of torment, how could he have the time to see her? Best she did not exist.

She had sat by the Thames at dawn when the tide was pushing down to the sea and wept that she could not ride on it to Dartford. There, she would walk to her village and go into the garden where she had best known her father and sit under the apple trees and wait for him to return from this war, as he had returned from others, and he would smile at her and give her a present and the world would be good again. Save it could never be good again now.

Her body hurt so much. Her body was dead now. But it hurt. Dead people could only hurt in Hell. Maybe her body had already been sent to Hell and this would be her punishment for ever and ever. She sat, defeated, her arms around her head.

What would her mother be doing now? She ought to be there, helping. But she would not be able to face her either. This ruptured body was unclean. She would be hidden inside the house for the rest of her life and who would want her? She did not want herself.

All this noise in London, these people, so many. Why had she left fields, woods, lonely paths, animals for this – this noise of men?

'Where have you been?'

The question carried blame.

Johanna stood above her.

'You lost us,' Johanna said. 'You should have kept with us.' To attack was her only way.

Joan looked up at the rough-tongued, fearless, handsome woman and bit her lip. She would not cry. 'I'm sorry,' she said, and made an awkward job of getting to her feet.

Johanna took it all in and opened her arms. The girl almost fell into her forgiving, fierce embrace.

'I would kill them if I could,' said Johanna. 'I would cut them up bit by bit. I would chop up their cocks. Every bit. Now then. Now then . . .'

At last Joan's quiet choked weeping let loose and her tears wet the face of her friend. 'Now, now,' Johanna said, 'you will stay here. You won't lose me again. I will leave some women with you.' The girl's racking sobs subsided and abruptly Johanna pulled away. 'We are going into the Tower to join the men,' she said, and she indicated about two dozen women nearby, women Joan recognised from the journey.

'My father . . .'

'Your father sees no one now,' said Johanna, with worship in her voice. 'He has eyes only for the traitors. I want to see them too.'

Tyler felt a resurgence of rage over the humiliation at Greenwich, and at the evidence all around of the wickedness of those advisers who threatened the King and were destroying the kingdom. Destroy England? He walked up towards the Tower. The war-cries of victors ghosted through the decades. England had to be saved! She had to be victorious again, what she once was. Tyler's resolution was set. And for that to happen, the King had to be rescued. He strode up the steep stone steps to the chapel. No quarter. No prisoners. England would be reborn through justly shed blood. Now was the time.

'You can have no quarrel with the mother of the King.' Tom's flat pronouncement siphoned off the pressure of alarm that had beset those in her chamber, who had witnessed what some thought was the death of Princess Joan and on their account.

'I, too, am her son,' he continued, unarmed now, but not to be denied. 'I will take her back to her palace. Your chief, Walter Tyler, will not want her here. You know that. He would want me to take her away from here to safety.'

He went over to the bed and touched her shoulder, none too gently. She had heard every word. The sham had worked but what she must do now was just as difficult.

'You,' said the young aristocrat, to four of the knights who had allowed their beards to be patronised, 'help her. There are enough boats drawn up. We will take one.'

Joan's exit was steadier than her condition might have suggested. The rebels stood aside, abashed but relieved. Joan's safe exit took away a problem. They did indeed know of Tyler's respect for her.

'This way,' Tom instructed the men. He beckoned to the ladies-in-waiting to follow.

'When first I saw Tyler,' said Joan, on the barge, miraculously restored, 'I thought of those stone Roman heads we saw in France. Men of high rank.'

'He has made his own rank here in London,' said the young man, with unconcealed admiration. 'And it is we who are turned to stone now.'

29
Tower Hill

The sight of the candle flames was calming. Fire could soothe. And the thick walls of the chapel shut out the agitation elsewhere. The 'traitors' still seemed safe. Outside the chapel the rebels were waiting for Tyler.

Dressed in his full episcopal majesty, Archbishop Sudbury was serene. He had made his peace with God. God had given him time to confess and to pray. His soul was now purified and that final mass had surely gone straight to Him to whom he had given a lifetime of service and obedience. He would enter Heaven unblemished and surely take his place among the martyrs. For that was his destiny. The shock force of the ever-increasing strength of the peasants pointed to only one conclusion. He had chanted prayers for the dead. He had recited the litany asking for protection from the saints. His refrain became 'Omnes sancti orate pro nobis' – all the holy saints pray for us.

Finally there was the hammering at the door. He turned to his small congregation, which, in that constrained space, held some of those whose tyrannical intemperance had done most to provoke the initial uprising – himself, John Legge, the King's master-at-arms, and the treasurer, John Hales. There was also a son of John of Gaunt, Henry, Earl of Derby, a boy of Richard's age, and several other courtiers who had been invited into the Tower for their safety.

As the doors opened, Sudbury spread out his arms and said, 'Let us go with confidence, for it is better to die when it can no longer help to live. At no previous time of my life could I have died in such security of conscience.'

Tyler stood four square in the doorway. On both sides of him the rebels surged forward. It is said that they cried out, 'Where is the traitor to the kingdom? Where is the despoiler of the common people?'

Sudbury replied, 'Good my sons, you have come. Behold, I am the archbishop whom you seek but not a traitor or a despoiler.'

Satan, they cried, was before them! Ignoring traditions of the sacred and sanctified nature of the chapel, ignoring the sacrament on the altar and the words of the archbishop, they grabbed him and dragged him by the hood out of the chapel. As he passed Tyler, Sudbury managed to loosen the grip of his captors and looked him in the eye. Tyler's face was set. There was no pity. His gaze, bright in the burned skin of the soldier face, was unmerciful. Sudbury had intended to display his own mercy by blessing this man but he hesitated for too long and was dragged on his way. Sudbury had seen an executioner. Tyler had seen a tyrant.

They dragged him and other councillors up Tower Hill, where crowds were already baying in anticipation. As John Ball had told them, 'This is the true hand of God. The blood of traitors must be spilt for England's prayer to be fulfilled.' Johanna was among those who organised the executions.

Fires were still burning from the previous night. Crowds were on their way back from Mile End where the news of the taking of the Tower had ended the King and his court's benign performance in a riot of revolutionary joy. Checked in their budding triumphalism, the King and his party skirted Tower Hill and headed for St Barnard's Castle to the south-west of the city.

From Tower Hill Tyler looked over the city. Now it was truly theirs. He could not weaken now. In Chancery, the

King's clerks were already writing out dozens of pardons, proclamations and promises, all to be sealed. The London streets belonged to the rebels. As he saw Johanna, axe in hand and seized by joy and vengeance, as he was fed reports about the murder in the streets, as the sun burned hard, as if itself joining in the fire to end all the vanities of the ancient regime, in that moment Tyler dared to feel that he was master of all before him. This was a cleansing. This was the fury of the God of John Ball. Without this destruction there could be no resurrection. Blood sacrifice was the instrument. Tyler succumbed to its intoxication.

Tower Hill was where the great were executed. No skulking off outside the city to Tyburn. Here, in the blaze of power. But he must take care to tread carefully. Battles could be lost if you did not follow the plan. First he must demonstrate to the world that the killing of traitors was not an empty threat. This hour, he thought, would show to the True Commons and the court alike that he could seal his promises.

They made way for Tyler and his entourage as he walked to the execution block. The prisoners were already there, protected with difficulty from those who wanted to hack them to pieces . . . What anger! It was as if the injustices compacted over years had been made molten and just now become a volcano. Axes were brandished, spears, swords, pitchforks: some of his men wanted to kill, kill today, every one of those who had forced them to live as slaves.

Archbishop Sudbury, who had found reserves of inner faith to sustain him as he was half dragged, half carried through the crowd, had striven to keep his soul pure, his mind calm. But as he reached the executioner's block and saw the former servants of the Crown, the executioners with their long swords and axes, huddled apprehensively to one side of the death spot, and as he shielded his eyes from the full sting of the sun in the south, John Ball stepped into his path and ordered that Sudbury be unbound.

Sudbury called upon God to help him and tried with all his strength to extinguish the scalding fury that raged through him at the sight of this worthless man, this tormenting creature of Satan. Perfect hatred drove out love. They were a few feet apart.

'What sin have I committed against you that you want to kill me, John Ball?'

'You have used God to crush His people. You have sought only wealth. You have flouted the words of Jesus Christ. You are no man of God.'

'I am your pastor.'

'No! You have become the messenger of the devil!' There were cheers for Ball. 'You are the lie. We cry for truth! You brought us chains. We cry out for freedom. Now we have the power, we say blessed are the poor.' The cheers intensified. 'You were no rock. You betrayed your flock. God wills you die.' Ball was silent for a moment. 'Repent to save your soul.'

'I am your archbishop!' Sudbury's anguished fury against the cur, this less than man, this wicked priest, would not be contained. 'I am your prelate! If you kill me, God's vengeance will fall on all of you! The pope will spurn you! For such a deed all England will be laid under an interdict.'

'We do not love the pope!' someone shouted from the crowd. 'KILL HIM!'

Suddenly Sudbury shrivelled. It was over. Fighting for his own death, he raised his hand to John Ball, made the sign of the cross and wanted to say words of blessing, but he could not utter them.

The archbishop was led to his nervous executioners. For what they were about to do, he forgave them.

What a noise there was! A sudden gust of it as Tyler reached the place of execution and the rebels screamed 'Kill! Kill! Kill!'

Sudbury knelt at the block. The executioner, weakened by such a public lust for vengeance, struck his neck but not fatally.

The archbishop put his fingers to the wound and said, 'This is the hand of God.'

The executioner struck again, cut off the top of Sudbury's fingers and severed an artery. But still he did not die. It took eight increasingly wild blows to kill him. Eight blows, each one counted by the crowd, sung out each time the bloodied blade thudded into the full flesh and sinewed neck of the heir to Augustine. All order was overthrown. Had the sun turned black the crowd would not have been surprised. The other traitors from the chapel were brought up in their turn. The crowd gazed on their blood, seeing it as washing away the sins of those who had crushed them. The executioner went mad and blind the next day.

Tyler, who had seen much worse on a battlefield, believed that there, now, the new order had begun. The severed heads of the King's councillors lay in dark blood on the bright green summer grass. Sudbury's body would not be buried that day, or the next. The body lay, headless, an untouchable holy corpse.

Other heads were spiked on wooden poles, then carried through the city and on to Westminster Abbey. The acclaim for this high-held display matched that of the acclaim given to the high-held crosses for Corpus Christi carried through the city on the previous day.

Finally they were brought back to London Bridge and above the gate the heads of Archbishop Sudbury and the others were displayed for all to see. Sudbury's red mitre – which declared his rank and authority – was nailed to his skull.

30

The Heat of the Day

Tyler looked out from the Tower and considered his next move. Most of those who had once guarded it had joined his cause. The lesser members of the council, reprieved, were in the dungeons alongside the court clergy, now praying for their souls. There was no food, no water, no telling what would happen next. The prayers and pleas of the archbishop and his doomed company had shredded their nerves. If the anointed head of the Church could be beheaded on Tower Hill, what hope could anyone have? Tyler saw a Tower once invulnerable that was now under his command. He would not let any army into such a place. For such a Tower, you fought to the death.

First there was the rest of the day to organise. He needed to be with his men. They were becoming harder to control. Heat, conquest, drink, fatigue, the lust for a quick final victory and an imminent home-going combined to create a fret, a restless buzz, like the noise of the big horse-flies circling the open sewers. There was still sufficient loyalty to see it through, he thought. But quickly.

Was it just over one day and one night that they had been in London? How long it seemed. By pausing now, he allowed drowsiness to squat inside him. He had to push it aside and move on. He had seen that in France. Once the enemy was on the run, there must be no hesitation, no pause: the pursuit was all. What he had done in London was, in blood and executions, in numbers, no great matter. But in the signal it sent out it would change a kingdom.

Yet the drowsiness and the heat had seeped into his senses, as if they had found a chink in his concentration. Nights without sleep. Weeks without let-up. As he stood there, seeking a space for solitude, a spot for calm, he saw the petitioners and messengers circling his tent on the hill, waiting for the sign to be given that he would come back to them.

He walked to the tent. Residence in the Tower could wait until everything was settled. He could see John Ball approaching, but not, as was usually the case, shadowed by his giant guard; he could see a group of women. One of them was Johanna. She had fought like a man. And was that his Joan? So she had disobeyed him. But all seemed well. There were his bowmen, even better armed now from the Tower. They would not leave. But were Straw's men drifting back to Essex after the King's promises at Mile End, or hovering around Chancery for their royally sealed documents? Did they believe the battle was over?

It was not good, Tyler thought, as his sleepiness thickened, that there had been no battle. How could you tell you had won unless the dead could be counted and there were hostages and prisoners? He needed to meet the King face to face. He needed to talk to Ball. He drew in a deep, rich, warm draught of morning air. He stank.

He would wash, then be alone in his tent to think. That was what he would do.

As if sleepwalking or numb he organised pails of water, stripped down, immersed his head and rubbed away the dirt of days. Then he upended the pails and the cold water streamed all over him.

Johanna drew nearer, leaving Joan behind her, well protected among the women. She drifted to the far side of the tent and crept under its loose hem.

'You are a terrible man, Walter Tyler.'

She stood against the canvas wall of the tent and spoke with unusual nervousness. In the presence of Tyler she felt disarmed.

'You are a terrible woman, Johanna Ferrers,' he said, lightly. Out of the bone tiredness and the hornets' nest of his thoughts, there arose a spring of calm, a spot of un-demanding affection and need that sank his memory back through time, to his young manhood and youth, the woods by the river in Colchester, Margaret . . . Johanna walked towards him.

Outside the tent the noise of the real world drifted away. For this brief unexpected time the world of the two of them was all that there was.

Dog was loose. Dog was free. And they would never lock him up again. Before they left the prison, he and his gang brained their gaolers and stole every weapon they could find. They swarmed into the sunlight and saw London ripe to bursting.

Dog stopped and took in a huge breath, dizzy on the deep disorder of the street. Dog, dragged up in the gutters of the city, filthy and hungry from sunrise to sunset, clawing for bread, fighting for scraps, had eventually gathered a gang whose speed in the alleyways secured them for some time. He had known the lash and beatings and just escaped hanging but learned how to steal, assault and frighten those who stood in his way. But never, until now, aged eighteen and built like a young bull, had he seen such a paradise as this London day! Drunks, shops smashed up, local fights going on, clusters of unchecked men moving up and down the street aimlessly, casks of wine freely available, no soldiers, just mayhem and, best of all, not much further up the street, in Cheapside, an executioner's block and a happy mob cheering the severing of heads.

'It's ours,' he said. His black-toothed grin split a white stretched face of dug-in bitterness, and his half-dozen gang were glad to be on his side.

He led them to the nearest tavern and they drank for England. Pies were demanded and brought. No money changed hands. Word was already on the street that Dog was out. Old acquaintances hurried along to pay their respects and try to cadge admission to his pack.

Dog went back onto the street, looked and listened. He saw that ordinary Londoners, or worse, like himself, were running his town now. There were some out-of-town accents, like those of the men who had released them and told them to follow John Ball and Wat Tyler. But Londoners were running it. Or they would now he was out.

Tyler's name had already breached the prison walls. Dog, who liked no one he could not subdue, wanted to meet up with this Tyler. But 'I'm for Tyler,' he said, knowing it was a password as he shouldered his way through the crowd to secure more drink.

As he scanned the street he saw a bounty of easy victims, and no men of high rank. Perhaps Tyler had already got rid of the rich, the knights, the guards, the city men and their armies . . . Their absence was strange. Dog's usual tactics of strike, run and hide were not needed. He could walk down the middle of the street now, take what he wanted and shout, 'I'm for Tyler.'

He saw one alderman – Joyce – and luck was on his side for a second time that day. This was the man who had pursued, persecuted and put him in gaol. There he was, in full swagger, his henchmen alongside, making a little wave through the streets. And then the man Joyce was face to face with Dog, one hand held out for appeasement, the other on the handle of his sheathed dagger. Dog glanced over his shoulder and his men came closer. He did not take the offered hand.

'The prisons are empty,' said Joyce. 'You are all free men now.'

The lack of a reply spurred him on. 'Tyler will be our king,' said the switched-sides alderman. 'Those who ruled over us dare not come out of their houses today.' He waved at the houses rather royally and looked around at the ferment in the streets, as if bestowing a blessing on the new natives of liberty. 'We rule now.'

Dog had taken the gaoler's dagger. He plunged it into his enemy under the ribs and drove it up to the heart. Blood gurgled from the victim's mouth. His gang set on the henchmen. The corpses were kicked into the clotted gutter. No one intervened when he took the dead man's purse.

This, Dog thought, was truly a land of free men. Thoughts of making for Cock Lane, visions that had tormented him in prison, were, with effort, set aside. There was too much to be had on these streets. He would come out of this day a rich man.

'They want Smithfield,' said Tyler.

'Who chose Smithfield?'

'Does it matter where it is, Henry?'

'Smithfield is in the city. It is near the palaces. Is there enough space for us?'

Tyler smiled at Long the lawyer's entry into battle tactics.

'We will have all we need. There will be the King and a few from his court. It is the King alone we want. He has to hear what John Ball and I have to say. He must know that we come to rescue him and England.'

Tyler's tent and others were some few yards behind them as the two men stood and faced the Tower. Long was drawing up Tyler and John Ball's demands.

Rumour had become a whirlwind. It told the turbulent new world that the rebels had captured every castle, sacked all the monasteries, beheaded all corrupt lawyers and tax collectors the length of England, seized Church lands and the ancient estates of the aristocrats, burned down the pride of England's houses and brought knights and burgesses by the score under oath to the side of the rebels. John Ball was the new Archbishop of Canterbury. Princess Joan was dead. Walworth had fled London. The King would ride with the rebels around his kingdom. Tyler would be lord chancellor. Henry Long would be the treasurer.

'We must wait,' said Tyler. 'Until tomorrow.'

'We are giving them time,' said John Ball.

'They will not meet again today. The Essex men – and our own – are content to wait for the documents he promised at Mile End. They want to see if he keeps his promises. So do I.'

'Once they get them, many will leave London. Some of those who can go are already on their way home,' said Long, ever-anxious. 'You say "speed", Walter. We are here with half the day still to come.'

'And London is being taken over by the devil,' said John Ball.

'They need a little time to enjoy their victory, John. We always did after a battle. It's the reward. There's no devil in London now, John. You scared him off.'

Ball was perturbed, not so much at his friend's words as by his manner. There was a slackness in his body, which he had not seen before. Worse than that, there was about him what John Ball felt could be dangerous, a sense of peace, as if the struggle was over.

'God is only with us if we listen to Him,' he said.

'Well, John, what is He saying?'

'Strike now. Strike harder. Destroy our enemies in London who have armies. Our strength is in the multitude, Walter. If the multitude melts away we will be chickens to the wolves.'

'We have them.' Tyler closed his fist. 'Like that.'

'Not while they live.'

'What do you see, John?'

'I have seen you,' he replied. 'I saw one chosen to say to Pharaoh, "Let my people go". I saw a man like yourself walking ahead of the enslaved people of England, across her meadows, through her villages and towns, fording her rivers until he reached the citadel of Pharaoh himself. I saw him storm Pharaoh's city and, with the help of God, cleanse the city, meet Pharaoh and convert him. I see fire and palaces burned down. I see the one chosen talk to the King and he will set the people free.'

Tyler, hearing himself being chronicled, shook his head. It was too grand for him.

'But it is not yet concluded,' said the priest.

Tyler leaned forward and, in an uncharacteristic demonstration of physical affection to the lonely priest, he grasped John Ball's right shoulder tightly and held it. Out of the face of weathered bronze, his eyes softened to as deep an affection as he had felt for any man. For some moments he stayed still. 'All will be well, John, as long as you are here.'

And he grinned. Ball felt the impact of that, though at first he tried to dislodge Tyler's hand. But the hand was too strong for him. And within moments he felt his resistance dissolve at this force of reassurance.

He was a man who avoided being touched. Since those early days in the York school when he had been transformed from an innocent, brimful-of-willingness child into a frightened, confused boy, he had avoided physical contact with all the skill and determination he could muster. It had led him to be thought of as 'the strange one', the 'peasant runt', but his fellows had learned to leave him alone.

Tyler had soon noted the way his friend would flinch at any attempt to put an arm around his shoulders, or even to shake hands. But he wanted John to feel, to feel through to his bones, the depth of the affection he harboured for him. Unable to break free of the warm grip, the strange priest yielded to the affectionate hand on his shoulder and would nourish the memory of it.

Tyler called some of his men and struck north-west though the city to Mile End where Jack Straw and the men of Essex had their camp. He had to persuade the more able ones to stay in London for longer. He was hailed all along the way. In the heart of the city a drunken young pack, whom he could see were criminals, hollered at him with greetings that sounded like taunts.

Their leader bowed.

'Tyler!' said Dog. 'They call you the king of the True Commons. I am Dog, the king of the Fleet Prison.'

He pulled in his gang to watch as he held out a challenging hand. Tyler hesitated for a moment. But too many people had witnessed the challenge for him to duck it.

Tyler took his hand and felt the immediate tightening of the young man's grip.

Dog had played this game many times, and if ever he felt he might lose he would use a knife, his knee, his teeth or anything available to make sure he won. He had to win. He had to remain king of the Fleet. But by the time Tyler was fourteen he could handle a seven-foot bow and bend it near double to send an arrow a third of a mile. Between times his work for his father was heavy lifting.

Dog's hand, sinewy, muscular, gave him a fine grip but he realised that Tyler was stronger.

He looked around for help, and Tyler's big hand tightened around his opponent's with such ferocity that Dog thought his fingers would be broken. He bit back a cry of pain. Tyler pushed it a little harder, threatened to force Dog to his knees, then released him.

The crowd was impressed.

Dog's good hand rushed to comfort its bruised twin.

'You have a good grip on you,' said Tyler. 'Make sure you use it well.'

31

Into the Dark

John Ball had to find Will. The pain at the thought of losing him sucked in more and more of his energy and pushed out all other concerns. He had not felt like this before. He had not let himself feel like this. Merely human feelings had been frozen. But his friendship with Will had thawed them. For the first time in many years his boyhood warmth surfaced and he let it in.

Since leaving home when he was thirteen, John Ball had not known friendship. As a boy in Colchester he had spun like a top, whirring in the hum of his contentment at just being who he was and in that place.

St Mary's in York had put an end to that. He had seen the world through God's eyes and he had seen that the world was not good. It was not what God had intended. Even the priests had not been good. And they had liked to torment him. The world should not have been like that. Therefore, the unhappy passionate boy thought, his sole duty was to bring home to God's people, at whatever cost, the world as it should be. The Great Plague was clearly God's punishment for the sins of mankind. Ball knew that, unless people mended their ways, God would plague them again and again. They would all die in sin and be condemned to Hell.

He bore physical deprivation without complaint. He could make a shelter in the woods. He could live on the leanest diet. He survived as the early Christian ascetics had survived.

Everyone he encountered, even Walter Tyler to whom he was now uncharacteristically close, he saw primarily as part of his mission to save souls. To save your own soul was the first purpose of your life on earth: to save the souls of others was his vocation.

Will had become his first true friend since he had left the spiritual adviser in York so many years before. Why that was, Ball could not wholly fathom. He thought it must be the man's holy innocence – that gift from God, as his Samson-like strength was surely another.

He had never encountered, since he had become a man, such unqualified devotion. He had never been wholly at ease in any company before. Perhaps it came from the desperation of the times he lived in. Ball, unused to thinking in personal terms, knew that such an explanation was not enough. Will had touched his buried heart.

He knew now that Will had the plague. He saw clearly the uneven walk, the strained and sweating face as he had carried the dead body of the Lollard boy at Lambeth Palace. Why had he not recognised it then? Will had known it and had left him to protect him. When Ball realised that he experienced a new sensation, the sick fear of loss. He had to find him. After Tyler had left for Mile End, Ball did not march after him but headed for the slums beside the river. He guessed that Will would have gone there to hide.

John Ball was afraid. As he searched increasingly frantically through the walled-in poverty of slit alleys and infested yards, deeper into the disease, he wound a piece of cloth around his mouth and nose. He passed boarded doors and the dolorous graves of fast-decaying bodies, the cries of the comforters, the occasional incantation of a priest.

He asked everyone he met who looked as if they could answer. Had they seen someone of Will's unmistakable description? He raked the cramped area, lodged in Thames sludge. Just a couple of hundred yards downriver he found the vast warehouses of the wool trade, the Flemish merchants, great wealth cheek by jowl with poverty, like an illustration of the World As It Was and the World As It Could Be. Ball saw, yet again, here as all over England, the rich seeming to need to confine and cramp the poor. And the poor had agreed to endure it until now. Back he went into the rat-run of tunnels, dark even under the clear June sun. Will would surely not have been hard to spot. Wrong directions diverted him until he was sent to a door, unboarded, in as hopeless a street as Ball had ever seen.

His friend lay on the bare, filthy floor. Ball, who had been with many plague victims, saw that Will had the strain at its most savage. A few hours were all he had left. He knew that the fever was violent even before he put his hand on the sweating, swollen forehead. Will tried to restrain the spitting of blood when he saw who was ministering to him. His eyes battened lovingly on the priest's face and he tried to speak, but another retching gout of dark blood came from his mouth.

Ball knew that prayer was all the help he could give. And powerful prayer would surely help this good, trusting soul, help speed it to its assured place in the heavenly kingdom. The priest knelt beside his friend and whispered the prayers into his ear. About them in the diseased house, there was the weeping horror of other deaths and harsh gasping for air, even foul air.

As he prayed he felt a surge of feeling so new and so painful that he did not recognise it. Good Christian men like Will should not die like this! Yet such a thought had to be banished and he had to prepare himself for later punishment for allowing himself, however fleetingly, to question God's greater purpose.

Will turned his head and shifted his trembling body a little so that he was face to face with John Ball. He indicated his hand and Ball took it. The love in his expression was unmistakable. Ball's eyes stung and, again, he had no recollection of this happening to him before.

'You are my good friend, Will,' he said. He found it hard to speak. He had first to swallow.

He said, 'Do you remember, Will? "Our Father, Which art in Heaven, hallowed be Thy name . . ."' He could not go on. Then he paused and, with difficulty, added, 'I bless you in the name of the Father, the Son and the Holy Ghost. May God receive your soul.' And then there was a small miracle: Will mouthed 'Amen'.

Ball held his hand until he heard the death rattle.

He went to look for a funeral cart. For some minutes he thought he, too, might have contracted the plague: dizzy, unstable in his walking, a feeling of ravenous emptiness. He must find a cart. The churches were inured to the untraditional nature and brevity of a plague victim's funeral. He made for the river, hoping for better air.

He would not get the plague. He had been beside too many of the dying over the past two decades. God must have protected him. But why him? He could not take on that question: its load was too heavy for him.

Ball looked at the river, away from the sludge around the bank out to the middle of the Thames, which flowed so freely and simply, so like the way men could be, he thought, if only they followed His commandments. Perhaps the river held a lesson.

He would find a church. St Martin Vintry was the nearest.

Near St Martin's there was a substantial settlement of Flemings, who controlled much of the lucrative wool trade, which came to and went from London. Like the Lombards and the Genoese, the German and Baltic traders, they had been given royal blessing and favours unbestowed on native merchants. This short-cut to short-term taxes had helped build wealth for the King and resentment among their long-established London competitors. But the King's writ, or that of his ill-advising councillors, ran weightily in that largely law-abiding city and the resentment had been controlled. No longer.

The houses of the Lombards, the Genoese and the Germans had that day been raided, looted and hacked by packs of frustrated, vengeful Londoners, led by the English wool merchants whose day of justice, they reckoned, had come. The foreigners could at last be dealt with as they deserved. The Flemings, the rich, clever, brothel-owning, guild-darling Flemings, were the greatest prize. The avenging gangs came together, a violent congruence of different currents, and swung south to the unprotected citadel of the Flemings, next to St Martin Vintry.

They saw it as the new legality. They would ask the Flemings who they were for. If they could not reply, 'I am for King Richard and the True Commons of England,' they were condemned. Or they would ask them to say, 'Bread and cheese.' If they said this with a Flemish accent, they were condemned. Or they would ask them nothing but condemn them because they said nothing. The gangs had become feral and the Flemings had become prey. The London mob, aided by a few from the counties who had deserted Tyler's rule, had turned barbaric. The summer sun, the drink, the thrill, the licence given by the executions of great men on Tower Hill, had whipped and intoxicated them to a self-righteous fury, which fed on all the fantasies their oppression had dreamed of.

John Ball walked towards the church and saw a cart that had been abandoned in the churchyard. He took it, but before he could leave to push it back the way he had come, the gangs crashed through the feebly defended doors of the church and went in with a howl for blood that curdled his mind.

Ball stood like a ghost at the battle. A church was surely a place of sanctuary. Not on that day for the thirty-five Flemings who had fled there. A frenzied sense of justice had melded with the ancient and visceral vengeance of the mob, to kill those you feared, envied and hated.

He ought to preach. But what was he to say? Were not these merchants, now being dragged from the church by their hoods, now being stabbed by swords and daggers, and slashed by axes, now being forced to kneel, were not they, too, part of the oppression, forcing starvation wages on those who clipped, washed and combed the wool while they who merely transported it walked the streets in rich clothes and lived in splendour? He was too confused to answer his own questions. He needed to bury Will.

He would not have been listened to even had he spoken. More than thirty Flemings were executed outside St Martin Vintry that afternoon, and the wild dogs went berserk at the blood. Men are the wild beasts now, Ball thought, as he stood in horror before them. Oh! See how far we have fallen. God have mercy on us all.

Heads were kicked along the gutters, then stuck on poles and hoisted like captured standards in a war. The bodies pumped out blood. The thieves ripped off the fine clothes before they were too stained. The screams of the Flemish women rose above the rooftops. The streets were a slaughterhouse in London that day: more than a hundred and forty Flemings were executed.

Ball looked until he had had more than his fill. Only God could solve this.

He went slowly back the way he had come, pushing the cart before him. He would seek out a small, unrich, undesecrated churchyard.

32

Through the Night

P rincess Joan heard it all. La Royal, her London palace, was just a few hundred yards from St Martin Vintry, so the screams of fear and the shouts of triumph came to her as she looked out to catch sight of the murder of her hopes.

Those fatal words at Mile End – how could he have said, 'Seize the traitors'? This was permission to murder his closest councillors. The King must have been trapped in sympathy for the peasants who worshipped him so fervently. But any pact between them had disintegrated as the day had worn on. Over in the south-west of the city, in Castle Baynard, she could visualise the King and his advisers urging on the clerks to write out scores of pardons, each sealed and offered as a guarantee of concord to stem the tide of blood. Meanwhile this rabble was butchering the wealth and burning the law.

Her messengers were all over London. There were two at St Martin Vintry. One observed and noted the blood frenzy; the other scurried to the Queen's Wardrobe at La Royal, delivered the news, then hurried back for more. Joan sent this information to Richard and would add to it intelligence of the most recent movements of Tyler, Straw and Ball. Her son Tom roved the capital alone on foot, now perfect in his ability to be part of the rebel mass. Joan thought proudly that there was no one in London with a wider knowledge of the state of things. And with his reports her mood darkened by the hour.

The truth facing her was that the initial demand to seize the traitors had swiftly turned into indiscriminate executions, the settling of private grudges and bloodlust. Walworth had been right. They should have been assassinated in their drunken sleep.

Who would be next?

At the same time as the madness over the Flemings ripped them from the church, one of her closest allies had also been murdered. Her messenger told her of the fate of Richard Lyons. Lyons was one of the richest men in London, familiar to her since the days of the Black Prince's court in his last years in England. He had been a benefactor to Princess Joan. She had ignored justified accusations of corruption against him and surrendered happily to the rewards of his extravagance and good company. Sometimes, she thought, a little wickedness was the making of a man.

Lyons was dragged through the streets to the executioner's block in Cheapside where two blows of an experienced axeman severed his head. His blood ran into the blood-soaked earth and the burning midsummer sun immediately began to vaporise it.

Reports came to La Royal of cemeteries desecrated, houses and shops robbed, tradesmen assaulted for trying to barricade themselves in. Even if these reports were only part-true, and Joan was shrewd enough to understand the infection of rumour, they were true enough to make her mind uncharacteristically anxious.

She was now convinced that Tyler would burn down all London. She had heard that the plan was to seize the King and take him around England on show to subdue the people and win them over to the peasants' cause. Outside London, she had been told, imitation Tylers were taking palaces and towns without resistance. John Ball was to be the only priest in England. All the jewels and ornaments of the Church and the Crown would be divided among the poor. Some of the English earls were seeking an alliance with the French Crown to come to London and help their cause. John of Gaunt was bringing the Scots to save England. How had her world collapsed so quickly?

The wild beasts must be stopped. They must be killed as they were killing 'us', she thought. That was the only way. She wanted night when secrecy could plan retribution. She requested the King come to her palace with all speed as soon as darkness gave him a cloak.

After he had buried his friend, John Ball drifted through London. He was recognised wherever he went. Some knelt for a blessing, which he gave. Others wanted a sermon, which he could not find it in himself to deliver. What he had seen and done in the past few hours had hollowed him out. The act of walking on his own seemed to offer some ease of mind.

The smell of burning was as welcome to his nostrils as it was to his sight. Wicked cities deserved fire. But there was in him an unease he could not identify.

This drift was taking him where he neither knew nor cared. He could have been a lost soul. As if he were searching for someone among the dead.

Slowly, as night finally overcame the June day, he found himself in a state of unaccustomed agitation. He sobbed for breath. He felt he might choke. He could not remember feeling like this before.

There was a deep doorway in a quiet street and he lay down there, hoping that sleep would blot out the events of the day. He found it difficult to articulate his prayers and the ancient mantras in Latin gave him little comfort.

As night settled in he began to piece together movements of men high-mounted on warhorses, which stepped on muffled hoofs along the street, which, like those nearby, though he did not know it, was the centre of a network housing the palaces of rich, well-armed merchants. John Ball imagined he could sense a new mood. He gave up the hopeless search for sleep and moved carefully through those few streets where he picked up fragments – of messages to and from the King, who was now, he learned, harboured with Princess Joan, of numbers available, two hundred and fifty here, five hundred there, more than a thousand men-at-arms, of men in full harness, the kingdom to be saved at any cost, Smithfield, Tyler, Straw, the King to lead them, the King. Their final chance.

As a crimson dawn rolled slowly up the Thames, luxuriant Nature and the multitude of birdsong made the city and all of England seem a sceptred island. Meanwhile John Ball warmed himself at the embers of the Savoy Palace.

Scavengers were picking what they could from the ruins. The warrant of restraint of two days before no longer held. He was offered meat and beer, which he took thankfully. A hunger had grown in him, which he had ignored until now. This, he comforted himself, looking at the ruins, was how the mighty were fallen. Take away their appearances, their outer show, and they would be revealed as naked as any other wretch.

He went towards Westminster, which some of the rebels had attempted to reach the day before in what had turned out to be a half-hearted and unsuccessful assault on the Exchequer. It was just possible, Ball thought, as he strode out, following the tide of dawn light, that the men of Kent and Essex had quailed before the might of Westminster.

Ball went into the abbey and, in the cool morning gloom, made for the shrine of Edward the Confessor. He regretted its ostentation – plated with gold, embroidered with rare jewels. Too worldly for his taste. Why was such extravagance thought necessary? Would God care? But of the King's religious nobility he had no doubts. Edward was truly a king from God. His holy life had been an example to all his countrymen, abroad in France and everywhere his reputation reached. He was wise, he had loved his people before himself, and this small room in the centre of the great Ark of Westminster, a small space inside that immense abbey, was where the core of the godly power of the kings of England resided and from where it emanated.

John Ball prayed that God remove the doubts that had swarmed into his mind after the death of Will. He prayed for His kingdom to come in England.

On the previous evening Richard had arrived stealthily at his mother's palace, more like a thief than a king. Even on the short journey, riding swiftly with few retainers to avoid challenge, he had noticed the deepening disorder. It was impossible not to sense the danger to his realm.

Joan had rested her aching back, sought relief in a prolonged massage, corseted her wavering spine as fiercely as she could endure and decorated her blood-red gown with her best jewels. She was ready for him.

She dismissed her courtiers. Richard followed suit.

They were alone in her bedroom, deep in the comfort of treasures, exotic cloth, tapestries, choice furniture, fine pictures and tall candlesticks giving glitter and lustre to her voluptuous retreat. It was late, and though the day had been hot, there was a fire against the coolness of the night and the broken flames embossed the brilliant surfaces on which they played.

Joan had planned to let Richard speak first, but her impatience was too pressing for her to entertain delay.

'So what will you do . . .' she paused '. . . Your Majesty?'

He did not smile but she saw again in his eyes the hope of a victory. It would be, she thought, her victory.

'We meet Tyler and his men again tomorrow,' he said.

'Your father used to talk to me about his battles. He knew I liked to listen. Sometimes he would take notice of what I said.'

'This is not like a battle . . . It is . . . a negotiation.'

'What does the council say?'

'It is still divided.'

'Salisbury against Walworth?'

'In the main. Salisbury fears that any offensive action we take would rouse all the Londoners against us. Walworth wants them cleared out as soon as possible, and if there has to be a battle, so be it. He is pleased with the choice of Smithfield. He says it is the perfect pen for sheep.'

'I do not like William Walworth.'

Richard shrugged agreement.

'But now I think he may be right.' She had persuaded herself to be fair-minded. 'If only we could be sure of the strength of support Tyler commands.'

'The rebels call him king of the True Commons.' Richard was offended. 'He walks through the crowds to huzzahs! When I see them, I try to ride around them.'

'Are you afraid?'

'They smell.'

Joan smiled, to indulge him. But there were urgent things to be said. 'They do not know how to rule. We have bred them to obey,' she said. 'This – revolt, this uprising has sent their heads spinning. They have swallowed too many draughts of "freedom". They are drunk on it.'

'Yes.' Richard looked closely at her. 'My advisers are also full of such descriptions. But what's to be done? Do we attack and risk in battle the elimination of all the present leaders of our kingdom? Or do we continue to surrender and watch as more and more liberties are claimed and taken? We have no army in London. They now say that Tyler will take all the land, all the wealth, make all the laws, collect all the taxes . . .'

'Only you can stop him.'

'How?' He was petulant. 'How can I stop a rabble that is now pulling down and burning some of the most beautiful parts of London? How can I stop all that? What can you suggest?'

'I say what I have said before. You can replace him as their leader,' she said severely. She did not enjoy criticism, even implied criticism. 'You alone.'

'How?'

Still that trapped anger, that petulance. Joan held on to her patience.

'You must appeal directly to your people,' she said very firmly. 'They are loyal to you. "We are for King Richard," they say. It is their oath. They want you to listen to them. If you do that, they will be led by you.'

'I did listen. I listened at Mile End. And I gave them all they wanted. Didn't I?'

And more, she thought. Too much more. They think that you gave them permission to murder 'traitors', or anyone who stood in their way and whose murder would enrich their cause. But she stayed silent. He knew it was thought that his exuberant youthful promise, so full of comradely feeling when he had made it, had set off the storm of murders in the streets. It was too painful for him to face so he dismissed it. Joan would not scratch that sore.

'Salisbury says that if we provoke even a skirmish then one sole arrow could end my life. My father, I am told, loved the bowmen. They won his battles. Tyler was one of them and there are others. No one can win against them.'

274

'Save the King! Save you! You cannot give up now.'

Eventually he nodded. Then he looked away from her. 'Will you be with me?'

Joan took a deep breath. 'No. You will have your councillors. There will be an escort. But, Your Majesty, you are now on your own.'

He turned to her, his eyes pleading.

But she did not give in.

After prayers at the shrine of Edward the Confessor, John Ball went into the abbey's grounds. It was a tranquil morning, already dappled with early sunlight. He needed solitude. He had begun to lose himself in the crowds and also lose his intense personal communion with God . . .

He was drawn out of the grounds by the sound of violent blood cries, like those that had pounded his ears at the slaughter of the Flemings. He went towards the west door. It seemed to be much the same mass – loud, still drunk, largely Londoners, bold apprentices, with a few accents he recognised from Essex and Kent, all clagged together in an unstoppable rush into the abbey.

He followed them.

Their shouts rang up to the high Gothic ceiling; the stone bounced their cries back in exhilarating echoes. He soon learned that they were on the track of Richard Imworth, the gaoler and torturer from Southwark Prison, who had eluded them for the past two days. Word was that he had made for the shrine of Edward the Confessor, surely no sanctuary more inviolable.

Ball stood in a confusion both approving and appalled, as the gaoler was torn from the golden coffin to which he had clung as his last hope and out of the abbey to meet cries of 'Cheapside! Cheapside! Cheapside!' He was dragged by the hood to Cheapside for execution.

Ball followed the death procession at a distance, feeling cut off from the main. Then he went towards the river to visit Will's grave, which needed more heavy stones to secure it. With two pieces of wood he made a cross and lingered a while, trying to reignite the anger and conviction that had brought him from Maidstone to London.

Up from the river he came to Charing Cross, where he witnessed a procession such as he had never seen before.

Heading it were about a score of the flagellants who had come into the city the previous night. Their whipped backs and bloodied chests, their cries to God not to end the world shocked those who had come to see them. Most of the crowd knelt and prayed. Following them were more than a hundred monks and clerics of all ranks, all barefoot, but robed in their finery, carrying crosses. In resonant union, they chanted the psalms, moving towards Westminster, to the abbey they had come from.

Behind them rode the King, dressed in gold, with an escort of at least two hundred men, high on horseback, harnesses jingling, intent, locked into themselves. The horses walked at a funeral pace so as not to challenge the flagellants and the monks.

He saw the King turn to talk now to this nobleman, then to another. Although he was solemn, there was no mistaking his friendliness with the men, his councillors, these traitors, his deceivers.

They seemed to be his closest companions.

And then, quite suddenly, Ball realised that the King was not to be trusted. He murmured those words aloud to give the shock a physical reality. 'He is not to be trusted.' Surely that was inconceivable. But the revelation was in him, and it had been given to him in that moment and it could have come only from God.

It was plain to see. The King was not from God. The

King was no exception to those at his court. The King was no innocent among the wicked. The King was no different from his traitorous councillors around him on horseback now.

The King had to be killed with the rest of the traitors!

33

The Preparation

'What do you think, John? How does it look?'

Walter Tyler, spruced up, washed yet again, grinning broadly at his tense, contained friend, opened wide his arms, perhaps in an unconscious imitation of Ball's habit at the beginning of a sermon. He had procured a new set of clothes. When Ball looked around, he saw that others of Tyler's council were also dressed above their station. They could have been a cluster of merchants, he thought, but for the context of grubby tents, servantless clutter, scattered fires and mounds of litter.

'Don't look like that, John. I'm going to meet our king today. And this time Salisbury will not be able to send me away because of what I wear. I'll ask him just what you said I should ask him, and tell him just what you and I and all these men here want me to tell him. Then all will be well, John, and our England will be God's country again. And we shall have you for our archbishop, like it or not!'

You are speaking too quickly, Ball thought, unlike your true self. And in those new clothes you do not look yourself. In the background, approaching with confidence, he saw Johanna Ferrers, accompanied by Tyler's daughter. Innocent though he was, Ball was not blind. He feared for Tyler's soul. And there was a general looseness, even a little tipsiness, about his friend as he prepared for Smithfield . . .

'Drink some beer, John.' He handed over his tankard. 'It will do you good. Water can't be trusted. It's like the King's council – it sparkles but poisons. Here.'

Ball sipped gratefully. The sun was beginning its decline to the west but the excessive summer heat persisted. He was troubled. And here was Walter preening himself! It was harmless. Clearly, Walter wanted to mark this day in a dignified manner. To parley on equal turns with a king while looking like an infested peasant outlaw would be an insult to both sides. Tyler was right in this, Ball thought, as he had been right in every move he had made so far. And why should there not be joy on a day such as this? Had there ever been a day such as this? England seizing England for the English.

But the King . . . Ball could not let go of the question of their loyalty to him. Was it well founded?

'Here she is,' said Johanna, proprietorially, presenting Joan to her father as if at a court. 'She took some finding, Walter.'

Joan was mute with shame. Surely her father, who had seen through her all her life, would see now that she was ruined. She hung her head and tried hard not to let him down further with public tears.

'She was caught up in one of the riots,' said Johanna. 'You'll have to see to them, Walter, after you've met the King.' There was still guilt about her parting from Joan to take loot from the Savoy Palace downriver, but she went on the attack: 'There are some bad men on the streets, Walter. We think that John Ball opened too many prisons.'

Tyler had not taken his eyes off his daughter. He walked across to her and gently chucked her under the chin. She looked up in despair. He stroked the cheek on which the cruellest bruises remained. He guessed what had happened and, for the flare of a moment, he wanted to find the rapists at any cost, castrate them, rip them open from groin to throat and feed their genitals to the dogs. He steadied himself, put his arm around his daughter and took her aside.

'You should have gone home,' he said, 'but you always said you were better than a boy.' He tried to smile at her. But his mind was full of the rage. Why did he not go and kill them? 'After today, Joan, I do want you to go home. There will be work for me here for some time to come. I'll give you a note for your mother. Tell her I will see her soon and that I am with good men. I will talk to the King and all things will be well.'

Joan now looked fully at her father and, with difficulty, she stopped the tears. She had to be brave.

'Good girl,' he said. 'You still have the dagger?'

She searched for it inside her filthy gown.

He took it and looked at it. 'I remember when I was given this,' he said. 'I have never been so proud before or since that day. We had an England to be proud of then. An England of true kings. And we shall again, after this day. This, too, will be a proud day.' He handed back the dagger. 'Kent will be beautiful on a day like this,' he said. 'London is nothing to it. But it is here we have to be to win, and it's here I shall stay until we are sure of it.'

She bit her lip. The tears would come and now they did. How many tears had she shed over the past two days? He had not reproached her. He was still the same father.

'Now,' he said, 'I have to go. Johanna will take care of you.' Once more he stroked her bruised cheek and she tried not to flinch. 'You make sure the garden is well cared for.' He let his mind drift to his village. How fine it must be there on a day like this.

For an instant they looked at each other a few feet and a world apart. He smiled one last time and she returned to Johanna.

'There,' said Johanna, hugging her. 'Good now . . .'

'John!' Tyler called, switching his tone instantly. 'You want to talk?'

The men found a space and sat down. Tyler looked at the White Tower. How many times had he sized it up? And now it was his.

'Some of them wanted me to set up camp in there,' he said.

'You were right not to.'

'That's what you said when they pressed me. It is not what we want, is it, John? We don't want to show that we can conquer London and England. We want to change it. We don't want to replace them or to copy them. We want to banish them. We stay out in the open to show to our own people that we will always be part of them.' He paused. 'So what is it, John?'

'The King.'

'We shall soon be face to face.'

'Who will you be facing?'

'John?'

'Walter. This morning I saw the King with his retinue. He is one of Them, Walter. He is not apart, as we have always thought. And afterwards I had a vision. I saw the King and his advisers, the traitors, the oppressors, cut us all down, slaughter us, the True Commons, and the King was in blood with them. I could not interpret this at first. Was this a warning from God that we must be careful not to transgress? Was this a fear of my own that it would be impossible for us to win? Or was He saying that we could not trust the King?'

'But we are for the King,' said Tyler, puzzled by this change. 'And he is for us.'

'And so I, too, thought,' said the priest, 'until I saw him and his retinue this morning, riding out to Westminster. He was of their company, Walter. Not ours. He was riding to pray for their victory. Not ours. He is not our king, Walter. He is theirs.'

Tyler was winded. John Ball had become his oracle. 'You cannot be right this time, John.'

Ball was silent.

'He is a king, John. You told me that God created kings. And look what he did at Mile End. The Essex men were waving their pardons all over London today. It was difficult for me to get Jack Straw to hold enough of them here for the meeting at Smithfield tomorrow. The King gave us everything we asked for.'

'But will he keep his word?'

'At first I feared they might not let him. But then, I thought— But he swore!' said Tyler, angry now – anger was his only escape. 'He is a king – he swore on his oath! That is sacred, John. And we will kill the councillors who try to make him change.'

Ball hesitated. How could he break this man's faith? And should he? Tyler had his own path to follow and he would surely follow it. Why wound him now when he most needed strength?

'Could you be mistaken, John? Could the young King not be riding to the abbey to renew his vows? And those who were with him, could they have been of a mind that the closer they stayed, the safer they were? Could he not have been just . . . good-natured? He knows we will not harm him. For what are we without our king?'

Ball was moved to be prepared to doubt. After the death of Will perhaps he had not been in his right mind. Now that he was here, once more in the middle of the rebels he had helped mould, he felt their pride in achievement all around him; he could see the hope of people who had been without it throughout their lives. His loyalty to them vied with this revelation. Perhaps it had been sent to test him. Maybe it was a temptation of the devil – to destroy all that was so soon to be gained. Get thee behind me, Satan, Jesus had said. Get thee behind me.

'Without a king,' Ball replied carefully, as a man emerging from a deep weariness, 'without this king, I agree we would be lost.'

'And you believe that, John?'

'I believe that.'

'Then we are set, aren't we? We are set.'

'You are a brave man, Walter. I am with you.'

Tyler reached out and clutched his friend's arm. 'We will do this, John. We will make a good place where we will all be with one another as brothers.'

Ball knew that Tyler wanted the final reassurance. 'There is no other way now,' he said.

Tyler's mood switched again. It had passed through anxiety, touched on anger and concluded in renewed reverence for this holy man. Now was the time to fulfil their destiny.

The closer they drew to Westminster Abbey, the more silent Richard grew until he became impervious to the self-serving overtures of the nobles in his council who rode nearest him. They were used to his withdrawal and the way in which he seemed to have no need of them. It was never comfortable. On this day it made them afraid.

What was in his mind? Even the dullest among them now knew that only the King could stave off this rebellion, save their hides and secure the kingdom. They had failed to act like the armed warrior class they had been born into, then trained and rewarded to become. Bellicose suggestions offered by the martial party had been rejected. Salisbury's pacific policy of retreating with bribery had won the field. But now, as their tall horses jingled their way down the final shallow slope to Westminster, they saw that appeasement had not worked. From reports coming their way, the situation was worsening. What was to be done?

It always came back to the King. This half-boy, half-man, this curious son of the Black Prince, was a stranger to most of those men. When they were almost at the abbey, they fell back, just a yard or two. They fell back so that the King alone was at the front, the most wholly exposed.

Now, Richard thought, was the time that he had to be like his father.

He knew very well that he was not as his father had been. Tom Holland, who shared their mother and had a different paternity, was much more like the Black Prince than he was. Richard saw the love of this in his mother's eyes. His jealousy was constant. His need for her good opinion had become an addiction. He longed to be free of it. Now here he was, with the opportunity to be free, followed by his sword-bearer, his council, and the ghosts of the archbishop and the chancellor. They were all behind him. Before him, the abbey, the stage of his great boyhood triumph. In the chapel of Edward the Confessor he would be made free.

Beside the coffin of the Confessor, Richard knelt, prayed, thought hard of his father and wept. In the deep historic echo of the sanctuary of the saint, he lost himself to find himself anew. How could he do what was expected of him? How could he prevent the throne of England being taken by peasants, his realm toppled by a rabble, all that made England what she was crushed under the heels of serfs? All over the country, he was told, they were victorious, tearing up the traditions of centuries.

The boy did not try to restrain his sobs. The copying sobs of some of the council who had overflowed the small chapel only slightly disturbed him. But he had learned how to ignore what he did not want to hear. He pressed his brow against the cold gold frame of the tomb and willed his mind to gain strength from this saintly king and from his soldier father. Gradually the tears dried. The weight of his slim young body was lightened. His prayers were done . . .

In the grounds of the abbey there was an anchorite. The hermit had lived there since the time of Edward III and the monks considered him a talisman. They fed him, and one or two visited him daily; his life on earth was devoted to prayer.

The two men could scarcely have been more of a contrast. There was the young King, who sat on the ground beside the hermit at the mouth of his cave, sipping from the small beaker of water he had been offered. Richard had ordered his men to leave him and they stood, disconsolate and fatalistic, beyond the abbey, frustrated, waiting.

The anchorite was old, parchment-skinned, calm, stick-thin, attentive; Richard was in gorgeous pageant-battle array, with the peach bloom on his skin, his exquisite formality and a deference that threw in high contrast the easy egalitarianism of the hermit. The odd coupling might have provided a subject for allegorical paintings – Youth and Age, Innocence and Wisdom, Pupil and Master, Hope and Learning, Yesterday and Tomorrow.

The anchorite soon overcame the young man's reticence and talked to him of the power of prayer, the love of God for his king, the eternal faith of the people who had been led astray but would be brought home by the Good Shepherd. He offered to share bread with Richard, and when Richard ate it, he thought he had never before experienced such a rich and sustaining meal as that bread. He thought he could feel it giving him bodily strength, just as Edward the Confessor had given him spiritual support.

The sun was well past its zenith. The time was near. He left some coins in the anchorite's bowl. The anchorite did not offer to kiss his ring.

For a few moments Richard stood still in the soft-aired, well-groomed grounds. He let his soul feel purified. His eyes closed, he swayed slightly in the shade of the high abbey walls that reached up towards the heavenly kingdom.

Then he was ready. He was shrouded in an invisible but inviolable cloak. He had been divinely appointed by God Himself. He was God's will on earth. And God's will would be done.

34
Smithfield

S ir John Newton walked his horse through the crowds
of armed men who were streaming into Smithfield.
This large open space, just outside the city walls, was
London's liveliest market – an open slaughterhouse, a venue
for horse-traders and fairs, for farmers and for occasional
tournaments and executions as a national spectacle.
William Wallace, the hero of Scotland, had been dragged
across Smithfield by a horse, strangled, castrated, disem-
bowelled and executed.

A blood field and a broad field of trades and drama,
monks and beggars, a field flanked on the east by the bulky
Norman church of St Bartholomew the Great, with its
hospital. There were shops and tumblers, a graceful copse
of elders, a horse pond. It was a field pullulating with all
the glitter and vivacity, the commerce, gore, poverty and
piety of the age, controlled by an English law enforced
violently. Newton was exhilarated by it.

He was preceded by two young gentlemen from the court,
two others behind him. They were not armed. When conges-
tion threatened, one of the young men would shout,
'Messenger for Walter Tyler from His Majesty the King!'
and the crowd would move aside.

Newton noticed a change in the mass of the rebels.

On the march to London, they had been fierce, a few
ruthless, often beyond the call of the majority, but throughout
all there had been the buoyancy of expectation, a sense of
spring. Now he saw tiredness. He saw the physical dirt

of nights sleeping in the open. He saw rifts among them – squabbling, infighting, even here on such a day in Smithfield. He thought he could detect some guilt for the bloodletting, which was becoming the brand of the insurrection.

Yet he also saw a certain growth in confidence. There was a weary sense of achievement: a patient last assembly where they would hear the final word of the King. Many thought that the concessions so swiftly granted the day before at Mile End, so royally followed up with documents, seals and pennants, had answered all their questions. But they trusted their leaders, and the weariness was sweetened by rumours that the King would hand over to Walter Tyler the keys of the kingdom and John Ball would this day make everyone equal.

Newton drew up at the site of Tyler's camp. Tyler looked up and smiled.

'Ah! Sir John. Still the messenger?'

Despite his better judgement, Newton could not but smile back. This was a rare man even though he was wrong-headed, guilty and a greater danger to the state (as Salisbury had said in council) than the French, the Scots and the Spanish combined. Newton expressed admiration for Tyler's new clothes. Tyler did not know how to respond to such a compliment so he ignored it. John Ball still looked like the outlawed hedge-priest.

'The King wishes to know when you will be on the field.' It occurred to Newton that this phrase was very like that used in the formal notice of a deadly joust.

'The King must be patient,' said Tyler, evenly. 'We are talking about matters we need to settle before we meet.'

He sees himself as the King's equal, Newton thought. A few weeks ago he was a former soldier who tiled roofs in the Dartford area. How could this have happened? And so quickly – they had been in the city for less than two days!

'Wait over there,' said Tyler, and turned back to his councillors.

There were almost thirty of them now. Henry Long, who had increasingly become his chancellor; the burgesses of Colchester, who were his core advisers; leaders from other counties, towns and villages; and still some of the men who had been with him in that now distant purge of the Dartford robbers and outlaws.

Against the royally authorised revenge taken on traitors and the blood spilt in personal grudges and viciousness against foreigners, his council was working to construct an alternative government. Change would be radical. They had struggled with the idea of imagining it. It would, some thought, have been much easier to imitate what existed. But they had confidence that they could make it different. As experienced burgesses, tax collectors, keepers and instruments of the laws of the land, they believed they would have few difficulties once they were recognised in office.

They were comforted by the thought that they could scarcely do worse than those they were to succeed. Ideas for the way in which the Church's lands could be divided among those in the parishes, how ecclesiastical treasure could be used to ease taxation, how the land holdings of the aristocrats and the rich could be taken into the common wealth – these had been talked through every night along the way around the campfires and written down by Long and his scribes. The King would rule. Tyler would be his leading councillor. Everything else would follow.

'But what will happen to our own towns and villages?'

'You will have to appoint your successors. You know who they are. All those young men already knocking on your door!'

But did that mean they would have to live in London? Yes. The palaces and houses of the wealthy merchants would be made available. How would they live? Out of the taxes they would take sufficient for their needs. How would the city function? As now, but on licence from us, from you. What about the laws governing commerce and movement of people, even the style of dress? What would happen there?

'Where the laws are good laws, we shall keep them,' said Tyler. 'Where they are bad laws and customs, you shall abolish or change them. And the city men will help you. Why should they destroy all that they have?'

'Can it be so simple?'

The Colchester elders had discussed this thoroughly and their spokesmen expressed their common apprehension about the speed at which they were being asked to do all this.

'Yes,' said John Ball. 'But when William of Normandy came to England and conquered the Anglo-Saxons, he replaced their aristocracy, the Church's leaders, the landowners, the language and the lawyers immediately after his victory. He made his own new world out of what had been ours. The greatest change always comes about violently and rapidly.'

Tyler nodded. Ball could always find words that reassured and emboldened his listeners. And Tyler sensed that, even at this ultimate moment, the rebels needed every ounce of practical reassurance.

'The word is that Waldegrave himself,' Tyler said, 'the speaker of the House of Commons, said yesterday that he understood our cause. He said that the King's councillors had set out crippling taxes. These were to support wars they showed no talent for winning – and they had allowed French and Spanish pirates to raid our Channel towns at will and leave us undefended. This is one of their own party. This is Waldegrave. He can understand why we are here.

He is the speaker of the House of Commons! We now have allies in high places!'

Newton came across again.

'Not yet!' Tyler was peremptory this time. 'Not yet!'

How long would they keep the King waiting?

Finally, Tyler released the council and they went to organise their formation on the field, town by town, county next to county, pennants and flags of St George to be held high.

Tyler needed time alone. He had been told of the Black Prince's habit of deep and long prayer before battle. Tyler stood aside and alone, seeking in himself the inspiration of religion. He did not find it easily. He was not convinced that his belief was strong enough. He took comfort from the certainty of John Ball.

Ball had heard his confession earlier in the day. That meant he was as ready as he would ever be. They were so many who wanted him to speak for them. He must not fail them. He must not fail England. He was daunted by what was expected of him. What if, after all the victories, he failed now? What if . . .? He must not betray this fear.

Newton waited.

The King and his entourage waited. They were outside Smithfield. Richard could not be seen to wait on Tyler. One strain that increasingly characterised his court was the insistence on protocol. When Lord Salisbury had complained at Greenwich of the poor dress of the rebels, which had made it impossible for the King to speak to them, he had been expressing that insistence on the outward recognition of the King's absolute and divine power.

Over the past two years the court had become increasingly barnacled in protocol. Each bow, step forward, cut of jib, place in the order of arriving, leaving, eating, seating and meeting was embroidered into the daily routine. It was the realisation of a fantasy that acted out the obedience and duties the King could demand from his court and, by extension, from all those outside the royal circle. And the King could not be seen to wait on any person.

Walworth had joined them after organising his forces at Aldersgate. He kept his distance from the King, the aristocrats and the knights. His group, the city financiers, were a small squadron sufficient to themselves. Walworth, still scorned for letting in the rebels, still smarting from the refusal of the council to take up his plan of a night massacre (though he had been right!), had made his own plans for the meeting. He revealed them only to the few who were to act with him. Despite the injunction to bear no arms – save the King's sword, carried by his sword-bearer – Walworth had a long dagger in his cloak, and under his unmartial clothes he wore a coat of tightly knit chainmail.

Salisbury had given the advice that had worked so well at Mile End. Give them everything they ask for. Agree to sign everything. But in return they must go back to their homes. Walworth had pointed out that the Mile End agreement had not staunched the bloodletting. Salisbury's response was that, unfortunate though it had been, such excess was inevitably the price of war. Moreover, he added, in comparison with battles in France, in which he and so many other English nobles had taken part, the number of deaths in London was small.

Tom Holland appeared through the jostle and whinnying of the impatiently moored horses and made for his half-brother. Richard's heart lifted. This was a day to be shorn of jealousy. Tom recognised this: he was used to provoking love, and he, too, felt a warmth of feeling as he pulled alongside his king and they manoeuvred their horses skilfully a few yards away from the others.

'We have a fine day for it,' Tom said, as if they were out in Windsor Forest for a day's hunting.

'What are they saying?'

'The people are most pleased that you went to the abbey,' he reported. 'There are stories of tears in the chapel of St Edward, your own, and some now say tears were shed from the eyes of the saint himself. And they say you look very regal, such a splendid young king in all your majesty. They cheer on the boldness you are showing. The people love you and are with you.' Tom had calculated that it was no time for reality.

Richard could not have asked for more.

'And this.' Tom handed over a beautifully embossed small box. 'This is from our mother.' Richard took it carefully.

'The Princess Joan asked me to say this,' Tom said, and his brow clenched a little as he strove to remember every word. 'She said that she did not want to write a note because it could not say all that was in her heart. Inside the box is the ring your father wore at the Battle of Crécy. It was the first present he gave to her. At Crécy, he was sixteen years old. His father had him lead the battle, and when his nobles called for help, his father refused. This was to be the day he would win the glory alone. When he did so, on that very day he became the Black Prince and the leader of Christendom.'

Richard opened the box and found a broad ring, gold and silver subtly plaited. It was very simple. He thought it was beyond price. He kissed it and put it on the central finger of his right hand.

Sir John Newton came up and announced, 'Tyler is on the field, Your Majesty.'

Richard turned his horse towards Smithfield and led his men forward.

What a wonder of a king the boy is, Tyler thought, as Richard led his two hundred magnificently dressed men into

Smithfield to take their place on the east side and face the re-disciplined ranks of the rebels. He would hold on to such an entourage, Tyler thought, but it would come from Tyler's own men.

The bowmen flanked Tyler. At his command, the bows, many of them from the Tower, were unstrung. John Ball was to his right. A few yards to his left, having wheedled her way there, using Joan as her pass, was Johanna. Joan, still shocked, still dazed, gazed at her father adoringly. She took out the dagger and passed it from one hand to the other as he had done. She had polished the sheath and it reflected the sun.

Even in the shadow-encroaching late afternoon, it was hot. Smithfield seethed. Tyler in his new clothes, gallant and appropriate though they made him look, missed the loose comfort of his normal dress. He felt beads of sweat on his neck and brow.

He waited. He would be summoned by the King. He – a soldier, a tiler – was about to talk man to man with the King of England in whom he had put all his trust, as had those he led. They were amazed that in such a few days they had reached London and in three days in June it had fallen to them. The King himself was now before them, waiting for their leader to talk to him. Tyler had decided to go unarmed.

Richard called forward Walworth to summon Tyler. Walworth thudded across the field, high on his warhorse and pulled up abruptly, with deliberate provocation, a couple of yards in front of Tyler.

'The King commands your presence,' he said, with as much contempt as he could summon. He added words of his own: 'You are to come alone.' Then he wheeled away and galloped back across the field to the royal entourage.

Tyler got onto his horse and looked around him. What a fine sight! And they had followed him! They trusted him; they trusted John Ball now standing near him, looking out keenly as if he were a pilgrim in sight of the gates of Heaven. Tyler felt he knew all of them – the bowmen, those who could bring swords, those who had seized axes, those with chains, pitchforks, staves . . . what John Ball called 'the good people'.

He caught the eye of his daughter. She looked so beseeching, so stricken. He smiled at her, and it was as if she had been redeemed. She threw him the dagger, which he caught and tucked into his belt.

Then Tyler set off to meet his king. Behind him came a great cheer from the many thousand hopeful, longing mouths. On and on it went, this sound, as Tyler's horse walked steadily across the wide open field to an entourage that quailed as the sound of the rebels slapped into their faces.

Tyler drew up some yards before the King. His understanding was that the King would come forward to meet him and that the two of them would talk unattended. He dismounted, and waited. He held onto the reins of his horse.

35
The Speech at Smithfield

Tyler was half a dozen steps from the King. He looked up and for a few moments, which seemed to become a freezing of time, he was assailed by a sensation he had never before experienced. For this was the King of England, looking down on him not unkindly. This boy with the peach skin of a girl, this upright slim figure enrobed in gold and embroidered splendour, this divine messenger of God, was his king.

He wanted to say, 'Your father's son is safe with me.' He wanted to say, 'I called my daughter after your mother.' He longed above all to say, 'I fought with your father at Poitiers.' He wanted to say, 'I can see in your face traces of his and so all is well.' His hand found the dagger sent to him by the Black Prince. He heard the noise of battles in France rise up from his memory, but this was no battle. He struggled to find his words. He had rehearsed this speech with Henry Long as well as John Ball. Now words failed him.

The sweat prickled around his new collar. The sweat trickled down his forehead and into his eyes. The King seemed unblemished by sweat.

He glanced about. The two hundred men in the King's retinue, who, from across the space of Smithfield and set against the thousands Tyler had under his command, had seemed a meagre force, now seemed powerful. He knew that he had victory-rich and dedicated forces behind him but he had cut himself off from them. He stood alone. He had delivered himself to the protection of the King. Too late to ask why. Total trust and faith were good. But . . . as he stood on Smithfield ground he was one against two hundred.

It was not difficult to sense the disdain and hatred directed at him by most of the King's retinue. He was, to them, vermin. But he was to be feared as they feared the plague. They held their horses back. The King spearheaded them, apart from them: it was only the King who mattered.

Richard took a long look at him. So this was the 'king of the True Commons'. This was Walter Tyler. This rough, strong man standing before him. Beware of him, his mother had said, but respect how your father admired and trusted his kind. Richard held on to that as he looked at the broad-shouldered, bronze-faced, independent figure, who as yet had not acknowledged that he was in the Royal Presence. It was, he thought, a deliberate defiance of protocol and so of his authority.

A change in the King's expression brought Tyler back to the moment. It became clear that the King would not move.

Tyler took the few steps forward, half bent his knee and doffed his hat. Richard extended his hand, one finger ringed now by the gift from Poitiers. Tyler did not kiss the ring. He took a strong grip on the King's slender forearm and said, as he had memorised so determinedly: 'Brother!' He heard the high pitch of outrage that emanated from the tightly exhaled breath of those in close attendance on the King. But now he was set. Now he was speaking for all those who were with him.

'Be of good comfort and joyful!' he continued, his grip firm on the boy, who felt he was being pulled down to earth. 'For you shall have, in the fortnight that is to come, fifty thousand more True Commons than you have at present, and we shall be good companions.'

Tyler then let go of the King, sprang to his feet, and

smiled welcomingly. Richard righted himself and repeated, coldly, what Salisbury had advised him to say at Mile End on the previous morning. Without any acknowledgement or, perhaps, awareness of this being a different situation, he once again employed the Salisbury tactic, but this time in a rather waspish tone as if he were put out that he had to meet again with these rebels only to say again what he had said the day before.

Tyler's heart, as well as what he saw as his true allegiance, had been poured into his own warm words. He had expected a sympathetic response.

'Why will you and your – people not go back to your own county?'

It was a slap.

Tyler stepped back. His horse was restless: he tightened his grip on the reins.

But then he thought, This is a boy. The boy would be understandably fearful about the ranks of armed men facing him. And he was a king. He needed to be taught to know his people and how to speak with them. There would be time. Yet as these calmer considerations were working through his mind, Tyler's own nervousness and sense of the importance of this meeting broke out.

'God's my witness!' he said, so that all about the King could hear. 'I will not leave this field, and nor will my men move from where they now stand, until we have the new charter we now wish to have on this day.'

His anger was heard as a threat by many of those in the retinue. The more reckless murmured aloud their disapproval. Their horses took up their aggressive mood and shifted their ground, a jingling of spurs, a rippling of restive bodies, the impatience of forced restraint.

'And you,' Tyler, in his stride, continued, this time not looking at the King but deliberately scanning the retinue, 'if you stand in our way, we will be as merciless to you as you for so long have been merciless to us. You have led this noble king and England to ruin. We have come to rescue him. Do not stand in our way.'

This open threat chastened them. The bowmen across the field could surely reach each one of them with arrows that would penetrate armour.

There was a private murmur from the adjacent Salisbury. The King reset his mood. 'What are the points you wish considered?' he said, in a softened tone. 'You shall have them freely, without contradiction, written out and sealed as they were for your fellows yesterday. Even now they are carrying them back to their homes.'

'We are here to ask more of you, my lord. We seek to protect you and to guide you. We will have you as our king with no let or hindrance and we will bow down to you.'

Tyler stood encircled by a space beyond which was an arc of the King's men, horsed, several secretly armed. They brought forward their horses ostensibly to listen, but closing in on Tyler. The sun was moving into the west and flat on Tyler's face. He stood, planted in the ground, it seemed, while he laid out demands surely never before put to a king, demands that, if accepted, would root and branch and for ever change England.

'We want there shall be no law but the law of Winchester,' he began. 'In Winchester Alfred the Great and the Anglo-Saxons made laws to help the commons. We ourselves in our towns and villages will keep the peace. There will be no hanging for every small offence but punishment enough still if the offence is bad. We had good order under the law of Winchester. No one was spared but we did not take life unless for the greatest crimes. We could carry arms. We had land. We were not slaves. Anglo-Saxon England was free. It was the Norman King William who brought in the

serfdom, villeinage and bondsmen. All this must be undone.'
Tyler was making one of the biggest efforts of his life. But
now it was as if the well-rehearsed words possessed him.
The brooding and often unfocused talk of the long nights
now found shape.

Tyler beckoned for a tankard of water, which was quickly
brought to him. Salisbury had ordered that such small
demands be expected and immediately met. Tyler swilled
out his mouth and spat. Once more an angry murmur came
from the retinue. To spit before a king! Richard made himself
appear unaffected.

Tyler took a deep breath and again went into battle.
'There will be no temples and chanceries but the King's
law in agreement with the True Commons and they who
carry it out will be the leaders in the towns and villages.
They know the people and they know when to be hard
and when to be merciful. They will collect the taxes
because they know what the people can bear and they
know, too, that the King must have full coffers when he
goes to war.'

Salisbury nodded at the sense of some of this. He could
see some advantage to the King. But now he himself was
attacked.

'And we shall have no lordship,' said Tyler, now confident
and speaking in the secure faith of John Ball. 'We need none
save the King. And all the land of the lords is to be divided
among all men.' He paused and was gratified by the silence.
'The King alone shall keep his lands, his forests and castles,
his palaces and all his treasure.'

Richard, caught up in this drama of demands, only just
restrained himself from open gratitude for this unique
bounty.

'The Holy Church must be stripped of its wealth and
titles,' he went on, as John Ball had instructed him. 'God

does not say the Church must have wealth, jewels or serfs, make bishops, have a pope, or keep the tongue of the people away from the word of God . . . Those of the lowliest clergy and the friars shall have sufficient sustenance and their few goods, but for the rest, it must be divided equally among the members of the parish.'

The world that was emerging from Tyler's steady, determined list of demands was now beyond the imagination of his audience. It was further away than the descriptions of Heaven and Hell. Their fear began to rise. How could this world exist? How could it be allowed to exist? How could they prevent its existence?

Tyler had not finished yet. 'All the lands and tenements shall be taken from bishops and prelates. There shall be in England only one bishop – if such he may be called – one prelate.'

He took another mouthful of water and, while the retinue watched agape, he swallowed it. Then he stopped, looked boldly across the gilded retinue, found for himself the voice of John Ball and concluded, 'Now is the time.'

The man called 'king' by so many in the streets, and who had described how he would be rid of the old court, stood plainly before them. And behind him line upon line of men who would not hesitate to obey him.

In the mind of Walworth and his close allies, who had not let go of their contempt for the rebels, the demands of Tyler further inflamed a fear that longed to be given the opportunity to act.

Richard backed his horse expertly until he came alongside Salisbury. On the other side he summoned Walworth, whose bellicosity his mother had urged him to heed but harness. He took counsel from the two men. Yet again it was conflicting. This time he did not so easily yield to Salisbury. 'This is not war,' Salisbury murmured, as one who had

301

fought in real wars. 'We will gain everything by not doing battle here today.' But Richard now believed that his previous surrender and retreat had gained him nothing but humiliation. And Walworth's blunt council of battle appealed to the aroused instincts of the boy. In this Smithfield simulacrum of a battle, with his father's ring on his finger, his mother's exhortations fresh in his mind, he would win his spurs.

Let them talk, Tyler thought, and asked for beer. He felt a curious compound of depletion and exhilaration. It was done, just as John Ball had wanted. There would be a new England.

He drank some of the beer. How would the King respond? He set the mug on the grass, took out his dagger from his belt and passed it from his free hand to the hand slung through the reins of his horse as he waited for their reply.

From across the field, John Ball strained to follow events. He saw Tyler plain. The only man standing. Beyond him, though, if Ball was right, edging forward, a few dozen men – was that Walworth, the man around whom they were jostling? Walworth was dangerous. What were they saying? He wanted to call, 'Danger!' But Tyler was too far away.

Johanna had come closer to him and peered into the distance, as immobile as Ball himself.

The King came forward, and Tyler noticed that the Walworth flank had moved forward with him. His hand tightened on the dagger but he did not cease to toss it from hand to hand.

'Beware the dagger,' said Walworth, quietly. The King was all but converted.

'My message is not changed,' said Salisbury, who was no friend to what he saw still as the coarse Walworth's appeal to the King's baser instincts.

Richard pulled a few paces ahead of them until his horse all but nuzzled against Tyler. Walworth moved stealthily, thinking it was unnoticed.

Tyler got back on his horse.

'We will give whatever we can fairly grant,' the King said coldly, 'reserving only for myself the regality of the Crown. Now I command you and your fellows to go back to your own county.'

Tyler shook his head. He wanted to talk. He wanted to believe that the King had understood his demands and would willingly go along with them. He studied the solemn, long-nosed face of the young man and saw the vanity in the arrangement of the hair, the over-embroidered cloth . . . Was the King still poisoned by those councillors who would not let him be? Why did he repeat for the third time – once at Greenwich, once at Mile End and now here at Smithfield – the request that they go home and leave the city? What would his council tell him to do when they were gone?

'We will stay in London, my lord,' said Tyler, 'until our demands are agreed, and here, in London, we will set up our government.'

'You trust your king?'

'I do, my lord.'

'You have the King's word. All that I can fairly grant, I will do.'

Again Tyler shook his head. And now he saw that the Walworth flank was moving to cut off his retreat and screen him from the rebels across the field. He made ready to move away.

Walworth looked behind him and nodded: it was the signal.

'Tyler, you are the greatest thief and robber in all Kent!' A thin but clear voice emanated from the third or fourth rank of the retinue.

Tyler looked to the King to squash this slander but the King said nothing.

'Bring me that man!' said Tyler. And then, in a voice that carried the triumph of the past three days, 'Bring him to me now!'

Walworth hesitated, and he and Tyler locked eyes. Walworth beckoned and the reluctant young plant nudged his horse gingerly through the ranks, drawing up just behind Walworth, whose creature, Tyler saw, he clearly was.

'Say that to my face.'

The man's face was pale. He was transfixed by the toss of the dagger, from hand to hand, hands of strength, he noticed, hands he feared, hands that could break him in two.

'Am I to let that slander stand, my lord?'

The King was silent. Tyler saw Walworth's right hand move inside his cloak. There would be a dagger there.

Could he not trust the King?

He waited for a sign but there was none.

Tyler caught the fragment of a whisper from Walworth to Richard and saw the King incline his head. He saw betrayal.

He unsheathed the dagger.

'Put away your weapon,' said Salisbury, fierce in protocol and fearing the worst. 'It is not allowed in the presence of the King.'

Tyler switched his gaze from the King to Walworth, backwards and forwards just as the dagger had passed from hand to hand.

Surely he could trust the King. He must trust the King.

'You have heard the Earl of Salisbury,' said Walworth.

Tyler should turn and go. He knew that. He was all but surrounded, he was hopelessly outnumbered. The danger to himself was full in his face. And yet. Surely the King would not betray him.

'Arrest him!' said Richard. 'Arrest this man!'

Arrest this man? For a moment Tyler could not believe 'this man' was himself.

Walworth pulled out his own concealed dagger and rushed towards Tyler, who drove his own weapon up into Walworth's chest only to find the blade foiled by tightly meshed mail. Walworth's long dagger was driven into Tyler's neck. As Tyler reeled and tugged the reins to turn his horse back, Knolles came and plunged his sword into Tyler's side. Yet somehow Tyler turned the horse and it raced some way across the field, Tyler wildly swaying. Finally, less than halfway across, he slithered down the animal and fell to the ground.

Johanna's scream alerted all the rebels. 'Look after her,' she told the other women, and pushed Joan firmly towards them. Then she ran across the field. 'No!' she shouted. 'No! Let him live! Please, God! Let him live!'

Walworth instantly galloped back to the city. Alarmed and confused by his flight, the fainter-hearted in the retinue also tugged their horses away.

John Ball turned to the bowmen but he had no need to speak. They were stringing their bows and the sound of anger grew among all the others.

Richard seemed to wake from a trance. 'I will go to them,' he said. 'I will go alone.'

Some of those nearest made as if to accompany him.

Tom Holland rode across them and shouted, 'The King will go alone! The King will go alone!'

They watched him, their king, as he galloped across the hard ground, passing by the small cluster of rebels who had lifted their leader and were carrying him towards the priory and its hospital, passing those who had raced across to help him. And the bowmen fitted their arrows and took aim. Had they loosed them, had they killed the King and the chief councillors, they could have walked back into London, an unopposed entry, and set up a victorious government – their government. Why did they not loose the arrows?

36

Summer Lightning

The King felt that he was flying. He was alone, on fire with the sense of his heroism. His fine horse, urged on across the easy ground, stretched its speed. And Richard's spirits surged with the excitement of the splendid animal he commanded. There was joy in this glorious gallop to which he would return again and again throughout his life. This and the ecstasy of coronation were twin pillars of the edifice he built of himself – the King by God and now a king in battle.

Later the alchemist swore that some said they had seen him as a golden bird, whirling out of the dazzling westerly sun. Many saw an aura illuminating the crown. Disbelief shocked the members of his court. This boy, this fragile king, riding alone, unguarded, towards the rebels, delivering himself into their hands.

The bowmen paused as the figure came into focus. Some began to kneel. The King pulled his high warhorse to a dramatic halt just a few yards in front of the menacing phalanx of bows. Such a light, slender thing, they thought, on that mountain of a horse. Their king, brilliant in fine colours and brave. That could not be denied. They were proud of him. More and more of them knelt.

He raised his right hand, a gesture of pacification, but also, it seemed to many, a blessing, a pardon, an absolution. Led by those who, at the front and nearest were fullest witness to the King and who knelt or bent one knee to him, the whole host, like a slow scything of acres of corn, now bowed down. And as Richard saw this, it was as if a dove had descended on him and once again declared him the beloved son of God.

Now, he thought, he knew what his father had known and what had made his father's name immortal. He thought of himself now as a warrior, who had gained honour in war. He made no distinction between murderous savagery on those foreign battlefields and the workaday market character of Smithfield. He was a king who was facing an army. And he was facing it alone. The story of David and Goliath rose in his mind. God was everywhere. In him, guiding and protecting him.

When there was sufficient silence and a widespread visible sign of obedience, he spoke. He spoke in English. He left a gap between the sentences, as he had been schooled by Salisbury for Greenwich in the speech that had been unspoken. No one could advise or restrain him now.

'Your captain is dead. Surely you do not wish to shoot your arrows at me, your king,' he said. 'From this hour you will have no captain but me. Be all in rest and peace.'

He rode along the front of the army repeating, 'I am your king. I am your leader now. Be all in rest and peace.' The death of Tyler was being instantly swallowed in this new life offered by their king.

This was the king they had come to save and now he was to be their saviour. How had it come about? It must be through God's grace. He was in front of them: reach out and they could touch him. He would be their captain. No nobles, no council, no lawyers, tax collectors or men-at-arms, just the King and themselves, the True Commons of England. As they had dreamed and demanded, so it was done.

Jack Straw turned his men away with a message that they must move back to Essex and regroup. But many of the rebels wanted settlement. Who could guarantee that better than the King? There was something somnambulistic about them, those men and women, rough-slept for days, grab-fed and often too abundantly wined, gratified and amazed that such a moment as this had come at all, unbalanced by the welter of unexpectedness, confused by success. And Tyler dead. No time to mourn. Replaced by their king. His right arm raised, the reins held loosely in his left hand, the horse obedient to every touch. In front of them.

Across the field was a reduced huddle of the King's retinue. In the middle of the field the body of Tyler, still not dead though viciously wounded, was being taken into the priory itself.

But the new world of the rebels was here with the King, their new leader, their captain. No time to mourn.

Richard turned and smiled as he saw three men trotting unthreateningly across the field towards him. Salisbury, Newton and, in the middle (and, no doubt, Richard thought, the instigator of this move), Tom Holland. Richard's warmth for Tom grew even stronger. Tom always knew what he needed. One day he vowed he would make Tom his greatest councillor.

Taking care to keep his action emollient, Richard turned his horse, beckoned the three men and rode some way – not too far – to meet them.

Tom looked at him with what he knew the King needed – passionate admiration, which was returned. Richard reached out to clasp his hand.

'And now?'

Salisbury, as was his manner, which had become his right, spoke first.

'We cannot leave them here,' he said. 'There will be riots in the name of their leader and then more burning. The London mob will once again be inflamed. These men must go back to their own counties tonight.'

'And Walworth?'

'He will be in the city by now,' said Tom. 'He is raising arms. At last.'

Richard smiled at the disgust in the last two syllables. 'Newton?'

'May I propose that Your Majesty lead them out to the cornfields of St John at Clerkenwell? They are only a few minutes away. If Walworth comes in any strength, he can best encircle them in Clerkenwell.'

'They are yours now,' said Tom, cutting through. 'You have them at your command.'

Richard turned, rode back to the rebels and pointed them towards Clerkenwell. Slowly, but without protest, the long lines drained from the field, past the pond, past the elm trees, and quite soon the meat market went on as before. Beasts were slaughtered, bread was sold, the taverns were as busy as they had ever been, and small boys played at being soldiers.

Tyler's bed was saturated with blood. His head lolled on his shoulder, but Walworth's thrust had not proved fatal. Nor, it seemed, had the stab of the other assassin gone in as deeply as death required.

Johanna knelt beside the bed. If will and unconstrained longing could have saved him, her silent cry for his life would have mended him.

Henry Long tried to direct matters. Those who had brought him into the hospital talked of revenge. The monks from the hospital staunched and attempted to seal the wounds.

Tyler had said nothing but his faint groans gave them hope. John Ball prayed for his soul and feared that the man, the day, the cause could be lost. Tyler – who had led them – could not die. Why had he let himself be trapped? Why had the bowmen not fired their arrows? Where were the arrows?

Walworth rode through Aldersgate and into the city as lathered in sweat as his horse. Their strategy planned on the previous night, which had interrupted John Ball's attempt to sleep, had to be implemented immediately or all could be lost. Walworth thrived on the energy of panic. There was no telling what might happen.

There was John Ball, there was Jack Straw, there were rumours of new rebel recruits coming from Norfolk, Suffolk, Hertfordshire. The only way to stop this was to kill them in such numbers and hobble them in such a way that . . . Never again.

Just beyond Aldersgate, as planned, the men were assembled. The city, Walworth thought, unlike the pusillanimous nobles and the King's councillors, had finally turned out to defend the Crown. The aldermen in the wards had carried out his instructions and called out their armed men. Other city financiers contacted through the night – Phillpot, Brembre, Knolles – who had so far kept their men inside their palaces, had also been persuaded out onto the streets. Walworth saw Smithfield as the last chance to seize back the initiative.

The men fully armed before him gave him all the hope he needed. Now it was Walworth's time to speak out. His words were well calculated and effective. In the hubbub and the proximity of failure he dug deep.

'Most noble, generous and pious citizens,' he began, believing that many of them still despised him for letting the rebels into their city, 'I beg you to go and help your king without delay for he is threatened with death. Assist me, your mayor. Even if you decide not to help me because of my failings, at least do not abandon your king.'

311

'The King! The King! The King!'

'I have asked Sir Robert Knolles to lead you,' he said. Knolles rode forward on his warhorse, armed for full battle. He, too, was cheered and followed in good order when, without a moment's delay, he swung his horse around and led the men to Smithfield.

Walworth let them start, then signalled to the two score of lancers he had instructed to wait nearby. They fell in behind him and went pell-mell for Smithfield, passing the marching citizens of London, lifting their spirits with their galloping splendour, the long lances, the heavy mail armour. Walworth, at their head, shouted them on and, at last, felt forgiven.

First there was vengeance.

But Tyler was gone from the field.

He must be in St Bartholomew's hospital, only a few score yards from where he had fallen.

Walworth led his men there. Some stayed with the horses. The others strode into the priory, calling for the hospital; the sound of their clanking march menaced the chaste corridors until their blood hunt burst in on the desperate scene of the attempt to save Tyler.

Tyler's men, four of them, stood in a semi-circle at the foot of the bed. Tyler's bloody body was besieged by blood-spattered monks silent, doing their best to keep alive this Christian body. To one side of him, kneeling as if in prayer, was Johanna Ferrers. She had unclasped Tyler's bloodied hand and taken the dagger: she would give it to Joan. John Ball stepped forward but was pushed aside and penned against the wall.

Walworth's men barged away the unprepared followers of Tyler and stabbed those who resisted. The others, led by Walworth, went for his body and dragged it from the hands of the monks and out of the room. Johanna's shouting attracted the anger of a soldier, who smacked her away. After Tyler's body had been dragged out, three of Walworth's men stood in the doorway, weapons ready, preventing any other exit.

A track of blood, from the trail that had brought him there, carpeted the path to the door. Near the spot where he had fallen, he was propped up and, with axes taken from his men, he was hacked to death and decapitated.

His head was jammed onto a lance and Walworth had it carried before him. He led his men towards the King, just as he saw Sir Robert Knolles in the near distance lead the private armies of London onto the golden cornfields of Clerkenwell.

The rebels still left on Smithfield saw Walworth, the lancers and Tyler's head but they were in an irresistible current. They were being led by their new captain, the King, and whatever doubt and sorrow might be stored to surface in the future, this was not the time to stop and mourn.

The King beckoned Walworth to come close to him. Salisbury flanked the transcendent King. Behind these three were the council and Tom, whom Richard also kept near him. The lancers, men from the city, began to spread out with the armed men from the palaces and the attendant foot-soldiers from the boroughs until they had encircled the rebels, whose numbers were depleted now. There had been those who could not bear the loss of Tyler, those who had stolen away for safety and those who had decided to regroup and fight another day. But thousands remained. The lancers and the well-armed men, under orders to be restrained, contained them.

There was a thickening atmosphere of confusion: sadness and fear at the loss of Tyler, sadness that it was not as they had hoped, but pride that the King was now their leader, was indeed at their side and had promised them immediate pardon and the future resolution of their burdens. They flinched when they glanced at Tyler's severed head. But sadness was distant, like the faraway roll of thunder. No time to mourn. They were hurried on.

The city armies congratulated themselves on their patience in waiting instead of feeling shame in hiding away. Now they saw the counties, the peasants, the True Commons, subdued by the mere presence of the King – their king, one of them – and further cowed at the high-held severed head of their leader. Whose was the victory now?

Walworth took his leave quickly of the King to speed up the encirclement; Salisbury once more whispered caution, even more necessary now, he pointed out, with Essex and Kent not yet peaceful and up country more and more rebellions, often inspired by Ball's prophecy and Tyler's leadership. How would they respond to this severed head? It could be seen as a martyrdom, a rallying point. And who was to say if these men now peacefully walking to Clerkenwell would not recover their original purpose once back in their villages and march again on the city?

Even though Salisbury kept close, others came up with requests to execute immediately some hundreds of the rebels who, in their peaceful obedience to the King, were easy game.

The King knew, and Tom reinforced his conviction, that those who made the most violent suggestions did so to redeem the dishonour they felt at letting down their king from their palaces in the country as the rebels had marched to London, at the bridge into London, or in the Tower, in the streets, at Mile End or until now at Smithfield. Many had dissolved into thin air when the hard call had come. It was Walworth, the King thought, and his untitled friends

314

of the city who had finally displayed the warrior loyalty to which the aristocrats claimed a monopoly.

'Resist these wild opinions. Kill no one today,' said Salisbury. 'They have their own and not your interests at heart.'

'Cowards!' said Tom, of the newly valiant. 'Look at them rattle their swords, now that it seems easy. Why should you listen to them?' Tom's contempt was far from the battle experience and diplomatic skills of Salisbury, but the two were in unison, which steadied the young King.

He needed it. Only an hour ago the rebels had seemed indestructible but were now vertiginously submissive. Richard struggled to absorb the cascade of pleasure it brought to him. This was to be a king! His people at his feet! An army at his command!

'But I will have my banners back,' he said. A petty thing, Salisbury thought, but he would not be dissuaded and the knights went to the departing rebels with this demand. Though some saw it as the breaking of a pact, the banners were returned with little dissent. Could they any longer call themselves the King's men? They were slowly being shepherded away in their lines. There was no time to gather together and consider the implications of this lightning stroke. What would Tyler have done?

Richard's eye was never far from Walworth who, across the field, was shepherding the armed men as they shepherded the rebels. He found his dash and command exhilarating. This was his man of the day.

To Salisbury, after consultations, he said, 'Very well. Have it proclaimed that Londoners are to have no further communication with the rebels. Nor will they be allowed in the city this night. Some are leaving Clerkenwell now. I will provide men to escort them from Clerkenwell past the city to London Bridge for Kent and to Mile End for Essex. Tell

315

them I have brought with me the written and sealed charters that they had requested and I have had made. These will be given to their chiefs and leaders.'

Those proclamations were carried across the lush summer fields where the long shadows had started to grow.

Walworth signalled for his forces to hurry the rebels along, but no swords were to be drawn, no lance pointed. After a hesitation, and understanding that their local chiefs would be given the King's sacred charter, they took that as a God-sealed promise and left the field – left the scene of what some believed had been an amazing thing, the birth of another Eden, now promised in England.

Tyler's head was carried through the city and rammed on a spike on London Bridge.

No more than a dozen gathered to witness the event.

37

Sunset

The charter that had been given to the leaders of the rebels was a solemn commitment. With the names and counties changed as appropriate it read:

Richard, by the grace of God King of England and France and Lord of Ireland, to all his bailiffs and faithful men to whom these letters come: greetings. Know that by our special grace we have manumitted all our liegemen, subjects and others of the county of Kent [or wherever]; and we have freed and quitted each of them from bondage by the present letters.

We also pardon our said liegemen and subjects for all felonies, acts of treason, and transgressions performed by them or any one of them in whatsoever way. We also withdraw sentences of outlawry delivered against them or any other of them because of these offences. And we hereby grant our complete peace to them and each of them. In testimony of which we order these letters of ours to be made patent. Witnessed by myself at London on 15th June in the fourth year of my reign.

So, whatever their anxieties as they headed for home, they were safe. And they were free. The King's seal, the King's word and the King's charter, had granted them all they had demanded at Mile End and in terms so plain they could not be misunderstood. They slept in the warm fields that night, saw home drawing nearer and could feel that an unprecedented thing had been done. Now all would be well in England.

'Walworth!' Richard called him out loudly even though, with three other financiers – Brembre, Phillpot and Robert Launde – he was just a few paces away in the fields of Clerkenwell. 'Wear this.' He held out a small metal helmet, a bassinet. Walworth, rather breathless from his activity in the field and alert to every incident that might halt his redemption, was puzzled, but he took it and did as he was commanded.

'Dismount,' said the King, hugely enjoying the theatrical moment. 'And your friends.' He waved to Brembre, Phillpot and Launde. 'You, also, dismount.'

They obeyed, but warily: they had not a seasoned opinion of the character of this young man. In so far as they had heard about his obstinacies, his whims and his inordinate love of jewels and paintings, they were not convinced.

The King beckoned to his sword-bearer. 'Kneel,' he said to Walworth and, with a slight wave of the heavy, jewelled sword, he included the other three in the command. They obeyed.

It dawned on Walworth first. 'Your Majesty, I am not worthy of the honour I fear you intend to do to me. I am of no family. I am of the Company of Fishmongers. I have no lands. I bring no ancestral honours. We were not at Poitiers or Crécy . . .'

Richard took the sword in both hands and tapped Walworth first on the right shoulder, then the left, and then on his newly protected head.

'Arise,' he said, 'Sir William Walworth, knight of our realm. Arise,' he repeated, because Walworth had looked up as if he had suddenly seen a star shooting out of the dusk of the sky. But he stood up and, without command, passed the bassinet to Robert Launde. And so it went down the line. Four new knights, dubbed, as in the finest tales of chivalry, after victory on the field of battle. For this, Richard was for ever convinced, was his great triumph of war.

'We meet tomorrow,' said Richard, 'at the palace of Princess Joan, at seven.'

The four knights stood in a line of unconcealed gratitude and bowed deeply as the King mounted his horse, beckoned Tom to ride alongside him and with his entourage made his way back through the city which was now, once again, his city. Savaged, burned, despoiled . . . On that evening he vowed again that he would one day make it the most beautiful city in Christendom.

'Come away, girl. Come away with me.' Johanna put her arm around the shivering girl's shoulders. Joan – she could feel it as keenly as a sudden stream of freezing air – was beyond words of comfort. The pain was fixed as solidly in her as her father's head was rammed onto the centre spike on London Bridge.

Joan looked up at it, Johanna thought, the way people gazed at the coloured windows in churches, seeking to fix their eyes on the saint who could save them. The head looked so small. The heads of those killed in the White Tower had been removed and were being reunited with their bodies before a Catholic burial. Tyler's was alone.

Johanna, too, looked up, but only for a moment. She could not bear it that the man she had known was now an exhibit. A small gathering was gawping at the trophy. She tugged at the girl's limp arm. 'We must come away.'

Joan turned to her with such a look of sorrow that Johanna's layers of toughness were pierced. The girl was utterly lost. For his sake she would take Joan home. She could be alone with her own sorrow later.

'We must go quickly,' she said. 'My brothers' boat is over there. The tide has just turned. We can be in Dartford while there is still some light.'

Still Joan was battened to the spot, still transfixed by the small severed head.

Johanna stood in front of her, blocking her view, and stared fiercely into the blue eyes that were her father's. 'It won't be safe here,' she said. 'Believe me. You will be in danger.'

Danger meant nothing to the girl. The shock had driven out everything but loss.

'Your father,' said Johanna, fighting to get out the words, 'needs to be remembered. You must go back to your village, and when they come to ask you about Walter Tyler, you can tell them his story.' She knew that she had kindled Joan's interest. In what became a dream of her own, Johanna continued, 'You can tell them how strong he was. How true he was. You can tell them how the people followed him as a leader and how he led them from all the villages and towns and into London, and made the King give him what he wanted. You can tell them he did what no man in England has ever done before. Then you can tell them that he was betrayed and murdered by the King's councillors. You can be his book, Joan. Now be brave, girl, like him.'

The girl looked up one last agonised time, then followed Johanna to the shore of the Thames. Barely out into the river, a small boat was skilfully handled by Johanna's two brothers. The women stepped in from the shallows and the men swung the boat out to take full benefit of the tide at its deepest in the middle of the Thames.

The women looked back to the west. The bridge was silhouetted against the growing sunset in clear lines, but soon it was impossible to make out the severed head of her father, and Joan sought refuge from her grief in grasping the dagger as the sun's last colours shot across the sky in strands of silken mauve and slowly deepening crimson.

John Ball struck north. It seemed that even in death Tyler had gained everything he had wanted. But Ball knew better. He had seen the collecting and burning of the banners, the knighting of Walworth and his friends. He had seen the growing swagger of the city armies, and the escorting of the compliant rebels out of London and back into their county kennels. All this he saw as evidence of a prologue to defeat.

Yet in the north, going by reports and rumour, the rebellion was still strong, gaining cities and abbeys, burning great houses, beginning to put into practice the call to strip the rich and enfranchise the poor. Norwich and St Albans were said to be in flames. Around York he knew a few he could trust. The people could still be led out of captivity. Nor were those men of Essex downhearted. They would fight another day. Jack Straw, it was rumoured, was already making new plans. But there was no place for John Ball in London.

He mingled with the Essex rebels, who were headed back to their base beyond Mile End. They were tired and perturbed. But, also, they were well pleased. The death of one man, Ball tried to tell himself, was not the end of the struggle. But what a man! He grieved for Walter Tyler. His friend. His good friend. It was so very strange that he must now be thought of as dead.

Princess Joan made her deepest curtsy, rose and opened her arms. Her pride in her son and her love, new in its intensity, engulfed him, and he walked into her embrace like a lover.

'We will talk,' he said. 'You and I only.'

Joan had anticipated that. She led him into her bedroom – extravagantly candlelit as ever. There was her best food, her finest wine and she wore her most valuable ring of blue and white diamonds. She slid it off her finger.

He looked at it, shook his head and held up the infinitely plainer ring she had sent him at Smithfield. 'This is my ring for today's victory,' he said. 'I need no other.'

She smiled. That was the perfect response. He was a true aesthete. Her happiness increased by the minute. He had become a man. A victor.

'You have had a triumph,' she said, as they sat opposite each other.

'I have,' he said.

'Now the histories will honour your name for evermore.'

'Like my father?'

'Like your father.'

Richard sighed with brimming contentment. To bask in her praise, to feel the fullness of her love, to be at last the dearest son . . . To be compared with his father! 'I will stay here until the morning,' he said.

'Whatever Your Majesty wishes.'

Now at last he let loose a smile, a full, boyish, charming smile, which buried itself in her. 'Like my father!' he repeated.

Walworth and the other new knights met at the palace of Sir Robert Knolles with their friends and feasted ravenously. A huge unnecessary fire threw out the flames as if fire itself celebrated their triumph. Servants moved rapidly to keep up with the demand for wine, for game, for meat and fish. It was as if they had been on a true battlefield and at great risk routed an enemy superior in everything but the cunning and courage they in that hall possessed.

There was music, there were speeches, there were congratulatory embraces between embroidered men. The noise from the palace defied the thoughtful mood of the London streets.

'But we are only half done,' said Walworth, who was beside himself with delight that everyone now called him Sir William. 'We will see the King in the morning and we must try to persuade him that we must strike hard. Now! Our time has come.'

Tankards were raised to applaud and assent to Walworth's words.

'The King is a fine man,' he said, in a tone of drunken piety. 'See how he flew at them – alone. Against all that rabble. The thousands. Bows drawn. The true son of our Black Prince.' Wild praise for the King rose to the ceiling. 'But I fear he might want to pardon them. Salisbury is for that. Our duty to him and to our kingdom is to follow one single course.' He paused dramatically and the pause drew together a most satisfactory silence.

'Revenge,' he said quietly. And then the newly knighted Walworth, with fathomless pleasure in his fresh greatness, added, reverently, 'For the sake of our honour.'

Joan had waited on the King. She passed him his food and wine, and listened, like a confessor, to his self-entranced repetition of his actions that day. He told her of his visit to the tomb of Edward the Confessor and of his tears. He spoke about the anchorite and his confession, and how the anchorite had blessed him. He described his apprehension as they approached the city. He dwelt on how much he loved Tom, how Tom loved him, and how they were true brothers at last. He took her to Smithfield and described how patient he made himself be in the wait Tyler had imposed on them. He told her excitedly of the sight and noise of the mass of rebels pitched against him. He spared no detail of Tyler's impossible demands – Joan insisted he try to recall every phrase – and then came his charge against the rebel army, himself alone, their submission and his control of them. He spoke of the death of Tyler as if he had personally slain him.

But again and again he went back to his glorious and heroic confrontation with the army of the rebels. He remembered every word he had said to them. He had led them to Clerkenwell fields. The head of Tyler had been hoisted on a lance and carried beside him. Walworth had brought his own army . . . It was a slow uncoiling of the greatest day he would know. As she listened, he felt her love and admiration for him grow even deeper. He was now what she wanted him to be. Now he was free. In her one intervention, Joan said, 'After some of his battles your father said, "Take no prisoners."'

38

The Revenge of a Plantagenet

R ichard woke up radiant with thoughts of revenge. He saw from his window the early dawn shot with bars of delicate rose as, he knew, the poets loved to describe it. He lay in the deep comfort of fine linen and the cushioned cradle of goose down and felt unboundedly free. Nothing could be forbidden him now.

Now he was master of himself. Now he was a tested king. He would heed but he did not need his council. Now he, Richard, could rule. And how he would rule! He wriggled luxuriously in the cocoon of bed. Smithfield had proved him. The memory consumed him.

Yet again, all but squirming at the ecstasy of the recollection, he saw himself ride out across the open field towards a vast rebel army. Through God and by his own courage he had spurred on his warhorse and when they were sure of who he was – they had bent their knee! They had lowered their bows. They had accepted him as their leader, their new captain. And, even more ever-to-be-remembered, they had obeyed him, thousands of them, and let him lead them off the field on which their champion had fallen.

Now he must come out of the timid huddle that had avoided all battle. Now he could strike back. And take no prisoners.

He called for his servants and scribes. Within the hour, while London was only moving slowly, he was dressed, refreshed and dictating drafts of proposals for documents that would draw England into his image.

On the previous evening he had ordered Salisbury to set up a Royal Commission to work through the night and report to him by dawn. They joined him just as he concluded the dictation of his own proposals. After the formalities of welcome, Salisbury read out a near comprehensive list of the destruction, murders and robberies done in the name of the rebels since their entry into London.

Richard was outraged afresh and more strongly. How dare they? Those ignorant peasants! Who were they to challenge the majesty of a king? To desecrate my abbey of Westminster, to burn down my uncle's palace, to violate the bedchamber of my mother! To murder my archbishop! What vermin were they?

As he gorged on his anger, so his pleasure in it grew. He felt that he could burst with a wonderful fury and he loved the feeling of power it gave him. He handed over to Salisbury the scroll that he had dictated that morning. Then he stood aside to allow time for the earl and others to read his proposals.

He was sure now that there had been a flash of light on Smithfield, a flash of pure whiteness, like summer lightning. It had been a sign. And it had been meant for him! He had been granted that singular sign from God Himself. He was no ordinary king.

The memory kneaded into the ferment of luscious wrath by which he was now possessed and with which he would be armed for the rest of his life.

By the time Walworth and his colleagues had arrived to join the council, Richard was prepared, and he would not deviate: he would bring justice, obedience and due awe of the King's majesty back to this broken land. He would pursue revenge.

'This,' said Salisbury, after a second glance through the King's document, 'is unprecedented, Your Majesty.'

'I will set a new precedent.'

'We may have to answer to the House of Commons.' There are laws, Your Majesty, he wanted to say, but now was not the time.

'They are not sitting. And we will defy the House of Commons, if they try to thwart us.'

'Is it . . .' Salisbury hesitated, looked again at Richard's document and searched for the least inflammatory word he could find '. . . too harsh?'

'It is meant to be harsh, my lord.'

Salisbury looked at the four new city knights – Walworth, Brembre, Phillpot and Launde – and their friend Sir Robert Knolles. Capable men, he thought, though not one of them was as diplomatically experienced as himself. A new breed of advisers. Here in council they stood apart from the King's old friends, the aristocrats. But Salisbury calmed himself. They were capable men. It was they who funded the King's wars and stood guarantors of the King's debt. That claimed respect.

Sir Robert Belknap and William Cheyne had been assigned to them by the King as their lawyers and they, too, were capable men. Yet what these seven men were being commanded to do was more, Salisbury thought, in the sphere of tyranny than kingship. Great charters had been drawn up to prevent that. The Earl of Salisbury was not inclined to boast. But did they not realise the insurrection that could have overthrown the kingdom had been averted not by the exercise of brutal tyranny but by cunning, caution and an awareness that these were the valued common people of England and should be allowed to have their grievances heard in law? Yet when he looked at this new breed he saw that, for the moment, he had lost. It was his first defeat in the whole affair. He did not like it but there was a time to retreat and he decided that he would do so. It was unsettling.

The King was full of anger, yet he had never seen him so happy.

'We are of different minds, Your Majesty,' said Salisbury, sadly.

'We have made our purpose plain.'

Salisbury nodded and looked again at the document. He read aloud: 'The King to his beloved and faithful William of Walworth,' Salisbury bypassed the other names, 'greetings. We desire with all our heart especially at this time of disturbance,' 'disturbance' struck just the right note at this stage, he thought, 'to duly protect, save and securely rule the city of London in the face of the invasion of these men who (as you know) have recently risen . . . we assign, appoint and ordain you [Walworth] . . . to keep, protect, rule and govern . . .' To rule and govern? That, Salisbury thought, was far too broad a guide for Walworth: it was unlicensed. Bluntly, it meant that Walworth and the others could do whatever they thought fit. '. . . govern the said city of London, its suburbs and other places without . . . at our command but according to your own discretion.'

That was what Salisbury thought unjustified and possibly unjustifiable severity. 'According to your own discretion'? Would that be outside or above the law? He read on, aware that to most men in the room this was news. Perhaps there was a chance they would right it. 'You are to punish everyone who makes, or presumes to make, riots, rising and assemblies against our person . . . either according to the law of our kingdom of England . . .' That was good, Salisbury thought. It showed due respect for the law. '. . . or by other ways and methods, by beheading and mutilations of limbs, as it seems to you most expeditious and sensible.'

That was not good. 'Other ways'? That was not his country's law. There should be trials. There should be proportion. And the King in this new document, a king of England, had just broken his recent and solemn promises to the rebels. Salisbury, no matter that he had advised the King to consent to these demands and later break them, felt ashamed at such a sudden vicious and comprehensive betrayal. Proportion was everything: peace fed on mercy.

He could read no further. 'The last few words are distressing, Your Majesty.'

'They are necessary, my lord.'

'So we become as them? We ignore the law. We behead and mutilate at will?'

'By this we will make them ours. Because they will learn to obey us, as before.'

'Does Your Majesty withdraw his own great powers and the law from all but these men around us here?' He looked across at the capable men of the city and now he could not quell a certain contempt. New merely rich rabble, he thought. Men of no honour. Honour had to be won on the battlefield. This had been no war.

'My lord Salisbury, it is done. And this order will carry in all directions within seventy miles of London. Sir William, I charge you to leave this council and begin your work. God be with you.'

So, Salisbury thought, we send out murderers to murder those whose names and the facts of whose crimes we do not know. Is this the way a king should use the law? And the sacred law of England. The noble old warrior felt this keenly but he kept his silence.

Walworth and his colleagues bowed their way out. As he passed Princess Joan, Walworth bowed again and was rewarded with a smile that he would later boast about to his wife.

'And now, my lords, we have other plans,' said the buoyant King. 'Sir William brought to Smithfield loyal citizens of London armed for us. I have now decreed that messengers will be sent all over London and into the country to command all who love me and honour the realm to come to London also well armed and on horseback. No one is to come weaponless. No one on foot.'

This released an army. Within three days up to twenty thousand armed horsemen had joined the King. They met on Blackheath. Every day Richard went to greet the new arrivals, riding among his men on his warhorse, his standard carried in front of him, his sword of state behind. His open enjoyment of the part he had adopted gave confidence to those men, many of whom had come as a desperate last measure to stop the local upheavals from which they still suffered. They loved the determination of their elegant young king.

News came that the Kentishmen were conspiring to rise again. Richard took his new army into Kent immediately, vowing to remove the entire race of Kentishmen from the face of the earth. Only entreaties by those local magnates who had been loyal to him and their willingness to stand surety for the 'True Commons' prevented mass slaughter. The new army felt cheated, but they obeyed. Richard assured his men that there would be other opportunities to kill the former rebels.

'There are many more Tylers prepared to threaten and murder us,' Richard declared. He drew up another commission, this time addressed to 'the sheriffs, mayors, bailiffs and other faithful men of the counties . . .'. After itemising what had already happened – that people 'have formed various gatherings and assemblies in order to commit many injuries against our faithful subjects' – he concluded 'you must command all and each of our liegemen and subjects to desist completely from such assemblies, risings and injuries and return to their homes to live there in peace under penalty of losing life and limb and all their goods. Witnessed by myself in London 18th June 1381.'

The sound of hoofs was loud in the land. The King's men went high-mounted and war-armed into the country to destroy the nests of rebellion. Children and the innocent were caught up in this. On the one side were the dispersed and deceived rebels, most of them expecting peace and betterment, on the other their bristlingly armoured oppressors, reverting to the kill and earth-scorch tactics employed since the colonisation under William of Normandy. Much of England was made once again to feel like occupied territory as it was bent to the will of a tyrant king.

For as William the Conqueror had notoriously laid waste the north, so the rebels in the south and east, who had shown most courage in their initial opposition, were to suffer the worst of it. Depleted by the plague, diminished by wars, England was terrorised further by Richard's merciless retribution. Mercy, he told Salisbury, could wait.

Outside London, Richard himself led several campaigns. Essex was still the most troublesome county and he took his army there. He hunted down Jack Straw, tortured him, then had him executed. He appointed Sir Robert Tresilian, who presided over bloody assizes at which dozens of men were convicted and executed. In Essex at Havering, a king now intoxicated by blood was met by more than five hundred former rebels, barefooted, heads uncovered, seeking mercy. Mercy was promised on condition they named the local elders and leaders of the Essex rebellion. Richard, like a connoisseur of humiliation, watched the enforced betrayals as those who had marched together were compelled to fight for their lives, like gladiators of the tongue, and keep them only by condemning their fellows to death. Tresilian sent

331

scores of rebels to their deaths. Trials were corrupted by the prevailing tyranny.

The Earl of Buckingham had brought back his army from France and now the south and east swarmed with men-at-arms, lancers and knights with their companies. They tramped over the countryside, discovering hiding places and killing, it was said, hundreds of men who tried to escape the tightening noose. Sometimes the more determined of the rebels would find a spot for a last stand and build barricades with felled trees and furniture, anything that might break the galloping squadrons of warhorses. But these were no defence, and again and again the small bands of resistance were scattered and, if caught, executed.

Kent and Essex were overrun by the King's men, whose armour and numbers they could not resist. The blood they had shed was shed from them many times over. They were slaughtered, as Walworth had suggested they should be on their first night in London, like pigs.

On 2 July Richard put out a proclamation dated at Chelmsford, which formalised and made legal what had been the case since the morning after Smithfield. All the charters of amnesty and enfranchisement he had granted at Mile End on 14 June were revoked. All the sealed documents handed out at Smithfield were worthless.

The King, whom Tyler and the 'True Commons' had worshipped and trusted, had broken his sacred oath to them. Richard rode at the head of his army, like a barbaric and merciless conqueror. His new-found love for his valour knew no limits.

Walworth went through London with an avenging sword. While Richard's progress left gibbets across the countryside and England's summer pastures became fields of death, Walworth turned London into a butchery.

First he went with a company of lancers and sergeants-at-arms to the Flemings. He authorised them to seek out those who had killed so many of their number. He gave them deeds of pardon in advance for all the killings they would do. He stirred into their grief and anger his own passion for vengeance against those disloyal Londoners and let them loose. If they needed support from his men, he promised, he would provide it. He gave them twelve heavily armed men-at-arms to be at their service.

The Flemings took full advantage. Now it was their turn. Their persecutors were hauled into the street by their hoods or by their hair and mutilated or executed. Dog and his men were found drinking by a wharf. By now Dog had a short sword, a dagger and, most cherished of all, an axe. His gang of five faced about two dozen well-armed Flemings. Dog ran straight into the body of them, his axe whirling in his right hand, the sword in his left, his exultant yells and war-cries inspiring his own men and at first terrifying the Flemings. In those moments Dog had never been happier. This was a battle! He had longed for this! But they were too many . . .

When he was finally hacked to pieces, the narrow street was a stream of blood; the headless bodies of himself and his men were hurled into the Thames.

Walworth tortured the Londoners whom he reckoned had been sympathetic to the rebels to make them squeal on others and had them lead his men to their prey. Dozens of men by the day were dragged through the street to Tyburn and arrived skinned raw to be executed. Richard's command unleashed a barbarity that the new city knights embraced to show their loyalty. Their city had been burned, despoiled, looted and occupied. Never again! This retribution would be known the world over.

The carts that took the dead bodies daily through the streets were also used at night to hurry away those dead of

333

the plague. Within a few days of Walworth's medicine, the city was brought to its knees, bled to impotence and, through its weakness, stabilised. Ruined buildings could be rebuilt. Damage could be repaired. Trade and the normal daily lives of those who had been trapped in the maelstrom could be restored. Walworth, their mayor, their new knight, was now their champion.

Like his king, Walworth thought of himself as having been in a great battle. Like the King, he now thought himself to be one of England's historic warriors.

The prisons were refilled. The prostitutes were requartered. The old curfews were reintroduced. The Flemings were now to be feared. Boys plunged into the Thames beside the Savoy Palace looking for jewels on the bed of the river. Walworth had retaken the city, which now honoured the fishmonger for those vengeful days and praised him for centuries after his death.

The White Tower was reoccupied, the stable stench removed. Repairs were carried out. Kitchens cleaned. Future embellishments planned. New linen, curtains . . . Richard took up residence. The previous pusillanimous guards were expelled, all punished, some mutilated, several executed.

Yet still, well after the herding of the rebels from London, requests would come to the King from the more intransigent or innocent. One came from Essex, whose envoys asked whether the King planned to allow them the liberties he had promised, and whether they should be equal in liberty to the lords and should not be compelled to attend courts with the exception of the review of frankpledge twice a year.

The council had been called to address this and Salisbury, still an advocate of conciliation, led a murmur of hesitation. But now the King was in no state to be his pupil. He had changed. Could those Essex rebels not see that he had changed? They would now.

334

The King sent Thomas Woodstock, the Duke of Gloucester, the Earl of Buckingham and Thomas Percy into Essex to deal with those who had sent the message. The men of Essex chose their ground, used ditches as defences, woods for refuge, carts and stakes for barricades. The King's heavily armed troops, gathering in numbers and confidence every day, crushed and dispersed them, executing those they captured.

The King had commanded them to 'take no prisoners'.

At the same time he sent the Essex men the following answer, an answer that went out to all England, an answer that chilled men's souls and chained their minds for centuries.

Oh! You wretched men, detestable on land and sea, you who seek equality with Lords are not worthy to live.

Peasants you are and peasants you will remain. You will stay in bondage, not as before but incomparably harsher. For as long as we live and, by God's grace rule over the realm, we will strive with mind, strength and goods to suppress you so that the rigour of your servitude will be an example to posterity. Both now and in the future, people like yourselves will always have your misery as an example before their eyes: they will find you a subject for curses and fear to do the things you have done . . .

39

A Death at St Albans

John Ball had soon peeled away from the Essex men and struck across country on his own. He knew the ways well. For more than twenty years he had made this area his roving parish. He needed to be alone with his thoughts.

He found solitude in the fields and barns of summer England. There was still evidence of the scything of the plague in deserted villages, abandoned cottages, meagrely manned monasteries. The plague was back but not with the virulence of previous visitations, and though there were some dead beasts in the fields and houses boarded up with a cross on the door and death inside, it could, for stretches, seem a green and pleasant land. He allowed himself to accept this for a few days. It nursed his melancholy.

Ball could not articulate the sadness that shrouded him. He mourned Will, and he felt only half a man now without Tyler. He had seen people with friends, envied them and sometimes wondered at the purpose of it or the need for it. Now he knew. Will and Walter Tyler had been his friends. Round and round the loss of them distressed him, and only in time did the memories comfort him.

God had called him to be alone, as one crying in the wilderness, and he had willingly taken up that lonely vocation. Now, without the devoted presence of Will, he was again outside life. Solitude had once been his natural state, but it had been breached by warm feeling, and this trek across the middle of England was a journey of mourning. He had come to care deeply about the all-but-wordless man.

He had felt protective, pleased when Will was pleased, glad to be able to give him happiness.

Walter Tyler had been different from any other man Ball had met or known. He had watched him grow. He had seen the unfolding of qualities that neither he nor Tyler knew he had. God, he thought, must have given these gifts to Tyler while he was in the wars in France, but only on English soil did they seed and flower.

And he had brought Tyler to the Truth. Once he had seen the light, Tyler was like Paul on the road to Damascus. He did not preach. He bowed to Ball for that. But he carried out the work of the Lord. He acted. He showed faith in his deeds. How else could he have inspired and led such huge numbers?

There must be other men like him, Ball thought desperately, as he tried without much success to force sleep to suppress his seething mind. Surely there must be other leaders ready to rise up as Tyler had done. Reports that had reached him from the north had been jubilant. Surely the rebellion was living on.

Like most of those whose lives are obsessed with an idea, John Ball had had, until recently, no room in his character to look at himself. He had not employed the empathy that would enable him to see himself through others. 'Others', to that fractured, lonely, passionate Christian, were souls to be converted. Perhaps to protect himself he had cut himself off from the aspect of imagination that wants to know and understand what is human in those apart from themselves.

But the devotion of Will to him and his own devotion to Tyler had changed that, and he was in a new and, for him, bewildering world of confusing ordinariness.

He thanked those who offered him bread and shelter with a new understanding of their generosity and even of the

337

danger they were courting. Again and again he pictured the bloody body of Tyler and the long, subdued procession of the rebels to Clerkenwell, like the Israelites, he thought, being led into captivity.

As he walked across the middle of England he saw a faithless wilderness, himself like one of the ancients in the desert, and he remembered the words of the cenobitic St Anthony, 'Good Jesus, where were you?' He chastised his memory for allowing these words to come into and stay in his mind.

But the thoughts were lodged there as he wended his slow way northwards. How could he question Jesus? But, then, how could Jesus have let them kill Walter Tyler and how could God have sent a plague that ended the life of Will, one of His innocents?

He knew the answers. He was unworthy. England was unworthy. This was justifiable punishment for centuries of sin. As he tried to sleep in a hastily built shelter in the woods, in a barn or, if lucky, in a house, he was driven towards despair. This sinful despair was new to him and it broke into his mind like a knife stabbing into an egg. He returned to his spiritual exercises and tried to find his old certainty. The certainty that had once been the foundation of his life . . .

He walked slowly, sadly, as if wounded. Good Jesus, where were you? He hoped for visions to put him once more on the right path but they had deserted him. He felt emptied of struggle. Why not live and die in prayer in the woods? Why not disappear into a hidden life, which would not be difficult, in one of these isolated hamlets, these remote half-empty villages?

But gradually, the sights of people and their children, many unblessed by life and seemingly unheard by God, stirred him in some way as they had done in the past. He talked to them. He prayed with them. What he had been returned to strengthen him. His mission was to save souls.

Finally his prayers were answered. He heard the words 'Thy will be done.'

What else was there but to do God's will? To hide, to retreat, to give up would make him a coward to Christ.

Eventually the priest of St Mary's, York, found the will to lift himself up, not to let himself be destroyed by this burden of merely human feeling.

After more than three weeks at large, he made for the holy city of Coventry.

'Thy will be done.'

John Ball did not realise how famous he was. Over the years report and rumour had elevated him far above the ranks of other hedge-priests. Who else had been imprisoned at the command of Edward III himself? Who else had been excommunicated three times, once by the Archbishop of Canterbury? His letters and rhymes were on the streets. At a time when some outlaws were celebrated for their daring, and their rumoured chivalrous robbing of the rich to give to the poor was seeping into the mythology of the Middle Ages, John Ball stood alone, an outlaw for God.

Who else had been so defiant? Who else cared nothing for possessions, a home, a family, money, friends or the company of other priests, some of whom were inspired by his rhyming tongue? He was a free man! His name was loved by the people, hated by the few. He did not realise that, in those days following Smithfield, he was a prime target, a hunted man.

As soon as he arrived in Coventry he went into the market-place and began to preach.

'John Ball, priest of St Mary's, greets all manner of men and bids them in the name of the Trinity, Father, Son and

Holy Ghost, stand manly together in Truth and help Truth and Truth shall help you . . .'

John Ball was alive! Within minutes a crowd had begun to grow. He had been handed a bench, which gave him the height he needed, and they cheered him. Then, at his gesture, they were silent.

He raised his arms. 'Beware of treachery even in this holy city. Stand together in God's name.' Once again, each sentence was punctuated by a loud 'Amen'. 'Take heed of yourselves. Beware of woe. Know your friend from your foe. Do well and better and flee sin. Seek peace and hold you therein . . .'

John Ball was preaching in the centre of Coventry! The news raced across the city and galloped across the county. Local lords who had failed to stand up to the rebels saw a chance to ingratiate themselves with the King. Who would be the first to capture the traitorous priest?

John Ball was given lodgings and asked for pen and paper.

Here he wrote his last letters. Previous letters had been thought sacred by the rebels. One such letter fluttered from a rebel's sleeve as his hanged body swung in the wind. Others fastened the letters to their clothes, like decorations or charms. He claimed no miracles, nor attempted any. He had no disciples. By words alone he worked his good.

And in Coventry he spoke out. Somewhere, he thought, there might be another Walter Tyler, who would hear him and join him. For the present he had to preach. God's patience would not last for ever. England's fate had to be resolved. 'When Adam delved,' he could say, and the crowd would chant back, 'And Eve span,' and the chant would grow louder, 'Who was then the gentleman?'

He was easily captured.

Two local lordlings claimed credit and their men began a bloody feud.

They took him in a quarrelsome procession of sinister triumph to St Albans, which commemorated the first English martyr. It was a town riven by the tyrannies of the abbot and his monks in the opulent abbey, and the relentlessly exploited townsmen, whom Tyler had helped to drive out their oppressors. But soon after Smithfield, the King's army had come to St Albans, purged it and reinstated the privileges of the abbey, which included reclaiming their monopoly on the grinding of corn, which had destroyed the local artisans.

The King, who had been present at many of the mass trials, came to St Albans on word of Ball's capture. For three days Ball was imprisoned. There were many to be tried. Richard, when he was in attendance, always demanded many trials, however summary and pre-ordained the verdict. The rounding-up of victims included those who thought to make themselves safe by betraying their friends. Already, at this early stage, Richard was being criticised for the intensity of his vengeance. Although he had no intention of easing the pain of those who had set themselves against him, he had decided to repel criticism by appearing to hold on to traditional legal observances. But these, in effect, were show trials. It would be many months and a new year before the politics of marriage provoked the politics of mercy and made the King change course.

Richard became a connoisseur. He took particular interest in how long a man could hang before he was counted dead. Records were kept. In the matter of executions, he was displeased when the executioner took more than two strokes of the axe to sever the head. He noted that blood spurted out more copiously from the severed necks of some men than from others. He discussed such matters with his doctors. He often felt excitedly disturbed by what he saw. He enjoyed those sensations.

He studied, intensely, the expressions on the faces of the condemned. He nodded approvingly at resolution. He almost applauded an expression of what he thought was courage. Babbling and crying made him laugh. And the sound! *Thud!* Such an uncommon *thud*. The axe blade into the neck. *Thud!* Flesh, sinew and bone. A soft, dull *thud*! He loved to hear it. As for the monks and the last rites, the incense and the chanting, he thought that was always very well done and he would make the sign of the cross every time a head fell to the ground.

And now he had John Ball standing before him.

Richard studied the man. He was said to be a mystic and a prophet. His visions were believed by the peasants. Richard was disconcerted by his resemblance not to a mighty figure from the early history in the Old Testament of the Bible but to the sparely built anchorite of Westminster Abbey. He conceded that there was about him an unmistakable sense of holiness. He had expected, he had wanted, a raging and ignorant apostate, whom he could cut down in an elegant display of royal authority. He was confronted by a holy man, a John the Baptist, an ascetic man, and a man unafraid.

Ball examined the King, the divine representative of God on earth, who had broken his sacred oaths. The royal presence who had been party to the assassination of his friend Walter Tyler. The boy who had killed hope. Put no more trust in kings.

The apparatus of execution had been laid out near the west door of the abbey on a spot called the Rome Lands. A throne was always brought for Richard. He had come with an entourage of two hundred armed men. He feared an attempt to rescue John Ball. Walworth and his colleagues were in London engaged in their final clearances. Salisbury had retreated to protect his estates, following information that one of the King's favourites, and one of Salisbury's rivals, the Earl of Buckingham, was in that part of the country looking for treasure with some of the army he had taken to France. The King had brought Sir Robert Tresilian with him. He was very proud of his notoriety for making bloody judgments and even more proud of how much his skilful bias pleased his king. Tresilian had high hopes of further preferment.

Ball was his choicest victim yet. The King had said he would not be fully satisfied until this traitor to God had been brought to justice. Tresilian saw this as an unparalleled opportunity to impress the King. The trial had been held back for two days, partly because William Courtnay, Bishop of London wished to persuade Ball to repent, partly because Tresilian wanted a crowd. Ball would not repent, but the crowd had built up.

Tresilian was disappointed that Salisbury was not there. And he thought he deserved the archbishop rather than the Bishop of London. Walworth's absence he considered inexcusable, but what could you expect from a fishmonger? Tom Holland's was a welcome absence: the young man was unreliable. But he had the King, now comfortably seated and waiting for his chief justice to perform.

Tresilian was learned and well briefed, fierce in examination, unrivalled in exposition, and renowned for his rage.

Taking a swill of beer to clear the dust from his throat on another baking hot day, he weighed into Ball with relish. He told the King, the jury and the people of St Albans that, for more than twenty years, this dangerous and wicked man had so badly misrepresented the truth of religion to the people that he had endangered their souls. He had scorned the sacred Bible of the ancients and embraced the common English tongue to seduce the ignorant into a knowledge they did not need or deserve that had led them astray and into rebellion.

Ball stood, shackled.

The King found that his attention was too often swerving from the thundering accusations and torrent of instances produced by the garrulous Tresilian to the still figure of John Ball. How slight he was. How calm he was. How did he find such calm?

Tresilian railed on to the jury about Ball's widely known challenge to titles – to the pope, the archbishop, bishop, dukes and earls – which the priest said were not to be found in the Bible and were therefore invalid. What pitiful logic! He had questioned the Trinity! He had urged the people to strip the Church of its treasures and land and give all to the poor. The Church, the anchor of life on earth and the life to come, the safeguard and succour of society, was to be destroyed! And after the Church, it would be the King!

It was strongly spelled out, but it was not going as well as Tresilian had anticipated. The crowd was not with him. He was fine-tuned to reactions to his performances and this reaction was tepid. He needed applause. He fed off it. He saw a dumb antagonism as his eyes swivelled across the listeners. Where were the acclamations for his powerful sentences? They were listening but they were not moved. He needed them to be! Like the King, they seemed more spellbound by the silent shackled figure of John Ball than by all of Tresilian's incomparable rhetoric.

But Tresilian had stamina.

And remember, he went on, how this man had roused the rabble and urged them to burn down all London. He had championed the followers of that traitor Dr Wycliffe. Think how he had driven on the murderers of Archbishop Sudbury and so many others that day on Tower Hill. Think how he had misled the poor with letters such as these – he waved a handful in the air – telling them they must fight on and overturn all that was held most dear to England!

And remember that he had been excommunicated three times!

Tresilian's speech earned him no cheers from the crowd. But it was more than enough for the tainted jury. From the King himself, Tresilian, the chief justice of the Court of the King's Bench, received only a crushing nod.

John Ball was allowed to speak.

'I did send those letters to the men of Essex,' he said, 'I sent many such letters and wish I had sent more. I did not execute Archbishop Sudbury and others, but I was there and I welcomed it. I have not met Dr Wycliffe, to my sorrow. He has given us God's word in our own true tongue. He is one of the greatest men in England. I have indeed been excommunicated three times, each time for telling the truth about God's word. On Blackheath I preached to men who had suffered from the new taxes and the wicked judgements of the King in his council, and I urged them to destroy all that which oppressed them. Save the King himself. And I plead guilty to the charge that I led men away from the false teachings of the Church. Their souls were in peril.'

This was said in a strong, high voice that reached far across the crowd. Its plainness and honesty evoked support, though in a muted way. The presence of the King, his armed men and the new omnipresence of spies and informers were too intimidating.

The jury's decision and recommendation were immediate. Guilty. Death. To be hanged, drawn and quartered.

'Do you have anything further to say?'

The King had been disappointed by the priest's words. He had wanted rage at the very least.

For a time, John Ball closed his eyes and bowed his head in prayer.

'I do,' he said, dispensing with any formal address. He spoke evenly, and the people listened.

'I wish to speak for the people I know. They are good people, the people of England. They love the Lord God. They work hard under cruel laws. They bow to their king.

'But many have been treated like slaves by those who rule over them. Good men and women and their children starve in this land of plenty. Their labour is so hard they cannot fully live. This is not God's wish. The earth is for all of us who are born on it.' Then, directly and fiercely to the King, he said, 'I see that you will die of your kin and cause endless wars in this kingdom unless you set your people free.' He looked so directly at the King that he flinched. 'Nothing else will serve. In your kingdom are good people.'

John Ball looked over the many faces turned towards him as so often in hope. 'I have tried to serve you,' he said. 'But I failed. Others stronger than I will come after me. Be ready for them.'

He waited.

The King said, 'Kneel and I will show you . . .'

'I will not kneel.'

Richard, rebuffed so publicly when he was about to proffer mercy, only just controlled the flare of temper that threatened him with a degrading attack against the peasant priest. 'You will now suffer the full force of our punishment.'

John Ball was led down the slope to the place of execution. The Bishop of London, troubled that such a man of God should be killed in this way, went by his side, murmuring the same prayers that Archbishop Sudbury had uttered in the Tower.

Ball's head was put in the noose. The stool was kicked away and he swung for a few moments. Then, like a rundown pendulum, he stopped. His hands had been tied behind his back. The executioner watched anxiously, and when the priest's face appeared about to explode, he lifted up his body. When Ball had regained some breath, he was sat down against a wooden board. His head was inclined so that he could see his body.

With a long knife the executioner slit open the priest's body from throat to groin, put in his hands, hauled out fistfuls of entrails and laid them where the priest could see them.

Once again the executioner took his time.

When Ball was all but dead, he took the axe, turned the body over onto the block and severed the head. Two strokes.

His assistant held the head up for all to see. There were no cheers.

Finally, he chopped the priest's still quivering body into four parts. One part would go to York, one to Coventry, one to Canterbury and one to Chester, to be nailed on the city gates as a warning.

Some swore they saw his soul ascend into Heaven.

Richard hurried back to London, confounded.

Throughout the execution, John Ball had uttered no sound.

40

The Women

Her carriage had been resplendently refurbished. Since the end of the rebellion, Richard had cascaded gifts over his mother. There seemed no end to them.

All was now well. This was a new year. Richard had married Anne of Bohemia, which Joan thought promised a succession, if not love. But now, in February 1382, Anne, surely the prettiest child in Christendom, would serve.

Tom was off to Spain with his combustible uncle, John of Gaunt, who had returned to his burned-out palace vowing revenge on all Londoners, only to be halted by Richard and his new closest allies, Walworth and his friends. He had turned his attention once again to Castile, of which he intended to be king.

The road to Windsor was not even but Joan was well cushioned. She had put her maids in the carriage behind her. She wanted to be alone to examine more closely the heavy diamond and gold necklace her son had just given her. How smoothly the diamonds slipped through her fingers. How they sparkled even in the dull Thames valley afternoon light.

She eased her back, which she had decided would never be mended. But it could be soothed at the hands of Mamoud and there was that to anticipate too. And music, wine, the sound of young laughter. And her chronicle. How rich it would be in praise of her son! How carefully she would write it to glorify him for all time. The anticipated pleasure of sending this account down through the centuries was almost unbearably delicious. He had triumphed!

And now back to the grandeur of Windsor. All was well. Her beautiful bed. The coming and going of well-bred intelligent men, though no more Lollards, alas. They were too dangerous now.

Richard, her son, had won the day. But enough, now a new year was here, of this revenge. The House of Commons had criticised his vengeance and that man Waldegrave, the speaker, had had the insolence to declare that the grievances of the peasants had some merit. She, too, considered that the vengeance had been over-prolonged. But the general pardon her son had just granted would bring the wretched peasant clamour to an end.

They always fell back, the peasants. They would never win. The strong did what they could. The weak had to suffer it, she thought. This was the way of it, and God, as had just been demonstrated, approved it. God was on their side. He ruled, and so did they.

'You took some finding.' Johanna was exhausted. Normally she carried her swollen belly before her with ease. But the last mile on the winter path through frosty woods had been too much.

She made herself comfortable in the small dwelling. 'The last mile is the hardest,' she had been told. There was a fire; soup was warmed.

'You took some finding,' Johanna said again. 'I was weeks getting your new name.'

'We were told to change it,' said Tyler's wife, 'that it was the only safe way.'

'And they wanted us out of the village,' said Joan.

'They acted as if they were ashamed of him.'

'I told them stories,' said Joan, 'like you said. But they said it was too dangerous for us to stay.'

'How do you live?'

Tyler had given Margaret instructions on where to find a substantial and carefully accumulated treasure of coins and other marketable objects gathered during his service in the French wars.

'We will live,' said Margaret, 'and we have faithful friends.'

Johanna took the soup and warmed her hands on the bowl.

'I have you to thank for looking after Joan,' Margaret said. 'She talks of you often.' She touched the brooch Walter had brought her from Maidstone Fair as she looked intently at Johanna. Her eyes tracked down to her belly. She made no comment. 'I must look to things before dark,' she said. 'You will stay with us tonight?'

'Thank you.'

'You are welcome.'

When she had gone, Johanna looked closely at Joan. The young woman was still not recovered. Her face was repaired, the skin fresh, even glowing. She was in less of a trance. But she was not through it. One day, perhaps. But most likely she would never be right.

Johanna had come to bring money from the haul she and her brothers had smuggled from the Savoy Palace. But Tyler's wife had reassured her. It seemed that money was not needed. She would keep it for herself and the child.

Joan wept silently.

'There,' said Johanna, quietly. 'Cry away, child.'

Her sobbing grew more intense as if she were frantic for it.

Johanna reached across and held her. 'There,' she said. 'Cry away.'

'I miss him so much. Every day I miss him.'

'There was no one like him,' said Johanna, as steadily as she could.

'There will never be,' said the girl.

'Well . . . I hope there is, child. I hope he comes again. We have all suffered from his loss. Someone has to help us to end it . . . Someone has to come again.' She bit her lip to hold back her own distress.

'He gave me this dagger,' said Joan, holding it out. It sparkled by the light of the fire.

'I know,' said Johanna. 'He wanted to protect you.'

'And he did. Didn't he? He wanted to protect me. Didn't he? And I did help him, didn't I? Didn't I?' Her sobbing was growing softer. It was difficult for Johanna to hold back her own tears. But she must. She was here for his child.

'Hush,' she said. 'Hush now.'

—+— —+—

Tyler's head was pecked to the skull. The sun blackened it. Storms wore it down. Many other heads of rebels were hoisted alongside it on the bridge above the untroubled Thames. The warning was in plain view. For months Tyler's head could be pointed out. And then it was just a small dark clump on the spike. And then it was no more.

Brief Timeline

This is the sequence of events in 1381.

6 June	Rochester Castle attacked
7 June	Maidstone: beginning of march to Canterbury
10–11 June	Canterbury
11 June	Archbishop Sudbury flees from Canterbury
12 June	About noon, Tyler, Ball *et al.* make for Blackheath; evening, Sudbury flees from Lambeth Palace
13 June	Morning, Ball preaches sermon at Blackheath; Tyler meets the King at Greenwich; march from Blackheath to Southwark; ransacking of the Marshalsea prison; burning of the brothels; entry into the city of London; destruction of the Savoy Palace; court in crisis – decision to meet next day at Mile End
14 June	Mile End, Jack Straw, burning palaces and legal documents; Tyler and his men enter the White Tower; beheading of Sudbury and others; John Ball searches for and finds Will; Joan escapes to her own palace; murder of the Flemish wool merchants; murder of Lyons; preparation for Smithfield
15 June	Westminster, John Ball and the King go to the abbey; Smithfield, death of Tyler
June–July	Revenge of King Richard II
15 July	Death of John Ball

Author's Note

This novel is based on the mis-called 'Peasants' Revolt' of 1381. Like all novels, it is fiction, a work of imagination. Like all historical novels, it willingly takes on the events of the time as recorded in chronicles, trials and letters. This remains the biggest popular uprising ever experienced in England.

The broad outline is largely consistent with the accounts given at the time, but the accounts are not themselves consistent. They can be patchy, contradictory and sometimes merely propagandist. There is a persistent and, as it has later proved, mistaken denigration of the motives and actions of the rebels.

I have taken some liberties with history. For instance, there is only one reference to Tyler's service in the French wars, but his overall generalship was well recognised at the time and by commentators since, so I thought it valid to build on that reference. There is a minor reference to the 'election' of a leader for the Kent rebels at Maidstone. I took the word 'election' at its face value – and we have an election. Some circumstances are wholly made up but, I believe, tally with the characters and their roles in this short, spectacular drama. And there are encounters, conversations, characters I have invented to enrich the story as I saw it. This brought me Will and Dog, the Lollard scholar, Henry Long, John Ball's spiritual adviser and the good men of Colchester.

In at least one case I pursued an historical character: Joan, the Princess of Wales, who has been meagrely represented in the chronicles. Yet when you look at the chronicles and read around, Richard her young son was forever staying with her or she with him; her connections were unequalled, she was a friend of wealth and power. I thought that she would have been a major influence on king and council in that June crisis. I also thought she was intriguing and represented the force of riches and entitlement of the day more vividly and rootedly than anyone else.

Johanna Ferrers, one of the four thousand women said to have been involved, was a gift. Court records gave me a bounty. Ferrers' trajectory seemed inevitable. I developed Tyler's daughter, Joan, from a minor reference to her existence. And Tom Holland, the young Earl of Kent and Princess Joan's favourite, I imagined beyond his weight in the chronicles – one day, when I was thinking about the heavy composition of Richard's council, the young buck Tom took off and I followed.

The characters based on historical persons are: Walter (Wat) Tyler, his wife and their daughter; John Ball; Jack Straw; Johanna Ferrers; and Abel Ker. Joan, Princess of Wales; Richard II, her son by the Black Prince; Tom Holland, Earl of Kent, her son by Thomas Holland; Sir Simon Burley, the King's tutor; Friar Thomas Rushbrook; Simon Sudbury, the Archbishop of Canterbury; Sir Robert Hales, the treasurer; William Walworth, Lord Mayor of London, and his colleagues Sir Robert Knolles, Sir Nicholas Brembre, John Phillpot, Sir Robert Launde; Sir John Newton and his two sons; Sir Richard Waldegrave, the speaker of the House of Commons; Sir Robert Tresilian, the lawyer at John Ball's trial, and all those named in the King's council. Off-stage: John of Gaunt, uncle of the King and brother of the Black Prince. The challenge was to retain their historical integrity yet turn them into characters in a novel and, if in doubt, exercise the Rights of Fiction!

354

I studied history at university and somehow the 'Peasants' Revolt' was hopped over; the waters of history soon closed on that violent uprising. Perhaps it was too dangerous for establishment historians to dwell on, too revolutionary, too egalitarian, too radical, altogether un-English. Chaucer gave it a few dismissive lines and set the tone; Shakespeare mixed it up with Jack Cade's rebellion and was also dismissive. It was the neglected child of English history until the Civil War, then the French Revolution in the late eighteenth century. In the late nineteenth century William Morris gave attention to it. Even then it did not fire the wider imagination, did not become a trophy and cherished marker on our history. Perhaps for some it was too disturbing. Perhaps it always will be. Had they fired the arrows . . .

I began working on this novel about fifteen years ago. I made a radio programme about John Ball, a BBC2 film about John Ball . . . Some books take a long time to land.

SOURCES

The essential book for me has been *The Peasants' Revolt of 1381*, edited by R. B. Dobson (London, 1970). This includes the contemporary chroniclers Henry Knighton, John Walsingham, the Anonimalle Chronicle, Froissart, which range from the vivid pace of Walsingham to the steady hand of the Anonimalle Chronicle to the helpfully copious and often convincing realism of Froissart, who saw himself – with some justification – as the master chronicler of the day.

The Peasants' Revolt: England's Failed Revolution of 1381, by Alastair Dunn (Stroud, 2004), provides an essential and thorough backbone account to the rebellion.

Summer of Blood: The Peasants' Revolt of 1381, by Dan Jones (London, 2009), is an exhilarating and excellent history. His other fine books on the Plantagenets provide a valuable wider context.

The Time Traveller's Guide to Medieval England, by Ian Mortimer (London, 2008), is rich and continuously entertaining in its travels through a distant time. Indispensable.

The Lives of the Princesses of Wales: vol. I by Barbara Clay Finch (London, 1883)

Richard II and the English Royal Treasure by Dr Jenny Stratford (Woodbridge, 2012)

Revolt in London 11th to 15th June 1381 by C. M. Barron (Museum of London, 1981).

ARTICLES INCLUDE:

'The Imaginary Society: Women in 1381' by Sylvia Federico, *Journal of British Studies*, Vol. 40, No. 2 (Apr., 2001) Johanna Ferrers features strongly here.

'Edward III's Prisoners of War: The Battle of Poitiers and its Context' by Christopher Given-Wilson and Francis Beriac, in *English Historical Review*, Vol. 116 (Sep. 2001)

'The Organisation and Achievements of the Peasants of Kent and Essex in 1381' by Nicholas Brooks, in *Studies in Medieval History: Presented to R.H.C. Davis* (London, 1985)

'"The Hand of God": The Suppression of the Peasants' Revolt of 1381' by A. J. Prescott in *Prophecy, Apocalypse and the Day of Doom: Proceedings of the 2000 Harlaxton Symposium* (Lincolnshire, 2004)

I am indebted to the producer of the Radio 4 programme about John Ball, Simon Elmes; to the producer of the BBC2 television documentary on the same subject, my long-time colleague Gillian Greenwood; to Hannah Whittingham; to

Carole Welch, Publishing Director of Sceptre, whose close, analytical comments were, after an initial jolt, very much appreciated; and, as always and with unending gratitude, to Vivien Green, my agent and close friend; and Julia Matheson, another very good friend and help for more than fifty years. Finally, to Cate Haste, for her support over many years.

The poll tax was not imposed again for six hundred years. In the 1980s, Margaret Thatcher reintroduced it. It provoked violent riots and was quickly withdrawn.

$$18440$$

$$
\begin{array}{r}
720 \\
105 \\
\hline
825
\end{array}
$$

$$
\begin{array}{r}
320 \\
170 \\
125 \\
80 \\
40 \\
\hline
735
\end{array}
$$